"*Vivid*"

The New Yorker

"*Full Bodied*"

Chicago Tribune

"*Full of Action*"

Fort Worth Star-Telegram

"As the plot buds, blooms and bursts into its climax, each event and character fits so beautifully into the scheme that one has an almost uncontrollable desire to underline certain passages, parts of which deal with truths of life in any age . . . Shellabarger has surpassed *Prince of Foxes, Captain from Castile* and *The King's Cavalier*"

Memphis Commercial Appeal

Samuel Shellabarger

Author and educator, he was born in Washington, D.C. He studied at Princeton, where he received many prizes, and later obtained his Ph.D. at Harvard.

Dr. Shellabarger was an assistant professor of English at Princeton and a world traveller. Known for his painstaking historical research which contributed so much to his books' authenticity, he wrote such widely-read bestsellers as *Captain from Castile*, *The Prince of Foxes*, *The King's Cavalier* and *Lord Vanity*.

Tolbecken was published after his death in 1954.

TOLBECKEN

Samuel Shellabarger

POPULAR LIBRARY · NEW YORK

TOLBECKEN

PART ONE

TOLBECKEN OAK

1

A month of hot weather preceded the storm; it was called the Great Storm of 1898 for the lifetime of a generation. In the town of Dunstable it set an all-time record for damage.

The heat was leaden—the sort that in summer gives the Middle Atlantic states a flavor of the tropics—weather-breeding heat, everyone admitted. For several nights the sky had been full of heat lightning and a muster of clouds, but nothing happened. The mosquitoes whined undisturbed in the darkness; the drugged trees hung low over lawn and side-walk; people sweltered in their beds, and the next day's fever sent the thermometer up. The tension had to break—somewhere, soon. Finally, on the night of July fourteenth, it broke over Dunstable.

From his bed, Jared Tolbecken could hear the voices from the lawn; the family was sitting up late. He could distinguish his grandfather's full laugh, his mother's exclamations, Aunt Joan Maylin's downright voice, Uncle Vincent's drawl, and Aunt Sophia's plaintive argufying. The last two were guests for the night. Even Grandmother, whose broken hip usually kept her indoors, had been carried out to enjoy the imaginary coolness of the lawn. Her serene, modulated voice contrasted with the others'.

Jared envied them all with a child's passion. Grownups had all the fun; they didn't have to go to bed while it was still light. When he was grown-up, they told him, it would be different. But hadn't he been growing up for eleven years, and wasn't he still a little boy? To him, looking forward, the wait seemed endless.

Grownups were spoiled by their own privileges—they didn't half taste the mystery of things. On great occasions, like the Fourth of July, his birthday in June, or special family celebrations, he had learned what night is like outdoors. Grownups wasted it sitting on the lawn. If he were free, he would be exploring the garden paths—utterly changed at that hour—blind paths, velvety black, and sweet with the smell of cedars or the dry odor of box. He would dare to visit the spring in the far corner, overhung with willows and wild cherry trees, where the Negroes said the ghost of a woman walked. The approach to the spring was through high dank weeds, fearsome even at midday. Or he would cross the wide oval of lawn between the elm-shadowed house and the stable to the sundial. Or, skirting the grounds between fence and shrubbery, he might come as far as the front gate, to gaze at the distant façade of the house, pearl-vague in the darkness. Here in the center of the lawn, alone as befitted its dignity, stood Tolbecken Oak, and hanging from its lowest branch the new swing that Grandfather had just had put up. In his thoughts Jared savored the delight of swinging there now, back and forth, higher and higher, feeling the sweet rush of night air.

From his bed he could see the mass of the oak blacker than the surrounding darkness; at times, in a glimmer of far-off lightning, it stood out distinct and gigantic. It was older even than the house—they said it was three hundred years old. Three hundred years! Before the country was settled, when the town of Dunstable itself was a forest! Grandfather had once showed him a book printed in 1760 which described that part of the state; such and such a place was said to be five miles from Tolbecken Oak, another place ten miles. As far back as anyone could remember, it had served as a standard of comparison: an old man was sound as Tolbecken Oak; a tree was half as large. Its lowest branch, to which the ropes of the swing were fastened, sprung from the great tree fifteen feet up.

How he would like to be swinging now beneath its canopy —higher, higher. . . .

A new sensation wakened him, a draft of cool air filling the room with a scent of honeysuckle. It billowed the window curtains. A shutter banged. From near and far outside came the swish of leaves, and with it the shiver of advancing rain. Then, white and perpendicular, a streamer of fire lashed through the sky, revealing for an instant citadels of cloud suspended above the earth, and, somewhere close by, a bolting crash, clear-cut, riveted home the first shot.

Storm. Jared sat straight up in his bed, tingling. He could hear a racing of footsteps through the house, a slamming of windows; from below on the side porch the creak of awnings being pulled up, and the rasp of chairs being drawn out of range of the downpour. Aunt Joan's voice sounded here and there in command as usual—"Elmira, have a look at the attic. Carrie! Fetch in Mrs. Tolbecken's shawl. It was left on the lawn. Afraid? Oh, hurry up! You ought to be ashamed. . . ." Tolbecken prepared its defenses.

The draft of air leaped into a gale. Between the nearing bolts of thunder, sheets of rain filled up the intervals with the roar of a torrent. The storm shouldered against the house. Its lightning, more and more vivid, showed it grappling with Tolbecken Oak, which looked foursquare and unbending as ever.

Jared's door opened before a woman's heavy figure that crossed the room and shut the window. "Mercy on us!" she muttered. "The floor will be ruined! Children can sleep through anything."

"I'm not asleep, Aunt Joan. Can I get up?"

"All right," she said, mopping the drenched floor. "Get up, but put your clothes on. Don't catch cold."

With a bound he was out of bed and pulling on his trousers. He felt wonderfully excited; storms at sea and beleaguered castles were jumbled together in his mind.

"Electricity's off," said Aunt Joan. "There's no relying on these newfangled inventions. We'll have to light candles."

This was even better—the gale outside, the shadows wheeling on the walls, the uncertain flicker on brass and mahogany.

Candle in hand, he hurried out. Through the arched colonial window of the hall, blinking on and off in the lightning, he could see the rain whopped sidewise by the fury of the wind like a host of flung lances. Earsplitting, almost continuous detonations shook the house.

"Rufus!" called the voice of Grandmother downstairs. "Rufus Tolbecken! The stable's hit. That last bolt . . . I saw it myself. You'd better get the horses out."

And in answer, the even steadier voice of her husband, "Why?"

"Fire!"

9

"There'll be no fire with this cloudburst. What end was struck?"

"The North Street end."

"No harm done. Gregory's there. But I'll go over and make sure."

There was comfort in these voices, and something that gave the boy a feeling of pride. It would take more than a storm to make Aunt Joan or Grandfather and Grandmother afraid. But the group huddled at the foot of the central stairs and dimly apparent in the flutter of a candelabra was something else again. Here sat his mother with Aunt Sophia and the maids, caricatured by their shadow dance on the wall. Before them, irresolute, stood Uncle Vincent Tolbecken; the center of the house was supposed to be the safest from lightning, and he himself should protect and reassure his wife. The droop of his sandy mustache reflected the droop of his shoulders.

"It won't amount to much," he was saying. "It's almost over. Lightning never strikes twice . . ."

As he spoke, the place rocked and flashed. The rain pounded on roof and windows like drumfire.

"It's all right," croaked Vincent. "Only a thunder shower."

"It's nothing of the kind," said Aunt Joan, descending the steps and pushing past them. "It's a hurricane, and it'll be a mercy if the roof holds. I've never seen anything like it. But a peck of help you people are, hanging on to the stairs. Do you think that if the Lord wants you, He can't reach you there?"

She stood confronting them, square, muscular, hard. Her face, humorous and shrewd, showed the chiselings of sixty years.

"I don't understand young people these days," she continued, eying her nephew and the others. "No spunk. When I was young, there was nothing on earth I liked better than a storm. Still do, except for the damage. . . . Vincent, you ought to go to the stable with your father. He shouldn't go alone."

A sudden flash and roar stunned them. The women on the stairs screamed. Vincent Tolbecken clutched at the banister. Even Aunt Joan exclaimed, "Great Governor! That struck close—one of the trees, likely. I'll have to see." And turning away, she hurried along the hall.

"Vincent," said Aunt Sophia, "you stay where you are. Husband and wife belong together. If the Judge is fool enough

10

to go out on a night like this, your being along won't help him."

Vincent stayed. His tractability was one of the many traits which had left him what he was, a kindly nobody, wistful for the manhood he had never had courage enough to earn.

"Come here to mother, Jare," called Bella Tolbecken. "You'll be safer here."

But the boy, afraid of capture, stole off to the rear of the house and down the service stairs. At the door to the pantry he encountered Aunt Joan.

"Where are you going?" she demanded.

"Out with Grandfather."

"The idea!"

"Yes, I am. Please, Aunt Joan . . ." He squirmed under her grip.

"I should say not! What do you want to get soaked for?" And when he answered like the hero of a favorite book, "My place is with him," she burst out laughing.

"You're an idiot. You're not a fraid-cat, though. Come along and don't make trouble. There's something queer about this storm—it's the worst I've ever seen. Maybe the house'll be struck next. If it is, it is; but we've got to be ready for anything." She pushed him along in front of her. "We'll watch it together," she added. "There'll be a lot of wreckage in town tonight."

"Is that little Jare?" queried a voice from a nearby room.

"Yes, Grandmother."

"Come here. Having a good time? This is a July celebration, isn't it?"

Mrs. Rachel Tolbecken sat apposite one of the windows of the drawing room, unlighted except by the flashes of lightning. She watched the disorder of nature with a sort of amused surprise. Her tranquillity, in part the result of long invalidism, was too deep to be disturbed by what she called fireworks. Her hands, with their touch of lawn at the wrists, lay quiet on the arms of the chair; her head, with its tulle cap, rested a little languidly against the back. The portraits on the wall of Great-grandfather Jared Tolbecken in his stock, of Great-great-grandfather Rufus in his wig, and of Grandfather in a frock coat looked no less disturbed than she.

"A fine spectacle," she observed. "Reminds me of the storm in *Macbeth*. I'll never forget how Edwin Booth played it. I'll have to read you the parts about the witches."

11

"Reminds *me* of Judgment Day," put in Aunt Joan. "Come on, Jared, we can see more of it from the hall window."

Side by side there, they stood looking out at the night, now black as pitch and again bright with veins of fire that showed, beyond the gardens of Tolbecken, the circle of the town. Points of light appeared dimly, for the whole population was up, the inhabitants of each house cut off in the welter of wind and water and forced to watch out the night alone. Far off, several barns were ablaze, in spite of the downpour. The lightning bolts were striking within the town itself. Close at hand, the familiar outlines of a tree had altered; a great limb dangled beside the trunk. And everywhere, houses, trees, the very earth seemed to be bracing themselves against continued shock.

" 'Behold,' " said Aunt Joan, " 'the name of the Lord cometh from far, burning with His anger, and the burden thereof is heavy.' If it isn't Judgment Day and we live through it, you'll remember this all your life."

She broke off at a blast of wind behind them which was abruptly cut off by the closing of a door.

"Well, Rufus, I'm glad you're back. Began to worry about your going alone. Everything all right?"

"Some bricks knocked down, and a considerable leak in one corner. The horses were frightened, but Gregory and I calmed them."

"You're wet through, I suppose."

"Only my feet. Get me some slippers, will you, Joan?"

In oilskins and sou'wester, with his square white beard showing beneath it, Judge Rufus Tolbecken looked like a frigate master just coming in from the quarter-deck. But when he unclasped his slicker and removed the hat, which he hung carefully above the iron base of the umbrella stand, he appeared in his usual summer suit of pongee, a tall, loose-limbed figure, gaunt but still powerful, topped by the dome of a massive bald head. He belonged to the angular American type that Abraham Lincoln represented. There was a leonine dignity in his bearing and voice, but something childlike and gentle in the eyes, and sadness in the deep lines above the beard.

"Why, little Jare," he said, beaming, "up and around? Making a night of it?"

"Yes," snorted Aunt Joan, coming back with the slippers, "and wanted to follow you out to the stable, what's more— said his place was with you."

12

"And so it is." Bending down, the Judge caught up his grandson and swung him back and forth.

"Heavy! So heavy! Eleven years old! But I can lift you yet. Eh, can't I?" Then, releasing him, but with a hand on his shoulder, "Where are Vincent and the others?"

"On the stairs," said Aunt Joan.

Rufus Tolbecken laughed. " 'Cowards die many times,' " he quoted, "but I'll say this for them, that I've never seen the equal of tonight. Here, Jared, give a pull, will you?"

Seating himself, he presented an old-fashioned half boot, which Jared, braced at the other end, worked off. Having changed to his slippers, he strode hand in hand with his grandson to the study, a room lying secluded in a wing of the house, smelling of old leather and books. An oil lamp with a green shade stood on the desk.

"It seems to be blowing over," said the Judge, as the intervals between flash and thunder lengthened. "A good thing, too, for there've been a lot of people tonight caught short and a little uneasy. Nothing like a storm to remind folks of their last hour. We'll sit here awhile and then go to bed. It's getting late."

A renewed pelting on the roof and booming of wind interrupted him. They preluded a fresh outburst of the storm, which had either circled back or was being reinforced by a second gale from the north. Shorter than the first, but more furious, it fell upon the town with a general discharge of lightning. It was as if all the resources of the elements, baffled thus far, were being thrown into a last attack.

From the door of the study, at which she had appeared as if from a crash of thunder, even Aunt Joan confessed alarm.

"It's pretty bad, Rufus, and it's getting worse. But it's not so much the lightning as the wind—I don't know whether the walls can stand it. The roof's split open in three places. I've been mopping so much water that I'm tired."

The Judge smiled. "Don't worry about the walls, Joan. People built homes to last in those days—twelve-inch timbers strong as Tolbecken Oak. As for lightning, if Bella and Sophy are scared, let them go down to the cellar. I've been told that's the safest."

"It's flooded," said Aunt Joan.

"Well, then, let them stay where they are. Tell 'em they won't know it if they're hit. . . . I'd better step in and see Rachel. With her heart trouble, she oughtn't to get worked up."

13

"Rubbish!" returned his sister-in-law. "She's asleep. We Maylins never took any stock in nerves."

Turned toward the window with Jared between them, they stood absorbed by the splendor and savagery of the storm. An almost continuous illumination disclosed mass upon mass of clouds surging toward the horizon, disclosed details of house and tree ghastly and forlorn, but it showed also, unswayed by the wind, solid as a tower, the great oak in the center of the lawn. Tempered by countless storms, it stood assured by its centuries of life, keeping its watch, an assertion of the past, an assertion of vigor and continuity.

The flagstaff midway toward the gate had been splintered; bolts had maimed several trees.

"I wonder what's happened in town," said Rufus Tolbecken. "Jerry-built modern houses won't hold against this. We'll have bad news tomorrow. Besides, the river's rising. There'll be damage from flood. But, you know, I think our place has been the bull's-eye, and we've lasted it out."

They remained staring at the window.

Then suddenly, as if all the fire in heaven were focused in one ball of flame, the lightning struck again, obscuring what it had hit by its unbearable vividness. The concussion of the report sent them staggering back, ears ringing, bewildered for a moment by the interplay of filaments across the retina. Hard upon this came a succession of crashes, a thudding and a rending, and a fountain of sparks in the night.

Too frightened to cry and still dazed by the shock, Jared heard his grandfather speaking in a voice entirely new to him.

"Look," he was saying, "the oak!"

Some echoing flashes, glancing back from the clouds, once more lighted the lawn. Its immemorial sentinel had been stricken. A splintered trunk, a remnant of branches sinking in their turn, the glow of a thunderbolt at the heart were all that were left.

Aunt Joan gave a low cry, but said nothing. Urgent entreaties from the hall asking whether the house had been struck passed unheeded.

"The oak," repeated Grandfather in the same odd voice. And after a long time, "I remember coming back from the war . . . I could see the top of it across the houses. . . . I remember how Father and Mother used to sit out there in the evening. . . ."

"Well," said Aunt Joan suddenly, "everything comes to an end. You can't alter that. We'll plant ivy around the

14

trunk—there'll be that much left. A kind of monument.
. . . I'll go along now and tell the others what's happened."

Silent because Grandfather was silent, distressed by what
he could not wholly understand, the boy remained leaning
against the side of Rufus Tolbecken's chair. The strong
profile of the man stood out against the lamplight. One hand
smoothed his beard, but Jared could see—as one by one the
remaining branches of the oak crashed down—the hand
tightening as if in pain.

"Sounds like the snapping of a cable," said the Judge at
length. "And that's what it is—one strand after the other."

He threw out an arm and lifted the boy to his lap. The
thunder rumbled far off; the rain lessened, became at last
a pattering, followed by the splash of drops among leaves. A
cool night air stirred.

"Time to sleep now, little boy," he muttered. "The storm
has passed."

2

An indenture hanging framed above the fireplace in Rufus
Tolbecken's study bore witness that in the year of Our
Lord, 1753, the twenty-sixth year of the reign of our gracious sovereign, King George the Second, certain lands thereinafter described, whereon stood a house thereinafter described, were to be ceded by the party of the first part, one
John Gresham, to the party of the second part, one Jared
Tolbecken, as full and sufficient payment of the dowry and
jointure of Mistress Mary Gresham, beloved daughter of
the party of the first part and betrothed wife of the party of
the second part, to be held and enjoyed in freehold by him
and his heirs or assigns forever . . . whereunto both parties
had subscribed their names and affixed their seals.

This in its copperplate handwriting was the Tolbecken
patent of dignity—evidence of the long possession of land
handed down from father to son. And toward the end of the
nineteenth century in America this was in itself a rarity and a
distinction. Five generations, including young Jared Tolbecken, had been born in the house described in the indenture. It did not matter that in a hundred and forty-five
years the house had grown and the land had dwindled; that
the house had become a mansion and the land a town block.

The same hearth in the now modernized sitting room warmed Jared and Mary's descendants; the same trees or their aftershoots shaded them. The core had been preserved; they were still the Tolbeckens of Tolbecken.

Dutch by origin, forthright and public-spirited, they had served America and had prospered with her. Jared Tolbecken of 1753 had been a farmer. Rufus Tolbecken, his son, had been a farmer and an officer in the Continental army. His son, Jared Tolbecken, had been part farmer, part lawyer, and had fought in the War of 1812. His son, the present Rufus Tolbecken, was a lawyer too; had commanded a regiment in the Civil War; had been thrice elected to Congress; had been a friend of Lincoln, Sumner, and Grant; a federal judge; a foreign minister. With him, the Tolbeckens had reached their zenith. He was the single national figure in the country, its most respected attorney, a wealthy man, the embodiment of all that was good in a family identified from the beginning with the history of the state.

On Tolbecken land the town of Dunstable, at one time no more than a relay station between Philadelphia and Baltimore, had grown up and now flourished. It was the Judge's grandfather, Rufus Tolbecken, who, around 1800, stimulated river traffic and made a shipping center of Dunstable. It was Jared Tolbecken who in 1830 sold a right-of-way to the railroad and thus put Dunstable on the commercial map. It was he who, realizing that the region henceforth was committed to industry rather than to agriculture, split up his remaining farm into lots, encouraged building, and gave the town its present shape. It might more appropriately have borne the name of the family which had created it, but in any case it remained proud of the Tolbeckens, proud of the Judge, who after a brilliant career had chosen to reopen his office there rather than accept a more lucrative practice in Philadelphia, proud also of the Tolbecken homestead itself with its five acres of lawn and garden, extravagantly occupying the most valuable block in the business center.

But in the late nineties business centers of towns which had not yet become cities were less than turbulent. An air of rural leisure lingered around hitching posts under trees not yet condemned in the interests of traffic. Although banks, stores, and offices grew thicker about this square, and were at worst unsightly, they were still fairly unobtrusive. Newcomers to Dunstable were sure to inquire, and were eagerly informed, about the handsome colonial house which in the

16

past had entertained so many distinguished guests. A brass plate nailed to a post of the front gate bore in old-fashioned script the one word *Tolbecken*.

This place, the family's last real holding, best revealed its spirit. The square frame house of Mary Gresham's dowry had long since been extended to form part of a generous façade. The plain doorway had been remodeled upon more graceful lines. In short, conditioned by the changing problems of each generation, the utilitarian farm and home had become a gentleman's residence, but slowly, almost reluctantly, with each successive addition the family had been at pains to retain as much of the old as could possibly be salvaged.

The result, of course, was that the place, however irregular in architecture and planting, acquired an ever-deepening individuality. It was an organism rather than a construction. It expressed and repaid a century and a half of love and tending; it bore the curious coloring which inanimate things acquire from an intimacy with human destinies. Many of its details had been copied for use in period houses elsewhere—the staircase with its many landings, the elegant dining room, the octagonal room, the sundial on its circle of lawn in the rear garden—but, however faithful, the copies bore only a pale similitude to the original. The separate features of Tolbecken were facets of a single gem; the self-consciously planned period house with its studied graces could display them only as fragments of mosaic.

Judge Rufus Tolbecken, who gave permission for such copying readily, at the same time mildly ridiculing it, on one occasion visited a client in Washington the hallway of whose house had been meticulously modeled from the Judge's own.

"This," remarked Tolbecken in his stately Victorian manner, "is a compliment, a very handsome compliment, Senator."

"And pretty successful, don't you think?"

"I do, sir. My place at Dunstable wouldn't know itself."

"What do you mean?"

"I mean it's rejuvenated. Your house is as much like Tolbecken as a new shoe is like an old one. But when your shoe has worn down and been resoled, it won't look like mine."

On the large-scale map of Dunstable in Karl Kirschbaum's real-estate office, Tolbecken, a square of green on a pink background, challenged the eye. Once spotted with green, the map had grown steadily pink around this steadfast center. For years it had faced the desk and, stared at a hundred times daily, had burned itself into Mr. Kirschbaum's consciousness. At home on his porch, at night in his bed, he was never quite free from its pink and green shadow. The pink consoled him as the green distressed him.

Karl Kirschbaum was a prophet and a dreamer. Twenty, thirty years before anyone else in Dunstable, he sensed the possibilities and the trend of expansion. He smelled with his long nose, as it were, the future factories, more-serried means of transit, a denser population—his visionary city beautiful, into which, if acumen and effort counted for anything, his native town would be transformed. But, though first a prophet, he was even more fully a businessman bent on effecting his prophecies. It was chiefly he who, by dint of organizing, promoting, scheming, advertising, had cleansed the map of its disturbing green and made it so harmoniously pink. When he had started, forty years ago, the place had been a sort of feudal dependency of the Tolbeckens. It was dependent no more, thanks in great part to the zeal of Kirschbaum and others inspired by his dream. Philanthropy, politics, and competition, powers harnessed by him, had paved the streets, dug the sewers, assured the water supply, installed power plants and a streetcar line, built factories, schools, churches, and a Y.M.C.A., and quadrupled the population. What Jared Tolbecken founded, Kirschbaum developed. It was not wealth that tempted him; he had wealth enough. It was not personal ambition, for he lived modestly, even obscurely. It was essentially the urge of creation, which he himself would have called "business sense" and "keeping up with the times."

Meanwhile, old houses and gardens disappeared; noise increased; banks and slums multiplied; and an ever-deepening cloud of soot drifted over the town, which was slowly becoming a city.

But not quite; there was still a good deal to do. Here and there waning conservatism resisted the prophet. Kirschbaum was patient; conservatism was thinning out; progress was steady. But there was one thing of which he was intolerant, a thing that like a green, malevolent eye defied him from the center of his map, and baffled him—Tolbecken.

"Every sensible man," he observed to Albert Reiger, the Judge's son-in-law, "ought to listen to reason, and the Judge is a sensible man." He proffered the syllogism in a tone of exasperated inquiry. "Don't you think so, Al?"

"Think what?"

"That the Judge ought to listen to reason."

Albert Reiger was a big, square man in his late thirties, with heavy, regular features, gray eyes, and sandy hair. A

18

down of lighter shade covered the backs of his hands. His jaw, like the rest of him, was square, his mouth straight under a blond mustache. He owned the Reiger underwear factory, one of the most considerable plants in Dunstable.

"There's no use discussing what the Judge ought or oughtn't to do, Ike."

"But don't you think he will?"

"Will what?"

"Reconsider this business of holding on to Tolbecken?"

"No, I hardly think so. He has a mind of his own. Mary and I have done all *we* could. So has Vincent—what with hinting about the value of the place, and the taxes and the expense. But the subject's like a red rag to a bull. We have to back off pretty quick every time."

Kirschbaum grunted. "I thought the storm and the repairs he's been in for might have shaken him."

"You're always hopeful," said Reiger. They had gone over this problem for the last ten years, whenever, as today, occasional business brought them together. "I'm not," he added. "It's no use."

"Well," sighed Kirschbaum, "the Judge is getting old, after all."

"He'll probably outlive you," replied the other. "He's sound as a bell."

The real-estate man calculated, his hands triangular at the tip of his nose. "Might try a jump in the tax rate," he mused.

"No, you don't!" Albert's voice was polite, but there was controlled anger in it. "You can't jump taxes on Tolbecken without affecting business property in the neighborhood, and we—" Albert spoke collectively for the business interests— "we won't stand for it. Besides, I don't intend to stand by and see the Judge subjected to petty persecutions of that sort, am I'm not alone in that. The town owes him a great deal, don't you forget it. Taxes'll have to go up," he continued, "but they'll go up in the natural course of events and not for the sake of ousting Rufus Tolbecken!"

"Who's talking about ousting him?" grumbled Kirschbaum. "It's simply a business proposition, advantageous to both parties. The Judge's practice isn't what it used to be. It must cost him a good deal just to pay his son Maylin's way out of scrapes in New York. And he's half supporting Vincent, not to speak of Maylin's wife, Bella. Oh, that's all right," he waved impatiently at a frown on his caller's face, "everybody knows about it. But the point is, in view of everything,

19

wouldn't he like to capitalize on Tolbecken, make an asset out of it instead of a liability? Isn't he spending more than he can afford, eh?" prompted Kirschbaum.

Albert had a habit of humming, and now he hummed a trifle grimly. He was a coolheaded, progressive business-man, but he was honest and forthright. Moreover, he belonged to the Tolbeckens by marriage; though he could not claim an exaggerated delicacy, it chafed him to discuss family affairs with an outsider. He hummed on, but when Kirschbaum repeated his "Eh?" for a second time, he replied bluntly that it was none of the latter's business. "And it's none of mine, either," he added.

Kirschbaum rose and strode over to the map of Dunstable. His stained thumb, spreading itself out, covered up Tolbecken; he pressed so hard that the nail turned white.

"Look there! Do you see any sense in that—one whole block, maybe two, of such valuable business sites given up to grass and trees? People say, 'Expand back from the center.' But you know what that means: narrow, inconvenient streets, buildings still in good condition having to be bought up and torn down. And then, admitting we go ahead along that line, what happens in the end? Why, Tolbecken will have to be sold some time or other; and then, of course, every up-and-coming firm will want a location there. What's the result? Duplication, overbuilding, waste. And all because one man is bullheaded."

He removed his thumb from the obnoxious green, which once more seemed to stare out at him; but turning his back on it, hands in his pockets, he fixed a fanatic eye on his companion.

"We need a hotel, a really grand hotel ten stories high, with space around it. We need a first-class department store that'll bring in trade from every county not supplied by Baltimore and Philadelphia. We need some banks that look like banks and not like Quaker meetinghouses. And, by George, we could have them, all of them! I could organize it. I've had feelers out and I could find the backing. There comes a time, Al, when property gets too valuable for any one man to hold unproductively. He can't afford it. He *won't* afford it unless he's crazy!"

Reiger approved these sentiments, but lacking Kirschbaum's imagination, he took facts as they came and remained outwardly cool.

"Well, what of it?" he remarked. "There's no use going over that again."

"There certainly is. I'm going to make the Judge a new offer. And I want you to back me up."

"How much this time?"

Kirschbaum paused dramatically, then, giving each syllable its value, answered, "One hundred and seventy-five thousand."

Calm as a codfish, in the approved manner, Reiger met Kirschbaum's inquisitive eyes without blinking. As a matter of fact he did not even see them, being absorbed by a row of figures strung across his mind which he was multiplying by five per cent. One hundred and seventy-five thousand times five hundredths. Result: eight thousand, seven hundred and fifty dollars. But add a thousand for taxes, plus a thousand for insurance and upkeep. Total: ten thousand, seven hundred and fifty dollars. Practically eleven thousand dollars in rental, eleven thousand dollars' loss of income, to retain Tolbecken at its present value. He reckoned that his father-in-law, what with practice and investments, had between fifteen and twenty thousand a year. If so, the disproportion between income and cost of residence was ridiculous. It hurt his business feelings.

"It's worth considering," he remarked finally. "The Judge might want to think it over. When did you plan to take it up with him?"

"Any time, but I'd like to have you along. You're a member of the family, and could put things in a way I couldn't —that is, if you think as I do that the Judge, for his own sake, mind you, ought to sell."

But to Reiger, strategy forbade enthusiasm. "Might pay him to hold on," he demurred.

"It might," agreed Kirschbaum. "But I've got a feeling," he murmured, "that Judge Tolbecken is hard pressed, that he's more up against it than most people think. The question is, can he afford to hold on?"

The other capitulated slightly. "Ask *him*. I think it's a fairly reasonable offer, and if it'll help you any, I'll call on him at his office with you."

"When?"

"This afternoon. We'll go over together."

"Good work," said Kirschbaum.

When Reiger had gone out, the prophet of progress sat with speculative eye on the map, like a painter before his masterpiece. It was a good deal to expect that the final touch of perfection could be applied so soon; but at all events, there were two things in which Kirschbaum had unlimited confidence, and they had never failed him—Money and Time.

21

3

Everybody in Dunstable showed respect to Rufus Tolbecken, and not chiefly on account of his name and career. These, though contributing to the deference paid him, did not fully explain it; among strangers and in other towns, he commanded the same respect. He had a spiritual quality perhaps best described as the reverse of everything cynical and worldly-wise. He believed in men and he believed in God—it was his faith that glowed within him, that kept him young, eager, and steadfast. And to this had been added age, the authority of work well done, and wisdom born of experience. Absorbed in interests greater than himself, he shared in part the greatness of those interests, more impressive in his simplicity than by any pose or strutting of self-assertion. And it was an awareness of this superiority that had prompted Karl Kirschbaum's insistence that Reiger accompany him to his interview with the Judge.

"I hope," he observed to Reiger, after they had put on their hats with a certain grimness and set out, "I hope that the Judge will take it easy. We've known each other for forty years. He ought to understand that I wouldn't try to put anything over on him."

The other, who, though a man of some importance at the council tables of his own and other companies, had never quite rid himself of a small-boy feeling in the presence of his father-in-law, cleared his throat. "He'll realize that, all right; but I hate to tackle him, anyway, on the subject of Tolbecken. It seems almost like interfering with his religion." Then, pointing up to the second floor of the National Bank building, "He's in, all right. There's young Jare at the window."

It was a hot day in late July, but when they had climbed the narrow old-fashioned stairs to the office, it was not the heat alone that made both men take off their straw hats and run a handkerchief over their foreheads. They paused a moment in front of the glazed-paneled door, bearing in somewhat frayed lettering the words *Rufus Tolbecken, Att'y at Law*.

"Is the Judge at leisure?" asked Kirschbaum of Ed Coales, typist, clerk, and student, who sat coatless, cigar in mouth and feet on desk, in the outer office.

Time was when there had been three such clerks and apprentices at desks now vacant, who read the law, copied briefs, learned the ropes, and finally took their bar examinations from that office. But that had been ten or twenty years earlier, when Jared Tolbecken, Rufus's eldest and ablest son, was alive, and when the Tolbecken practice had been the most extensive in the state. Since the death of Jared, many changes had taken place. Younger men, better hustlers and better mixers than the Judge, had established themselves in Dunstable and in the rest of the county. His clients, although still sufficiently numerous and loyal, had dwindled. Students nowadays preferred law schools to office reading. Coales, therefore, a somewhat fat and placid relic of an older day, read his case books by himself.

It appeared that the Judge was not engaged and would be glad to see the gentlemen. He sat at a long ink-stained desk in a horsehair swivel chair that had served him and his father for sixty years. Because of the heat he wore a black alpaca coat, without collar or tie. When they entered, he was craning over his desk, his bald dome of a head only a few inches above a reference page he was copying. "Just a moment," he murmured, "just a moment. Have seats, Mr. Kirschbaum and Albert." The large, finely shaped hand, that seemed too heavy for the pen it held, pressed down, showing the veins; it moved deliberately, laboriously over the paper. Then, when he had marked his place and raised his steel spectacles to his forehead, he wheeled in his chair, stood up, and shook hands with his visitors.

"Mr. Kirschbaum," said the Judge, "I want you to meet my grandson, young Jared Tolbecken, named for his uncle, you remember. Come over here, Jare. This is Mr. Karl Kirschbaum, the most prominent man in Dunstable and my old acquaintance."

He had called him "Mister," and he had not called him "friend." It implied kindliness, but no familiarity.

"That's saying a good deal," replied the other, parrying the compliment, "a good deal, particularly in this office." And taking the small hand lifted up to him, "Here's a fine boy, Judge—has the family look about him. What're you reading, Buddie?" for Jared had left a small buckram-covered book on the window ledge.

"Guy Mannering."

"Ah, yes." Kirschbaum was plainly at a loss.

"By Sir Walter Scott," explained the boy.

"That's right," said Kirschbaum hazily. "Nothing better

23

than a book." But it struck him as queer that a lad of eleven should be hanging around his grandfather's office, reading books, when he ought to have been out at a swimming hole or doing chores at home. He liked boys who were fighters and hustlers, as his own sons had been. Still, young Jared was certainly well grown and good-looking, with his brown hair and dark eyes—he had the aristocratic Tolbecken look, all right.

"We came to see you on a matter of business, Judge," Kirschbaum continued, lifting his pale face and nose toward the taller man.

"At your service. Jare, get back to Sir Walter. The boy's my little partner," smiled Rufus. "I'm training him early to the law . . . unless your business is entirely confidential?"

Kirschbaum hesitated. "It's about your place—about Tolbecken."

"Why, then he can listen. It concerns him as much as it does me. He'll own the place when I'm gone."

The boy listened, gradually aware of conflict between these men. Once more, as on the night of the storm, he felt that his grandfather defended some threatened past, valiantly, but hard pressed. Or was it only later that the import of the scene became clear? At all events, he would never forget it, and as time passed, it would grow more vivid, more dramatic in his mind. He would recall the details of the setting, the dusty office, lined with its calf-bound law books, the black stone mantelpiece with Daniel Webster frowning above it, and outside, the drowsy peace of summer afternoon.

"This is the proposition, Judge Tolbecken," said Kirschbaum solemnly. "I'm prepared to offer you one hundred and seventy-five thousand dollars in cash. Now, wait," he added, staving off rejoinder, "I think that's fair, but price would never be the chief consideration with you, I know. I'm asking you to sell in the interests of the public, in the interests of Dunstable. Everybody thinks you ought to sell; *I* think so, and Albert Reiger here agrees with me."

"He does, eh?" interrupted the Judge.

Reiger flushed. "That's not correct," he protested. "I told you that in my opinion the terms were reasonable and that the Judge might want to consider them."

"And who, sir," returned his father-in-law, "has given you to understand that my home, that Tolbecken was for sale at any price? Have I ever even suggested it? When you, Mr. Kirschbaum, offered me a hundred thousand some years ago, I declined and told you then that the matter was closed. I considered your proposal fair at that time; I consider your

24

present offer fair. But what of it? Tolbecken is not for sale. And let me tell you one thing more," he went on in a deeper voice, his jaw squared, "I have not reached the stage where I permit others to think for me and tell me what I should do. Public interests!" he snorted. "Interests of Dunstable! Who has worked harder for the interests of the public than I have? What do you *mean* by the interests of the public?"

Cringing a little, Kirschbaum stuck to his purpose. The pale lips, crossed at times by an apologetic smile, moved rapidly; he spoke with growing eloquence. He reviewed the history of Dunstable, forecast its future, explained the strategic location of Tolbecken. Then, veering to another angle, he pointed out the inevitable rise of taxation, the loss in income involved in retaining such a property, the necessity of looking at things as they were *now,* in the year 1898.

"Of course you're fond of the old house, Judge—we'll all of us be kind of sorry to see it go. But that's just sentiment, if you'll excuse my saying it, just feelings that aren't worth a hundred and seventy-five thousand dollars. Or look here, I'll stretch a point and make it two hundred thousand simply to show you that we look at this deal in a big way."

"Tolbecken is not for sale," repeated the Judge.

"Well, sir," exclaimed the other, "do you mind telling me *why* not?"

"I do mind, sir. I can't see what affair it is of yours." Then, suddenly, the older man smiled. His native warmth broke through with a softening of the eyes. "You must excuse me, Mr. Kirschbaum. I intended no discourtesy and you intended none. You asked me why Tolbecken is not for sale and I'll tell you, though it won't sound like sense, I presume, not business sense, anyway."

He leaned back and crossed his legs. "It's like this. First about Dunstable: there's no use going over what our family has done for the town. You and Albert know all that. I think you'll admit it's a little hard to be swallowed up by the place we founded. Still, if it were a question of real benefit to the thousands of people here, I don't think I'd be selfish enough to stand in the way of it. But the point is, I don't see the benefit. Will your banks and hotels make up for my lawns and trees? Everybody in Dunstable enjoys them now, feels cooler, breathes freer around that square than they will between your walls.

"But here's another thing. People walking outside my grounds look over into the past. Usually they don't think about it, but the consciousness is there. And often they do

25

think. They say George Washington's carriage drove out through these gates once. John Marshall stayed here, and so did John Quincy Adams and Tippecanoe Harrison. In 1862 there was a torchlight procession up to the front door there, and President Lincoln made a speech from the steps. Longfellow, Prescott, Beecher Stowe, Emerson were here; Sumner, Sherman, Horace Greeley, James G. Blaine. It gives them somehow the flavor of America, reminds them of their birthright. Can your banks and hotels take the place of this—will they give the people something better? To build in your way is to wipe out this feeling for the past, and in my opinion you are building on sand."

"Wait a minute," interrupted Kirschbaum, "doesn't every child in the public schools study history? Don't we make a point of Washington's Birthday, Decoration Day, Fourth of July, and so on?"

"Yes," said the Judge, "and which do you think makes the deeper impression: reading that trees cast shadows, or sitting in their shade?"

The promoter shrugged. "It seems to me," he grumbled, "that the present and future are a little more important than the past."

"Of course," agreed Tolbecken, "but the trouble with you and Albert is, that you act as if the past had no present or future value at all—at least not enough to be worth the sacrifice of a building block, not worth the sacrifice of any immediate advantage."

"Oh, now," protested Reiger, "that isn't fair. The fact is, whatever we think about this sort of thing, that America *is* speeding up. We may like it or not, but the *fact* is that business sections of towns like this have *got* to be used for business sooner or later. We've got to keep up or fall behind, and we don't want Dunstable out of the race, that's all. That's the point."

"You've said it, Al," nodded Kirschbaum with a grateful glance at his ally. "There's the point."

"Not in the least," answered Tolbecken. "The point is that you were urging me to sell my place for the benefit of the town and I refused to agree that it would be a benefit." He laughed. "You took the conscientious line with me, gentlemen. But you took another line as well. You said that mere sentiments aren't worth a hundred and seventy-five thousand dollars to me personally, that a sale would be to my own great advantage. Well, I deny it, in spite even of two hundred thousand dollars, and I'll tell you why—because it would be

26

impossible for me to invest the money you offer in anything that would yield as satisfactory dividends. What are those dividends? A home. You say, 'Build another home in the suburbs that would cost less to keep up.' But homes aren't built—they grow. They take form through the years. I could build a house there, but that's all. Why, the very word 'home' is dropping out of use. Men say, 'My house is on such and such a street,' or, 'I'd like to receive you at my house,' or, 'Come back to the house with me.' And for good reason—because they do not give themselves time to have a home. I have one and intend to keep it."

He stopped, suddenly aware of the glazed eyes of his listeners. They were as uncomfortable as deaf men who have to pretend they understand what they cannot hear. Kirschbaum nodded politely from time to time, and Reiger crossed and uncrossed his legs. If anyone but Judge Tolbecken had talked like this, they would not have put up with it. Since it was he, they felt that what he said probably meant something, but it sounded very foolish.

"Of course, Judge," said the real-estate man suavely, "I see what you mean. Some men like to spend money on horses or traveling; you prefer to spend it on your place. No quarrel with that. All we claim is that there's such a thing as too much extravagance. Look here, can't we leave the matter at this? Think it over, talk to the family about it. I understand you're going to have quite a reunion this week—Mrs. Lehman back from France, your son coming down from New York, and of course Mrs. Reiger and Vincent will be here. Don't you think they and Mrs. Tolbecken ought to be consulted?" He smiled and added tactfully, "We're both of us getting along. It'll be the young folks' turn after us. And an advantageous offer like this mayn't always be possible."

But the Judge had stiffened. "My family, Mr. Kirschbaum, has nothing to do with it. A man must think for himself and make his own decisions. Tolbecken is not for sale. And now, unless you have some further matter of business . . ."

He paused, completing the insinuation with a glance at his desk. Kirschbaum got up dejectedly; Reiger, humming a little, reached for his hat.

"Good afternoon, gentlemen. My best regards to Mrs. Kirschbaum. Albert, bring Mary and the children over this evening."

The real-estate man lingered, however. "I'm sorry, Judge . . ."

"Not at all, you haven't disturbed me in the least."

"I mean, that you refused to consider . . ."

"Oh, I see. No, quite impossible, Mr. Kirschbaum, as I explained. Good afternoon."

"Is it really true, Grandfather," breathed Jared, when the door of the outer office had rattled shut, "that that man wanted to buy our place?"

Rufus Tolbecken nodded and began pacing the office, his hands clasped behind him. But the boy, trained to his moods and aware that questions must wait, saw in his face not the expected anger, but a look such as often crept over it when he spoke of Uncle Jared's death, a look of faltering and desolation. Up and down he walked, slowly, leadenly. Then he squared his shoulders.

"Let's be going home, Jare. Time to break off, anyhow. And what do you say to some ginger ale at the drugstore? Seems to me I'm kind of thirsty."

4

It was hot in the street, which exhaled a smell of newly laid asphalt; but Ogden's Pharmacy, on the corner facing Tolbecken, shaded by its awnings, was all the cooler and more fragrant. Here an electric fan with propellerlike blades revolved on the ceiling and kept the cool air in movement. In the boy's mind Ogden's Pharmacy, with its awning, fan, perfume, and soda fountain, personified summer. Perched side by side on their stools, the Judge and his grandson confronted Mr. Ogden himself, who, having served his customers, leaned against the back bar and prepared for small talk.

He chatted now with the Judge about Hobson and the Battle of Santiago, which had been fought several weeks earlier, and about how Admiral Cervera from all accounts was a nice old gentleman, and what a national disgrace the commissariat of the army was turning out to be; how it was said that the boys were dying like flies at Tampa.

"A foolish war," grumbled the Judge, "like every other war. People get drunk on heroism and they stampede. They stampeded McKinley. It was the same thing in the Mexican War, same thing in the Civil War."

Ogden respectfully agreed—he usually agreed—and conversation drifted back to Dunstable, the recent storm, local

28

trifles. Jared's straw made a sucking noise at the bottom of his glass.

"They tell me Miss Elizabeth's coming back on a visit, Judge," hinted Ogden. "Terrible long time she's been away. Used to be my favorite. So full of life. What's the name of the fellow she married—Bowman? Breman?"

"Lehman," said the Judge, a trifle shortly, "an artist."

"Six years ago, wasn't it?"

"Seven."

"That's it—1891. I remember her wedding as if it was yesterday. We could hear the orchestra and lawn party all the way over here. Been living in Europe, hasn't she?"

"France. Paris."

The same clipped tone sounded in Rufus Tolbecken's voice. Elizabeth was his favorite daughter. He would have felt aggrieved at her marriage to anyone; but he distrusted artists with an old-fashioned American distrust, and above all he despised Frederick Lehman, artist, expatriate—a Frenchified middle-aged satyr, he called him, in spite of his Legion of Honor ribbon and his gold medals. How Lizzie had taken to such a man, he could not see.

Then, aware that his curtness might be misinterpreted, and with characteristic horror of disclosing one shred of intimate family affairs, he took pains to add, "Yes, she's coming tomorrow, but unfortunately without Mr. Lehman. She's bringing her stepdaughter, though. Her name's Clarice, and she's ten years old. Lehman was a widower, you recall"—he said this with an air of carelessness. "She's had no children of her own. Clarice's mother was French."

"Somebody told me," said Ogden, "that your son Maylin . . ." but glancing at Jared he coughed, and changed the subject. "Kind of a birthday party, isn't it, Judge?"

"Yes, I'll be sixty-seven. Strange thing, this matter of age. First impressions are the lasting ones, and the first impression with all of us is youth. I can't seem to remember that I'm old. Well, so it goes. . . ."

He selected a dime from the loose change in his pocket, put it on the counter, and stood up. The glare beyond the awning outside had faded into rays slanting between trees and houses. The summer evening had begun to drift over the town. In place of carts, drays, buggies, and other vehicles, a smart buckboard or two, drawn by a high-stepper in bright harness, rattled by, and family surreys with their fringed tops followed more demurely, for it was now the hour of the afternoon drive.

29

Judge Tolbecken lifted his hat in reply to greetings as he and Jared crossed the street to their gate, but the shadow which had fallen upon the Judge after his interview with Kirschbaum seemed to have returned as he followed the winding driveway up to his house. Slower than usual, and silent, he moved on in deep thought. What the subject of this might be the boy had no means of knowing; but when his grandfather spoke at last, Jared felt that the remark had little to do with what had absorbed him.

"Your father will be here tomorrow," observed the Judge. "Did you know that?"

"Yes," said Jared indifferently.

"You don't remember him, I suppose?"

The boy did not. He remembered only an occasional gift that the mysterious person called Father had sent, and he had seen a miniature of him on Grandmother's bureau. Recently, of course, he had begun to question what had so far been taken for granted and wondered why, unlike the fathers of his schoolmates, his own should be living in New York or elsewhere; but all his questions had been met by evasions, and after a time, putting two and two together, he had formed a confused idea of something wrong and incomprehensible, which did not as yet, however, greatly preoccupy him.

"He was a handsome boy," said the Judge unexpectedly, "but you look more like his brother—like Jared."

"Will he be staying with us now, Grandfather?"

Again the familiar hesitation crept into the old man's voice. "I hope so. . . . We'll see. . . . He has business in New York."

Following their custom, they did not immediately enter the house, but continued along one of the erratic side paths which led through the grounds—past the ruins of Tolbecken Oak, through a group of willows and wild cherries, between a length of box hedge ending in a disused garden, and so finally to the lawn between house and barns, with its girdle of elms, and the old sundial at its center.

Here the Judge paused, as usual, drew out his late-afternoon cigar, and leaning on the dial looked up at the high gable of the house, overarched by trees and mellow in the light of sunset. It was almost the look of a lover who finds peace in the presence of his beloved.

5

The Judge and his wife had had five children, among whom Jared, the eldest son, had most completely represented the family type. He had been well balanced, forceful, intellingent, and slightly ponderous. But he had died some years ago, at the age of thirty-five. Of the remaining children, the daughters, Mary and Elizabeth, more than their brothers, were Tolbeckens of the pure tradition; but they had, so to speak, divided this heritage between them. Mary, substantial and Saxon, had the physique of her stock together with its common-sense qualities; while Elizabeth, on the other hand, displayed in concentrated form that strain of brilliancy which had distinguished her father and had been interwoven with the family homespun.

It was in the persons of the second and third sons, Vincent and Maylin, that the breaking-down process of the family became evident.

Vincent was merely a genial, feeble, lackadaisical man, with the capacities of a clerk, who, by the Judge's influence, had attained the position of cashier at a Dunstable bank, and would stick there to the end. He was the typical small-town citizen, hectored by his wife, jog-trot in his habits, taken for granted by everyone. Maylin, however, was better and worse than this. He was sometimes spoken of as the black sheep.

Opinions differed as to the exact depth of his blackness; but even those women who admired his looks and had been flattered by his gallantries admitted that his character was quite off-white. As for the men, they considered him vaguely a scamp; Dunstable puritans set him down flatly as a blackguard.

The essential facts of his life were these: after a joyous career at college, he came back laden with all of the social and none of the academic honors. It was the day of striped blazers, mustaches, and yachting caps, the day of cotillions, fine horses, and lawn parties, and Maylin Tolbecken was nonpareil in Dunstable, its chief beau, the biggest catch. He had a splendid way with the ladies, and started a number of fires in feminine hearts. But his incendiary fling was brief. Always readier to say yes than no, he said yes to the oglings and languishings of Bella Lawton; that is, of course, she induced him to make her say yes. And the bird was caged.

She had very melting eyes, creamy skin, and flaxen hair that she knew how to show off to advantage. She had also a way of putting herself under people's protection that was affecting and flattering—up to a point. But she had nothing else, and her limited scale tended to become tiresome, as the cooing of a dove becomes tedious. Bella Lawton was much like a dove, a soft, stupid dove.

All the Tolbeckens opposed this marriage on every count. The cuddling type of woman did not appeal to them, and they were unmoved by prettiness. The girl had neither fortune nor family; she was, in fact, an orphan under the weary wing of an aunt, and although her dependency seemed piquant to a lover, it was unromantic in the eyes of his relatives. They opposed, argued, entreated; Bella languished in the protecting arms of Maylin. In the end they were married.

And then the nonpareil came to his senses. He was no longer beau of Dunstable, but a married man, chained to his father's office and to the lifelong task of petting his dove. But Maylin, though he may have been a goose, was a wild goose, and domesticity suffocated him. The first year went by tolerably enough; he put up with the second; during the third he pecked at his cage. Meanwhile, Bella, secure of her nest, curled her hair less diligently than before, put less of adoration in her eyes. And then there was a baby and Maylin was expected to play second fiddle to the child, to be helpful and devoted. But it happened that his college class was to have a banquet in New York.

And to New York Maylin went. At the banquet they sang "Drink Her Down" and "A Capital Ship for an Ocean Trip." With every song and with every mug, Maylin's determination grew clearer. The goose had slipped his cage and would not again be caught.

There were telegrams and letters, appeals, threats, and finally anathemas. But he did not return. He simply would not come back to Dunstable, and he was through with Bella, let everybody say what they would. He rode the crest of the wave for the most part, being saved from the trough of it by an occasional check from home, a furtive check of which the Judge was ashamed, but which he could never bring himself to withhold. On one occasion, Rufus Tolbecken went to New York, interviewed the prodigal, and almost prevailed. Maylin promised to come back, but he never did.

From time to time he hinted by letter that if Bella saw fit to divorce him, he would be glad to cooperate. And Bella indeed saw fit; she would have liked another protecting arm, if any could be found. But on this point, they struck an absolute wall. There would be no divorce in the Tolbecken family. The record had remained clean of that, and must remain clean. The Judge would support his daughter-in-law and his grandson, would support them gladly, but he would not endure the blot of a divorce. And Bella, daunted and helpless, agreed.

She lived on at Tolbecken, therefore, a pale, inconsequential shadow, inclined to plaintiveness and the role of martyrdom, in which she found her only sense of importance. In the effort not to neglect her, the family spoiled her punctiliously. They found themselves in the position of making up for Maylin to the wife of whom they had disapproved. But the spoiling did her no good. She dawdled and shirked the responsibility of Jared as much as possible. The injustice of her desertion, the pathos of her sorrows were all that gave her life color, and almost instinctively, she played them up. No wonder that she was sometimes forgotten in a house where her only function was to be pathetic. Her mother-in-law, Aunt Joan, and the others did their best; but she kept slipping out of mind, to be recalled, as it were, with a jerk. Even her son reckoned without her.

So, as in most things, there was a balance on both sides of the Maylin-Bella question. He should have been true; but it is hard to be true to a wax figurine. There was no extenuation for his act except her fatuousness. Between them, it was the family, as usual, that suffered most.

In those years Rufus Tolbecken felt more than the chill of age. For, bitter to a distinguished man, the son and grandson of distinguished men, is the thought that after him his name will fritter off into the mediocre. The name, the justifiable pride in it, had become almost religion. Of all his hopes, there remained to him only one, and that one problematic—little Jared.

And yet miracles sometimes happen; there was always a chance that the lost son would return. For years the Judge had alternated between diatribes and appeals; but of late he had given up thundering, and had been content to plead. He and Maylin's mother were old; Elizabeth, the favorite sister, would be arriving from France. Would Maylin not come? Could they not try to patch up this wretched grievance? At least, would he not come for old love's sake? And to the

33

Judge's astonishment. Maylin had written that he would come.

Now that the day had arrived, Tolbecken went about in its various ways to prepare the fatted calf. Aunt Joan looked to the baking and house cleaning, Bella to her clothes and curls; Mrs. Rufus Tolbecken, dressed as for Sunday in her best tulle cap, sat for once without book or handiwork in the parlor; the Judge scanted his office to meet the late morning train from New York; even the servants looked solemn and self-conscious.

At length the surrey appeared, in a last flourish of speed along the drive, and the whole of Tolbecken stiffened. Grandmother limped from the parlor to the hall; Aunt Joan in her satin dress opened the front door; Jared hovered behind them; Bella, waiting upstairs, peered down through the window curtains.

But as the carriage approached, they saw that the Judge was alone.

"Maylin didn't arrive," he said tonelessly, in answer to the silence that greeted him, "probably missed the train."

The family, joined now by Bella, trooped into the drawing room, where they sat crestfallen and baffled, their preparations hanging in vacancy.

"There's another train at half past twelve," said the Judge, consulting a timetable. "I'll meet that."

But almost at once a messenger boy with a telegram put an end to the possibility. SORRY UNEXPECTED BUSINESS DEVELOPMENT MAKES COMING IMPOSSIBLE. THOUSAND CONGRATULATIONS TO FATHER ON BIRTHDAY. LOVE. MAYLIN.

Bella began dabbing her eyes with her handkerchief. The others excanged glances of cold comprehension. "If it's like that," said Rufus Tolbecken after a while, "perhaps it's just as well that he didn't come."

And the silence to which Jared was accustomed with regard to his father closed in once more.

6

There was no silence that afternoon about Elizabeth Lehman when she hurried down from the steps of the parlor car into the arms of Judge Tolbecken, and from them into the arms of her other relatives. Between embraces, she presented, to be hugged and kissed in turn, a slim, dark-eyed girl in a straw bonnet. Then a crowd of friends surrounded and exclaimed over her. Next she shook hands with the stationmaster and with Gregory, the Tolbecken coachman. Then the whole family, installed in various carriages, escorted her up Green Street to Tolbecken Avenue, and at last along the drive to Tolbecken itself. She radiated and absorbed high spirits, was so brilliant, alive, and electric that it was not until later, and then grudgingly, that the boy discovered she was not beautiful—a short, round person, like Grandmother, with too small a nose, too heavy eyebrows, and too large a mouth. Her eyes, hands, and complexion, her taste in dressing made up for this; but what distinguished her most was personality.

And yet . . . perhaps the aura of Paris, something foreign in voice and manner, perhaps her very independence separated her a little from the house and the others. Not in the same way as Maylin Tolbecken, but obviously, even to a boy, she represented a curious divergence that both charmed and disturbed him.

"Frederick's doing well, as usual," said Aunt Elizabeth in answer to a question about her husband, after she and the children had changed clothes and were in the sitting room grouped about Grandmother. "Frederick's doing very well. His nudes made quite an impression at the last *Salon,* you know—one *hors concours,* one gold medal, and two *mentions honorables.*"

"Nudes!" exclaimed Grandmother, in the general silence. Rufus Tolbecken looked blank, Aunt Joan smiled, and Mrs. Reiger, with a glance at her husband, blushed.

"I wasn't aware," said Grandmother formally, "that Mr. Lehman selected subjects of that nature."

Elizabeth, who had forgotten that nudes at the *Salon* and at Tolbecken were two different things, changed color herself. But she laughed and said, "Now, Mother, it's not so shocking as all that. The paintings are lovely—and besides it's an artistic convention."

"A fig for artistic conventions!" returned Grandmother. "Why should people be naked in pictures and wear clothes everywhere else, or be arrested if they don't? Lust of the eye is the only name for it. Art should be chaste; it was chaste in my young days. But I'm surprised at you, Lizzie, actually *approving* your husband's painting such things."

"Shhh!" warned Aunt Joan, with a crushing look familiar

to Jared. "Little pitchers . . . ! Now, Jare, you take Clarice out and play. Show her the garden."

"And you be careful about your dress," Aunt Elizabeth bade the girl. "It's your best one, remember."

Nudes? What did it mean? Jared had the notion of something vague and terrible. He consulted Clarice.

"What were they talking about?"

"Papa's pictures. Ladies going swimming."

"You can't wear clothes when you swim," mused Jared. "I don't see why Grandmother got so mad about it. They ought to have put on bathing suits," he decided.

"Prob'ly they forgot 'em," said Clarice. "Anyhow, they're only picture ladies, so it doesn't matter."

This seemed to Jared the right solution. He felt a kindling approval of his guest.

She was a strange-looking girl, at least to his Saxon eyes. She had sallow skin, but fine-grained as silk and with a glow under it. Her eyes were dark, almond-shaped, with long lashes. Her nose would be longer sometime, but was now short and gave her a look of self-assurance. A tentative smile seemed always to lurk about her mouth. Her legs were long, gawky, muscular, and as she wore socks and her dress was short, they showed bruises and scratches which, to Jared's taste, heightened their attractiveness. With her straight black hair in a bang, she differed completely from the blonde little girls of Dunstable.

Two other cousins, the daughters of Aunt Mary Reiger, hopped about; but they were older, very shrill and patronizing. After a while they started whispering to each other and giggling. The sights of Tolbecken were an old story to them. Finally, they strutted around the corner of the house on their own pursuits.

"Hello, Jare," came a timid voice from the shadow of some bushes.

It was David Mansen, a little boy two years younger than Jared. He was the son of a ne'er-do-well civil engineer degraded by drink, who, when sober, wasted his time on fruitless inventions, and drunk or sober indulged a grievance against society. His wife supported him by doing laundry, sewing, or whatever work could be had, and by dint of borrowing, begging, and scrimping, managed to keep her boy at Mr. Baker's Select School. David Mansen was regularly dressed in Jared's castoff clothes. He was a painfully timid and feeble boy, narrow-chested and thin-faced, with large, fluttering blue eyes. Out of his element at the private school,

36

he was the constant butt of the young Indians who naturally pursued any quarry that showed itself weak or afraid. Jared, who hated bullying, and had, as well as a strong physique, the prestige of his name, had saved David from some of the worst ordeals, and had become his idol. Like a stray dog, David haunted Tolbecken, his only sanctuary, awaiting the young hero's pleasure.

"Hullo," said Jared carelessly.

"I'll come back," stammered David, confused at the presence of Clarice.

"What'd you come over for?"

"Just to play."

"All right. I don't mind." And to Clarice, "Want to see my pony?"

"Pony!" she breathed ecstatically. "Have you got a pony?"

"Yes. His name's Hugo. And Diana's had a whole lot of little puppies. They're at the stable."

"Oh, Jare, please show me."

Followed shyly by David, they started trotting down a side path from the front.

"Race you!" she challenged.

And they sped off, David toiling valiantly behind. They reached the stable side by side. Jared looked at her with greater respect.

"It's mean," she said, glancing back, "we oughtn't to have left him." And then, *"Mon Dieu!"*

For already the misfortunes of the afternoon had begun; David had tripped on the gravel of the walk and come down flat. Although he had risen before they reached him, his knees were bleeding and his chin was cut; he clenched his teeth, but the tears stood in his eyes.

"Pauvre petit!" said Clarice, consoling him in French. Jared told him not to cry.

Clarice, fishing out a handkerchief from her pocket, applied it to the cut on David's chin. He was not used to such attention. The very surprise of it overbrimmed his eyes. She transferred the handkerchief upward, and as a result smeared her sleeve with blood.

"Regarde-moi ça," she exclaimed forlornly. "Oh, well, come along," and with David this time between them, they entered the stable.

It was cool, pungent, and mysterious, as a stable should be. The odor of hay, oats, leather, harness polish, and Gregory's pipe was mingled with scent of manure into one heady fragrance. They passed through the carriage room

37

with its coupé, victoria, surrey, landaulet, and pony cart—
the place for clambering—into the feed room with its chutes
for oats and bran, and thence into the darker aisle of the cattle
stalls, among the sounds of munching, stamping, and rattling.
Three tails swished at intervals in the dusk.

"They're Exeter and Jill and Star," said Jared. "They're
Grandfather's. Hugo's farther along."

A box stall had been contrived for the pony. He peered
over the top of it at them, as Clarice and David stood in
attitudes of worship on the other side.

"Can we go in?" she whispered.

"Of course," said Jared, and opening the door a little, they
squeezed through. They fell on Hugo's neck, they pressed
themselves against his furry sides, they stroked his nose.
Trifles like clothes could not be remembered at such a moment. Squeezing through had left marks back and front;
Hugo, in search of sugar, slobbered on them.

"Could I ride him once?" begged Clarice.

"Yes—any time. It's kind of late today, but tomorrow
morning you can."

"I wish I had a pony," she yearned. "I'd sleep with him.
You're so lucky."

It was good to have his treasures admired. "Come on,
let's see the puppies," suggested Jared. They were newer and
more interesting than the pony.

Diana, the setter, lived in a tool shed next to the stable
and had to be approached with tact. They stood outside
while Jared cajoled her. After a while, she stuck her head out,
deliberated, let herself be won, and wagged her tail. She
sniffed Clarice, apparently liked the smell, and putting two
paws on her shoulders, knocked her down. Then she made
amends by licking her face, and glad of a respite from puppies, galloped off around the barn.

"There they come," shrilled Clarice. "Oh, dear me!"

Hugo was forgotten. Five droll objects with long ears
came flopping out of the shed. Down went the children in
the none too clean grass and rolled with them. A half-hour
passed before Diana returned, whining, and led them back
again into the shed.

"*Ciel!*" Clarice exclaimed, holding out her dress. The
starchy white linen of an hour earlier, with its embroidered
belt, rosettes about her neck, and little puffs at the shoulders,
was now limp and filthy. As she looked at it, her lips began
to tremble.

"Want to see my knife?" Jared consoled. "It's a mighty fine knife."

He hauled out his Kohinoor. It had a horn handle and a chain for fastening to a trouser belt. It was as big as a dirk. Beneath their absorbed eyes he opened its cluster of blades, marked I.X.L. Sheffield—a large and a small blade, scissors, an auger, a saw, a nail file; the back of it opened out into a hook for removing stones from horses' feet.

"Isn't it lovely!" Clarice admired.

"Sharp as a razor," said Jared. "Let's cut our initials on that tree."

And they set to work on the smooth trunk of a copper beech. Jared scratched C.L., J.T., and D.M., and carved half a letter.

"See how she cuts?"

But Clarice's thoughts were wandering. "It'd be a wonderful tree to climb."

"You like to climb?"

"Yes."

"All right, come on. I'll finish this later."

They left David behind and worked their way up, Clarice's calves on a level with Jared's nose. She was better at it than he and scissored aloft at a great rate, adding new scratches to her legs. It was a small copper beech, but from its top they seemed to be looking down from a great height. The tree swayed deliciously in a light breeze. The full summer-afternoon breath of cinnamon roses, new-mown grass, and a thousand spicy unknown scents blew across their faces, somehow becoming identified with Clarice in Jared's mind. They perched close together, swaying back and forth with one motion.

David called from below, "I'm going to come up."

"No," she exclaimed, "we're coming down. He doesn't look strong enough," she added, and began slithering down from fork to fork, while Jared followed.

But misfortune had not yet done with them. Clarice reached David and, telling him to wait, jumped from the tree; there was a ripping and tearing sound. She landed on all fours, but most of her dress, like a battle flag, hung over her head in two long tatters.

"Are you hurt?" panted Jared.

"No, I'm all right." Then, perceiving the extent of the damage, she stood fingering her rags. By the time he reached her she was blinking hard. "I didn't mean to"—her voice was pinched, her lips drawn. "You saw how it was, Jare. Tell Mama I couldn't help it. I'm scared. What'll we do?"

He put his arm around her in a gesture of comradeship.

"Don't you worry. I'll tell you what—we'll go to Grandfather. We'll sneak around the corner of the house to his study. I'll tell him all about it. He'll fix it up with Aunt Elizabeth. What are you crying for now?" he added sharply to David.

"Because I don't want 'em to hurt her," struggled the little boy. His thin face grew pinched with a sudden resolution. A new light mingled with the fear in his eyes. "I'm used to being licked—every day," he went on with a pitiful attempt to swagger. "It don't mean anything to me. I'll tell 'em I did it."

"And they'd believe you, wouldn't they!" scoffed Jared. A curious resentment at the other boy's officiousness welled up in him. "You go on home," he added. "I'll take care of her. You go on home."

David shrank away from this threat.

"All right," he mumbled.

But Clarice gave him her hand.

"Good-by, David."

He kept his eyes on the ground.

"Goo'by."

In a childish fashion, he realized that he had been put in his place, but he would have liked to do anything for her. From behind a tree he watched the others scouting toward the refuge of Judge Tolbecken's study.

"There's Grandfather's window," whispered Jared. "We're all right. We can crawl through . . ."

Around the end of the house, billowy in a lawn dress and garden hat, strolled Aunt Elizabeth, flanked by Aunt Mary Reiger and her two daughters. At the sight of the children they stopped short.

"Clarice!"

"Yes, Mama." With rounded shoulders and hanging head, Clarice waited.

"Your dress!" gasped Mrs. Lehman. "Your expensive new dress! What's happened?"

Clarice swallowed and stared back.

"Will you answer me when I speak to you! Very well, that settles it. You promised to be careful, but you're just naughty, thoughtless children. Clarice, you go straight upstairs and get in bed. I'll be along in a minute."

40

"Don't!" shrilled Jared passionately. "Aunt Elizabeth, it wasn't her fault. It only happened."

But Mrs. Lehman's eyes flashed. "Didn't you hear me tell you to go upstairs? I'll attend to you in a moment and I'm going to attend to you good."

Experience had taught Clarice what to expect from this sentence. Her face showed the beginning of tears. Digging at her eyes with one hand, she walked slowly away.

Little David mourned in the shadow of the tree.

"As for you, Jared Tolbecken," continued Aunt Elizabeth, still at white heat, "I'm very angry with you."

But Jared was gone. He raced around the house with a thumping heart, dashed through the front door, and came upon Grandfather, Aunt Joan, and Grandmother in the drawing room.

He squeezed himself between Grandfather's knees and pressed his face against his coat.

"She's going to punish Clarice," he sobbed, "for spoiling her clothes. . . . She couldn't help it. . . . I took her to see the pony and the puppies . . . we climbed a tree. Don't let her punish her! Grandfather, please don't let her do it." He broke out into a wail.

"Nonsense!" exclaimed Aunt Joan, already up. "I'll fix it."

"Ridiculous!" growled Grandfather. "That's just Elizabeth's temper. Tell her from me I won't have it, Joan. Don't take it to heart, boy. It's all right."

"Shame on her!" cried Grandmother.

An altercation broke out in the front hall between Aunt Joan and Aunt Elizabeth. Jared listened with bated breath.

"No, you don't. You shan't whip that child."

"I certainly shall."

"Lizzie Tolbecken!" There was a threat in Aunt Joan's voice. "I say you shan't, and you know I mean it."

"Aunt Joan, I'll ask you to let me go. You mustn't interfere. It's a question of discipline."

"Fiddlesticks!"

"Her new dress. In *rags!* It cost a fortune!"

"And I'll buy her ten dresses like it," called the Judge, pushing Jared away from him and striding out, "if you'll let her off. Come, Lizzie, you mustn't be obstinate. I insist."

"Shame on you!" cried Grandmother again from her chair in the drawing room.

A gay laugh reached Jared's anxious ears. Aunt Elizabeth's ire vanished. "Of all the old tyrants! How could a person

41

bring up a child in this house! Very well. You make me feel like an executioner, and Heaven knows I love her, but she's such a trial sometimes. You didn't use to let me off like that. There's one thing I do intend, though—she's going to stay in bed."

"Now, Lizzie," protested Aunt Joan, "just this once . . ."

"No, I mean it. And only bread and milk for supper. She's had a hard trip and tomorrow is Father's birthday— she'll be sitting up late. This is a good excuse. Besides, it was thoughtless of her. No, I won't listen to anything more."

And her light steps sounded on the stairs.

So she was going to be punished after all. Clarice was going to be punished. A lump stuck in Jared's throat. He had saved her from the worst, but he realized that nothing he could do would bring complete acquittal. An excuse! She would be lying there alone when it was still daylight, smelling the cooking, hearing the others' voices. Put to bed like a baby in disgrace. He slunk off somewhere to brood.

Talk at supper depressed him. The family actually joked about his concern for Clarice. They were all heartless except Aunt Joan, who looked disappointed. She had ordered an especially good supper, and kept wheedling in vain for permission to send up various dishes.

Afterwards he prowled off again behind the house and gazed up at Clarice's window. They might have been playing now. He felt terribly alone.

The sight of Diana frisking around the barn gave him a sudden idea. He ran down to the shed, kidnapped one of her puppies, went back up the service stairs, and stole along the upper hall. At the same moment, equally furtive, Aunt Joan tiptoed out of her room. They startled each other.

"What are you up to?" she whispered.

"I was going in there," breathed Jared, struggling to keep the puppy quiet under his coat.

"All right, *you* go. She'd rather see you. Give her these." She brought out a plate of cookies from behind her back. Then, discovering the puppy, she chuckled. "Wait, I'll open the door—you're a good boy."

Clarice lay facing the wall, her head dark on the pillow; a forefinger of one hand was tracing the flower pattern on the wallpaper. He crept up behind her, a board creaked, and she turned round.

"Jare!"

It was a single note of delight in his ears.

"Look what I've brought you," he said, extracting the

42

puppy, "and Aunt Joan sent you these, and"—fumbling in his pocket—"here's my knife. I want you to have it."

Cookies, knife, bedclothes, and puppy slid together. She sprang to her knees, and throwing her arms around his neck, kissed him.

7

Rufus Tolbecken's birthday dinner was an institution which in the eyes of his grandchildren seemed as venerable and permanent as any national feast. It rivaled Thanksgiving and Christmas, and outdid Washington's birthday, Easter, and the Fourth of July. It was the family's tribute not only to him, but to itself.

The Judge's home and his law practice were almost exclusively his life. Though he entertained at his table friends from many states, he seldom visited them. For professional reasons, he belonged to clubs in Washington, Philadelphia, and New York, but he had never been a clubman. He had shared in politics and held office as tasks imposed by his citizenship, but he had gladly withdrawn from them. Work at his desk or in court, attendance at church on Sunday, the company of his household, a game of checkers in the evening, and his books were enough. He was, therefore, the center of the family, which revolved around him, and his birthday had become the yearly occasion for expressing this relationship.

Of course Grandmother and Aunt Joan shared in the anniversary. Earlier it had been they who, together with him, celebrated the birthdays of his father, Jared, or of their own parents, the Maylins, in the West. Now they stood alone as the extreme rear guard of their generation, and for them at times like these a throng of vanished faces stood about the board. "That reminds me of Aunt Letitia," they would say, and bring up an anecdote; or, "Do you recall when Papa came back from Louisiana just in time for Grandfather Maylin's golden wedding? They had run aground off Vicksburg, remember, and he paid the steamboat captain to make up time. That was in 'forty-eight, no, 'forty-nine." So the dead remained living and the family saga spun itself out further. Aunts, uncles, cousins, and great-grandparents whom none of the younger ones had seen except in portrait or daguerreotype retained their individuality by much-repeated, intimate details. The children and grandchildren of Rufus Tolbecken imbibed the past at gatherings like this, where the family paid honor to its own continuance.

Nor was it difficult in the long, white-paneled dining room to conjure up figures and voices once familiar there. It would have been difficult *not* to do so when everything— hearth, table, china, silver, the chairs themselves—had its individual history. So and so had sat here, and another there. Irate gentlemen had taken sides here for Federalist or Democrat. Here Jared Tolbecken had scandalized his guests and neighbors sixty years ago by championing the heresy of abolition. Wigs and silk stockings, high stocks and cravats, checked trousers, pantalettes, hoop skirts, Prince Alberts, crinolines— the wardrobe of a century—had each in turn passed through the room and given place to newer fashions. A shadow lingered here; the family gathered beneath it.

And here Judge Rufus Tolbecken, sixty-seven years old, stood waiting at one end of the long table until the rest had found their places and the clatter of talk was hushed.

Then he bowed his head. "Heavenly Father," he prayed, "who holdest our times in Thy hands to lengthen or complete them as seemeth best to Thee, receive my thanks for life and all Thy gifts which have enriched it hitherto; receive our thanks that once again Thou grantest us to meet in this loved place to share Thy bounty. As in the past, we crave Thy blessing upon us now and forever."

Talk burst out again; chairs were adjusted. Then from his place the Judge smiled down the board.

"Hurrah for Joan's cooking! I hope everybody's hungry."

To his right and left sat Aunt Elizabeth and Aunt Sophia; to Grandmother's right and left were Vincent Tolbecken and Albert Reiger; the others sat in a well-established order, which Clarice disturbed by squeezing in between Jared and Aunt Joan. The best china, with golden centers, which the Judge had brought back from Paris, was on the table; the Tolbecken silver, heavy and old; candelabra as yet unlighted, for the sun still shot long rays through the garden window. These fell on metal, crystal, and lace, on roses in the silver punch bowl, on ice in the cresents of cantaloupe, and in the amber of sherry. It was a rich, luxuriant table, the special province of Bella Tolbecken, who was considered artistic and had spent an hour arranging it that afternoon. The Judge paid her his compliments.

Plates were changed, were filled, emptied, refilled. Course

followed course. Hospitality consisted in making people eat; appetite was the highest flattery, and the lack of it an affront.

Clarice and Jared, shoulder to shoulder, worked on together. Piles of drumsticks, boats of gravy, mounds of mashed potato, peas, asparagus, tomatoes, radishes, browned rolls with butter and crab-apple jelly, uncounted condiments—they progressed through them all, sighed, and had room for dessert. For once no one remarked that children should be seen and not heard. Only at one point did they become the object of conversation.

Mrs. Lehman was spending two months in America, and during that time it was planned for Clarice to remain at Tolbecken.

"It's a great thing for Jare to have a playmate," said the Judge. "He must take her with him to Sunday School tomorrow."

Mrs. Lehman hesitated. "You know, Father, Clarice is a Roman Catholic."

A hush fell about the table, of which Clarice herself was unconscious, but Jared, at her side, felt stricken. A distance, not of inches, but of taboo, opened between them; for in the family of Rufus Tolbecken three words expressed the trinity of evil: Devil, Democrat, and Catholic.

"Indeed!" he said, a trifle coldly. "No, I didn't know."

Aunt Elizabeth explained that Frederick Lehman's first wife, a Frenchwoman, had asked him on her deathbed to bring their daughter up in her own, the Roman, faith and that Fred felt bound by this request.

"Of course," affirmed the Judge unexpectedly, "he ought to feel so bound. He has acted properly in the matter."

Tension relaxed; dread of the Scarlet Woman waned. . . . "Clarice hasn't been confirmed yet," added Mrs. Lehman. "We thought the choice should be left to her when she's older."

"But, Mama," interposed the girl, "can't I go to Jare's church?"

"What would the Abbé Thibaut say to you when you got back, Clarice?"

"He won't mind. I'll kiss him behind the ear. He loves it."

And laughter, for the moment, silenced prejudice.

The candelabra were now lighted and the curtains drawn. Ice cream, rich and studded with peaches, appeared together with angel and chocolate cake. The children attacked it. Talk in general grew louder—but it was Elizabeth who absorbed the Judge. "Birthdays are well enough," he said,

45

"but like everything else they can be overdone. It's about reached that point with me. Sometimes it scares me a little. I'm lonely without you and your brother, your brother Jared."

"I'm lonely without you," she answered, taking his hand beneath the table. "It isn't always gay in Paris. I have to shut both eyes sometimes. Wife, diplomat, and dupe," she said, and in parody of the recently produced *Cyrano*, "Here lies one who was everything and still was nothing."

The Judge's face darkened.

"Oh, yes," she went on, "why did I marry him? Love's queer. I'm not sorry. I'm sticking to the bargain."

"Aye," he muttered, thinking of Maylin, "you're the right kind."

The end of dinner had come. Rachel Tolbecken looked inquiringly at her husband. "We'd better leave these gentlemen . . ." she began.

"One moment," he interrupted, leaning back in his chair. "Something has recently come up about which you should all be informed, and this is as good a time as any. Albert knows about it already. I was offered two hundred thousand for Tolbecken by Mr. Kirschbaum and, of course, declined it."

His voice was casual, but his gaze circling the table hesitated. Two hundred thousand was a great deal of money. And yet, when it came to the preservation of Tolbecken, he might expect . . .

He was met by silence, averted faces, except on the part of his wife and sister-in-law, who echoed his "of course." The others showed no such certainty; with them the unuttered echo was Mr. Kirschbaum's price.

"Well," he challenged, "you don't seem greatly interested after all."

"I wonder," began Vincent, with a glance right and left for support, "I wonder if it's wise to turn down a proposition of that kind without a little thought—on the spur of the moment, don't you see. I wonder."

He looked the picture of deprecation; his mustache drooped; he mumbled his words. The Judge eyed him with distaste.

"You seem to forget," he retorted, "that I've had offers like this before. What do you mean, *'on the spur of the moment'?*"

"Yes, Father," said Vincent, "but the present proposal is more handsome, more adequate. Now, two hundred thousand at six per cent . . ."

"Pshaw!" fumed the Judge, "don't teach me arithmetic— What do *you* think, Mary? Like Albert, I suppose?"

"Why," said Mrs. Reiger, "you've got to admit that Al's a

pretty level-headed businessman. He thinks the offer was really advantageous." ("Now, Mary, don't mix me into it," interjected her husband.) "And of course," she went on, "Tolbecken's a big place to keep up."

"You haven't asked my opinion," said Elizabeth. "I think you're right in keeping the place. You love it, and it means everything to you."

Rufus Tolbecken remained silent, his eyes on the table; but the others, knowing him, knew that a storm was brewing. He looked up at last, a flush on his forehead.

"It's incredible," he began. "Am I to gather, then, that the place means nothing to *you*, that for two hundred thousand dollars you would sell what is part and parcel of yourselves? I don't understand you."

"Now, Rufus," said his wife, "keep cool."

But Jared got up and, rounding the table, stood by his grandfather's side. They were being hard on him, he felt, and somehow he knew he belonged with him. Mechanically the Judge's heavy arm went round him and drew him closer.

"There's no use getting angry, Father," said Mary. "Of course we all love the place, but you asked what we thought. It isn't our faulth that Dunstable's not a village any more and that times have changed. We've simply got to make the best of it; it isn't sensible nowadays to own more land than necessary—at least in a town. But you must decide. Nobody can force you to sell Tolbecken."

"You're right about that," nodded the Judge, "you're exactly right." And sharply, "That's all. I told Kirschbaum the matter was closed. I won't sell my home whether times have changed or not, and I was wrong to invite discussion on the point. I had hoped . . ." He made a vague gesture with his hands, and let them fall. "When I'm gone, do as you please; but I prophesy that the sale of Tolbecken will yield no one anything but a mess of pottage."

He rose with his hand on Jared's shoulder, patting it once or twice.

"Gentlemen, we'll have coffee and cigars in my study."

47

8

Elizabeth Lehman's arrival had upset Bella Tolbecken. She went through the Paris dresses and inhaled the talk about Paris like one entranced by an intoxicating perfume. She reveled in descriptions of the shops and theaters, of the opera on gala nights, of receptions and dinners. It interested her particularly to hear of the men one met, hinting with a flush that, being foreigners, they were probably very unprincipled and attractive. "Aren't they, Lizzie? They must be frightfully risqué," she would sigh. And she liked to talk about the "*vie de Bohême*," savoring such words as free love and mistress with a shocked delight. *Trilby* and an old Baedeker's *Paris* appeared on her bedside table.

But her infatuation went farther. As Rachel Tolbecken observed, she took to mooning about, referred more than ever to Maylin's desertion, and could not be coaxed from martyrdom. The family, as usual, mustered its sympathies. Elizabeth gave her one of her newest dresses, and the Judge bought her a hat, but nothing would do.

Finally one night, when Maylin's name happened to be mentioned, casually enough, she burst into tears, gathered her skirts, and hurried from the room.

"She mustn't be left alone," exclaimed the Judge anxiously. "I'm concerned about her these days. Poor Bella!"

"I'll go up to her," said Aunt Joan, filling the breach. "You're right, she oughtn't to be left alone."

Her heavy tread sounded on the stairs.

She crossed the unlighted bedroom to the figure by the window, pulled up a chair, and sat down, but said nothing for a while. The light of an early moon filtered through the trees outside.

"You mustn't take things too hard," she began after a time. "You feel bad, but it will pass."

The figure of the younger woman stiffened. "Please don't," she choked. "That's only talk. When a woman's been cheated out of living, out of all the things she cares for, won't every day remind her of what she might have had? How's it going to pass? Do you mean I'll forget?"

48

"No, but sometime it won't hurt you to remember so much as you think it will."

"How do you know?" retorted Bella in the same compressed voice. "You were never married. Besides, I'm not old, either; I've still got a few years and I want to live. . . . I do want to live."

The square face of Aunt Joan in the moonlight confronted the hungry, distorted face opposite her, but lost none of its gentleness. It had been her portion in life to put up with people in order to help them; and petulance like this did not disturb her.

"Well, then, Bella," she answered, "if you want to live, why don't you begin?"

"What do you mean?"

Aunt Joan was silent a moment before answering. She sat looking out of the window, her hands unclasped on her lap.

"I can explain better," she said, "if I tell you what happened to me. My family, the Maylins, you know, used to live at Thebes, Ohio, near Cincinnati. Until the railroads and one thing or another cut down river traffic, Thebes used to be a lively place and full of very genteel people; but afterwards it went to seed; those who could afford it moved to the city; even the boat didn't stop there, except now and then. I was a young woman around twenty-five at that time. Rachel married Mr. Tolbecken and went East; my other sisters married and left; my brother lived down South. Somebody had to stay at home and take care of Father and Mother. I was the youngest and unmarried, so it had to be me.

"Lonely? When the hired girl had left in the evening and Father and Mother were in bed, I used to walk up and down our yard wringing my hands. There were letters from Rachel and the others about what they were doing and the places they saw. And I was young and hadn't anything at all except Thebes, or Cincinnati a few times. Naturally I'd kind of been shut out of things, being the youngest. When it came my turn Father and Mother were old and the others gone. I used to amuse myself by imagining that I was in Rachel's place or Letitia's, and what I would have said to Mr. So-and-so or what I would have worn at General Scott's reception. I hadn't more than a couple of dresses to my back and 'reception' was a grand word in Thebes; but I really think I had as much fun thinking about Rachel's or Letitia's good times as they had themselves.

"Then Mr. Henderson came back to town on a visit. He

had been a schoolboy friend of mine and had been appointed to Annapolis."

Bella momentarily forgot herself. "Was that the Admiral Henderson," she interrupted, "who called on you several years ago?"

"Yes, he became an admiral and had a very distinguished career; but he was only an ensign then. He was the handsomest young man I ever saw, Bella—so dignified and noble-looking. He fell in love with me, and you can be sure I was in love with him. One night, when we were walking back from church, he proposed to me."

Aunt Joan, breaking off for a moment, gazed at the moon-patched trees. "Well, so it was. He proposed to me. I wanted to have him; I'd have given anything to have him. But of course it was out of the question. Father and Mother couldn't spare me. He said he would wait; and he did wait several years; then he married a young lady from Lexington, Kentucky.

"I'm only telling you this to show you that I know what it is not to get what one wants. I'm sorry that I couldn't have married James Henderson. But you see right well that I couldn't. I had to stay where I was. And you talk about living: I nursed Father and Mother to the end; then I came here and brought up Rachel's children after she was crippled; I did some nursing during the war. I've done a good deal, by and large, and I'm not sure that if I'd been married I'd have done more or as much. That's what I call living, Bella—being of use. You've got Jared to bring up; you've got friends you can help here in Dunstable; you can lend me a hand with the house. That's better than grieving about what can't be helped, though Heaven knows you have cause enough."

She leaned forward and put her hand on the other's knee. "It's just life, dear—happiness, sorrow. Neither of them lasts."

But character can only be profitable to character; it cannot strike fire from dough. And poor Bella was merely a soft, poorly educated woman, who had once been a small-town belle with the knack of making herself agreeable and with no idea that anything else could be expected of her. When something more was needed, she remained helpless and incapable of being helped.

In the silence of the room a sob jerked now and then, convulsing her shoulders. It was the only answer she could make, the whimpering of a child who half expects that its

50

weeping will accomplish what it wants. And Aunt Joan sat pitying her.

"Come, Bella," she said at last, "let's go downstairs. We'll get Lizzie to play one of those French tunes you like on the piano. That'll cheer us up. And don't worry any more. It mayn't be as bad as you think. I rather expect Maylin'll come back sometime."

"I don't care whether he comes back or not," sobbed Bella. "It isn't that. I'm just tired. There's no use your talking to me about being useful. I'm not like you. I wouldn't get any happiness out of bothering around with people, like you do. I want a man. I want to be loved. I want to dance and wear pretty clothes and go to nice places before I get too old."

Aunt Joan considered her a moment. "Well, then," she said gently, "what do you propose?"

The sobbing stopped. Bella straightened up, leaned forward. "I'll tell you what," she whispered, "I'd like to go back to Paris with Elizabeth—I'm sure she'd have me. Don't you think Judge Tolbecken would be willing to give me enough money for that?"

"He might. But what about Jare? Rufus wouldn't want to be separated from him very long. Besides, it would mean taking him out of school, having him miss a year. I'm not sure . . ."

"Jared could stay with you. He'd be much better off, and I'd be much freer to have a good time for once. Don't you see?"

Yes, Joan Maylin saw. She saw indeed much more than Bella did, as she kept silent and pondered the matter. She looked at it and found nothing to approve. Bella was a weak woman, she thought, eager to make a fool of herself; she wanted to be transplanted from the only environment she knew to one utterly different—and Aunt Joan saw what would happen: at best, silliness involving expense that could ill be afforded, but also likely enough something worse, when the corset of the Dunstable repressions had been taken off. Aunt Joan, though a Puritan, was not a prude; she had a keen perception of physical facts and called a spade by its name, but she had been brought up in a world that believed in the repression of natural impulses. She believed in them herself, particularly when anyone as weak-willed as Bella was involved. Restrictions made, she thought, for the ultimate happiness of such people.

51

Another prejudice affected her. She had no patience when it came to the shirking of duty. Bella's only remaining duty was to Jared, and no matter how eagerly the rest of the family might cooperate with her, it was not proper or good, according to Joan Maylin's code, for a woman to leave her child with others and go off for months in search of amusement. It was not only not proper, it was contemptible. Aunt Joan's attitude might have been compared with that of a commanding officer who has borne the brunt of service all his life and is solicited by a subaltern to be allowed to sneak off in the heat of action. The idea shocked and disgusted her.

"Paris!" continued Bella, misinterpreting her silence. "It would be so wonderful. You'll speak to the Judge about it for me, won't you?"

The other's jaw set hard, but still she spoke gently.

"No, I won't, and you must get the notion out of your head, Bella. I don't approve of any such plan and I'm certain he wouldn't. If you'd like to take Jare to Atlantic City or to the mountains for a change, I'm sure that could be managed. I'd even pay your expenses myself. But Europe's out of the question just now."

Of course, there was pleading, there were tears; but equally, of course, against this rock they came to nothing.

9

If history repeats itself in children, Clarice and Jared were at the medieval stage, the stage of wonder-working imagination and sensitiveness. On one hand, they created and lived in a world of make-believe; on the other, they absorbed actuality with undulled perceptions. Facts mingled with fiction and both were vivid. Like medieval romancers, they magnified and colored and transformed. They shared a breathless life—thrills, hopes, punishments, delights—and child love made it magnificent.

Jared used to go to sleep thinking of Clarice; she took part in his dreams. He would lean out of his window in the morning calling to her, impatient for the first sight of her.

They always drifted together, side by side, crowding into the same chair, holding hands absently as a matter of course. They romped and wrestled and raced, but he was very careful of her, would even let her win on occasion. The thought that time was passing and that she would have to leave was unbearable.

They were medieval in another sense. Bellicose adventure still lurks for children; duels and knight-errantry continue. Grown people lead sheltered lives.

There was a young swaggerer in the neighborhood called Eaby Ellis who lorded it at school and had fought his way to sovereignty. Little boys truckled to him and big boys let him alone, for he was a stout young bulldog. He was two years older than Jared, and had licked him more than once, though the victory had never been decisive. The authority of the name Tolbecken galled Ellis, who longed to show that snob, as he called him, a thing or two.

He passed by the back gate one day, and caught little David Mansen on his way in. It was an opportunity for tormenting a weaker creature that could not be missed.

"Where you going?" he demanded, collaring the victim and enjoying the terror on the other's face. It was responses like this that made bullying David such fun.

"In there," piped David. "Please lemme go, Eaby, please!"

"No, you don't," returned Ellis. "You're coming with me. I'm arresting you. I'm going to take you over to our barn."

The goggle look of David's large eyes was infinitely amusing to Ellis. The boy was so frightened that he could hardly breathe.

"No, you don't," said Ellis again, forestalling David's feeble attempt to pull away, and twisting the child's arm. "How do you like that? Going to be good?"

"Yes!" shrieked David. "Don't . . . don't!"

And at that moment Jared and Clarice emerged from the bushes on the other side of the fence.

"You let Dave go."

"You come and make me."

Jared hesitated, a little white.

"Fraid-cat," said Eaby, "dirty little fraid-cat! Hangs around with girls and babies. Ought to wear a little petticoat." He eyed Clarice. "Hello, Frenchie—or are you a Dago?"

Jared flung open the gate and came out with murder in his eyes. But what can ninety pounds do to a hundred and twenty, the muscles of eleven to the muscles of thirteen?

53

Even love could not make up the difference. All love could do was to give Eaby the tussle of his life, black his eye, and bloody his nose. In spite of it, Jared went down at last with Eaby on his chest.

"You say 'nuff."

"I won't."

"I'll lick you till you do," and Eaby struck him in the face.

At this point a brick catapulting through the air grazed his head. Stiff and bristling, like a cat about to leap, Clarice approached. Before her tense advance, Eaby staggered back, scorched by words he did not understand.

Her nails drew down across Eaby Ellis's face; one hand buried itself in his hair; her foot, driven with fury, cracked on his shin; her teeth, unfanged, sought a spot to close on. No demon from the pit could have been as frightful as this thing in skirts, hissing strange oaths, who had fastened on him to rend limb from limb.

Eaby's heart turned to water; his eyes rolled; he fell back waving his hands. Then, profiting by a recoil of the monster, who was gathering for another spring, he turned and bolted down the street. But even so he did not escape. He was coatless, and a hand clutched his shirt, ripping a trophy from it. A stone thumped on his rear. *"Salaud!"* yelled a pursuing voice. And at that moment two schoolmates appeared at the corner watching his flight, causing his bitter cup to overflow. At the sight of them, he hesitated, half turned, but a glimpse of the fury bounding close after him sent him on again and out of sight. His comb had definitely been cut. *He had been licked by a girl.*

Clarice, still demented with rage, caught sight of his straw hat in the road and trampled on it. Then in vicious ridicule she planted it on Tolbecken gate, where, sneaking back an hour later, Eaby found it. Nor had he at the family assizes that evening any excuse to offer for his ruined shirt and missing headpiece. His lamentations echoed from the house. It had been a bad day from beginning to end.

Little David Mansen would never forget that day either, but for him it was merely one day of a whole rapturous summer. Under Clarice's patronage something vital and integrating seemed to inform his puny body, give a new steadiness to his eyes. For once he felt the warmth and the pride of inclusion. The perpetual fear in which he lived, the wrangling and poverty at home, the bullies on the street were no longer the sole reality for him. The thought of Tolbecken hovered con-

54

tinually in his mind, as the voices of Clarice and Jared did in his ears. Moreover, he had something of his own to give them, his adoration of them, a kindling imagination that enhanced their play, skill, too, with his hands in the making of things. They began to value him, to wait for him. It was not a one-sided love.

He would never forget their picnics near the sundial, the smell of hay in the stable loft, the tingle of hide-and-seek beneath the shade of the hedges. He reached the point of calling Joan Maylin "Aunt," as the others did. "You can drop the 'Miss,'" she told him. "I reckon I'm *Aunt* to all creation." On an awesome day he even found himself at table in the Tolbecken dining room itself, dazzled by the silver and linen, spellbound by the presence of the greatest man on earth, Judge Tolbecken, who beamed at him Jupiterlike through his spectacles.

As for Clarice, he knew that she belonged to Jared. In his humility nothing else was thinkable. But he could worship them both with the unstinted fervor of childhood. Every morning, like a small rabbit on the alert for dogs, but eager at the thought of the day before him, he would peep out from the shabby door of his house, make sure that the street was clear of enemies, and then flit from corner to corner, until with a last burst of speed he passed the Tolbecken gate into paradise.

The Middle Ages believed in phantoms.

Black Gregory, who lived at the stable and wore a rabbit's foot, was an expert in ghosts.

"I never heard of but one," said Jared. "Down by the spring."

Gregory lowered his voice. "Hush," he cautioned, "don't you talk so loud. I tell you dis hyah place's chuck full of 'em—same as de quality's houses everywhere. Bettah de quality—mo' de hants. De way dat Diana howls proves it—dogs kin see."

At the chilled look on the children's faces, he relented. "I s'pec' dese hyah is de good kind. But dey's one of 'em," he added earnestly, "dat I wouldn't trus' on no account, and dat's dat woman at de spring. No, suh, honey, don't you go foolin' round dat place."

The "woman at the spring" had a great fascination for the children. In spite of Gregory's warning, they would creep through the tall weeds that had grown up there into the canopy of vine-tangled trees covering the spring. Even at midday, it was dark there with a strange atmosphere of menace. The odor of lush growth had a hint of poison in it. The spring, black as a coiled snake, lay in the center. The rotted remains of a wooden bench, an urn of the 1840 period, lopsided on a decayed pedestal, gave an added touch of ruin to the spot. It had a curious isolation of its own, more psychological than physical, which cut it off from both Tolbecken and the encircling town.

"It isn't true," said Jared. "I asked Grandmother, and she says there aren't any ghosts. She says bad people go to hell and can't come back and good people go to heaven and don't want to."

Repeated trips to the spring encouraged them. They even wore a little path through the weeds, talked bolder and louder there, and bragged to Gregory of their exploits.

"Some day you get fooled and den you's sorry," he said grimly. "Dat dev'lish hant, she jes' playin' wid you all. She take her time, and den some day—*blap!*" Gregory brought his hands together with a crash.

"I'm going to go down there one of these nights and see if she's really there," Jared said.

Gregory looked at him in horror.

"Did you mean it?" asked Clarice, when she and Jared were on the way to the house.

"Yes," he maintained, "I'm going to settle it."

"You're awf'ly brave," she said admiringly.

The praise spurred his wavering courage. "I'll go tonight."

They walked on in a silence of doom. Clarice swallowed, and then finally, "I'll go with you."

"You wouldn't! Oh, Clarice, that'd be great."

"I don't want you to go alone," she quavered.

At last they worked themselves up to a spirit of adventure. They would have not only spectral but material dangers to contend with, for the enterprise involved slipping out of bed and escaping from the house when everyone was asleep. If the phantom did not catch them, Aunt Elizabeth might; it would be a very orgy of peril.

At bedtime they said their prayers with devotion and a tickling feeling in the pit of their stomachs. For once, Jared did not have to fight against sleep. As he lay there in the dark, the seriousness of the project grew. The crickets began their eery chirping, and the night sounds of the house multiplied. One by one, Gregory's stories recurred, their effect heightened by darkness and silence. There was no question about the reality of ghosts now. And he was going to defy them, the powers of the dead, the evil woman waiting at the spring. A bead of sweat trickled beneath his arm. He thought he heard something glide along the corridor, was relieved at the footsteps of the family going to bed. The clock on the landing ticked out the fatal minutes—half past ten, eleven, half past eleven. He bitterly regretted the undertaking and began to think of excuses. He could tell Clarice that he had gone to sleep, but that would not absolve him to himself. He could tell her that he had thought better of it, but what if, impatient with waiting for him as had been agreed, she should come and scratch at his door? The thought of that sound on the panels at this dead hour stiffened him. Suppose it were something else that scratched there! He wanted to make a break for Aunt Joan's room and plunge into bed with her. But pride gripped him; Clarice thought he was brave. He must go through with it. He reminded himself that Tolbeckens were never cowards.

He clamped his teeth together, and dragging himself up, pulled on coat and trousers. Then he opened the door and pattered down the hall; something followed along close to his shoulder, he felt. He made no attempt at quiet, for he hoped to be discovered and stopped. It was the only honorable way out. The worst spanking on earth would be heaven compared to this. He broke into a run. If he could only make Clarice's room before IT caught him! He wrenched the knob on her door and popped through just in the nick of time.

A flop sounded on the bed. In the moonlight, he could see a motionless heap of covers.

"Clarice!"

No answer.

"Clarice, I'm here." He put out his hand and shook the bundle, eliciting a gasp.

Slowly the tangle unwound itself. A head peeped out. "Oh, Jare, I thought it was HER." She got up, barefoot like himself but already dressed. "I'm so glad you've come."

They stood together at the window, looking out toward the spring.

"Let's go," he whispered, bolder on the score of company.

Then at that moment rose the blood-freezing sound of a dog's howl. It hung suspended in the air, rising, falling. Yes, there could no longer be any doubt. The WOMAN was there. Diana had seen her.

And now to confirm it came a wail, something gurgling and low lifted to a scream.

"Oh, mon Dieu, mon Dieu! Sainte Vierge nous aide!"

Clarice's arms fastened about Jared. Every limb shook. They staggered back from the window to the bed, their teeth chattering. And the demoniac sound came again, half moan, half screech.

"She's calling for us," babbled Clarice. "Where'll we go? What'll we do? *Oh, là, là, Maman!"*

They sat with thumping hearts for what seemed to be hours.

"Don't let's go," he breathed at last. "Let's give it up."

"Go?" she repeated. "I wouldn't go for anything. If she only won't hurt us . . ." They clasped each other convulsively.

"Oh, my Lord," exclaimed Jared, "what's that?"

It was the clock striking twelve, booming the hour when ghosts are set free to do as they will. And hardly had the last beat struck, when, unmistakably this time, came the sound of someone, something, creeping along the hall.

They had no courage to move or breathe. They could only stare at the door, like birds facing a serpent. The moonlight struck full on it.

Then the knob began to turn, the door slowly to open.

And they saw—the WOMAN.

Jerking back together on the bed, they began screaming for help, but their voices came only in a rattle.

Then the WOMAN spoke. "What on earth are you two doing? What do you mean by being up at this hour and dressed?"

The words were terrible, but the voice was familiar.

"Aunt Joan!" Jared leaped from the bed toward her.

"Aunt Joan!" piped Clarice, and flung herself at the apparition.

They clung to her nightgown, burying their faces in her sides. "Oh, Aunt Joan, Aunt Joan!" To feel her warmth, to feel her hand on their heads, to know that they were safe and that nothing could catch them! They sobbed in delight.

"Well, I'll be!" exclaimed Joan Maylin. "What the mischief! Why, you're shaking all over! Are you sick, darlings? What's the matter? Tell Aunt Joan. What is it?"

Through the strangle of voices, she finally learned the whole adventure. "That fool Gregory," she grunted, "he's going to get an earful from me. Ghosts! Poppycock! Diana got lonely and howled. And what you heard was a cat. I heard

it too." She hugged them and chuckled. "Now, you two get
undressed and get to bed. Hurry up and don't make a noise."

With sighs of happiness they obeyed.

The spectral problem remained unsolved. They decided that
ghosts, whether real or not, had better be left alone; and they
listened to Gregory with deepened respect.

10

Summer melted away: Blackberry season passed, watermelons
arrived. Corn on the cob got tougher and peaches sweeter.
Apricots, apples, and Delaware grapes began to ripen. Mornings had a bite in them that heralded frost. Smells changed
to the grapy, spicy odor of September, prophesying black-
boards and classrooms.

Jared felt like a poor man whose capital is dwindling. As
long as he could say "two whole months yet" he felt rich; a
month and a half was still comfortable; but when it came to
less than a month, he began to ache. There were no words to
match his thoughts about it. He could only sit knee to knee
with Clarice and pluck at her fingers one after the other,
constricted by something swollen in his chest.

"You'll be coming back soon," he repeated.

She looked at him with trembling lips, but said nothing.
They both knew that she would not be coming back soon. Indefinite time stretched before them wide as the stream of
death. If Clarice had been going to heaven instead of France,
the journey would hardly have seemed to him more irrevocable. Once, in dumb misery, he had leaned over and
kissed the hand on his knee.

"I won't have anybody when you're gone," he mourned.
And she had burst out crying and run away.

But there were still three weeks left.

Now and then of an early morning, a buckboard and a
pony cart drove out from the gate of Tolbecken—in front,
Exeter between the shafts, Gregory and the Judge on the seat,
the Judge in a farmer's straw hat, bamboo poles sticking out
from behind the seat; then Hugo, trotting like mad, Clarice
driving—her hands already dirty from the reins, her dark

hair tousled—Jared beside her ready to help if Hugo tugged too hard, and David in the rear seat holding tight. They were off for a day's fishing, Clarice in a gingham dress and boys in overalls, all happily barefooted. A hamper of fried chicken, bread 'n' jam, boiled eggs, sponge cake, and pop bottles bulged from the rear of the buckboard together with a feed sack and bait cans. They drove to Four-Mile Creek, which joined the Delaware in a sort of wooded cove, and there unpacked. Leafy banks wound off upcreek and there were pebble beaches along the river—a sound of trees and running water.

They fished for bass, ostensibly, but it was a great day when they actually caught one. Chub, perch, and sunfish supplied the slimy string they inflicted on the family at supper. But the thrill of a cork that twitches and then dives out of sight was all the sport necessary. By the end of a day their hands were muddy and wormy and fishy, their clothes smeared, their legs well bitten by mosquitoes.

The children occupied themselves apart. When they grew tired of fishing, they waded or climbed. Gregory, with a flair for the sport, did most of the catching. The Judge handled a rod at times, but mostly he basked or read or talked horses with Gregory.

When lunchtime came, they stretched out on the grass, beside the Delaware under its noon haze. Bread 'n' jam, chicken, and the rest circled the children's mouths, flies stung, sarsaparilla bottles dripped. Then the Judge smoked a cigar and took a nap with a white silk handkerchief over his face. Gregory dozed on the riverbank. The children, vaguely sick from overstuffing themselves, digested and watched the shimmer on the water.

"My stummick's bigger than yours."

"I bet it isn't."

They poked each other gingerly.

Afterwards, they fished again or waded or skipped stones until the shadows lengthened, the sky grew higher, and the lights more golden. Then home, dead tired, looking like ragamuffins, while Hugo and Exeter raced for the stable through clouds of dust. Scrubbings and bed awaited them. There was never any need for supper. Their hands still smelled of fish as they lay in bed.

The time Jared and Clarice had for being together dwindled. The equinoctial rains put an end to picnics. It was Grandmother now who entertained them with hours of reading in

Walter Scott and Dickens. Clarice would always be associated in Jared's mind with *Ivanhoe* and *Oliver Twist*. At exciting parts, they would clutch each other, hold their breaths, and lean forward.

"Now God be gracious to me," said Rebecca, "for the succour of man is well-nigh hopeless!"

"It is indeed," said the Templar, "for, proud as thou art, thou hast in me found thy match. . . ."

Afterwards they played "knight" in the attic, while the rain tapped on the shingles.

The last week came, the last day. They moped about together with no heart for doing much. It rained; they pressed their noses against the glass and stared out. More than ever it was impossible to say anything—possible only to feel numb and deserted. She was already dressed for travel, but for once the commands to keep tidy were unneeded.

After lunch the trunks departed, the valises and satchels were brought down. The half-hour of painful talk with an eye on the clock, which precedes departure, went on in the sitting room. Jared and Clarice sat together on the sofa feeling very small and helpless. Now and then he gave her hand a squeeze; she squeezed back.

"I'll write lots," she whispered.

"So'll I. I'll send you a Christmas present."

"I will too."

The carriage drew up in front. "There's Gregory," said the Judge. "Time to be going." Aunt Elizabeth put her arms about Grandmother. "You be careful, Mammy," she faltered, "keep well." Grandmother kissed her twice, and then abruptly, "You hurry up, Lizzie Tolbecken, and don't miss that train. You always were a slowpoke. Good-by."

The rest of them crowded into the station wagon; Gregory waved his whip. From the rear seat, Clarice kept looking back until the trees of Tolbecken were hidden by a turning in the street beyond.

Uncle Vincent, Aunt Sophia, the Reigers, a bevy of friends were at the station. Little David, in his best suit, turned up, wan and miserable. He could not even say good-by. Then, with a cold, smoky rush of air, the New York express thundered in. There was a last snatching of kisses, waving of hands.

Jared, struggling desperately among the hips of the crowd, seized Clarice's finger before she was pushed up the steps.

61

Then he followed along outside the train. She appeared at a window looking for him and waving, a dimming figure behind the streaked glass. The rear platform of the train faded and left blankness.

Too numb even to cry, Jared stumbled back with the others to the station wagon. Absorbed in a gloom of their own, they paid no attention to him. Back at the house, they exchanged banal remarks about the weather being bad for a crossing, sighed a little, observed that it had been a pleasant summer. Then the Judge took his umbrella and walked out to his office, Bella started tinkling on the piano, Grandmother took to her needlework, Aunt Joan called the maids and saw to the cleaning of the now vacant bedrooms. But upstairs, face down on his bed, Jared wept at last, sobbing his heart out against the pillow.

Later the rain stopped, and he crept out unobserved and wandered forlornly about the garden. Everything recalled his charming playmate to him. Now and then his mouth would draw in a sudden spasm and he would stamp his foot and struggle with himself and go on. When he came to the tree on which he had scratched their initials that first day, he set about carving them in earnest. He spent the rest of the afternoon at it.

"I wonder if the boy's sick," said Grandmother after supper. "He scarcely ate anything."

"No, he's just grieving," said Aunt Joan.

She went up and sat on the edge of his bed consoling him. Then he wept again.

"I want to grow up so's I can marry her."

"You'll be grown up before you know it. Besides, Aunt Lizzie may be bringing her back next summer."

He clung to the vague hope. "I'll write her a letter about it tomorrow. Do you think she misses me like I do her?"

"I know she does. And I'll tell you what, Jare, you and I will go out and buy her a nice present tomorrow. What do you think of that?"

"Oh, let's!"

She kissed him and left the room smiling. He would lie in the dark grieving for a while. For a few mornings he would waken to a sense of chill and loneliness. For a few months he would yearn. For years he might think of her as his sweetheart. But he would be consoled, the ill-spelled letters would gradually cease, life would absorb him. And yet something had passed that would never come again, something remained that would never be replaced. They belonged to each other as they would never belong to anyone else. The first impression would hold; the first love, integral with youth itself, would never be forgotten.

PART TWO

YOUTH

11

The Shakespeare calendar which had hung on a gas bracket in the sitting room had given place to Lowell, and this in turn to a Tennyson calendar for 1900. People now could speak of the last century without quite realizing what a distance and difference it implied. The scale of lead-pencil marks, each with its date, in a corner of the Judge's study climbed up the wall. Five feet four, five, six, seven. The Judge measured them with the greatest satisfaction.

"He'll be six feet if he's an inch. Slim and weedy yet, but he'll fill out. Spitting image of his Uncle Jared, only smaller boned. Same mouth and straight nose. Handsome."

And to Jared, "Hold yourself erect, sir. Don't stoop. Look the world in the face. Keep your shoulders back. That's the stuff."

One afternoon in late winter, they were walking along the ridge above Dunstable known as Gresham's Woods. The Judge wore a stiff felt hat and dark overcoat. He carried his gloves in one hand, his heavy stick in the other. Jared's long-vizored cap was perched on the back of his head.

There was a band of crepe around the arm of each. For with the changing calendars death too had passed. It was nearly a year since the telegram had come giving the news that Maylin Tolbecken had been drowned in a yachting party off the coast of Cuba. The Judge had closed his office that day, and had come falteringly into the drawing room where his wife and Bella were sitting. They stared at his face and at the yellow slip of paper in his hand.

After a while, he looked up.

"Maylin . . ." he began.

"What is it?" cried Grandmother.

He gave them the telegram, and walked blindly away toward his study. Grandmother, white in the face, limped after him, leaving Bella to her tears.

He was at his desk, leaning forward upon his outstretched arms.

"My son!" he kept repeating. "We parted in anger. God have mercy on me! My dear son!"

Rufus Tolbecken's old age began with that hour.

Maylin's body was never found; even his dust could not be brought to lie in the family burying ground. A memorial stone marked his empty place among the Tolbecken graves.

They walked at a good pace through the woods, which gave them an occasional glimpse of the town beneath them. The gray of winter had submerged sky and land.

"Grandfather," asked Jared suddenly, "what exactly does it mean to say a man is out of touch with reality?"

"Well . . ." began the Judge, and broke off. "Why do you ask?"

"I heard you and Dr. Craig talking last Sunday after dinner, and he said that was the trouble with my father."

For a while, the other walked on in silence. Then he said, "Yes, he was right—he *was* out of touch. Perhaps the fault lay in me. Perhaps I was remiss. . . . I'll try to tell you what he meant. I think it's important you should know." He pondered a moment. "Do you remember, when you and I went to Philadelphia, I took you to see that new invention—biograph, cinematograph, whatever they call it—like a magic lantern, except that the figures on the screen move?"

"Yes," said Jared, "it was wonderful. Seemed as if the locomotive would run right over us. And do you remember the picture of Niagara, Grandfather? You could almost hear the water."

The Judge nodded. "That's it. It seemed real—locomotive, waterfall, men, and horses. But there wasn't anything on the screen except shadows, a ray of light passing through film. Cut it off, and the screen was blank. No reality at all—a visionary world. I think that was what Dr. Craig meant about your father. Some men live on the surface of things. They forget or have never known the forces beneath that govern life. They are out of touch with them. Others put down roots, beyond the seen into something permanent and nourishing. We don't know what that something is. I call it God. It's the only reality

66

we have. And in proportion as we are in touch with it, we live."

They walked on, the Judge staring in front of him, Jared pondering what had been said, and but vaguely comprehending it.

"Your father was always dazzled by the new," the old man continued after a while, "new anything—clothes, scenes, faces, books, beliefs."

"Is it wrong to care for new things?" asked the boy.

"No, but it's wrong to be dazzled by them—that's the word I used. Don't be impressed, as your father was, by the slogan of 'up to date.' People run after every jimcrack theory as if it were an inspired gospel. Let them; don't you run. The old order must change, but if it changes too fast"—he made a sweeping gesture with his stick—"the Dark Ages."

They had come to the end of the ridge, a bald knoll overlooking Dunstable. Seen through the winter haze, the town, sprawled out smoking along the river, resembled a field of rock lava in the process of cooling.

"There's the New Order," he went on. "The more blotches we make like that on the face of the earth, the greater we are. I remember when it was only a country village. Gresham's Woods here were still a part of Tolbecken. Look at that—" he thumped with his cane on a real-estate sign that had been set up, directing purchasers of these residential sites to apply to Karl Kirschbaum—"the city will be up here in a few years. You'll be telling your grandchildren how you used to walk through it with me when it was open country, and how small the town was then."

They continued gazing down.

"There's Uncle Albert's new factory half up," said Jared, "and there's the United Blanket Company. That wasn't built when we were here last."

The Judge lit a cigar. "Yes, we're coming along. The Civil War, the opening up of natural wealth, waves of immigration made more of a break with the past than the American Revolution did. It's a break that's constantly widening. Old people like me are really exiles."

He stood looking out at the modern town, a bearded, massive figure. Jared would always remember him so—long after Gresham's Woods had become a city block and the ridge itself had been graded away.

"Let's be going," said the Judge. "We'll circle back across country."

But as they turned, a group of people appeared around a

bend of the road and approached them through the trees. One of them was Karl Kirschbaum himself in a shabby overcoat and black felt hat. Another, dapperly dressed, was Mr. Belknap, the publisher. The third, a handsome and clerical-looking man, Jared had never seen before. He walked hand in hand with a young girl equally unknown. Seeing the Judge, the group hesitated a moment and then came on.

"Gentlemen," said Rufus Tolbecken in greeting. And to the stranger, "Dr. Oliver, I'm pleased to see you again."

The clergyman bowed. He was of prosperous appearance, tall and pink-complexioned. The tones of his voice reminded Jared of the phrase "milk and honey." He presented the girl.

"This is my daughter, Frances. We call her Nan. Nan, shake hands with Judge Tolbecken—don't forget your curtsy. And this, I presume, is the grandson I've heard so much of —Master Jared. Splendid-looking fellow! Delighted to meet you, Jared. You and Nan will be great friends, I'm sure. Thirteen years old, eh? That makes it right, one year's difference—she's twelve. Ha-ha; there you are. Shake hands. . . ."

Jared backed away inwardly from this greeting. He disliked being called Master and gushed over. As for the girl, he felt a sudden hostility. She had managed to look him over and dismiss him with a glance which he repaid in kind.

"We've been taking Dr. Oliver through Gresham's Woods," explained Kirschbaum. "Thought I might talk him into buying a lot up here as an investment. It'd double in value in five years. But he's a little undecided. See what you can do with him, Judge."

The other smiled. "I'm convinced that you, sir, will give him all the advice necessary. So you've definitely accepted the call to Dunstable, Dr. Oliver? I hadn't heard . . ."

Kirschbaum and Belknap exchanged glances.

"Yes," said the clergyman, "I accepted yesterday after the second and more flattering offer made by the elders with whom I have been corresponding. I felt that I was no longer justified in declining so advantageous a proposal, and I decided to bring my acceptance in person. It will be a great pleasure to take up my duties here. They will be arduous at first, for between you and me, Judge, there's a good deal about the church that needs modernizing; but I'm very much gratified by the *carte blanche* I have been offered."

"Who offered it?" There was the flick of a lash in the Judge's voice.

"Why, the board of elders. Surely you must be *au courant* . . ."

"No, I was not informed."

The embarrassment of his companions becoming manifest to Oliver, he stopped and replied, "Ah?" on a note of surprise, then added diplomatically, "I intended calling on you this evening, as you're one of our most prominent elders."

The Judge bowed. "My wife and I will be delighted to receive you."

"I suppose," burst in Kirschbaum, fidgeting, "I suppose you've been admiring the new buildings of Dunstable, Judge. That new factory of Albert's is going to be a wonder, eh?"

Jared's attention wandered back to Nan Oliver. A knot of tawny hair showed beneath her hat. Her violet-blue eyes were startlingly deep, but they had a curious opaque quality that troubled him: they studied him without disclosing anything in return. "Stuck on herself," he chafed, "thinks she's pretty."

He compared this girl, as he did every other, to her disadvantage, with Clarice, the dim, idealized Clarice of lingering sentiment. It had become a habit with him. He was rather proud of his immunity among the riffraff of Dunstable schoolgirls. It distinguished him to be prepossessed by a distant Parisian sweetheart. He spoke of her at times to intimate friends like David Mansen or the now-converted Eaby Ellis, who passed on and embroidered her legend. Even then it charmed and exasperated the future belles of Dunstable. And now Frances Oliver paled by contrast. He could look at her with indifference slightly colored by irritation.

His scrutiny piqued her. She thawed a bit and smiled, but he turned away. The snap of her eyes and the toss of her head fell on emptiness.

Kirschbaum was holding forth on the glories of Dunstable. "Nothing can stop us now," he was saying. "American Wire has bought up those building sites to the east over there. In ten years we'll have a hundred and fifty thousand population."

"That's capital," exclaimed Oliver. "I like living in progressive centers. I like to keep my church abreast of the wave. People flatter me by calling me a hustler—you know, I glory in that title, gentlemen. Now, I take it that Mr. Craig —whom of course I respect as a Presbyterian of the old school—a very fine figure he is, too—I take it that he's not exactly a hustler. Am I right, Judge?"

"Entirely," said Rufus Tolbecken. "Well, I must be getting

on. I'll see you again, Dr. Oliver. Good evening, Mr. Kirschbaum." He bowed slightly to Belknap. "Come along, Jare."

"Who was that man?" asked Jared when they were out of hearing.

"The new minister."

"But Dr. Craig's the minister!"

"He's resigned." The Judge strode ahead, and Jared suddenly realized that he had never before seen him so angry. The anger of Rufus Tolbecken, though contained, vibrated. For once it burst forth. "And he did right. He refused to link religion up with the Dunstable business boom. There comes a time when the word of God should not be disgraced by preaching it to fools. They've replaced him by this—this hustler."

After a time, he went on. "They've shelved us both. I've been an elder of the church forty years, and they've met this fellow's terms, given him twice Craig's salary and a new manse, not only overriding me, but without even condescending to let me know that the bargain was struck. From now on, I'll have to get used to being ignored. That's what it means to be old."

Jared was up in arms. "But, Grandfather, aren't you going to do anything?"

"Yes—resign from the board. That'll be a relief to them; it's what they're hoping for. There's no use complaining. I won't give them the satisfaction of laughing up their sleeves at old Judge Tolbecken. Leave the church? I go there to worship God. What can an old man do about an insult? Why, bear it."

12

Donald Craig's resignation in the winter of 1900 represented the close of a chapter in the life of Dunstable. The North Street Presbyterian Church was the premier church of that denomination in town and hence as necessary to the Dunstable boom as the Y.M.C.A., the opera house, and Palace Hotel. Corporate Mammon felt a deep concern about Craig's lack of business competence. Services were neglected, donations cut down, death thinned his followers. He held on, despite heartaches and misgivings, preaching his rigid sermons to the end, and at last, forced out, he relinquished his pulpit in the proud manner of a captain relieved from too long a post.

After his final sermon, he walked back with the Judge to Tolbecken and stood warming his hands before the study fire.

"I'm a sinner," he remarked. "Aye, the more I think of it, the more reprobate I am."

"How so, Donald?"

"A good harvester should grieve at sunset, when there's work still to do, but I'm glad the day is over."

"There's a time for everything, Donald. There's a time for the nunc dimittis."

"Ah," said Craig, "I'm sorry that I couldn't depart in peace. Perhaps I'll find peace now."

The Judge frowned. "What do you think of this man Oliver?"

"You'll not expect me to answer that question, Rufus."

Again the Judge frowned. "But you know he was rail-roaded over my head and that I've left the board of elders?"

"I know. You did right. As you say, there's a time for everything, and our time is past."

Dr. Cary Oliver's first appearance was the signal for a gala reception. All the disgruntled sheep flocked back; even the galleries were filled; Messrs. Dunning, the distiller, and Belknap with their families attended; two palm trees and a vase of lilies decorated the platform; and a quartet of professional singers sat aloft in front of the organ. But Oliver himself outdid everything else. He wore a black silk robe with full sleeves. His face shone, his voice soothed, and his presence charmed. His tribute to Mr. Craig brought tears, not because it was felt that Craig deserved it, but because of Dr. Oliver's "sweetness and feeling." He preached on charity in such choice words and with such quotations from the poets that the ladies afterwards declared they had been listening to an English classic. Everybody except Judge Tolbecken and other intractables felt deeply moved.

Above all, he was brief. The entire service lasted only an hour, and this included an Offertory of high-class music by the choir. "It could have gone on for another quarter of an hour," said Mr. Dunning, consulting his watch, "I wouldn't have objected at all. I put five dollars in the plate, and I consider that I got my money's worth." In short, everything indicated that the North Street Church had entered upon a new and prosperous era.

As time went on, there were grumblings, to be sure, that for a man of God, Dr. Oliver was singularly preoccupied with his personal budget. His salary had to be raised from year to year. He required a fashionable turnout and two horses to make the rounds of his pastoral visits. A fortnight's vacation in the summer had been enough for Craig, but Oliver needed two months. In the end, he needed an assistant pastor.

On the other hand, he put the church on its feet. Pew rents were gradually raised to such a point that only the well-to-do could afford a sitting, and the church was packed. Episcopalians with a grievance came over to the still-more-fashionable fold. Socially as well as inspirationally, it surpassed anything else in Dunstable. An organist and singers were lured from Philadelphia; there were concerts of sacred music on Sunday afternoons; Dr. Oliver's prayers and sermons maintained a rhetorical level that was seldom lowered. And with this inner fire the church altered externally as well. It was painted cream color, the lawn in front was properly sodded and planted, damask curtains subdued the glare of the windows. An eagle lectern, discreet lighting, new hymnals, and new carpets were installed. In general effect, at length it had an appearance of severity—but it was richly, arrogantly plain.

Everything considered, therefore, Oliver was worth his salary. He had frequent calls from other parishes, and made no secret of his conviction that the laborer is worthy of his hire, which meant in plain language that he would not refuse a better bid out of any attachment for Dunstable. The best obtainable being the war cry of the boomers, they were proud to retain him. He published his sermons "on request" and got out a neat little calendar in red and black made up of cullings from his pulpit for the Christmas trade. It sold beautifully.

Meanwhile, among older parishioners, criticism of a different kind went on. Used to the meat and sinew of Craig's discourses, they found no substance in the new mellifluousness. They wanted salt instead of sugar, logic rather than phrases. They criticized him too for cultivating the rich, and maintained that his manner varied with the size of a bank account. Moreover, he played golf, played it fanatically. The sight of him in checkered cap and knickerbockers, followed by little Jim Oliver with an umbrella stand full of crazy-looking canes, stirred Puritan ire. It did not console them at the burial of their dead to be exhorted by a man who matched jokes with Paul Dunning in the club locker room. Perhaps they were hard on Oliver, but they were as hard on themselves. At all events, they did not like an ambassador of God in cap and knickerbockers.

For their part, the other members of his family did little to bolster his credit with these sticklers. They shone in society rather than in good works. Mrs. Oliver, indeed, spent half of her time on visits out of town. James Oliver, his son, a loose-mouthed Apollo, excelled chiefly as a dancing boy. About Frances, opinions differed, except on the point of her beauty. She resembled her father, most critics said, not only in appearance but in what appearance covered up. Then, too, the conservatives held that a man, especially a clergyman, ought to be lord of his own house; but Oliver was pampered by his family not as a lord but as a milch cow. They indulged him so that he might indulge them in turn.

To be fair, conservative opinion exaggerated. The truth is that Oliver, in his family or out of it, was no worse than most men—he was even a shade better in a cordial, bouyant way. Simply, he should not have been a clergyman.

Among the Tolbeckens, loyal of course to Craig, only Bella favored the new minister. She took to haunting the church with upturned face and ready handkerchief. Forgotten airs and graces blossomed out again in Oliver's presence. She even found occasion after a prayer meeting one night to pour out the story of her griefs to his sympathetic ears. He treated her with a pious gallantry.

"I don't care what you say," she burst out to the family, "I've never had such comfort. I adore him—he's a lovely man."

It was Oliver, glad of an opening at Tolbecken, who attended her during the last illness. Her funeral in the autumn was his first big function of that kind. Bella did not know that she was going to die; no one had mentioned the word pneumonia to her. She lay, her mind half wandering, flattered and consoled by the minister's handsome face and mellow voice. There was not more than a touch of calculation on his part. Beneath his worldliness, he could feel genuine pity for the vague, frustrated woman, drifting into death as she had drifted through life. He called with a solicitude that stirred the family to a kindlier estimate of him, gave Bella his hand to hold, and spent many an hour by her bed. In the midst of this pale idyl, she died.

Jared, recalled by telegram from Lawrenceville, which he had entered two months before, reached Dunstable too late. He found the house dark and hushed, permeated by the sickish smell of flowers. They led him into his mother's room, dim with lowered curtains, and drew back a cloth from the familiar face that yet seemed strangely unfamiliar—more beautiful than he remembered it, but terribly remote. He felt a solemn awe, stood timidly looking down, kissed the cold forehead, and then tiptoed away. It was the mystery of death rather than any loss that haunted him. Bella had stood only in the background of his life. Without knowing it, he was actually sorrowing over the first clear presentiment of mortality, of time and change. Henceforth, boyhood's assurance in the stability of things would fade; he would note differences and distance, grow conscious of a lengthening perspective.

The conventions of the funeral oppressed him without his understanding the cause. There was too much pomp and heaviness, too many wreaths, mourners, carriages, and speeches over poor Bella, as if, having ignored her in life, the world was conceding her an hour of importance at her burial. Tolbecken exacted its tribute of public sympathy, of black dress and flowery offerings. From the house to the church, from the church to the cemetery, a splendid hearse, a column of horses and coupés, coachmen in livery, men in high hats, and women in flowing veils escorted Bella to her final rest. Cary Oliver rose to the summit of his oratory in depicting her virtues and in consolations for her loss. Everyone suddenly perceived as never before the value of her life, a pattern of patience and devotion. The choir sang "For All the Saints That from Their Labors Rest," the women sobbed, the men looked solemn. Then lined up once more about the grave, they admired the minister's voice booming grandiloquently; they admired the expensive wreaths, and shuddered a little at the gaping earth.

They laid her, deserted in death as in life, next to Maylin Tolbecken's empty tomb.

13

From the vantage point of the second-floor sitting room in the manse, Nan Oliver and her friend Beth Bowman looked out on the come and go of North Street. A box of chocolates lay open on the window seat between them. It was

74

the Christmas holidays. Singly or in groups, boys and girls, at whom now and then they banged at the window and waved, sauntered past. They commented on and gossiped about them, giggling a good deal. The town had not yet quite outgrown its village gregariousness.

Presently the clip-clop of a horse unattended by wheels approached, and Jared Tolbecken curvetted by on his sorrel mare. But although both pairs of eyes quickened to intentness and a chocolate drop between Nan's fingers remained poised halfway from the box to her mouth, neither of the watchers rapped at the pane or waved. The profile of high-strung horse and booted rider drifted unhailed across the field of vision—with a shimmer of well-groomed flanks, ring of bridle chain, glitter of spur, a contrast of power and spirit with slenderness and grace. The watchers' eyes swiveled as they followed until their object disappeared from sight. Then the chocolate drop resumed its course; Beth Bowman's admiration exhaled in a sigh.

"Snob!" challenged Nan.

"I don't see that at all," maintained the worshiper. "I think he's wonderful."

"If you don't see it," retorted her friend, "it's because you people here enjoy kowtowing to the Tolbeckens. I don't. He's the great Dunstable snob."

"Jealous?" hinted the other.

"Jealous! Because he danced with you once or twice at Mary Reiger's German last winter and gave you a couple of favors? That's a lot to be jealous over! If you and he are such good friends, why didn't you knock on the window?"

Beth looked down. "I didn't think of it."

"No? Well, you'll have another chance. Do it when he comes back—I dare you. He'll be along in just about three-quarters of an hour."

"How do you know that?"

"Because I do." Nan caught herself. "I mean, I think he will," she added lamely.

They let the point drop.

"I never said that he and I were good friends," protested Beth. "I'm not going around waving at him. He wouldn't like it. But he has been awfully nice to me. And he's terribly bright—he's head of his form at Lawrenceville—and ambitious. Father thinks he's going to be as great a man sometime as his grandfather. He's simply not like the other boys in our crowd."

"I wonder," said Nan shrewdly, "I wonder if he *is* so

75

different. Being sort of high and mighty and a Tolbecken, he has all you girls bluffed. Since we moved here four years ago, all I've heard is how grand Jared Tolbecken is. I'm the only one that doesn't kowtow to him. I'll admit he's good-looking, though." Her square white teeth severed a chocolate nougat; she examined the remaining half abstractedly. "Yes, he's good-looking. Do you think he'll be at the Armstrongs' party tonight?"

"I don't know," sighed Beth.

About the same time, two young men held up the horse and its rider at a point in the suburbs. They were fashionably dressed in peg-top trousers, circular-toed shoes, overcoats tight at the waist and with flowing skirts. They wore oddly cocked felt hats.

"Yay!" they shouted.

Jared reined up his mount, guiding it to the sidewalk, where he swung off.

"Hi, fellows. Hi, Eaby. Hello, Josh. How's old Andover?"

"How's Lawrenceville? Gee, I'm glad to see you, Jare. How's the old scout? When did you get in?"

"Yesterday."

"Same here."

They shook hands and slapped each other's backs. With a trace of swagger, Josh Sedley pulled out a box of cigarettes.

"Coffin nail?" he asked.

"No, I haven't started yet."

"What's this I hear about your making the team?" put in Eaby. "Great stuff!"

"No," said Jared, "only sub quarterback. Got my letter, though. I'm not in your class for that game. Too light. You've got the Yale varsity cinched next year. I'll never make the first eleven at Princeton."

"Here's wishing us both luck," said Eaby. "I'd like to get another crack at you on the field, you old dude. Boots and spurs, eh? And take a slant at our riding togs."

The three of them exchanged friendly mockeries, patted the mare, expressed relief at being home once more in the old burg, and invited each other to drop around as soon as possible.

"You won't see much of me," declared Sedley. "I'm out on the trail of Nan Oliver. Golly, she's some looker! Going to the Armstrongs' tonight, Jare?"

The other nodded. "Yes, I couldn't get out of it." His glumness was so apparent that Eaby and Josh exchanged winks. They were both familiar with his dislike of parties,

76

which he dodged craftily and attended only on compulsion. At such times, he carried it off well, but he was actually on tenterhooks, well-mannered but miserable. He liked to believe that the chitchat and constraint at dances bored him, and that he was dedicated to higher things. No one, including himself, ascribed this antipathy to its real cause, bashfulness; he had camouflaged it completely. But a party in the offing cast its bleak shadow before; as it drew closer, he felt himself stiffening; his hands and feet went cold; there was an uncomfortable lift at the pit of his stomach. When it was over, the relief almost equalled the apprehension.

"Same old woman-hater," remarked Eaby. "What's happened to your sweetheart in Paris who tore the shirt off of me when we were kids? Great girl, that."

"Oh," said Jared, "we kind of stopped writing. Guess she's forgotten about me in all that time. Well, got to be going. See you fellows tonight, worse luck. So long!"

Maneuvering skillfully, he mounted; the mare sidled and reared; with a final wave of the hand, he rode on.

Yes, he guessed that Clarice had forgotten him. He had forgotten her a little himself—you can't go on with letters forever. The remoteness of six years stretched between them. He wondered what she was really like now that they were almost grown up, whether they could be such friends again. "Just kids," he sighed. The wraith of a childish longing dropped behind him as he let his horse out for a gallop.

Contrary to Nan Oliver's prediction, he returned home not along North Street, but followed a way that took him through the poorer quarter of the town—a section of narrow brick houses plastered one against the other in monotonous ranks. Leaving his horse at a tumble-down livery stable, he walked along with his eyes on the faded numbers above the doors, for there was nothing else to distinguish one house from the next, and although he had been here before, he could never remember whether the Mansens lived fifth or sixth from the corner.

The agitation of a curtain at the window and a hurry of footsteps inside revealed that his coming had already been noted. The door was thrown open by a scrawny, nondescript woman in a calico dress.

"Heaven's sakes, Mr. Jared! It's certainly nice to see you again. Dave—" her voice shrilled through the narrow house— "here's Mr. Jared come to see you. Walk right into the parlor. What a big boy you've grown!"

The mingled cabbage and onion smell that clings to the

walls of such houses closed in upon him as the door was shut.

"Herbert, here's Mr. Jared Tolbecken."

In the tiny parlor, that looked crowded with its sticks of furniture, an unshaven, collarless man put down the newspaper he had been reading and got up grudgingly.

"Hello," he growled.

Herbert Mansen hated his wife's to-do about the Tolbeckens. "As if they were little gods!" he chafed. "Because they happen to be born in a big house with silver spoons in their mouths! Patronize us, throw us a few scraps! The time's coming when there won't be any rich snobs in this country. You can't get me to lick their boots."

It had been Bertha Mansen, harried and desperate, who had pled for her husband at Tolbecken after his discharge for drunkenness from the Reiger underwear factory, and had gained him a brief reinstatement. It had been the Judge who had financed a promising invention of Mansen's that had come to nothing because of his inveterate shiftlessness. Time and again the Tolbeckens had paid the Mansens' rent and filled their larder. But nothing they could do would melt the defeated man's self-pity. Even more than drink, it was his consolation.

"Home from school, are you?" he went on. His heavy eyes rested on Jared's well-made clothes. "Been out riding, eh? I should think this part of town would hurt your horse's feet."

The rickety hall stairs shook with racing steps. David Mansen's thin, undergrown figure appeared.

"Jare!" It was the voice of the worshiper to his hero. "I thought it was tomorrow you were coming. I wanted to be at the station. . . . Gee, I've been looking forward to this! Gee!"

His father sulked out. A door slammed. But the two boys stood lost in each other.

"Come on up to my room, Jare, come on."

"You'll have to excuse the looks of things, Mr. Jared."

Bertha Mansen's eyes reflected the light in her son's. To see David in such company transfigured her. They stamped up the stairs. The floor shook above.

"Why can't you be nice?" she wheedled her husband in the kitchen. "He's Dave's best friend."

"You make me tired," grumbled Mansen. "Dave's got twice as many brains as that Tolbecken kid. You act as if he was doing our boy a favor to look at him." He sat with his hands clenched before him on the table. "Look at the chances he's got—boarding school, college next year, grand position after that, money, luxuries—everything. Because he was born in a family called Tolbecken. And our boy, our poor boy!" He struck the table. "God, what a world! But we'll see about it. We'll see whether Dave's going to get left. . . ."

He rose, stalked over to a cupboard, unlocked it and took out a bottle, which he held up to the light before pouring himself a drink.

"We'll see."

Upstairs in David's small room, the two friends sat on the bed and exchanged news. Two icons—a Lawrenceville pennon and a Princeton one, gifts from Jared—were tacked to the wall, magnificent objects in David's eyes. There was a surprisingly large bookcase, full of battered books. A boy's chemistry set stood on the table.

"Still messing around with stinks," commented Jared. "What good does that do you?"

"Just interesting. Won't have any time for chemistry after this year."

"What do you think you'll be doing?"

"Dunno. Get a job somewhere. It's time Mother had some help."

"Well, think of me plodding along with examinations and stuff four years, then three years law school after that. Wish I was in your shoes."

Although insincere, it was graciously intended and was so interpreted. David got up and sauntered casually over to the window, where he stood looking out into the boxlike yard squeezed between similar boxes. Something burned beneath his eyelids. He would have given his soul for those four years.

"Hello!" said Jared, catching sight of another object framed on the wall. "You aren't becoming a Roman Catholic, are you?" He got up to look more closely at a framed picture of a Madonna. Then after a pause, "Darned if it doesn't remind me of *her*, Dave."

"Think so?"

He could not see the light flush on Mansen's usually sallow face.

"Where'd you get it?"

"Oh, in a picture store. I made the frame myself."

"Nice work, that."

David joined him, and they stood staring at the picture.

"Yes, it certainly looks like *her*," repeated Jared. "The way she would look if she was older, that is. Aunt Elizabeth just sent over a photograph of her. I'll show it to you when

79

you come to our house. But I like this better. What'll you take for it—frame and all?"

"I wouldn't like to sell it, Jare." Then with a great effort, "Give it to you, if you like."

"Oh, no."

Jared turned away, and began whistling, as he fingered some books on the shelf. A long-forgotten warmth stirred in him. They talked about other things, but their thoughts were elsewhere.

"Wasn't that a great summer!" he said at last.

David nodded. "If I come over this evening, will you show me the photograph?"

"Sure. . . . No, I can't. Got to go to a fool party this evening. Show it to you tomorrow."

When he reached home, he stood for a long time before Clarice's photograph. She was half in profile, and with her hair drawn severely back, the delicate planes of her face were exposed. He recognized that tilt of the head, the challenge of the eyes; she had the look of temperament and fire that he remembered. Still, this was only a photograph. There was something finer about David's picture. It was an altarpiece.

*   *   *

That evening he danced punctiliously with Beth Bowman, Grace Armstrong, Mary Reiger, Jean Ellis, Daphne Sedley, and so on, whenever obligation required. He would have danced with Nan Oliver on the same terms, but she had always a plethora of partners waiting. It made no real difference to him who his partners were; he steered them creditably enough around the floor, and by practice had acquired the technique of making them think he liked it. As a matter of fact they were almost a blur—pale-colored dresses, hair newly put up or still gathered behind with a ribbon, tentative décolletés, the scents of soap or perfume. When he had done his bit and chattered through the same topics with each of them, he drifted back to a corner of the hall or any place where a group of trousered guests might be relaxing. His back ached, his face muscles felt stiff. He interpreted every glance or titter as directed at him and grew steadily more rigid. If those girls who considered him snobbish or mysterious had known the truth, they would have twittered indeed.

It was an old-fashioned party, the most dreadful of all, to Jared's way of thinking. Games followed the dancing. Charades were started. "Now, girls and boys," summoned

80

Mrs. Armstrong, "let's choose sides. Here, Jared . . ." He had to go through with it.

Creamed oysters, sandwiches, lemonade, ice cream and cake arrived at last. The guests distributed themselves around the dining room or in the parlor or on stair landings.

It was at this point that Nan Oliver tested a theory.

"I think you're mean, Jared Tolbecken."

"I'm awfully sorry. Why?"

"You didn't ask me to dance."

"You were so popular."

"That's no excuse. I hoped you would ask me."

She stood beneath a gas lamp in the hall and looked at him steadily a moment before looking down and then up again. It was a look that brought her out from the blur of other girls into a magic focus. He saw that she wore an exquisite pink dress, that her blond hair was plaited in an aureole around her head, that her eyes were enchanting, and that she had a dimple at the corner of her chin. No girl had ever made eyes at him before. It was a crucial experience. It melted his reserve, confounded his superiority, and brought him at once to the common level, deliciously, rapturously.

"I wish I had known."

"You ought to have known—I kept looking at you. You dance better than anyone here."

Flattery, whether true or false, always pleases as a tribute. In addition to anything else, it implies that the one who receives it is worth flattering. Jared did not dance better than anyone there, but he would have liked to, and Nan spoke as an expert.

"It's awfully good of you," he muttered foolishly. A novel idea struck him. "I wonder if we couldn't have supper together. Can't I get you a plate of something?"

"I'd love it," she agreed with another dazzling look. "I promised Josh Sedley, but that doesn't matter."

"Doesn't it?" he wavered.

"Of course not, I've had him around all evening. And now that I can get you . . ." She smiled softly. "Hurry up, please, Jared. It'll be fun to hide and have him looking for me. Quick! I'll slip up to that room on the second floor front. It's Mr. Armstrong's study, but he's not there—I peeped in a few minutes ago. We'll be all alone. Quick!"

He succumbed at once, pushing his way through the throng about the table with a new fervor inside him. He heaped two plates with tidbits. He contrived to manage them, forks

81

and all, with one hand, while juggling a pair of lemonade glasses with the other. Outside in the hall, he found Josh similarly burdened, wheeling about bewildered in search of Nan. "Where the dickens!" he was muttering, and then wandered off into the back parlor. Jared watched his chance and climbed unnoticed through an absorbed group on the stairs, tiptoed along the corridor above, reached the trysting place.

"Lock the door," whispered Nan, "then no one'll find us."

It was irregular enough to be very exciting.

"I call this cozy," she said. She nibbled the end of a sandwich, studying him the while and turning on a new variation in her eyes. "Sit down," she went on, moving a little on the divan. "There! Why haven't we been friends before?"

"I don't know . . ." he stumbled. "I wish we had been." And greatly daring, "I hope we will be from now on."

"Of course."

"Will you let me come to see you?"

"Of course." He thought her glance at him absolutely bewitching.

"Tomorrow afternoon?"

"Yes."

"Thanks awfully." He plunged on. "Do you like to drive? We could go over to Queenston and have something at the jigger shop."

"Oh, that's wonderful. I'm so thrilled!"

She reached out and gave his hand a little squeeze, then drew back and looked down. They were all alone. She was perfectly beautiful. He felt overcome by a strange, disturbing sensation, a sensuous awareness of her. His cheeks grew hot.

"I think you're lovely," he blurted out before he could stop himself.

"Do you, Jare?" She was not angry, as he had feared. Her hand lay open on her knee. "That's sweet of you."

He felt a wave of pride. He, Jared Tolbecken, had actually paid a compliment to this fashionable girl and had not been rebuffed. His heart beat in triumph. And yet at the same time he felt a little oppressed, without knowing why.

As for Nan, she had proved her theory up to the hilt. Jared the Aristocrat had turned out no different from Tom, Dick, or Harry, but had flopped into her net at the first dip. Pleased with herself, she thought none the less of him and glowed at the prospect of tomorrow's drive through Dunstable. But why didn't he hold her hand?

"I suppose you've rushed a lot of girls?" she said coquettishly.

"I certainly haven't."

"Didn't I hear about somebody in France? Clarice?"

"Yes," he agreed curtly. Somehow he disliked talking about Clarice with her. The hot wave ebbed. "You're not eating your supper," he observed.

Intuitively she drew the vagrant hand back. Yes, he was a bit different after all.

But their drive next day shook the Beth Bowmans and Grace Armstrongs of Dunstable. They tossed their heads and whetted their tongues about her; they grieved over him. Jared had crashed from his pedestal; he had fallen for Nan Oliver.

14

Dunstable lay within easy enough reach of Lawrenceville to permit an occasional week end at home during the school terms. A mysterious summons from the Judge recalled Jared to Tolbecken in the spring of his sixth-form year.

"What's happened?" he demanded of Gregory, who met him with the buckboard at the station. "Is anybody ill? Why did Grandfather send for me?"

"I s'pec' it's because we's havin' visitors, Mist' Jared. Some big fish. We's done been cleanin' house and shinin' silver like nobody's business. De Judge say he want you to meet Dr. Somebody-'r-other—say he's President, but de name wasn't Teddy Roosevelt."

That, of course, explained it. Jared's grandfather had always wanted him to meet distinguished men. Accordingly the boy had spent a good many dull hours listening to talk that he only partially understood, but he had sense enough to see the wisdom of his grandfather's policy. And he discovered that words and faces which have made little impression at the time have a way of coming back later, charged with meaning, like seeds which have taken root.

The driveway of Tolbecken had been newly raked and the hedges clipped; the house had a burnished look. Aunt Joan met him at the door. There was a sound of voices in the drawing room.

"Hello, Jare," called the Judge, "come in here."

His grandmother welcomed him from her throne behind the best tea set. After a brief hug, Rufus Tolbecken led him toward an erect, clean-shaven man who stood in front of the mantelpiece.

"I want you to meet Dr. Wilson, the president of Princeton, Jare. My grandson, sir. He'll be entering the college next year. Dr. Wilson," he added, "will be speaking at the alumni dinner tonight. We owe the honor of his visit to that. He's going to tell us what he intends to make of our alma mater."

"What we all intend to make of her, Judge," corrected the other. "I'm simply a responsible minister. Without your co-operation I should get nowhere. But a minister must have policies, must have a vision and assert it. Otherwise, you'll admit, he's not very responsible."

Dr. Wilson, who looked taller than he was, had an academic, almost clerical appearance. But Jared found nothing stiff or constrained about him; he was gracious and poised, without a trace of self-consciousness. What distinguished him was a certain dignity which forbade any familiarity, a certain intensity, too, in his controlled smile and alert eyes. On the whole, Dr. Wilson made an electric, masterful impression, the more so as he seemed entirely unconcerned about making any impression at all.

"You'll remember," he went on, "how President Patton used to say that it was impossible that Princeton should be other than a college for rich men's sons. We're going to see if it's really impossible. We won't discriminate against rich men's sons; but in the end, if I have my way, that's about all we'll do for them."

"Capital!" returned the Judge cordially. "But you may run into squalls, sir. It's the rich men that support Princeton. Most reforms seem to be based on compromise and conciliation. Beware of rousing the rebel which is in the heart of every American."

Dr. Wilson nodded, but the glint in his eyes boded no good to rebels. It was plain too that he disliked the word compromise. But he smiled, and said, "I'll follow your advice and try to conciliate a few of them tonight, Judge."

"The intellect," he said later on, when the conversation veered back to the reorganization at Princeton, "the intellect is well enough. We must have more of it and must have it disciplined. But without vision the people perish. It is great emotions, enthusiasms that drive the world. You know,

Judge, that, by the way, is what I miss in your Republican party—they do not seem to have any enthusiasm about anything. There is one thing I have got a great enthusiasm about"—his hands gripped the arms of his chair—"and that is human liberty."

Rufus Tolbecken shook his head. He was too good a Republican to let the challenge pass.

"The party out of power is always enthusiastic about human liberty. It can afford great emotions. The party in power can't. It's hampered by responsibility, and puts water in its wine, for the sake of business management."

But beneath their opposing political standpoints, the Judge and his guest were really at one; they harmonized on the much more important level of a common ethic and religious faith. Each in a different way reflected the same American tradition. The changes in the North Street Presbyterian Church and Dr. Craig's removal were mentioned, and drew a vigorous "Pshaw!" from the president.

"That's it," he exclaimed, "on the plea of making our churches more interesting, we make them merely entertaining. Did you ever know the theater to be a successful means of governing conduct? We should fill our pews on no lesser terms than by giving people to understand that the church is the place where life is dispensed, and that if they want life they must come there for it. I'm under the impression that your Dr. Oliver dispenses soothing syrup, not life."

"Exactly," approved Tolbecken.

It came out that Wilson had been a Presbyterian elder for many years, a fact that raised him still higher with the Judge. They fell to discussing modern religious tendencies. Jared, boy though he was, felt more and more, as the minutes passed, something supreme in Wilson that set him apart from others, that made him a great man and a leader.

When the hour came, they walked over to the Palace Hotel, where the alumni dinner was being held. The place resounded with Princeton cheers and spirit. The traditional clowns, of which every alumni association boasts a few, were in evidence and did their stunts. Jared, subfreshman as he was, humbly admired them, but he could not help noting the contrasts between them and the thoughtful face of the Princeton president. These were the supporters whom the prophet must somehow cajole into sympathy with his vision. To them, in large measure, Princeton was merely the setting of happy-go-lucky years, of friendships and escapades, flavored by a taste of already-forgotten study. Far from desiring to change the

85

college, they resented change. They wanted the scene of their boyhood to remain in detail as it had been. Only a few, chiefly the older men of the seventies and eighties, had training enough to grasp an educational program and to value, higher than the athletic, the intellectual status of a university. The mass, as usual, remained inert and vaguely hostile. But it was precisely this indifferent mass that must be converted and enlightened or the funds to support the president's measures would not be forthcoming. It gave Jared his first notion of the task of a leader—a task so difficult that it is usually shirked.

The after-dinner jokers did their stint; tobacco smoke thickened. Somebody near Jared had the hiccups, and faces in general reflected laboring digestion. Every now and then a college yell was called for and delivered with surges of tigers and sisses, booms and ahs that shook the building. Tunefully the crowd turned its memories back to the four long years of college, and the Orange and the Black. A recent graduate, who had taken too early a start on the evening, was overcome first with sentiment and finally with sleep. In the end, the toastmaster introduced, gentlemen, the president of Princeton, and called for a locomotive. Before the tilted cigars, stained coffee cups, and faces smoothed to attention, Wilson stood up.

He dealt in dreams, but dreams that were on the point of becoming realities. He did not talk down to his audience. Instead, by a peculiar magic, he raised them to his own level. For once, to many the idea of what a university may be, what eternal purposes it may serve, became manifest—not a playground or a cloister, not a social adjunct or a training school for selfish ability, but one of the distributing pulses of the nation, linked to the national heart, laboring for the national future. And they, the mediocre, the provincial, harnessed to little interests and humdrum tasks, were enriched for the moment by a glimpse of wider opportunity, by the summons to a great cause.

It was superb oratory not only by its manner and phrasing, but by its strategic skill. Wilson managed to hold this crowd spellbound; vibrant with enthusiasm, he communicated it to his listeners.

And we could make our dream real, he told them. He needed but fifty young men, fired with this vision, who would in daily, personal contact with the students teach not books but methods of thought, and instill the hunger for new ideas. The cost? A trifle—two and a quarter millions. His hearers might whistle; they must get over their surprise. He felt that

86

some in that room would be supplying these funds simply to get rid of him; they would get rid of him on no other terms. Two and a quarter millions? Why, he estimated that nothing less than twelve and a half millions would meet the needs of his program.

The first figure provoked amazement; the second drew applause. It was a tribute to courage, an appeal that they all be magnificent together. The very challenge captured their imaginations and won their support.

He closed on a still grander note. The cigars and coffee cups were forgotten; the college bravura was forgotten.

"I have heard," he said, "and my heart has echoed the fine cheers of loyalty that have gone up for Princeton in this place and in other places, and no man who hears those cheers can doubt the genuineness of the impulse that is behind them. But, gentlemen, cheers and good wishes will not make the fortunes of Princeton; these things will not give Princeton reputation; nothing will give Princeton reputation except the achievements of the men whom she creates. The reputation of a university is not a matter of report. It is a matter of fact. I should despair of producing a character for Princeton by praising her. We are here to praise Princeton by serving our day and generation. . . ."

Back at Tolbecken, when Dr. Wilson had gone to bed, Jared stood for a moment with his grandfather in the latter's study. The spell of the speech and of their guest's personality was still on them.

"I've had my doubts about your going to Princeton, Jare," his grandfather said. "I wouldn't have you go anywhere else now. Go where vision is, and power, in the person of some living man. The rest doesn't matter. . . . Yes, Woodrow Wilson will go far. Perhaps too far for many. I have the feeling that he's the kind of man who goes on at last alone."

15

An odd adventure in the May of that year troubled the serenity of Tolbecken. One late evening, the Judge, glancing up from his book, saw a face peering in at his study window and then vanish. He got up, went outside, and explored around the house, but discovered no one. He concluded it must be a tramp. There was no use in alarming the women by mentioning it, but he looked carefully to the bolts and fastenings thereafter.

Ten days later, he was roused one night about two o'clock by an almost imperceptible tapping at the door of his bedroom. Careful not to waken his wife, he opened to find the ever-vigilant Joan Maylin on the threshold.

"Rufus," she whispered, "there's somebody in the house— I think in your study. Heard the window go up, and then a tinkling sound. Whoever it is must be at the safe. What'll we do?"

"Look into it," returned the Judge, and started for the stairs.

"Nonsense," she breathed, clutching him. "He might shoot you."

"Fiddlesticks!"

"Call up the police."

"He'd hear that and get away. I propose to apprehend him."

Up from the depths of the Judge's being welled a long-forgotten glow. That some fellow had broken into his house and was opening his safe fired him with indignation. As for fear, he had no notion of it. He took down a heavy, flexible cane from a rack on the landing, and padded cautiously downstairs in his bare feet.

Aunt Joan did the same. In her high-buttoned nightgown, with her gray hair braided behind, her jaw set, and her eyes intent, she followed her brother-in-law down the moonlit stairs.

Rufus Tolbecken stalked along the lower hall step by step to the door of the study. A couple of yards from the threshold, he heard the sound of a movement, the shifting of something on the floor. Tightening his grip on the cane, he crept nearer, at last peered cautiously inside.

The room was dark except for a patch of light at the safe, which contained the family jewels and some silver. Its doors were open, and as he looked more closely he could make out, blacker than the darkness, a hulking mass which seemed to protrude out of it. There was a slight ring of metal. He could hear too a quick, heavy breathing.

In a few strides, he was across the room, but before he could reach the spot, there was a scrambling movement, and a voice cried, "God!"

In his surprise, the burglar had crouched away from his flashlight, which lay turned toward the safe, but he had no time to fumble for it.

"Switch on the lights, Joan, and step back," said the Judge calmly.

A click sounded near the door. Slumped in a corner between the safe and the wall appeared the figure of a man, a felt hat half shading his face.

"Humph!" remarked the Judge. And to his sister-in-law on the threshold, "You can call up the police now. I'll keep him here till they come."

"You better not," warned the burglar. "I don't want to harm you. But if you think . . ."

He braced himself with an effort, and began sidling along the wall toward an open window.

The Judge closed in on him.

"Look out," said the other, turning like a rat.

Rufus Tolbecken's arm shot out, long and heavy. He caught the man by the collar and took a twist in it.

"Let's have no nonsense," he rumbled. "I don't want to have to use this cane."

He swung the fellow around, half dangling, and shot him into a chair.

"You sit down. Stay quiet. Don't try any monkey business."

But as the other's head struck the back of the chair, his hat came off, showing a yellow and sodden, but vaguely familiar face.

The Judge stared at him.

"Great heavens!" exclaimed Joan Maylin. "Rufus, it's Herbert Mansen! It's Jare's friend's father!"

The captive's head sunk into his hands. He sat shriveled and spiritless.

The Judge continued to stare. At last he said:

"What's the meaning of this?"

Mansen, bent over, said nothing.

"I asked you the meaning of this."

"Call 'em up," shrilled the man suddenly. "Get it done with. For God's sake, get it done with."

"Step out a minute, will you, Joan?" directed Tolbecken. "I'd like to talk to him." He motioned her to close the door. Then to the other, "What's the trouble, Mansen?"

The fellow's twitching hands dropped to the chair arms, clamping on them.

"Trouble?" he repeated vaguely. "Trouble? Christ! Call up your police. What's the use of talking about it? I give in. I'm through." And, as the Judge said nothing, "I suppose I haven't even the privilege of blowing my brains out. We poor serfs haven't even that right. We haven't even got the right over our own bodies. Snitch a bone from our masters, and we've got to be sweated for it in the pen. Sweated and bullied some more. Ha-ha, that's the law." He broke into feeble, dry laughter. "Yes, that's the law. You're born either on the top or at the bottom."

"You were born a gentleman," put in the other.

"Don't!" cried Mansen. "Don't lecture me. Call your police. I tell you it's luck, just plain, dirty luck. Works like a steamroller. Great chance most of us have with it!"

"Pooh!" retorted the Judge. "Give it the proper name, my friend. No," he went on, interrupting another outburst, "stop that driveling. What did you break in here for?"

"Because I needed money," snapped Mansen. "That's why. Because I thought that for once I might get a little."

"Needed it for what? Whiskey?"

"No! That just shows what you people are. You think nobody has any decent feelings but yourselves. You think we're just animals. Well, it happens this time that I didn't want money for whiskey. But what's the use? You'd call me a liar if I told you."

"Maybe so," returned the Judge coolly, "maybe not." He had no doubt that Mansen would talk.

"Well, I'll tell you then," said the latter. "I don't care what you call me. I wanted money for my son David's education. Every boy he knows in that private school is going to college. He has more brains than any of 'em. He wants a profession. But what's his chance? The factory for him—the damn treadmill forever. He hasn't had much of a life. I wanted to give him something better."

Mansen's eyes lifted furtively to the Judge's, as if testing the impression he was making. A lie? thought Tolbecken. A play for sympathy? Yes, it probably was. He had a gentle heart, but it was tempered also by the experience of a long life. If Mansen expected sentimentality, he would be disappointed.

"Why didn't you or your wife come to see me about it?" replied the Judge. "Perhaps we could have arranged something. I've helped you before."

"I'm tired of begging from you people."

"You'd rather steal, eh?"

"Call it that, if you like."

"Why," returned Tolbecken, "there's nothing else to call it that I know of."

As his mind settled to its usual calm, a certain order of thoughts returned—the sense of stewardship, the sense of responsibility to a will other than his, the sense of his own shortcomings—an order of thought that integrated him. With his eyes on Mansen, he stood flexing the cane back and forth between his hands. At last he said:

"You wanted to give him something better, did you?"

"Yes."

"Well, it's right that you should. It's right that his father and no one else should give him his education, and should work to give it to him. Here's what I offer. You can do one of two things—go home or let me call the police. If you go home, we'll forget about this. I won't tell on you. But from now on, I won't raise a finger to help you or your family in any way. If I hand you over to the police, you'll be sent up for housebreaking. I'll appear against you, and your sentence won't be a light one. You'll do hard labor for several years. But if you take that course, I'll put David through Princeton and I'll look after your wife. You work and I pay. You won't owe me anything. They'll be owing what they get to you. It's a fair offer, Mansen. It'll show whether you've been lying or not. . . . What do you say?"

The other sat glowering, his eyes heavy.

"I suppose you think you're a grand Christian," he sneered, "doing a big thing, don't you?"

"No," said Rufus Tolbecken, "only a just thing."

"As if my boy would want his father in prison, so that he could have an education! There's mercy and generosity for you!"

He got up and regained his hat, but lingered.

"Think it over," said the Judge, intent on his cane. "You could be something more than a yellow dog."

Muttering, the other walked over to the window, straddled it, and sat looking into the night.

Rufus Tolbecken stared at the bookshelves.

Suddenly came a dry, jerking sound from the man at the window.

"By God!" he cried. "Call the police. I've been yellow all my life. Help me! Call 'em before I change my mind."

Bowed over, he felt an arm about his shoulders and a hand grasping his.

"Right!" said the Judge. "I call that gallant, sir. You have my respect."

The other straightened up with a new light in his face, tried to smile. "You'll tell my wife and Dave . . . ?"

"You can rely on me to tell them and to make them understand."

He walked over to the extension telephone on the wall, twisted the bell.

"Police headquarters, if you please."

Later that morning the Tolbecken carriage stood outside of the Mansens' narrow brick house on Fourth Street.

"I know how you feel, madam," he was saying across the dingy parlor inside, "and I know how you feel, David. But I wanted two things. I wanted him to make a great sacrifice for your sakes, and I wanted to get him away from drink. I could have found him a position, but you know he would not have held it. He'll be cured there. He'll get back into the habit of work. He'll find a position waiting for him when he comes out. It will require sacrifice on your part to accept his sacrifice. But you must do so—generously. You and I will visit him there together." The Judge smiled. "You see, we're involved in a queer kind of conspiracy—he and the rest of us. I think he's a prouder man this minute than he's ever been in his whole life. And we're going to keep him proud. . . ."

It was on these terms that David Mansen entered college.

16

September was in the air. The maple leaves on University Place were turning, and Princeton village was stirring from the drugged sleep of summer. Day by day forerunners of the approaching avalanche descended more thickly from the puffing little Junction train—boys in queer flat-topped felt hats, cocked or turned down, boys in wide-padded shoulders and tight-waisted coats. Express wagons loaded with trunks invaded the quiet campus. Hacks of every dilapidated sort plied to and fro. The eyes of the tradesmen brightened; boardinghouse landladies girded themselves for the year's campaign.

Then, as always, on a certain day everything swarmed. The train overflowed; the hacks bulged; files of young men with suitcases drifted through Blair Arch. The streets were clamorous with greetings. Bartenders swabbed their counters between rounds of "lights" and "darks." Dormitories and boardinghouses quivered with invasion. Huddles of boys pressed around bulletin boards to learn their class assignments. The bell of Old North began clanging. Somewhere the cry arose, "Hit it up, freshmen!" "Hey, you freshmen!" The adventure began again.

Far more pervasive and indelible than the curriculum of arts or sciences was the training in social nuances expressed by colors of the hats the students wore. Red, indigo, light blue, white, and green—each symbol, each tint, had meaning, expressed distinction or the lack of it, one's place in the social hierarchy. Too often it reflected the wrong kind of failure, the wrong kind of success, with corresponding attitudes of mind.

Two Prospects, happily named, confronted each other at Princeton. There was the Prospect House of Woodrow Wilson, who was launching a new educational system, who had enlarged his faculty by fifty new appointments, who pursued his adventurous dream of a democratic university. And there was Prospect Street with its upperclass clubs—upholders of the status quo, of the absorbing network of custom which extended from the hue of a student's garters to his philosophy of life, which eclipsed in his mind art, science, and every other consideration. In the phrase of the new president, they were the side shows which were swallowing his circus. He had set his hand against them. Princeton must choose between one Prospect or the other. It was a choice which would give the measure of her vision.

"Hey, you freshman! Come here!"

On the low fence dividing the length of University Place from the campus, a line of sophomores in grotesque orange-and-black headpieces, the so-called horsing hats, sat and doled out humility to the newcomers. A tall, well-dressed freshman obeyed the summons, not too quickly. He knew several of the "horsers," who had been a class ahead of him at Lawrenceville, and was in no way flustered by them.

"Make it snappy, freshman!" said one. "Wipe that smile off your face," commanded another.

A ferocious group closed around him.

"What's your name, freshman?"

"Jared Tolbecken."

"That's the hell of a name."

"Where you come from, freshman?"

"Dunstable, Delaware."

"Dunceville? That's the hell of a place to come from, Freshman."

An absent-minded horse drawing a milk wagon, which had forgotten that its driver had not returned from delivering

93

bottles at a house, came shuffling along dreamily without him. The horse was a fat, meek animal with a growth of sparse hairs foresting its nose.

"For God's sake, freshman!" yelled the sophomores. "You see that runaway. Be a hero! Be brave, can't you! Stop that horse! He might run over the old lady up yonder! Save her, freshman."

Jared stepped out in front of the approaching nag, which paused and looked at him inquiringly. Loud cheers burst from the sophomores. They slapped Jared on the back, pressed round to shake his hand.

"Gosh, Ed, did you see that? He's perfectly reckless. Just threw himself in the brute's path! Our hero! . . . But don't stop there, freshman. Be a Christian. You see what that poor runaway horse is longing for. Lays its chin on your shoulder, by gum. Aw, don't repulse it! It wants a shave. Put your arms around its good old neck and say, 'Let me shave thee, Maggie.' That's it. That brings tears to my eyes. Louder, freshman. Ed's deaf, you know."

"LET ME SHAVE THEE, MAGGIE."

At this point the milkman climbed into his wagon and drove off, despite loud protests from the sophomores.

"Due at football practice, are you, freshman? All right, then, beat it. But you're pretty damn fresh. We'll catch you again."

Jared contrived to thumb his nose furtively at one of the Lawrenceville men, and jogged off among loud yells of "Hit it up." But he had made a good impression. In terms of colors, they knew him to be a future Red or Dark Blue Hat.

"Hey, you freshman! Come here!"

His small black cap perched nonchalantly on the crisp, well-cut hair of the new victim. He was of middle height, but well built. He wore the dark clothes of his class with distinction. A broad, charming smile expressed ease, confidence, *savoir-faire*. He was from Exeter and, like Jared, knew several of the "horsers," who in turn knew and feared, almost as much as they admired, him. But the others did not know him—yet.

"Wipe that smile off your face! Never saw so many grinning freshmen in my life."

The other obeyed. It was a handsome face, cold as marble without the smile.

"What's your name?"

"Angus Grey."

"What kind of a name do you call that? Angus!"

It was a moment before the freshman answered. His gaze

94

lifted to the sophomore's cap, read the symbols of a poor club on it, and scornfully passed beyond. It was the gaze of an Olympian, that set the other in his place.

"I don't know."

The other flushed, embarrassed. He caught a wink exchanged by two of his classmates who belonged to a better club.

"You don't know, don't you? Well, it's the hell of a name."

"Think so?"

The tone was perfectly correct and indifferent. The sophomore lost his temper.

"Yes, I think so. What are you going to do about it?"

Something like a warning appeared on the handsome face; then the radiant smile quickly concealed. He half turned toward the others, blandly ignoring the question.

One of the men who knew Grey and wore a distinguished headpiece created a diversion.

"Here, freshman, sing us a song."

"All right, Mr. Jackson."

The pleasant smile this time expressed a sense of equality and deference.

They clustered about him. "He's got a dandy voice," whispered one of the Exeter men. "He's sure to make Triangle." Half leaning against a tree, evidently accustomed to the central place in any gathering, Grey's eyes circled the group and came to rest on the still-angry sophomore who had first accosted him. Then he began to sing with great feeling and power, but with an ironic undertone, directing the words toward this enemy.

"Oh, promise me that some day you and I . . ."

"Can that!" yelled the sophomore, aware that he was on the point of being made ridiculous. "It's stale!"

Grey stopped, and threw an appealing glance at the others. His voice was so fine that the interrupter was resented.

A chorus of "shut-ups" silenced him. "Let the freshman sing."

With a tolerant man-of-the-world expression, Angus Grey resumed his entreaty to the squirming sophomore.

With the second verse, he grew more wistful, extended his arm a trifle toward the other, let it drop with a hint of despair.

"Oh, promise me that you will take my hand,
The most unworthy in this lonely land . . .

95

And let me sit beside you, in your eyes
Seeing the vision of our paradise. . . ."

His voice rose to a magnificent climax, carrying his listeners with him on a current both of sentiment and buffoonery.

"No love less perfect than a life with thee,
Oh, promise me! Oh, promise me!"

The audience burst into cheers. The target of the song tried to cover his embarrassment by clowning that no one laughed at, and finally crept away, stricken. It began to be clear that anyone baited Angus Grey at his peril.

"Hey, you freshman! What's *your* name?"

"David Mansen."

In contrast to the elegant singer, the present captive looked humdrum and shabby. His shoes were scuffed, his hair was a little long; he wore glasses and had a studious, short-sighted appearance that bespoke the grind. He was too insignificant even to provide horsing fun.

"I bet you live in Edwards, freshman."

This was the cheapest dormitory on the campus, largely inhabited by grinds, who were known as "polers."

"Yes, I do."

"What did I tell you?" growled the disgusted sophomore to a friend. "You can spot 'em a mile off. Well, freshman, what you waiting for? Roll your trousers up. Take your garters off and tie 'em round your head. Then scramble like an egg. . . ."

It was evident from the start that Dave Mansen belonged to the species *sad bird* and would not make a club. He was poor, homely, unathletic, toiled at his books, and waited on table. But he was spared any chagrin on that score, for Prospect Avenue and colored hats did not enter his scheme of things even to the extent of a passing sigh. He was absorbed by a different objective.

Jared Tolbecken, who had spent the summer vacation with a Lawrenceville friend in Colorado, found his old playmate curiously changed. It came out particularly one night when Jared, braving the taboo overhanging such unfashionable quarters as Edwards, dropped in at David's room.

"You don't have to live here," he protested. "You don't have to wait on tables either. Grandfather didn't intend that. He wanted you to room with me." Jared's conscience hurt him a little for maneuvering out of this arrangement. It obviously would not have done. "You could at least have been over on

University Place—Grandfather would feel hurt if he knew what you're doing."

His glance wandered over the cracked walls which smelled of dust and lamp oil. The Princeton pennon, the print of the Madonna, a crowded bookcase recalled David's bedroom in Dunstable. His atmosphere and household gods had followed him.

Mansen nodded. "Yes, he's so generous that he would. But I intend to cost him as little as I can and to pay back every cent. My waiting at table covers the board; I'll have a scholarship next year; I'll do some tutoring . . ."

"What will you get out of college that way?" retorted Jared.

"Everything I want. I'm going to take the premedical course. They say biology's wonderful. . . ."

He fell into one of his waking dreams, his mind ranging over the Promised Land of science. But it was interrupted. A crash sounded on the door, which swung open before two second-year men in black caps with long vizors and an orange skull and bones embroidered on them. The intruders were slightly lit and evidently out for mischief.

"Hi, freshmen!"

Big-school man as he was, and already expert, Jared sized these two up as obscure members of their class. Equally expert, they took in at a glance Jared's maturity, stature, and good clothes. Then they remembered having seen him on the football squad. They had expected an easy quarry, and they were disappointed.

"Hi," returned Jared coolly.

He was surprised by David Mansen. The latter had never been able to face the rough and tumble of boy life. A year ago he would have quaked before such visitors, but now he received them as casually as Jared himself.

"Hullo," he said.

There is nothing so discouraging to a bully as *sang-froid*, and these were bullies who were not too sure of themselves. They rounded on David as the likelier prey. One of them, noting the picture on the wall, swaggered over to it.

"What do you know about that! Let's have a look at the freshman's girl." He unhooked the picture, squinting at it. "Can't say much for his taste, Bill. He sure picked a lemon in the garden of love."

Jared was getting hot. He expected his friend to turn white, and it startled him that, instead, Mansen smiled. It made the two visitors seem very young.

The sophomore called Bill looked at the picture over the

other's shoulder. Then he burst into a guffaw and began pounding him on the back.

"By God," he chortled, "that's a good one! Wait till I tell the crowd. You're so damn dumb that you don't know a picture of the Virgin Mary when you see it. Wake up, fellow!"

The dumbbell turned on Mansen.

"What's this place coming to, anyway! Why the hell do you want to go hanging up church pictures in your room for?" He muttered a while, then commanded, "Gimme the makings."

David returned the Madonna to the wall.

"I don't smoke."

"Oh, he don't smoke. Little Christer, eh? Well, you come along over to our room. I'm going to horse hell out of you."

David smiled again. "No, I'm not going with you. I've got to work on a chemistry test for tomorrow." He was matter-of-fact and serene.

"Come on, let's beat it," the sophomore said. "We'll collect some freshmen with pep. This one's a washout."

They stamped from the room, banging the door. Jared, fingering his pocket knife, recalled Eaby Ellis and the old days when Mansen played hare to his schoolmates' hounds. He threw the knife up and caught it.

"What's happened to you, anyway?" he queried. "You're different somehow. I can't explain it . . ."

The other pondered. "Yes, I'm different. I suppose that business with Dad, the talks I had with him . . ." Then he broke off. "No, that isn't honest. It was something more. I don't know how to tell about it. . . . The only thing I can think of is to call it a current that passed through your grandfather to Dad and then to me. It's made Dad a new man, and I'm changed too." He paused a moment. "Did you ever wonder why it is that your grandfather at every point makes the same impression? He's like an oak tree. Look at the roots, they're oak roots; at the branches, they're oak branches; at the leaves, they're oak leaves—never any doubt about it. Most men aren't that way. They fade out here and there—you can't tell what they are. Or they're different in different situations, or to different people."

Jared thought it over. "I see what you mean. I suppose it's Grandfather's feeling of responsibility."

"To what?"

"Why, I suppose you'd call it God. It's the same thing with Grandmother and Aunt Joan."

"That's it," agreed David, "or at least it's as near as you can come. It's the current or principle or energy I was talk-

98

ing about. Only whatever it is is intelligent, glowing. It sort of dominates and knits everything together."

"What you mean," pronounced Jared, "is religion."

"No. It's what religion is capable of meaning. All these old words are so dusty and worn out, Jare. I don't like to use them any more—they take the edge off of reality. What I mean is a tremendous, integrating force. You can talk to it, listen to it, become a part of it . . ."

"How?" queried the other, intent on the blades of his knife. "Does it just happen to you? Or have you got to do something yourself?"

"I don't know," returned David. "I feel like the first person that discovered electricity. I don't know much about the force or how it operates. One night in my room I just began to realize certain things, as if the thoughts that came weren't exactly mine. And I felt that I had to make a choice. It's impossible to describe that. It was terrible in a way. . . . I didn't sleep that night. It was as if I were dying. . . ."

In the silence that followed, Jared stared at his friend, once more possessed by the sense of change in him. He felt almost frightened, was driven to speak so that he could break the spell, but found no words.

"I suppose you could call ambition, pleasure, work integrating forces too," Mansen said. "But they're a different kind. At any rate, a man has to be something definite—he's nothing if he's patchwork. Now, if you don't mind, I've got to get busy for tomorrow."

Deep in thought, Jared crossed the campus to his freshman house. For some reason, he felt outdistanced and left behind. Why did he all at once have this sense of inferiority to David Mansen? What had David found that more than compensated for his disadvantages? Was he, Jared, a patchwork? The question troubled. What was he, anyhow, walking here through the night? What was it in him that called itself I?

There was a poker session in Angus Grey's room. He could hear the click of chips, an occasional outburst of voices. He dodged it, and climbed up to his own quarters. He undressed and crawled into bed, remembering that once upon a time he used to say his prayers.

17

As Mansen had said, life must have some principle of co-ordination. It was a certain American tradition which such a family as Tolbecken represented—a homespun schema of ideals, habits, prejudices, and beliefs that supplied Jared and others of his kind with a definite mainspring. But the current was running thin. Whether or not it would be sufficient to carry them through the changing age that lay ahead remained to be seen. Tradition alone is a brittle staff to depend on in the torrent of time.

Accordingly, at the end of freshman year Jared, in the local phrase, made Dark Blue Hat. It was just as inevitable that he should make that particular sophomore club as that Angus Grey should be a leading member of its rival, Red Hat. Indigo implied a slower pace than scarlet, a little more conservatism all round. They were equally distinguished. Among the upper-class clubs, Best had a preference for Red, but drew also from Dark Blue, Next-Best had a preference for Blue, but drew also from Red. The color expressed ethical rather than social dif-ferences. It came nearest to being the college equivalent for Tolbecken, and reflected this background.

Princeton was especially alive. Wilson's enthusiasm, vision, and leadership gave a tang to the air which the crowd could feel without understanding it. Even the most heedless were aware of progress and direction. To the more intelligent, the campus had become electric with a sense of ideal adventuring. To the zest of youth itself was added that of a renaissance. The crowded terms were like fugues of intricately interwoven themes.

There was the theme of work, which grew more dominant as the president's new system asserted itself—work, much of it that caught the imagination because it was treated as an individual challenge. A dawning interest in studies began to assert itself even among Blue and Red Hats in spite of die-hard custom; in the end this interest became not unfashionable. It was to Jared's credit, or, rather, to his tradition's, that he took a leading part in this movement. In the rooms of the young preceptors great hours were spent with poets and sages. Jared even decided to become a poet and sage himself. . . . Occasionally he would call at the august house of the president, albeit more because he knew the president's daughters than for the rare glimpses he had of their father. It was a young family, gracious, cultivated, and of infinite sparkle. The talk there was never dull, never banal. On one occasion, when he happened to voice the undergraduate religious skepticism, Wilson remarked, "You don't mean that, Jared. It isn't sincere thought. You're repeating a bromide of the crowd. If a man really has no faith, he is too bereaved to talk about it. Simpletons parade doubts because they consider them original or clever, but they're only a convention. In my experience the earmark of an unusual man is passionate belief."

Remote as this phase was from the horseplay of the campus, the terrible importance of athletics, of team prowess, it wove itself into the counterpoint of life.

In his sophomore year Angus Grey was section leader for Best Club. It devolved on him in conjunction with Best Club upperclassmen to corral the most desirable sophomores into a group that next year would put on Best Club hatbands. By intrigue and endless cajolery, he must prevent such desirables from falling victim to the blandishments of Just-as-Good or Next-Best Clubs whose section leaders were angling for the same fish. Other sophomores, all down the line to Worst Club, were similarly alert. Stealthy callers flitted here and there by night, spreading mystery and cabal. Every other theme dropped out, while wrapped in clouds of tobacco smoke and parley behind closed doors, the social fate of the second-year men was being decided.

Jared was one of the desirables whom Angus wanted—prominent in his class and with a background that Best Club favored. But with deep strategy Just-as-Good included a great friend of his, Dene Brett, in their section, to try to insure Jared's membership, whereas Best would not have Brett for any consideration. If Jared failed him, Brett would probably sink to such an unnoted outfit as the Mediocre Club. It was a delicate point of friendship. Behind his charming smile, Angus Grey did a good deal of cold thinking.

In the end, he called on Brett, who was duly flattered. Later they walked over to the Nassau Inn. It was Saturday night, and lively sessions at the tables had started.

"Join us," invited Angus, sauntering up to a table occupied by some of his section. "Pull up a chair, Dene. Drinks are on me."

Brett sat down. Swaggering a little, he noted with satisfaction that the leader of the Just-as-Good crowd was eying him from across the room.

After a moment, Angus strolled back to the bar, exchanged greetings on the way, smiled at this one, nodded at another. Everyone wanted to be noticed by him, but he did not notice everyone. Finally he chatted with one of the bartenders, winked slightly and laughed, tossed him a five-dollar bill. "Here's what I owe you, Lou," he said, and sauntered back to his table.

Beers were served.

"Bottoms up, boys," said Angus. "Last to finish pays for the next batch."

Dene Brett clapped his mug down first. He was a little proud of the feat, rolled himself a cigarette. Grey expressed admiration.

"How d'you do it?"

Brett explained that he knew the stunt of opening his throat. "Just let her go—pour it down."

"You got *us* stopped," grunted Angus. "Here, waiter, keep busy. Show us how you do it, Dene. Slow. I'd like to catch on to it."

Brett demonstrated. A couple at the table imitated him, coughed, got whacked on the back. Shouts of laughter. It promised to be a whale of an evening. They started a chorus:

"Won't you come home, Bill Bailey, won't you come home?"
    She moans de whole day lo-ong.
"I'll do de cooking, honey. I'll pay de rent;
    I knows I've done you wro-ong."

Lifted by Angus's bold voice, the song whooped through the haze of the room, sent the smoke drifts eddying. Other tables joined in.

Dene Brett was on the crest of the wave. He felt himself to be the center of this surge of good fellowship, a popular character. Angus's chumminess could only mean a bid to Best Club. He began pounding the table, taking charge of things, got noisy, and a little smart, flicked pretzels into the face of one of the others, looked the other way—kids' tricks. Glances began to be exchanged, cool and scornful. Angus repressed them with a wink.

It was queer that, for a man of such talents as the throat-opening stunt, Brett held his liquor so poorly. The session had just begun, and here he was tight as an owl. Usually mild enough, Brett grew quarrelsome, looked for a fight.

But nothing seemed to ruffle Angus Grey's good humor. He

102

coaxed him with a smile, started songs at the right moment, distracted him with another drink, and clinked glasses with him to the tune of "Bottoms up." After a certain round, one of the others looked pale, began sagging a little, and then took up Brett's challenge. Angus intervened, kept them apart, jollied them into shaking hands. But when he turned to the waiter, there was no smile on his face.

"If you swap those glasses again," he whispered, "I'll break your neck. You know which one is marked."

His broad white hand descended on the waiter's shoulder, tightened an instant, so that the man winced from the pain of it.

Then suddenly Brett went mad. He scrambled to his feet, kicked his chair over, and started staggering across the room. He swept the drinks from a neighboring table, struck somebody, and began milling around. He was chalk-white; his eyes looked blank and mad. People shouldered between him and the raging upperclassman; glasses toppled, shouts rose: "Fight! Throw him out! Cheese it—the proctor!" For an instant a circle formed around Brett; but before anyone could reach him, he collapsed and lay retching on the floor.

It was at that moment that Angus Grey called to the leader of the Just-as-Good section, who stood a few feet off.

"Take the bird home, Jimmy. He's one of your crowd, isn't he?"

Jim Ashton felt the stare of a score of eyes, and perceived that the maneuver of the evening had been aimed at him.

"Like hell!" he retorted.

"Oh? Somebody told me you had signed him up." And with a shrug, "Well, he's a friend of Jare Tolbecken's. Guess I'll have to take care of him."

Lifting Brett from behind, he got him to his feet, clamped an arm around his waist, and dragged him off.

The next afternoon Jared dropped in to see Angus at his room in Blair. The Just-as-Good invitation to Brett had been withdrawn. He had made a public spectacle of himself in such a way that they had no choice in the matter. They were sorry to lose Jared, but could not help it, if he stuck to Brett.

"Well," sympathized Grey, "it's darned tough. As I've told you before, Dene isn't our type—but he ought to do for them. Bunch of tinhorns, if you ask me."

Jared hesitated. "I think you ought to know what Jim Ashton told me, Angus. . . . He told me that you got Dene drunk, kept filling him up . . ."

"Matched him every drink," put in Grey, "as any of the crowd will tell you. We had some beer and two highballs. Nobody else got tight. How could I know he was like that?"

Silence fell between them. Then the Olympian continued, but without his smile:

"I guess Jim Ashton didn't tell you that he refused to take Dene home, though he belonged to his own outfit, and that I carried him all the way across the campus myself? I did it because he was your friend. If I hadn't, he wouldn't be in college now. Did Jim go into those particulars?"

"No, he didn't. I'm sorry. It was darned white of you."

"Forget it," said Grey. "Ashton is just a born snake in the grass. But forget him. What I want to hear is what you've decided. Your sticking to Brett won't help him now."

Jared thought it over. "No, it won't," he admitted gloomily. "Of course you know what my personal choice is."

"Atta fellow," said Angus approvingly, gripping his hand.

Perhaps Grey had a good many secrets, but nobody ever learned them from him; and in this case his Nassau Inn accomplices kept equally quiet. But there was something opaque about Angus. Jared admired and distrusted him at the same time. What Jim Ashton had said kept recurring now and then. As for Dene Brett, he made no club, and left college. From the diplomatic point of view he had been brilliantly managed.

But this year a shadow dimmed the club festivities. There was rage and indignation on Prospect, for the board of trustees, converted by Wilson, had issued a ukase against the clubs. There were to be no more clubs. The university was to be divided perpendicularly instead of horizontally. Freshmen, sophomores, and upperclassmen were to associate and eat together in various groups of dormitories to be known as quadrangles, or quads. The whole colorful symbolism of the system, the reds and blues and exclusive hatbands with all they represented of class and social distinction, was to be replaced by a drab, newfangled thing known as the quad system. After all the effort and suspense, the intrigue, heartburnings, and maneuvers, now that the upperclassmen had secured their hatbands, they were to lose them, and stand shorn of color on the same level with freshmen or the "sad birds" themselves. What would happen to class spirit? To Princeton spirit? The foundations of everything were rocking that June night.

But it was not primarily the undergraduates who raged. The young alumni, back for reunions, denounced the quad system as an attack on that most sacred of bulwarks, prosperity. The clubs represented not only privilege, but capital; not only social centers, but investment. Could anyone deny that the club system reflected the ways of the world? Did not people everywhere form more or less exclusive groups? Were there not everywhere fits and misfits? Why impose an artificial social system on youth?

But that evening, as Jared read the president's proposals and joined in the outcry, something beneath the surface disturbed him—an uneasy sense of disloyalty to a tradition greater than Princeton's, to an American ideal. He was not philosopher enough to define it.

18

There was a great deal about Nan Oliver that fitted into the life of a man who had made Dark Blue and, finally, Best Club. When she appeared for a week end in Jared's senior year, Angus Grey, who set the seal of Best's approval on girls, told Jared that he had picked a winner, and that, by God, it was a good thing he was a friend of Jared's, or otherwise he, Angus, would have cut him out.

"Easy to look at," pronounced the expert. "Ought to be easy to hold? Knows how to dress too, and she's got a pippin of a figure!"

She made a sensation at the club, charmed everybody, and raised Jared's stock several points by her visit. Decked out in fur coat and chrysanthemum, she made a marvelous football guest. In the prow of a canoe, reclining on cushions, she merged with the leafy stillness of Stony Brook or the Millstone. On summer nights, she belonged to the hot, spiced darkness of verandas.

Such being her versatility, it is remarkable that the affair with Jared did not make faster progress. It rose and sagged, like a top-heavy kite in a faint breeze, darting up now and then, as if in earnest, only to flop back and be kept flying by Nan with patient, skillful tugs at the string. She flew various kites, but this, on the whole, was the best, and she did not care to relinquish it. At times she felt hopelessly puzzled.

For example, there was that disastrous talk they once had about Tolbecken.

"What on earth," she was misguided enough to ask, "does your grandfather want to keep that old place for, right in the center of town? It's dreadfully unfashionable. Everybody's moving to the Ridge."

"Tolbecken's the finest house in Dunstable," retorted Jared.

"Dear me," she laughed, "that's a little strong, isn't it? What about the Sedley house or the Reigers' or the Bennetts'?" They were new, clublike mansions overlooking the town, Renaissance for the Sedleys, Gothic for the Reigers, and Spanish for the Bennetts. "What do you think of them?"

"Nouveaux riches," said Jared, sacrificing Uncle Albert to Tolbecken.

"Well," returned Nan, "Papa says the land is worth no end, and everybody's laughing at your grandfather for not selling."

Jared froze. "They don't laugh at him to his face; they don't laugh at him to mine either."

"I didn't mean to hurt your feelings."

"So you like new houses where nothing has ever happened? I wouldn't give a foot of Tolbecken for all of them."

After that he drifted out of her effective reach for about six months.

Experience taught her, at length, where and how far she might venture with him, but on one point she remained steadily at a loss. When he began talking about his books and ambitions, he talked Greek as far as she was concerned. If he had not been well dressed and good-looking and otherwise accomplished, and if these talks had not been rare, she would have dished him at once. For him to discuss dreadful old books with her seemed incomprehensible, little short of an insult.

If a graph could be drawn of their relationship, it would show that she succeeded best at what might be called a high temperature. She was not one of those who inspire, but who inflame. She was an expert at nuances—a look, a posture, sudden drawling of a word, tenseness of the fingers—things nothing in themselves, but which set up an effervescence of the blood. She had that power, too, that comes of dedicating mind and body toward a single object—in her case, pleasure in one form or another. She learned patiently to accept what she did not understand about him, secure of the moments when she understood him better than he did himself—far better, for she was as old as Lilith in some ways. Angus Grey discovered that much almost as soon as he met her. He was escorting her down from a campus tea party to the club, adroitly permitting Jared to plod behind with the chaperone.

Nan distinctly interested him. On her side, she found it thrilling to be squired by him. No one had more princely manners or more of a way with girls than Angus. As they walked, everyone knew and plainly deferred to him; everyone stared admiringly at her.

"Great chap—Jare Tolbecken," he remarked with his sunniest smile. "One of the best ever. We've had some grand times together. He's no-end popular, old Befo'-de-war is. That's my name for him—'old Befo'-de-war.' "

"Why?"

"Old-fashioned principles. Honuh. Chivalry, Miss Olivah, ma'am. But darned if I don't like it for a change—it's so refreshing." And with a chuckle, "He used to be innocent as the deuce."

"Yes," put in Nan unexpectedly, "I know what you mean."

He gave her a side glance. "Oh, Miss Oliver! You oughtn't to know what I mean."

They looked at each other—she with a half smile, he with a glint of speculation in his eyes.

"Oughtn't I?" she murmured. "All right, Mr. Grey. Perhaps I only thought I knew. What do you mean by 'innocent'?"

"Oh," he evaded, "when a fella doesn't know about certain things in the world."

"Do you think that's right?" she objected. "I should have said a person was innocent if he had certain things in himself that he didn't know about."

Angus thought this over, recognized the depth of it, and approved.

"By George, that's a fact, and no kidding. Where'd you pick that up?"

Nan smiled, shook her head, and was silent.

"Look here," he demanded with real cordiality, "may I call you Nan? I have a feeling as if we had known each other a long time. We kind of understand each other. . . ."

"Yes, don't we?" she murmured. "Of course, I'd like you to call me Nan. We're both such good friends of Jared." Then changing the subject as they walked, "Did you say your father was in Mutual Oil?"

Angus gave one of his dazzling smiles. "Yes, and the father of the girl I've a case on—you know, Betty Andrews—is in Mutual Oil too. Quite a coincidence."

Nan veered off. Evidently he understood her very well indeed.

A hot baby! he thought, beaming, and turned to wave encouragement at Jared, who was making what speed he could with the chaperone.

Thus, on the whole, the Nan-Jared flirtation went through phases like the moon. The fervent periods were so well scattered that his feminine relatives, who referred to her habitually as "that girl," stopped worrying. There were frequent partial eclipses, and at one time a total eclipse that under other circumstances might have been permanent.

In the late winter of junior year, a letter from Dunstable informed Jared that the Lehmans were planning a short visit to America. There was to be an exhibit of Frederick Lehman's paintings in New York. Aunt Elizabeth and Clarice, who had just finished her convent school in Paris, would visit a couple of weeks at Tolbecken, and counted on seeing Jared. He must arrange to spend a week end; it would be nice too if he could entertain Clarice at Princeton. . . .

The prospect excited him. Except through the family and for annual Christmas cards, he had not heard from her for years. The childhood attachment had long since faded to little more than a memory sustained by her photograph, which had grown to have the value of a mantelpiece fixture. Now he reread the letter eagerly and with a kind of reminiscent warmth.

Outside, an early March rain pelted the desolate campus. He threw another log on the embers, rubbed the dust off Clarice's photograph, and contemplatively filled his pipe. It was strange how a forgotten vibration began somewhere remotely in his mind, bringing with it a certain atmosphere, refreshing and ethereal; it seemed to him for a moment as if he had re-entered a lost world.

He thought at once of Dave Mansen, that he ought to walk over and give him the news. But he stayed to finish his pipe in front of Clarice's picture, allowing odds and ends of memory to seep back. Memory was a queer thing. You wouldn't expect it to recall the starchy odor of Clarice's Sunday dress after all these years. Then he put on his old blue hat and yellow slicker, and set out. David was a fellow you could be almost certain to find at home.

In a not unfriendly way, Jared had seen increasingly less of him during college. At his present rate, David was marked for the class salutatory; he was certain of Phi Beta Kappa, had an unbroken string of first groups to his credit, was a proverbial grind, and ate at the university commons with a group of other "polers." Between such things and Best Club, the Princetonian Board, an athletic managership, and a future place on the Senior Council, a great gulf was fixed. But more than this, Jared felt oddly young and uncomfortable in Mansen's company. The latter had continued to grow along his own strange line—more and more of a personality, not unrespected in spite of undergraduate scorn for first groupers. Of course, he was nicknamed "Professor." In freshman year it had come to him, as he put it, that he should exercise regularly; and with the effortless will that now characterized him, he had set to work in the gymnasium, to such good effect that by his junior year he could have had a place on the wrestling team, if it had not come to him to withdraw. But as a result of this activity, he had grown muscular in a lanklimbed, gawky fashion. By dint of tutoring and summer work he had long since made himself independent of Judge Tolbecken, who in turn had felt honor bound to establish a fund for his future medical training. Even the Best Club hatband had a faded, puerile look in David's room. Even Angus Grey, who had once called there with Jared, had been hard put to it to keep up his air of importance. It was not that Mansen objected to Best or to Grey, but that their rank obviously meant nothing to him.

"Poling as usual," remarked Tolbecken, seating himself in one of David's uncomfortable chairs. "Why don't you ever drop around? You know, this place is just about as cozy as a woodshed. Why don't you look *me* up?"

"I ought to, Jare. It isn't the regular work, but I've got twenty hours a week of tutoring."

"Bet you I can make you drop it," retorted the other. "Bet you in a couple of weeks you'll be pressing your clothes and getting your hair cut. Why, you'll even be cutting classes. What'll you bet?"

Mansen was no good at persiflage. He could only look fussed. "Wish I knew what you were talking about," he protested.

"Yes, sir," went on Jared, "cutting classes, escorting a girl round the campus and generally shocking the faculty."

"Girl?" repeated David. "I guess that's a safe bet."

"Done!" said Tolbecken. "You won't think it's as safe when I tell you that Clarice Lehman is coming to Princeton."

He had expected surprise, but nothing so inarticulate. David's awkward hands closed over each knee. A light dawning in his eyes made them suddenly beautiful. He echoed the name in a whisper. "When?" he asked.

Jared read him the letter. "You must come down to Tolbecken with me, Dave, that week end. Then the three of us will be there together."

Mansen got up and began walking about the room. He straightened some books on the shelves. The proposal had cost Jared an effort, but it had been made cheerfully.

"No," said David at last, "thanks a lot, but I couldn't do that."

"Of course you could."

Mansen shook his head. "No. I appreciate it, but I'd rather have you meet her first. I'll wait here." He contrived a smile. "You certainly win. I'll be getting my hair cut, my clothes pressed . . . You know, this is the first time I ever regretted not making a club."

"That's nothing," put in Jared. "She'll only be here overnight at the inn with Aunt Elizabeth. You'll dine with me."

"I wanted to do something for her, that's all."

He was straightening the frame of the Madonna. Jared walked over to him.

"Come on, Dave, be human. Run down to Tolbecken with me. You know you want to."

But Mansen turned away and stood over the desk. He pressed his hand down hard on his papers.

"No, thanks. Really. . . . You'll tell her how glad I am, how I'll be looking forward . . . It doesn't seem possible, after all these years. . . ."

He was staring at the papers and did not look up when Jared moved to the door. In an attempt to cover the silence, the other called back:

"Was I right about the classes, Dave?"

"Yes, you win all along the line."

19

The result of Clarice's visit might have been foretold; it was regrettably natural. The convent schools of France do not turn out young ladies who are equal in some respects to American girls. They do not know how to dress, dance, and mix as well. They are taught religion, the French classics and tradition of behavior, but an American subdeb of fourteen is more advanced in worldliness. It is only later, when a solid foundation has been laid, that Paris itself, in the case of Parisian girls, raises the superstructure and creates the *femme du monde,* a civilized and sparkling product. But Clarice had not yet gone through this finishing process; and Jared, raw collegian as he was, in spite of his undergraduate man-of-the-world pretensions, could not be blamed for his disappointment.

He found her overtall, overthin, swarthy, and too plainly dressed. Her nose, aristocratically prominent, showed character rather than beauty. Her eyes were almost too dark, too vivid and Latin, her mouth too large, her head too erect. She still wore a bang that somehow heightened the alien, Spanish modeling of her face. And her voice with its un-American musical pitch, the slight difficulty she had with her English accent seemed to him queer. There was between her and Nan Oliver's type the same kind of difference as there was between a Gibson sketch and a portrait by Goya; it takes a refined sensibility to relish the unconventional and subtle; and Jared's had not yet been through a refining process. By every one of his poor standards he could only disparage her. She would have looked odd in a fur coat and chrysanthemum. It chilled him to picture her at a prom. She belonged neither to a canoe nor veranda. And yet he could not for a moment get her out of his thoughts. Imperiously from the past, the old bond re-established itself. At the same moment that his conventional mind was pointing out how plain and bizzare she looked, a strange magnetism attracted him. It was peculiar how soon he found himself talking to her without restraint or apology about the things that most mattered to him, the ideal, secret interests which the undergraduate code ignored.

They were sitting on the worn sofa in Judge Tolbecken's study; her eyes were on his, her hands vital in their very quietness. She seemed to understand him before he spoke, her enthusiasm meeting his and inspiring it. With Nan and other girls, he had always the sense, at times, indeed, the oppression, of the physical. And yet the current between them here was warm and electric.

"David ought to be here. It isn't natural without David. He used to be a so timid little boy."

"Not any more," said Jared. "He's changed a great deal since then."

"Of course," she conceded. "You and I have changed so much too, haven't we? . . . Look! Aren't those the pencil marks on the wall where Grandfather used to measure us?"

With her old impulsiveness, she jumped up to look more closely, and he followed her.

"See—" she stooped down, her finger tracing the letters, one name above the other—" 'Jared—Clarice, September first, 1898.' How little we were, Jare! Think of it! So little!"

They stood looking down at two imaginary children. Then their eyes met, and the strange current leaped between them.

At that moment Judge Tolbecken entered.

"What are you two about?"

It was so much like old times that they both laughed.

"Please measure us, Grandfather," she begged. "Measure us again."

The old gentleman, delighted, took down a book, drew a pencil from his pocket, and adjusted his glasses.

"Back to back, now; head to head." Her hair pressed against Jared's neck. "Bless me, if Clarice isn't nearly as tall as you are." His lips working slightly, the Judge drew two marks beneath the book. "Only an inch difference. There you are. What a tall young lady!" And with his old-fashioned courtliness, "I have always admired stature in a woman, my dear— very becoming it is indeed. Let me see, what date do we have? March twenty-first, 1908. Yes, ten years."

Later they walked over to the stable, which had declined from its former pride. The carriages needed paint, the harness new buckles. A row of empty stalls commemorated the past. Even Gregory was gone. Jared explained that his grandfather no longer wanted to keep up a large stable; but truth forced him to admit that the family was no longer quite as well off as it had been. Only from one box stall did an alert head look out. It was Jared's hunter Astarte, with whom Clarice at once made friends.

It turned out that she had ridden a good deal during vacations at her uncle's place in Touraine, and they now set about preparing for a ride. The wardrobes of Tolbecken yielded an antiquated habit, the harness room an old side-saddle, and the livery stable a mount for Jared, who relinquished Astarte to his guest. As he tightened the girth, the thought of Nan Oliver occurred to him. If it was hard to think of Clarice at a prom, it was out of the question to imagine Nan on his thoroughbred.

"Look out," he warned, bringing the sidling horse around, "she's something of a handful."

But Clarice only smiled. It soon appeared that she was a better-schooled rider than Jared himself. They cantered along the country roads with the March wind against them, her bold, dark face a little flushed, her body at one with every

112

movement of the horse. And suddenly he was perplexed to discover that she seemed beautiful.

"Lord," he exclaimed, "I'd forgotten what you were like."

"I know, it's been that way with me, too."

Reaching out, her gloved hand rested a moment on his shoulder.

It was dusk when they returned. The lamps in the drawing room had not yet been lighted. She seated herself at the piano and let her hands wander from chord to chord. They drifted into a melody.

"Do you know this, Jare?"

She sang in a low voice; it was little more than a nursery song, yet somehow, because of her, because of her profile in the semidarkness, the grace of her hands on the keys, it was to him the voice of romance.

By the time the week end was over, the college point of view had been forgotten. He no longer considered her plain, or indeed thought about it at all. He was absorbed in something beyond that, something undreamed of. He put off leaving until the last minute, and at once began counting the days until her visit to Princeton.

Jared could not be expected to realize beforehand that Clarice on the campus, Clarice at Best Club, surrounded by girls trained in the Gibson school, would seem very different from Clarice at Tolbecken with its childhood background. It meant transferring her to the most unfavorable setting imaginable. Nor could he be expected at that stage to ignore the verdict of his own world.

Fired by the recent week end, he had planned every minute of her stay. She must have the best time possible. She must meet all his friends. It was the dead season at Princeton, with no particular functions going on, but it happened that two clubmates, Bert Gary and Ed Jones, were having girls down, and together with Jared they ordered a special dinner at the club. Angus Grey, impressed by Jared's enthusiasm, declared that Clarice must be a "lulu," and arranged a tea for the whole party at his rooms. She and Aunt Elizabeth were to call at the president's, attend a basketball game, and inspect the campus. Jared had never schemed so diligently for the entertainment of any other girl. In his best suit, he waited impatiently with David Mansen on the station platform.

But with the first glimpse of his guest, as she stepped from the train, the cloud which was to overshadow the visit began to gather. Tall, thin, and a little awkward in her schoolgirl clothes and foreign hat, she looked undeniably queer. The first impression he had had at Tolbecken, and which her personality had effaced, returned, and he felt his spirits sag. Aunt Elizabeth, also foreign-looking, short, middle-aged, and a little plump, did not help the picture. David Mansen, gawky in a store suit and dreadful tie which he had bought for the occasion, did not help it either.

"Da-vid!" she was saying, her hands taking both of Mansen's. "Da-vid, how nice it is to see you again! And how big you are, Da-vid!"

The other, flushed and beaming, dropped his hat in the confusion and stepped on it; but paying it no attention, he went on shaking her hands, unable to speak. Bert Gary, who had been meeting his guest and her chaperone at the same train—fur-clad, smartly turned-out creatures wearing violets —stared. If Jared had any doubt as to his own opinion, that stare settled it. A hot wave passed over him. But the comedy—if it were such—had only begun.

It was worse at the inn when Angus Grey called. Clarice had only one extra frock with her, a plain blue affair that brought out every angle of her awkward body. She did not know what to make of Angus's up-to-date patter. She sat bewildered, embarrassed, wanly reflecting his confident smiles. Too well trained to show anything but politeness, he included Mrs. Lehman in the talk, rejoiced that he was to have the pleasure of seeing them both at his rooms, regretted that Princeton was not at its best in March, chatted about his tour of France last summer.

But a covert glance at the clock, a waning interest showed what the real appraisal was. Jared, more and more ill at ease, could feel the impact of it. Not that he cared whether or not Angus liked her. She was worth a thousand of him. But his remarks at the club would be devastating. Very soon Angus regretted that he had to go.

And just at that moment David Mansen entered, face and glasses shining, with a great bouquet of American Beauty roses. Tongue-tied as before, he presented them stiffly.

"Oh, Da-vid, for me? How lovely! Look, Mama, how lovely!"

"Something for you to wear," he muttered. Angus Grey smiled. "And here's something for you to pin 'em on with," added Mansen. He brought out a small box containing a huge orange-and-black brooch with the Princeton seal on it.

"Da-vid! How dear you are! It's beautiful. Isn't it, Jare? Isn't it, Mr. Grey?"

"Marvelous," said Angus.

"And the words on it." She spelled them out—"*Dei sub numine viget*. Under God's power it grows. That will always remind me of Princeton and of you, Da-vid."

She set about pinning the roses at her waist. They were too long and too many. The blatant orange-and-black seal clashed with the red of the flowers.

"There! Isn't it beautiful, Da-vid? Isn't it becoming?"

Mansen glowed. Angus complimented her.

"Stunning's the only word for it," he said. "The Professor certainly has an eye for color. We call him Professor, Miss Lehman, because he's such a bright boy and we all admire him so much. Well, good-by again. So long, Jare."

Jared could have throttled him. A little later, when Mansen had gone, he summoned courage enough to suggest that Clarice leave off the brooch and a few of the roses. Mrs. Lehman supported him.

"Do you think I don't know how they look?" Clarice answered. "Of course I do. But does that matter? I'm wearing them to please Da-vid. He's very proud of them. Shall I hurt him because Mr. Grey laughs?"

So, she had seen through Angus. Jared boiled over.

"I should say not. You wear them."

She hesitated. "Perhaps I oughtn't to on your account."

"Ridiculous," he declared. "You look well in anything."

Clarice insisted that David accompany them—to the tea at Grey's, to dinner at the club. And she wore her plain dress, the Princeton seal, and the bunch of roses. She could not compete with the modish young ladies of Bert Gary and Ed Jones with their expensive gowns. They high-hatted her and then forgot her. The men clustered about them. She seemed to care as little as Mansen, who was equally left out, but talked with him and Jared—the three made a noticeable group, unnoticed in that company. They went back to the inn early. At last Jared and Clarice were alone.

"I'm sorry, Jare."

"About what?"

"About today."

"I know you didn't have a good time."

"Did you?" she asked.

"Well," he shifted, "it was such a rush. I didn't have a chance to see you, really. You talked with Dave all the time."

115

She shook her head. "It isn't that. I know I'm not pretty. I ought to have brought my other dress . . . but David didn't think of that. I was just Clarice to him. You were awfully good; you went through with it."

"You mean to say . . ." he began hotly.

"I mean that I'm sorry you had to go through with it."

Suddenly she turned her head, then got up and stood looking out the window.

He remained behind, stricken by her judgment, all the more so since he realized it was not unjust. Had he not done his level best, striven to give her a good time, stuck around with her and Mansen through the whole dreary day? Had he turned a hair at what the club thought, or acted like a cad? No, he had gone through with it. Her phrase, echoing in his mind, imposed itself with a sudden irony.

"I don't think you're very fair," he protested.

She did not answer.

"Clarice," he appealed humbly.

For the first time that day, the glow he had felt at Tolbecken returned. After all, this was Clarice. What did anything else matter? In a vivid flash, he perceived at the moment her central place in his life.

She turned and came toward him, but standing close to him, looked down.

"I think we ought to be honest with each other. It's hard to be honest. You know I'm fond of David, but you were different . . ."

"Were?"

"Yes." She looked up suddenly. "You were Jared. Of course we forgot each other a little. We couldn't help it. We were just children. But the other day at Tolbecken, I thought . . ." She broke off. "I can't explain it. You know what I mean."

"Yes," he said, "I know."

"I thought we were beginning where we had left off. I thought it was just the same—only better because we were older. Then today—that's what really hurts—the rest doesn't matter—I found it wasn't the same. A part of you was different—not all, just a part, that I don't know about. Tell me what it is, Jare. That's what I meant by being honest."

He could feel rather than express to himself what she meant, but did not know how to answer.

"Is it Angus Grey?"

The thrust of the question surprised him. Strangely, it called up a scurry of memories. A certain night in the New

116

York Tenderloin. Other nights. Compromises and locked doors. Nan Oliver last June. But these were a fellow's own affairs. The key had been turned upon them.

"I don't know what you mean. I've seen a lot of Angus. I like him."

"I despise him," she answered simply. "But it isn't just Angus Grey. He belongs to the part of you that I don't know. Tell me about it, Jare. Don't you see how important it is, if . . . Tell me, Jare."

Why important? What right had she to pry into these thoughts? The idea of talking to Clarice about them filled him with horror. And yet he hesitated. To have one person in the world, one person . . . No, there were certain doors that had to stay locked. The insight of a minute ago faded. After all, she was a plain, queer-looking girl. He made his choice.

"I really don't know what you mean."

"Then it's all right," she faltered. "Perhaps I was wrong."

He saw her once again before she sailed, attended the exhibition of her father's paintings, for the first time met Frederick Lehman, a man of the world as well as an artist. They had dinner at Delmonico's and she wore a new dress. The old attraction held; he could not free himself from it. After she sailed, they wrote for a time regularly, and Nan Oliver's attractions suffered complete eclipse.

But the weeks passed. Spring came. The club dances began, with their odor of fresh lawns and lilacs, the May moon on the lake. Someone else invited Nan Oliver. She had never been more beautiful or provocative or admired. Naturally he had to dance with her more than once. It was natural too that he should stroll out with her for a breath of air in the moon-checkered garden. . . .

20

Do you want to know who we are?
   We're the men of the senior class;
We've traveled near and far;
   We've emptied many a glass.
We sit and take our ease . . .

In the June darkness, cigarette tips glowed, a match flared occasionally; the paleness of white shirts or flannels outlined the otherwise scarcely visible mass of singers. For the seniors held the steps of ivied Nassau Hall, from which, conformable with custom, they luxuriated, musically, in the romance of summer and comradeship and the dulcet sadness of farewell.

> Where, oh, where are the grave old seniors?
> Where, oh, where are the grave old seniors?
> Where, oh, where are the grave old seniors?
> Safe now in the wide, wide world.

They clung together, singing the traditional songs, their rivalries and enmities forgotten in the lushness of good fellowship drawing to a close.

On the campus in front of them were shadowy groups of listeners, seated or strolling. The girls' frocks, forerunners of Commencement, glimmered faintly. The breath of new-mown grass mingled with wandering puffs of cigarette smoke. If the audience, innocent of decorum, applauded the singing, it was fiercely booed at and repressed by the singers, for the audience supposedly attended on sufferance and must not disturb the seniors' musical seclusion. For this night belonged to them; they sat in tuneful, sentimental meditation above the world. And when, at last, all standing, with a solemnity reserved only for that hymn, they sang "Old Nassau," then with clamor and shouting they broke up. Groups split off, but the major detachment headed, arm in arm, in caroling squads, to the inns, with their sociable cellars and frothing steins.

But Jared Tolbecken was not along. He faded out unostentatiously, rounded a corner of Old North, slipped through the library arch, and passed beyond the reach of calling voices. He turned into an entry with a characteristic dormitory smell of quartered oak and dust, groped his way up a dimly lighted staircase, and knocked at a door. "Come in," answered a deep voice.

Beyond this door yet another phase of college life made itself felt. To Jared it was the magnificent, transcendental phase. Here in Dr. Macklin's study, between books and etchings, in the glow of its reading lamps, hovered the mood of *Il Penseroso*. Here invisible banquets had been spread out—philosophy and letters, and new, strange thought.

118

"I'm not disturbing you?" he asked.

A form rose from the desk and came forward.

"You never disturb me, Nicodemus."

It was Macklin's occasional name for his pupil at such times, for calls on the faculty were not altogether orthodox. They smacked of the high-brow and eccentric, even of boot-licking; student opinion distrusted them.

"Besides, I was waiting for you," he added.

He was a tall, stoop-shouldered, old-young man with gaunt cheeks and sharp-cut mouth. Something clipped and English still clung to him from his Oxford training. When his guest had sat down facing him in the dim study light, he said, "Well, what news?"

"Bad," said Jared. "I'm afraid I'll have to give up our idea." He fished in his pocket and drew out a letter. "It's from Grandfather. You can read it yourself, sir."

Macklin, bending toward the lamp, puffed at his pipe and read:

As regards your literary ambitions, I am frankly opposed, though of course Dr. Macklin's opinion flatters you and pleases me . . . excellence is rare. . . . I do not care to have you at best an entertaining young scribbler. . . .

I believe that young men should put themselves in the way of usefully earning a living . . . in those pursuits which are essential to society. Unless it becomes a flame—and in your case, of this there can be no assurance—the divine spark yields only a precarious income.

Finally, I had hoped that you would follow my profession and take part in public affairs. You have a good mind and a name of long standing in this state. You are the last of us, and in your default, the tradition of one more family ends. You should not thoughtlessly reject this privilege. . . .

But while opposing your inclinations, I have no right to impose my personal desires. I love you too dearly for that. I insist only that you give due thought to the matter. Discuss it with Dr. Macklin in the light of this opinion; weigh it during the summer. Then, whatever your choice may be, I shall accept it and aid you loyally.

But is this not worth considering—that an experience in men and in life should precede the writer's interpretation of them, and that his work is valuable in propor-

119

tion to its wisdom? Would it be a mistake, before expressing yourself in print, to wait until you had something to say?

Macklin returned the letter and leaned back in thought. He was a man of books. To him the rumors of the world, its preoccupations and enthusiasms came from far off. He apprehended them from the watchtower of humanity's intellectual history, according the present with the past, noting directions, reinterpreting the tides of life. This he considered as the duty of letters, arduous, difficult to perform, but of supreme value. And in the youth opposite him with the keen eyes and sensitive lips, he had discerned one appointed by nature to such tasks, not to the forum, the senate, or the market place. He feared that Rufus Tolbecken's mantle would prove too cumbersome and ill-fitting for his grandson. He saw in Jared the delicacy and temper of steel, but steel too finely wrought for rugged uses.

Moreover, there was nothing vague or impractical about the plans they had formed, as the Judge's letter suggested. Macklin had arranged an apprenticeship for Jared on the staff of one of the more scholarly periodicals. Of course the pay would be small, but would that not be so in any profession?

The doctor was young enough to take sides in any case against the skepticism of age. Macklin perhaps overrated young men. To him Jared was a brand to be snatched from the burning of old-fashioned Philistinism.

At every point the Judge's letter chafed him; here were all the dogmas he combated—moral prepossession, pragmatism, and intolerance. Of what concern to a philosopher if one more American family ended its tradition?

"I don't agree with Judge Tolbecken," he said at last. "I think that with the best intentions in the world he is asking you to stretch out on a Procrustean bed."

Jared smiled. "It isn't as bad as that. I think he's simply asking me to be a man first and anything else second, and he believes that being a man consists in loyalty to whatever obligations one is born with. There's a lot in that letter you wouldn't feel unless you knew him. His idea of service to America, for instance—people don't speak of 'the republic' in that way any more."

Macklin suppressed a retort. He detested patriotic effusions. "There's more than one kind of service," he observed.

"Not in his sense of the word," maintained the other. "That's where the family tradition comes in."

"Precisely," Macklin took him up. "His are the formulas of fifty years ago. Do you think they're good for another fifty years?"

"I don't understand what you mean, sir."

"I mean this: the world is changing. Judge Tolbecken thinks in terms of a past America. He asks you to take from his hands a torch that is failing. But when it has failed, what light will be left for you and others who put their faith in it?"

"Well," replied Jared, "if America changes, we must change with her."

"Easier said than done," rejoined the other. "You start as a conservative, for that's what it amounts to, and suddenly you find yourself out of touch and sympathy with the age. What will you do then? You can't grow a new skin overnight. I was hoping to see you launch on a different course altogether, one independent of affairs and indifferent to change, one that's not likely to peter out."

"What would be your name for it, Dr. Macklin?"

"Why, I should call it intellectual appreciation, the emphasis everywhere on reason as a path to truth. Your office would be that of an interpreter who is concerned only with the accuracy of his interpretation."

Jared thought of Mansen. Here was his theory of the integrating principle again, only differently expressed—traditions, as one example of it; the search for truth as another. But was Macklin's cult of the intellect wholly satisfying?

"Do you think reason's the only path to truth, sir?" he queried.

"I don't know of any other."

"What about the emotions? Don't they have any place? Or are they just weakness?"

Macklin hesitated. He was too honest a man to evade honest objections. "You have to make a choice," he began. "You can't have everything. The *Homo sapiens* forfeits something of the plain *Homo*." Then he fell to pondering. "Yes," he sighed at last, "you have to make a choice. Of course, you can rationalize the emotions."

For the first time in their acquaintance, Jared felt a twinge of doubt as to his master's infallibility. Was Macklin deceiving himself? Was he by any chance putting the cart before the horse? Jared thought of one of the older professors he knew, a man of about sixty and eminent in the faculty—a dried-up, frozen man with a great, but wholly logical mind. He compared him briefly with his grandfather. There was no question as to which life made the richer impression.

"I'll admit," said Macklin unexpectedly, "that the Tolbecken formula is more complete while it lasts—it takes in more. But it's not philosophical. It's a fashion of living that becomes old-fashioned and at last obsolete. The rationalistic point of view may be poorer, but it is permanent. You can't have everything. Of course, all this has nothing to do with the choice of a profession. But in your case, brought up as you have been, to choose the law will be to choose tradition."

"Maybe," agreed Jared. "But there's more than that to Grandfather. There's the religious side. If you were to ask him what his guiding principle is he wouldn't call it tradition. He would say it was to do the will of God."

Macklin smiled. "What's that?"

Jared flushed. "I know I can't explain it. But Dave Mansen —you'll admit he has a good mind—would say the same thing. And I wonder if that isn't a formula which is more complete than any we have been talking about."

"Oh, quite," shrugged Macklin. "Only it's a little naïve. It's a part of the torch that is failing. What about yourself? Is that seriously your viewpoint?"

Jared flinched beneath the other's amusement.

"No, I'm afraid it isn't. I couldn't put it that way."

"Of course not," Macklin said approvingly. "You've come a little too far for that kind of thing. With all respect to your grandfather and young Mansen, that phrase, 'the will of God,' represents rather loose thinking. But to get back to the point of the letter, don't be misled by sentiment."

Something in Jared hardened. "I hope not, sir. But there's one thing Grandfather wouldn't mention. He's old and he needs me. He wants me with him. I can't dodge that—I don't want to."

"Ah," said Macklin, "you must decide as you think best about that. Where your own life is concerned, a little intelligent egoism is perhaps a good thing. My point only is this—" and, leaning forward, he laid his hand affectionately on Jared's knee—"you won't like keeping step with the legion. It isn't the legion of Judge Tolbecken's time. Perhaps you won't be able to keep step. If it can be managed in any way, you ought to follow your own bent. That's all, and it's saying perhaps more than I should, but we've become friends in the last four years."

"Thanks," answered Jared. "I appreciate it, sir."

He got up and stood leaning against the mantel. In the half darkness there was something about him, even to Macklin's eyes, of a mid-century silhouette.

"You're probably right," Jared was saying. "College has interested me in so many things that are hard to give up. I didn't know that Grandfather felt quite as strongly as he does about the law. I won't have him think that I am deserting him. For once I'd like to be as generous as he is." He stopped, and remained looking down at the hearth.

"Of course," he went on, "it's impossible to express my thanks to you—your teaching and kindness—everything— I'll always remember it."

Macklin rose in his turn and stood by the other's side. "I've a good deal to thank you for, when it comes to that. But as regards the future, things may clear up. If they do, I'll help you in any way I can."

For a while Jared lingered to discuss the summer's plans —he was leaving for Europe after commencement—but he felt a shadow between himself and his teacher. As one of the legion, he was no longer quite the same in Dr. Macklin's eyes; they had parted ways.

At the end, Macklin reverted for a moment. "You want me definitely, then," he said, "to write the *Review* that you cannot accept the position it offered?"

Jared cleared his throat. "Yes, sir, if you will."

Outside the night enveloped him. He felt somehow older and detached from the well-known surroundings, as if he were already adrift in the wide world of the college song.

21

A familiar voice hailed him from the darkness. "Hello, Jare."

"Why, hello, Dave. What are you prowling around for?"

"Nothing. I thought I'd drop in and see you."

Jared hesitated. "I promised some of the boys to meet 'em at the inn. And I'm right thirsty. Why don't you come along for once? A stein of beer won't poison you."

To his surprise, Mansen agreed. They strode along side by side.

The Princeton Inn was the seniors' stamping ground, particularly during senior vacation, when they had a last, grand, cordial time before the labor of Commencement. It was a period of get-together. Old divisions, enmities, or rivalries faded out, and the class spirit was dominant.

As Jared and Mansen descended the steps, a melodious roar greeted them. It was late, and the session was well under way.

Amid greetings, they threaded between the tables, dodged a waiter loaded with steins, tripped over the leg of a prankster uncoiled from ambush, and finally reached the table where Jared's party gave them high welcome.

"Look who's here! Befo'-de-war himself! And, am I drunk, or have we the Professor? Sit down, Professor, draw up. . . . Here's lookin' at you—drink happy!"

There were jokes about Mansen's falling off the wagon, regrets at his moral decline, and entreaties not to hit too fast a pace, which he met with his slow smile and quiet good humor. He had achieved a certain position in the class. None but the most featherheaded turned up their noses at him any longer. A number who were thumping the tables in the inn that evening would not have been there except for his tutoring or help in the courses. They felt real admiration for him, coupled with gratitude. But it was character rather than intellect which had established him. His steadiness and insight could be counted on. The little academic world of egoists instinctively valued the difference between him and themselves. His aloofness did not repel. For so quiet a man, it was astounding how many on the campus knew him. It was not a question of popularity; it was less and more than that.

Only Angus Grey had not been converted. The antipathy between these two had deeper roots than college conventions. Angus had evidently been drinking a good deal, for what his friends knew as the danger signal—a flushed band around his forehead—was out, and his smile, although jovial enough, had a trace of ugliness. As for Mansen, he leaned back and out of the circle, talking to Bert Gary, whom he knew well, and who was entered with him next fall at Physicians and Surgeons.

"So I looked at the dean," Angus was saying, "and the dean looked at me. Makes me think of the Great Stone Face —that fellow. He says, 'I hear you play cards, Mr. Grey.' Then I knew where the wind blew from, and I said, 'Oh sir, just a relaxation from study. You've got to give the mind a rest *sometimes*, don't you, sir?'"

124

Angus sweetened his voice into a bleat that sent chuckles around the table, and grinning into his stein, took a drink.

"But Stone Face never cracked a smile," he went on. " 'They tell me you play for money,' he says. I tried to look like Washington at the cherry tree, very serious, you know. 'Well, sir,' I told him, 'I wouldn't deceive you for the world. I have played for money a few times—just to see what it was like.' " And his gravity cracking at this point, Angus burst into a roar, which was echoed by the others. The flush on his forehead stood out like a crimson fillet. "Gosh, it was funny," he sputtered. Then, controlling himself, " 'They tell me you play pretty well, Mr. Grey.' 'Yes, sir,' I said, 'matter of fact, your course in mathematics helped me a lot —showed me how to concentrate and figure out chances. I've been experimenting with some of your formulas.' Pretty neat, eh? But Stone Face only grunted. 'That must be why you usually win,' he says."

Angus smacked his mug down on the table, and rolled himself a cigarette. "If it had been anyone else, I'd have landed him one for that. As it was, I remembered what Lord Somebody-or-other used to say in England: 'When you can't strike, smile.' So I smiled. Boys, I've made that my motto— when you can't strike, smile."

And suiting the action to the words, Angus shot his joyous grin around the table. It included even Mansen.

"Ain't that the Christian sentiment, Professor?"

"How did it come out?" someone asked.

"Oh, he gave me the works. Told me if I was caught playing again I wouldn't graduate. Then he ended up by saying, 'I wonder what a fellow like you gets out of college.' I was pretty sore but I kept on smiling. 'A lot, sir,' I told him. 'Latin, for one thing.' 'I never took you for a Latin scholar, Mr. Grey.' 'There's one line I'll never forget, sir.' We were standing close to the door by then. 'What's that?' he asks. So I let him have it. 'Why,' I said, *Plaudite, amici, comedia finita est'*—which, for the sake of you uneducated dumb-bells, means, 'Cherio, boys, the comedy's over.' Did he give me the glassy stare! 'Good afternoon, Mr. Grey.' " Angus bowed formally around the table, mincing his words. " 'Good afternoon, Mr. Grey.' "

He laughed, emptied his stein, and getting up, strolled over to another table a trifle unsteadily.

"Great fellow!" someone said admiringly. "He's sure got a load on tonight, though. You watch. He'll be up to some kind of devilment. Told me earlier that that Philadelphian Society crowd got his goat."

The Philadelphian Society, a student religious organization, was represented by a group at a nearby table. They were good fellows, a little quieter than some others, but they were taking part in the singing and engaged on a pleasant evening. Angus stopped to josh with one of them and then, turning away, winked back at his own party.

Time passed; the smoke thickened. Now the chorus of some popular hit, now a hullabaloo interrupted the general clatter. The young men poured confidences and good fellowship into their neighbors' ears. There were glowing arguments upon great topics that no one would remember next day. The room rocked with vitality and noise. Then somewhere began a call for silence.

"Angus Grey! Give us a song! Angus Grey!"

He was leaning against the bar with a crowd of others, his red hat of sophomore year on one side of his head, facing the room and smiling, as the hubbub quieted down. There was a magnetism about him, in his carriage and handsome face, a reckless, cavalier quality that would mean leadership almost anywhere.

"All right, all right," he called back. And taking a glass from the man next to him—"But give me a drink first; I'll have to clear my throat for this one,"—he emptied it, then announced, "Here you are, boys: 'Jesus, Lover of My Soul,' as sung by the Philadelphian Society." And launching out with great power and mock feeling, his voice throbbed through the room.

It was the hymn melody, but the words were a take-off, cleverly ribald. His passionate earnestness and acting made the drollery of it. Most of the crowd laughed, and grinned at the Philadelphian Society men, who sat embarrassed at their table. But a number looked black. For once he had slightly misjudged his audience. And yet at the end, the noisy part made up for the silence of the others. Jared frowned. "That's in pretty poor taste," he said. But what could be done about it? One couldn't make a scene. The Philadelphian men, apparently with the same thought, squirmed, looked uneasy, and kept quiet.

"Here's another," laughed Angus.

"Yay!" roared the crowd. "Atta fella!"

But there was an interruption. To everyone's amazement, a gawky figure stood between the singer and his audience.

"Just a minute," said a clear voice.

126

Then a babble of surprise sounded. "It's Professor Mansen! What the devil! What's happening?" A momentary silence fell.

He seemed curiously isolated in the open space where he stood confronting Angus. The latter, his elbows on the bar, stared back at him, half scornful, half amazed.

"Just a minute," repeated Mansen. "Before you sing another one like that, I've got to tell you something. I object to that kind of thing. It isn't humor; it's cheap dirt. But there's another point. You did that, knowing that some of us respect what you're ridiculing. You thought you could get away with it, and make what we believe in seem weak and cowardly. That was the act of a mucker and a bully. I don't have to defend religion. You're not big enough to insult it."

In the silence, the words were as distinct as the sound of a bell. To many in the room, it was a voice that expressed and liberated them. It was an act of courage for Dave Mansen, the obscure, to have dared publicly to reprove the biggest man in the class, the popular, rich, assured Angus Grey, a man with the temper and pride of a devil. Shame, admiration, and suspense accounted for the hush that followed. Jared himself, who had started to get up, remained spellbound.

From David's motionless figure, the eyes of the crowd turned to Angus. Perhaps, if he had drunk less, nothing would have happened; indeed, he would probably not have sung his parody of the hymn, because, for all his pride, he had a shrewd sense of public opinion. As it was, he stood quiet an instant, his elbows still on the bar, glass in hand, his red inverted bowl of a hat pulled down on one side. He still smiled, but his face had grown pallid as marble except for the flush across his forehead.

As David started to turn away, he said, "Wait, wait a second, my good little boy."

And so continuing to smile and stare, he closed in toward him with soft, catlike steps. There was something about the pallor of his face and the downcurving of his lips that kept people motionless.

"Do you think a nobody like you can raise his voice to me?" he said. "When I've finished with you, you'll know better. When you speak to me, talk low and call me 'sir.' You little Christer!"

His right arm shot out, but because of his drunken state or an instinctive movement on Mansen's part, his blow missed David's chin, cracking instead on his face; his heavy seal ring opened David's cheek. Drawing back for another swing, he stopped, paralyzed for a moment by the fact that the other made no motion, but stood looking him squarely in the eyes with his hands down. A return blow would have re-established Angus. The issue would have dwindled off into a brawl. As it was, he still had time to retrieve himself. Unwittingly he had run up against the greatest force in the world. If he had been wise, he might yet have drawn off, and submitted with a shrug. His four years of popularity depended on the next second. But he was not wise. With a sneer and an oath he struck again.

That broke the spell. Others closed in between them. Bert Gary was there, and Jared, who had suddenly become a madman. He did not hear David's voice begging him to hold back. He shouldered his friend away as if he had been an enemy. The unconscious hatred of Angus which the years had distilled became vivid in a moment. His shame and compromises demanded expiation. He found himself in the center of a milling ring face to face with Angus. He did not feel the blows he struck and received, nor did he hear his own raging. He did not know that his face ran blood. He could see only the distorted countenance of the other, white with fury, and then in its turn blood-streaked. He was on the floor and up again, grappling. They went down together, himself on top raining blows.

"By God," someone shouted, "break it up. They'll kill each other."

With a classmate on each arm, Jared glared across at Angus, similarly tethered. "Take it easy," a voice panted. "Hell's bells, take it easy, can't you!" An intervening body shut out Grey. He looked up at David, scarcely recognizing him.

"You're making a fool of yourself, Jared. Come on, let's go."

There was a sternness and mastery in his friend's voice that sobered him. A scuffle of feet crossed the room toward the stairs.

"Let me loose, will you!" raged a voice. A string of oaths followed, which were smothered by the closing of a door below. The tension relaxed. Someone clapped Mansen on the back.

"Served him right, the damned thug. He got his that time. And say, Professor, you were grand."

"Let's get out of this," repeated David. "We'll take a walk."

128

As they strode through the streets, Jared's fever lessened. They had a dip in Stony Brook.

"I suppose I did make a fool of myself," he admitted at length. "But, then, I'm not in your class."

Angus Grey awakened next morning to a Princeton with a difference. It showed in half-averted faces on the campus, in the curtness of hellos. It reflected itself at the club in the embarrassment at table, the constraint of friends. His forced jauntiness fell dead. He tried a joke or two about the preceding evening that failed to register. The incredible fact began to dawn on him, that he, the Olympian, was discredited. But he was not the kind of man to take that lying down.

"Look here," he said, thrusting into a group in the billiard room, "if you fellows have something on your chests, spit it out. You know I was pie-eyed last night. But if you expect me to whine around and apologize you're way off."

"Suit yourself," returned someone coolly, "and we'll suit ourselves."

"Is it because I poked that sad bird, Dave Mansen?"

The other chalked his billiard cue and turned away.

Public opinion is a powerful adversary. Angus Grey was too much a man of the world for defiance. He smoked a half box of cigarettes over the problem, and resolved to smile. But his smile meant patience, rather than submission. Certainly he did not whine or apologize. He simply took a few pains to be affable and allow people to forget. Within a week he had smiled back some of his popularity, though he never regained all of it. Then one day he approached Jared.

"Well?" he asked. "Are we going to keep on acting like kids?"

There were others present. Refusal to take the proffered hand would only have helped Angus.

"Whatever you please," said Tolbecken.

"Then shake."

But the grip was noncommittal, and cold as steel.

True to his motto, Angus smiled.

22

Commencement is a feverish time for the commencers, who are both lions and martyrs of their own circus. They meet trains, escort girls, dance attendance on families, and meanwhile pay official farewells to Alma Mater. Amid the clashing cymbals and costumes of reunion bands and carnival whoopee, they sell their furniture, pack their trunks, smoke a clay pipe at the final class meeting, attend a baseball game, a dance, and a sermon, are handed a diploma, are thrust bodily through car windows—until at last, dazed and incoherent, they find themselves, with a suitcase, amid new faces, other minds, in some railroad station, and realize that college is past.

In Jare Tolbecken's case, it was Uncle Vincent who first drifted, like an orange-and-black dragonfly, into the dormitory. For Vincent, of the Class of '83, was holding his twenty-fifth reunion, and his breath and costume were Scottish. Dutiful, but bored, Jared welcomed him to Princeton.

Then next morning he walked with his grandfather through the crowded campus. They were both of a height, the Judge still erect, broad-shouldered, his square white beard standing out in the surrounding tide of youth. His straw hat bore the alumni numeral of the Class of '52. More than once, Jared heard the whisper that identified the old man. Gray-haired notables stopped to greet him; the president, whom they met near Prospect, stayed for a chat and called him "sir."

"You've done great things for Princeton, Dr. Wilson," said the Judge. "You've infused a new spirit into the place."

"I've tried to make it more democratic," said Woodrow Wilson.

"Democratic with a big or a little *d?*" smiled the Judge. "I wish you'd let me convert you politically."

The other laughed. "No, sir. Not even your friend Mr. Lincoln, could have converted me in that respect."

His pride in his grandfather soothed for a time Jared's literary regrets. It was worth the sacrifice of the *Northern Review* to walk thus shoulder to shoulder and feel at one with him. There were artists and writers in that crowd, but who of them was clothed with more distinction or dignity?

Rounding the corner of a dormitory, they came suddenly on a group of three, at sight of whom the old man uttered a deep halloo. It was David Mansen with a man and a woman. But so changed were the latter in appearance that it was a moment before Jared recognized them as his friend's parents. He had known of Herbert Mansen's release a year ago, and that he had sought and secured through the Judge's influence an appointment connected with the state supervising board of prisons. It was well-known, too, that his own record in the penitentiary had been more of a triumph than an incarceration, and that he possessed the confidence both of wardens and prisoners to a degree that now gave him a real public value. But Jared was unprepared for the physical transformation he saw, the sense of power about the man. As for his wife, the frail drudge of four years ago was equally transformed by the magic of happiness. She stood between her husband and David, looking occasionally from one to the other, the three of them pressing close about the Judge in a glow of affection.

It occurred to Jared that here was something which Professor Macklin's vaunted reason could never have produced. The naïve belief that the intellectual scorned was at least capable of reconstructing human lives. He wondered whether any of the polished criticisms, the scholarly appraisals written by his preceptor had a fraction of the dynamic importance of such accomplishment; and he began to realize that life had things to teach him which were not dreamed of in the academic philosophy.

Judge Tolbecken beamed at the others with equal warmth. "It's a great time for all of us," he was saying. "Our two boys have both done us credit, madam. But I'll have to give the prize to David. There's no question about that, though I don't like to admit it." And laying his hand on David's shoulder, "You've won your spurs, young fellow. Jared hasn't, yet. Neither had I at your age. And what I mean by spurs is manhood."

At that moment Jared envied his friend as never before. Knowing Judge Tolbecken, he knew what such words from him meant. In spite of all his love, he would not have said as much to Jared. David's diploma and prizes were less significant than such a tribute. But the look in Herbert Mansen's eyes and that of his wife compensated for envy.

When they had parted, Jared spoke of the change he had noticed. "You ought to feel terribly proud of what you have done, Grandfather."

It surprised him that the reply was almost angry.

"Done? What do you mean? I was fortunate enough to be an instrument. I admit that was an honor—one of the biggest in my life."

Dr. Macklin, thought Jared, would have smiled at the assumption behind this answer. And yet it was an assumption that seemed to work. His walk with the Judge that morning through the campus was one he would long remember.

But there were other guests to be attended to, lodged, escorted, and entertained. Aunt Joan Maylin in her best crepe-de-Chine dress, red in the face and somewhat flustered by the crowd, Aunt Sophia Tolbecken, Uncle Albert and Aunt Mary Reiger were there; last of all, Nan Oliver arrived.

So, like a juggler who keeps big and little, sharp and smooth objects flying at once, Jared, with the rest of his classmates, darted about in tropical heat through a maze of bands, costumes, drunks, balloons, and general bedlam. He provided juniors to take Nan to the baseball game, a function which he must attend with his class. He made last-minute changes of names on her dance card to please her. He dashed to the drugstore for headache powders demanded by Aunt Sophia, fought to procure a cab for Aunt Joan, and at last, wilted and flushed, conducted the party to his club for lunch.

When he danced with Nan that night at Commencement Prom, her light gold hair was on a level with his nose. She drew back her head to look at him; her eyes and shoulders were magnificent.

"What's the matter, Jare?" Her eyes studied him.

"I was thinking that I almost wish I weren't going abroad this summer."

"Why?"

"You know why, Nan."

"It's awfully hot," she suddenly complained. "Couldn't we sit the last part of this out somewhere by ourselves?"

They threaded their way to the end of the floor, curtained off as a promenade and now almost empty. Standing at an open window, with the night air on their faces, they looked over grove and meadowland pale beneath the moon.

"But you'll have a good time in Europe," she said.

Then she fell into one of her strange silences, intense as a fever. Her bare arm was pallid along the window ledge. Then suddenly, her free hand raising his, she placed his fingers upon the pulse of the arm. "Feel how it beats!"

He stooped down, pressing his lips instead against the satin of the skin. And she stood quite still, half smiling. But when he raised his head, she drew back.

"No," she said, "not here."

"Nan, will you marry me?"

It was too dark to see the triumph in her eyes, and with triumph the glint of something else. She had landed him, but did she want him—at once? She must keep her head. She knew that law school takes time; she believed that there were a great many fish in the sea and that a girl must do the best she can for herself. Having once been brought to the point, he could undoubtedly be brought there again when necessary.

He waited, breathless. "*Will* you marry me, Nan?"

"Oh, darling," she protested, "how can I tell—for years from now?"

"Years?"

"Until you're through law school, until—you know—" she made a vague gesture. "We couldn't be married now, could we?"

"But you'll wait—promise me you will!"

"Why? I don't want to wear a ring and be left out of parties when you're not there, and just hang around. You know how fond I am of you."

"Nan, dear . . ."

But she shook her head. Then, with a glance about the vacant room, she gave him what she had refused a moment before, something much easier than a promise and tactically of greater value. It could mean so much or so little. His lips felt unskilled and shy against hers.

23

The next day, under a maple tree on Prospect Street, Joan Maylin fanned herself, and watched the classes marching by from the campus toward the athletic field. They marched in kaleidoscopic costumes, with a fanfare of bands, waving of banners, and general hullabaloo, while an accompanying crowd similarly bound for the ball game trooped along on the sidewalk. Joan Maylin planned a peaceful afternoon for herself. She was secretly indifferent whether Princeton beat Yale or not. But the procession interested her; she could review a good deal of her own life in it.

A feeble old man, flanked by two young standard-bearers, led the parade amid continuous applause. On the banner above him stood the year of his class, 1838. It was the year of her birth. Then came another also alone, with the banner of 1845. She had been seven then and had taken a trip to Cincinnati on the side-wheeler *Western Star*. She remembered her pride in her new bonnet and pantalettes. She remembered looking down at some slaves in irons who were chanting a strange song. And a gentleman from down South in ringlets and silk hat had carried her to the pilothouse. A lost world! And yet, more vivid, she thought, than even this procession now filing past.

Eighteen forty-eight—the Mexican War. Eighteen fifty-five—Rachel's marriage. The eighteen-sixties recalled regiments long disbanded, passions, anguish, distress. Then came the younger generation now middle-aged. 'Seventy-eight had been Jared's class. There was Vincent with 'eighty-three and Maylin's class of 'eighty-five.

She smiled at the costumes and laughed at the antics of the paraders; she pondered curious things.

She recalled a Fourth of July procession in the fair grounds near Thebes when she was ten years old. Daddy Goodrow had led it, hobbling after his cane and low-bent under the weight of his ninety years. At seventeen he had shouldered a musket in the Revolution. Thus her own life at its extremities spanned the whole of the national history. At least on the score of human contact, her single experience stretched back to the beginning. She had seen the devolopment of the West, the triumph of the railroad, the flood of pre- and postwar immigration. She had seen the invention of the telegraph, the telephone, the dynamo, electric lighting, wireless telegraphy, the cinema, the phonograph. She had seen revolutions in agriculture, medicine, household economy, travel, printing, and now came automobiles, even flying machines, people said, and submarines. New conceptions of the universe brazenly contested the inspired Word. There had been an avalanche of change in seventy years!

One by one the banners grew dim along the street, disappeared. These were the younger classes, undepleted as compared with the remnants in front. They bounded along, shouting, dancing, singing, luxuriant with life.

She smiled at their joy. There, at least, she reflected, was something that did not change. Machinery, science, progress, talk amused or harried, but changed by no iota the human heart. It was this that she loved with the wisdom of one no longer distracted by the blandishments of time.

Here came Jare's class. "My own boy!" she whispered to herself. "My darling!" She waved. How young they were and handsome—Lord God, be good to them all! There he was. He had seen her and was waving back. Dear Jare! He called out something; she could not hear him, but she nodded and waved again. The last of them trooped by. The street was vacant. Craning her neck, she could see their banner already dim along the street.

Then turning back into Jared's club, she found a chair on the rear veranda and sat looking out at the garden and trees. The procession unrolled itself once more in her mind, but fainter and at a distance. A languid breeze from the south crossed her face. She fell asleep.

From the gilded dome of the chancel next day, the painted archangels of Marquand Chapel looked down upon even ranks and a rippling of fans. Like everything else, they had the Commencement halo about them; their solemnity seemed more bland than usual. The class of 1909 was bidding them adieu.

But when the preliminaries were over, when the lights had been dimmed and the reading lamp of the pulpit showed vivid in the half darkness, one face became, as if symbolically, the center of attention. The imperious, challenging voice that expressed more eloquently than any other the idealism of their youth bade them godspeed.

The president spoke:

"The object, the standard you set yourself works by a strong alchemy upon the whole spirit of your life. . . .

"No man lives with his possessions. He lives with his thoughts, with his impulses, with his memories, his satisfactions, and his hope. . . . We must divest ourselves of the idea that men have souls. They *are* souls. They *have* bodies, and their bodies have material needs which must be supplied. . . . They are the mere vehicles of satisfaction, and it is the man himself, the soul, that must be satisfied. . . . Whatever you do, whatever comes from the natural fire kindled in you, whatever your spirit willingly undertakes and makes a satisfaction of, that is the thing which profits you. It at once contains and enriches your life. The more you are stimulated to such action the more clearly does it appear to you that you are a sovereign spirit, put into the world, not to wear harness, but to work eagerly without it. . . . You will be satisfied, you will be loved, you will have life and have it abundantly."

A fair promise! It remained to be seen how many in that place would achieve it.

Two days later Jared Tolbecken commenced his life in the world.

24

From the windows of a second-class carriage, Jared looked out at the pleasant country of Normandy. The sentimental, portentous ordeal of Commencement had curiously faded; its romantic sorrows had given way to a very robust interest in the present. He glowed with the thought that he was actually in France. This first glimpse of it—the villages, cathedral spires, men in blue blouses, cherry vendors on the station platforms, gardenlike fields, Lombardy poplars—would stamp itself upon his mind forever. And beyond, as climax at the journey's end, loomed the thought of Paris.

Jared felt himself tingle as the streets on the outskirts of the city began to drift by, as he caught sight of a fiacre, an omnibus labeled *l'Opéra,* with people on the roof, a kiosk, a dome.

The Lehmans would be waiting for him at the station; Clarice would be there. His heart warmed at the idea. This time there would be no disappointment. He had not romanticized her as before their last meeting nearly a year and a half ago. He knew now how she looked, what sort of impression she would make. He knew that they would be meeting simply as old friends. But, in spite of their neglected correspondence, in spite of the Princeton fiasco, there was a tenderness about that friendship which a person of greater experience would have found suspect. It was noteworthy that he had thought more often of Clarice than of Nan since leaving New York, that his anticipation of the visit to Paris had an added lilt because of her. Nan's beauty kept slipping out of his mind. What he called friendship apparently held a more durable, if less prominent, place there than what he called love.

The train plunged into shadow; the din of St. Lazare closed around it. He stood momentarily at a loss in the clamor of foreign voices and drift of travelers.

"Jare!"

Turning he found himself face to face with a stylish young woman who kissed him rapidly on both cheeks without interrupting her flow of welcome; he hardly recognized her. He had caught a glimpse of someone from the train as it glided past—a modish hat, distinguished carriage, exquisite dress—a vivid impression that he had not for a moment connected with Clarice. He still could not bring the two into a focus. This woman of the world—Clarice? He had seen her last as a schoolgirl fresh from the convent; he met her now after the alchemy of Paris.

She was waving at a couple farther along the platform who came hurrying up.

"Aunt Elizabeth!"

There were more kisses and exclamations.

"My dear nephew!" said Mr. Lehman. "This *is* a pleasure." He gripped Jared's arm and patted him on the back. "Welcome to Paris, welcome a thousand times!"

Almost everyone except Judge Tolbecken liked Frederick Lehman. He was the typical good fellow, the clubman, the man about town, who had a talent for putting his animal spirits on canvas. Like the moon, he went through regular phases between wealth and want, laxity and repentance. This was evidently one of his magnificent periods. Outside the station, an open carriage with coachman and footman waited. Passers-by turned to look as the party drove off.

But to Jared the wonder of Clarice eclipsed everything else. He could hardly find words with which to answer the questions about the voyage, America, Tolbecken with which everyone plied him. Clarice's features, though still bold and dark, had become harmonized and softened. To her essential self, her force and fire, had been added the allure of physical grace. In spite of the two years' difference between them, he felt younger than she, countrified, ill at ease. He saw the Princeton boys who had sneered at her in a new light—as crude, overgrown schoolboys. And he had been impressed by them, had looked at her through their eyes!

People sometimes grow by leaps and bounds. It was so with him now. As he sat facing Clarice and his aunt on the small seat of the victoria, the very tilt of her parasol against the noonday sun, the turn of her gloved wrist seemed to epitomize France. The faint aroma of her dress, a phantom of violets, pervaded and gave character to all the rest—the colors of the city now unfolding themselves on shop front and café, monument and palace; the blue of the sky, the glitter of the streets.

Aunt Elizabeth, eager for news, asked most of the questions, but now and then she stopped to point out and identify some building, place, monument.

Between double ranks of chestnut trees, carriages drifted

leisurely. Behind them the tables of an outdoor restaurant glimmered. The strains of an orchestra floated across. Frederick Lehman took off his hat, the ladies bowed to a handsome woman who passed them in her carriage—Réjane, they said. They bowed to a dandified gentleman who was strolling along with a woman on his arm—Rostand.

How, Jared wondered, could Clarice, a part of all this, condescend to him, the sulky collegian who eighteen months ago had let her see that he was ashamed of her—who had been too indolent even to keep up their correspondence. He dreaded indifference in her manner, but there was no trace of it. He still felt her two kisses on his cheeks. She was as quick, responsive, eager as he remembered her. Once or twice, impulsively, as she laid her hand on his knee, she called attention to something, and yet, perhaps because in that short time he had grown too vigilant, it seemed to him that something that he had once felt in her was lacking. He could not tell what it was—her smile, her manner were as warm—but something . . .

"Le Grand Palais," remarked Mr. Lehman. "They hold the *Salon* there. It's a pity that it's just over. I showed three paintings this year."

"One gold medal and one *hors concours*," put in Clarice loyally. "This is the Alexander Bridge, Jare. We live over on the other side. And if you look around now—Les Invalides."

He had a better view as the carriage turned right along the Quai d'Orsay. It was all superb—on one side, façade and dome, on the other, river and palaces, the outreach of the city. And she was with him, Clarice, who seemed the incarnation of it. What days were in store for them? His heartbeat quickened. It could only be a projection of his own fancy that he imagined some difference in her.

They drew up before an old-fashioned house overlooking the river. It recalled the days of the third Napoleon, with its stately front, long windows, and wrought-iron balconies, half shaded by the trees of the sidewalk. A generous circle of stairs led up from the entrance hall to the Lehman apartment. Aunt Elizabeth with another kiss bade him welcome again. Clarice's eyes glowed.

"We're so happy to have you here at last, Jare."

He felt instantly at home. It was into this epoch of formal rooms that he had been born. He liked the high ceilings, long mirrors, and chandeliers, the damask draping the windows, the massive paintings, one of which he recognized as having been sent over long ago from Tolbecken. They showed him

138

to his room, similarly tall and airy, with a vast double bed and wardrobe. Clarice brought in a vase of roses for the mantel.

"This afternoon," she was saying, "you and I will drive in the Bois. I want you to see my favorite place there. You'll love it. And then tonight we're giving a dance at Le Doyen's."

"But I have no dress clothes," he protested, "only a dinner coat."

She laughed. "That's my revenge. Do you remember my one poor frock at Princeton?" And, looking grim, "Well, I suppose I'll have to go through with it."

"Don't!" he begged.

"No," she said. "I'm sorry—I'll not tease you. I must have looked a fright. You were very good to me." And, arranging the roses, "Do you know, I have a surprise for you tonight."

"What is it?"

She was busy with the roses.

"You shan't know until tonight. I wish Da-vid were here too."

Suppressing a pang which he knew to be ungenerous, the other replied, "He sent you his love. Have you heard how well he graduated?"

"Of course I have. Though he's very modest. He's a truer friend than you are, Jare. He writes me sometimes."

"Writes you?" A fiber of jealousy glowed hot. "I didn't know that."

"Yes, why shouldn't he? Why didn't you?"

"I haven't any excuse, Clarice."

He looked so crestfallen that she laid both hands on his shoulders.

"You'll always be my friend, whether you write or not."

When she was gone, the word lingered in his mind. Friend. Only an hour ago he would have thought of her as that. Now the term chilled him. With a sudden insight, he began to realize what it was he had missed in her. Once there had been something more—the possibility of something more. It was this that had vanished. Friendship? Curious, how in so short a time the word had grown desolate. But what, if not friendship?

Thought stopped short, as if before a visible presence, someone who had entered and stood confronting him, whom he had read of and prattled about, but thus far never known. What of Nan in the June night, the fever that had burned him? It was not like this. This was wholly different, greater and more radiant. Desire, fear, ecstasy, longing, pride, reverence—all colors of one flame. Latent, unguessed, growing with himself, it stood mature and iridescent before him. In the curtained room beside the vase of roses he acknowledged *love*.

"Over there," she said, as the barge glided across the intervening water, "are the Flowered Islands, the *Iles Fleuries*. Isn't that a perfect name for them?"

They seemed to him the innermost jewel of a setting. First, the Bois de Boulogne itself, a circle about the blue of this miniature lake, and there, as a center, the little islands linked by a bridge, a seclusion of trees and lawns and flowers.

"Yes," he agreed, "they make me think of the Happy Isles, and this boat, of Charon's barge—a pleasant version of it. I wish it were that."

"Why?"

"Well, if it were, this afternoon would never end. You and I would stay on the *Iles Fleuries*. We'd remain just as we are and everything just as it is. Don't you ever wish that, Clarice?"

It is hard to keep the tempo of friendship when another pulse beat arches to be heard. He tried to speak casually, but a startled light fluttered in her eyes.

"Yes, I have wished that sometimes—not today, though," she added hurriedly. "It's nice to look forward. We might get tired of the *Iles Fleuries*."

"I'd like to take a chance on that," he murmured.

The boat nosed the landing.

He paid the boatman, and then caught up with her as she strolled ahead toward a little tea pavilion some yards back from the water. In her flowered organdy and white garden hat, she seemed the very spirit of the place. But she had grown silent. She kept looking out over the lake.

"Is anything wrong?" he asked.

She glanced up.

"No, of course not. I was thinking how strange it is to have you here—your real self. A lot of other afternoons and the thoughts I used to have about you were coming back. You've often been with me here without knowing it. And now I don't have to imagine you any more."

He felt a strange tension. Alert to catch one note of what he longed for in her voice, he remained baffled.

"That was years ago," she went on, "after the summer we had together when we were children. Mama would bring me out here to play, and I used to pretend you were here too. It lasted a long time—until I was quite a big girl—fourteen perhaps. And then—" she shrugged—"I began to forget how you looked. You didn't seem real any longer. Was it like that with you?"

"Yes," he faltered, "I suppose it was like that."

"It couldn't help being, Jare. But after that last visit . . ." She broke off. "I remember I wrote you in May. You didn't answer for a long time—months. What happened? Why didn't you answer?"

His cheeks flamed. How could he tell her about Nan, how admit the truth that Nan had supplanted her, that he had not cared to write? Without looking up, he felt her eyes on his face.

"You don't have to tell me. I oughtn't to have asked, really." To his surprise, her manner brightened, as if with a certain relief. "All that matters is that you are here, that we don't depend on letters. It's strange how quickly we're at home with each other, how we understand at once . . ." Her voice fell again. "Yes, that's strange . . ."

"No," he protested, "I don't think it's strange. It was like that when we first met as children. And I know now . . ."

She pushed her chair back from the table and stood up, once more with the fluttered look that he had noticed in the barge.

"Let's walk awhile outside. We'll have to be getting back . . ."

But as they walked, she began asking him questions about his plans, about the law school, about Tolbecken. There was a precipitancy in them that he did not understand. He felt the warmth of her arms against his, and his thought kept straying from their talk to the loveliness of her face.

"Will we be dancing together tonight, Clarice?"

"Yes, tonight . . ."

She looked hesitant.

"Are you tired?" he asked. "Shall we be going back?"

After all, he could wait to tell her what the vision of the morning had brought. And also he was afraid to tell her, was glad to put it off.

She stopped short.

"Jare, I told you that I had a surprise for you tonight. I think you ought to know about it now. . . ."

A couple, arm in arm, rounded the turn of the path. There were pleased exclamations. He found himself being presented to Monsieur, Madame—whose name he did not catch. They were evidently intimates of the Lehmans who knew that Monsieur Tolbecken had been expected, were ravished to meet him, and hoped he would like Paris. They were to be at the dance tonight, and (with a bow to Clarice) considered it a very special honor. Jared admired the ease of Clarice's manner, of her introductions. Did Monsieur, Madame have their carriage with them in the Bois? If not, it would be a pleasure . . . They accepted the invitation with gratitude and to Jared's chagrin. The four of them went over in the barge together.

After depositing these companions at an address in the Avenue Victor Hugo, and when the Lehman carriage had turned homeward, Jared took up the broken thread of their conversation.

"What about this surprise?"

"I think we'd better let it be now," she answered. "There isn't time . . ."

"Oh well," he smiled, "as long as I'm dancing with you tonight, I'm not curious."

25

In a city of temples devoted to the fine art of dining well, Le Doyen's is distinguished by its charm and location. It lies in the seclusion of the small park formed by Cours la Reine and the Champs Elysées as they branch off from the Concorde. Used primarily in summer, it is a white, circular building with a terrace of tables outspread before a fountain, a peninsula of trees and hedges embraced at night by the infinite sparkle of the city. Within are rooms for dancing or dining separate from the public.

On that June night, the fragrance of trees and flowers blending with the spice of distant pavements formed that inimitable odor which was characteristic of Paris. Jared filled his lungs with it as he stood outside, while the Lehmans made last preparations within for receiving their guests. It was glorious to be alone for a moment, to inhale this intoxication of night, to feel his youth and the tingle of the future. The vision of Clarice as she had appeared, dressed for the dance, a half-hour earlier in the drawing room of the apartment colored everything. The faintly rose-tinted silk of her evening gown heightened the darkness of her eyes and hair, the ivory pallor of her shoulders and throat. In her dancing slippers, she seemed taller, but still lighter, even more graceful, because of that. As her single jewel, she wore a diamond sunburst at her breast. The light rippled in rose and silver on her gown as she crossed the room.

"How do you like me, Jare?"

She was graver than usual, almost timid, he thought.

"I wish I had words to tell you," he said. And literally he had none—for what words were there to express the worship and the fire that possessed him? "I suppose," he added, "this is the surprise you meant."

Aunt Elizabeth, who had discovered some microscopic defect in the lines of Clarice's dress and was busy adjusting it, laughed.

"No, you wait and see."

Uncle Frederick, resplendent in his evening clothes and Legion of Honor rosette, gave Jared a portentous wink. Jared came to the conclusion that some famous guest they considered it a privilege for him to meet would be at the dance. They did not realize how little he cared, nor how incapable his mind was of any other impression at the moment than of Clarice.

Now, alone in the semidarkness, his whole being throbbed. He looked back over the day as the central point of his life, the day when *love* had made itself known to him, when he had first learned its infinite bearing and felt re-created by its presence. And as a fitting climax, there was tonight. But beyond it lay other days and nights, a beguiling vista. There would be several weeks in Paris; then there was Brittany, where the Lehmans had a country house. They had urged him to spend the summer with them and at once he had jettisoned his other plans. What did he care about the usual tour—Italy, Switzerland, the Rhine, and so on! He would not sacrifice another day like this for all of them.

He was glad he had not babbled his feelings to her that afternoon before their relations had been re-established. Evidently she had been hurt by his negligence about writing. She had every reason to feel hurt, and he raged at his own stupidity without any attempt at self-acquittal. A strange humility, the conviction of his unworthiness, that was also joy because it centered in her, possessed him.

Like a phantom of some other world, the thought of Nan Oliver passed through his mind. What if she had taken him at his word? Well—he would have broken his word, he realized that—he could not have helped himself. As it turned out, he was free.

He strolled to one side of the building where he could see

the terrace of the restaurant with its tables and lights facing the Concorde. Two officers in brilliant uniforms got up from one of the tables and passed him on their way toward the private entrance—evidently they were guests of the Lehmans. Several carriages rolled up: he caught a glimpse of opera cloaks, the sparkle of jewels. One tall man in faultless evening dress, with decorations on it, approached the door, his cape tossed back from his shoulders. The lamps of another carriage appeared on the drive.

Suddenly Jared became more conscious of his youth, his in-experience, his poor French, the inadequacy of his dinner coat. It was not even a new dinner coat; he had not only outgrown it, but outworn it. In the manner of shy young men, he stiffened and put on a lofty countenance, resolving to make up for his clothes by his bearing. He entered behind the others, wishing that he had not left the Lehmans; his grimness might, to the uninformed, have looked sullen rather than blasé.

But it was worse inside. The glow of costume in the entrance hall shrunk the sleeves of his coat further, brought out its youthful cut, and mocked the humble gold studs in his shirt.

Stiff and grim, he squared his shoulders, and with his head up, he made his way toward the stairs.

A somewhat hurried gentleman, with no more than a glance at Jared's black tie and vest, laid a hand on his arm.

"Garçon, le vestiaire, s'il vous plaît?"

Jared swung round on him speechless. He had been taken for a waiter!

Plucking the words from the grammar in his head, but trembling with rage, he managed to get out:

"Je ne . . . suis . . . pas . . . garçon. Le vestiaire . . . est là." And he pointed toward the cloakroom.

His interlocutor burst into pained apologies, bowed, hurried off. But nothing could restore the pride of bearing now. To be so ill dressed that people thought him a waiter! To be laughed at (for a witness to the exchange had turned away with a suppressed smile), to be ordered around! He felt hot with shame. He would not attend the dance to be a laughing stock! The Lehmans shouldn't have drawn him into it. They ought to have known . . .

He stood irresolute. But that was one thing he could not escape. He had to appear on the dance floor above. He thought of Clarice in her superb gown and again of his wretched suit, and he was still boy enough to feel a lump in his throat. Then, bracing himself, and swollen with self-consciousness, he climbed the stairs. The violins, screened in a corner, were

144

tuning up. As if he were walking on ice, he crossed the waxed floor.

"Where have you been?" whispered Aunt Elizabeth tartly. "I wanted to present you to the guests as they came in." And with a radiant smile, *"Chère Madame, comme je suis enchantée de vous voir. Permettez que je vous présente . . ."*

Numb and unseeing, Jared bowed, stammered. He found himself next to Clarice.

"Pierre," she exclaimed to a tall young officer in the scarlet and blue of the cuirassiers, "I want you to meet my cousin, of whom I have told you so much. Jare, this is Capitaine Delart."

Her voice was hurried and a little tremulous. Probably she was ashamed, as well she might be, of presenting her shabby "cousin" to such a debonair friend. Captain Delart looked about thirty, wore a small mustache, and was undeniably handsome. He made a virile impression, which his gentle smile just saved from being hard. With a word or two, he put Jared at his ease, and then, with another smile, turned away.

"What on earth was wrong when you came in?" asked Clarice. "You looked like a thunderstorm—as if you wanted to eat somebody."

Still out of humor and not sorry to vent his embarrassment he snapped about his clothes.

She laughed. "Think of me at Princeton with Da-vid's roses and the big orange-and-black seal . . ."

They were interrupted by new introductions—this time an elderly couple, General and Madame Delart. But her words kept ringing in his ears, and suddenly with a grin at himself he found release. The world slipped back into the right proportions. He was simply an inconspicuous youth of no importance; but at least he could keep a sense of humor. All that really mattered was Clarice's opinion, and if it was now her turn to feel ashamed of him, it served him right.

There was no shadow of a mental reservation in her eyes when the Delarts had moved on.

"The idea of your thinking about clothes!" she continued. "You're the best-looking man here. I do want you to have a good time, Jare. *Please* have a good time tonight."

Charmed by her words, he could not quite understand the urgency of them. It was almost as if she were asking pardon for something. Of course he would have a good time—now.

The orchestra swung into a melody. She lifted her arms. "Will you dance the first waltz with me?"

It was all forgotten—his recent embarrassment. He was back again in his dreams. They were drifting there together down the current of the rhythm. People and lights, the long mirrors of the room blended into a haze. Only she—the softness of her eyes and lips, her body against his arm—remained. Down an enchanted stream, while the melody of the waltz breathed love and the pain of love, its glory, its evanescence —away, far off, beyond time and space. And his heart cried out to her through the interweaving phrases of the music, and his arm trembled at the delicacy of her, and his eyes adored the dark curve of her hair.

"You are so beautiful," he murmured without knowing it, "so beautiful."

But she did not hear him for the music, and he did not know he had spoken. Then at last:

"What are you thinking of, Clarice?"

Her eyes met his, as if turned from looking into a distance.

"Of you," she said. And again, after a pause, "Of you."

Perhaps the fall of the melody gave its color to her voice. Somehow it implied the past, not the present, as if she were speaking of what had been.

"I'd rather not talk, Jare," she added, "not now."

He could understand that. The enchanted moment was too brief, too precious. Until the end of the waltz neither of them spoke again.

He watched her a few minutes later on the arm of Captain Delart, dancing in the more rapid French fashion. Perhaps he was making love, for she smiled, looked down, and half turned her face. He was handsome—even jealousy could not alter that—but Jared consoled himself that his own silence had been more eloquent than was Delart's speech. He must not be jealous—must not make a spectacle of himself, staring at them.

Aunt Elizabeth came up to him.

"Don't they look well together?"

"Clarice looks superb."

"Oh," she smiled, "I wouldn't expect one man to praise another, but I think he looks superb too. You know," she went on, "I used to believe that you and she would marry some day. You were so much in love as children. But of course you grew up apart. It's a long way between France and America. . . ."

Jared murmured assent. The summer would enlighten her, he thought. But he was startled when she added coyly:

"Tell me about Nan Oliver. You see, we know all about you, even in Paris."

His blood had frozen.

"There's nothing to tell."

Mrs. Lehman smiled. "All right. I'm not asking for confidences. But I'll tell you something, now that it doesn't make any difference. It was after our last visit to America. Your Aunt Mary wrote us how attentive you were to Miss Oliver. I didn't think anything of it, of course. . . . It was quite natural. But you know—" and she smiled again—"I found Clarice crying over that letter. You see what a heartbreaker you are. Doesn't that cheer you?"

Something in his face stopped her.

"You needn't look concerned. She's forgotten about it long ago. You'll always be one of her closest friends. She's so glad you're here, especially tonight."

Her words had become drops of molten lead. He understood everything now—what he had missed in Clarice's eyes, certain tones of her voice. But it was not too late—surely he could make amends.

"You must believe," he begged, "and so must Clarice. There's nothing between Nan Oliver and me—nothing."

"Why, of course I believe it," she soothed, a little surprised by his earnestness. She moved on to some other guests.

No, it did not matter. He stood looking out across the changing colors of the room, the beat of the music in his ears, toward the ever-changing center of a rose-colored gown and the loveliness of one face. They passed near him. She caught his gaze and smiled. His love for her had become the breath of his spirit. What *could* matter except that? And Elizabeth Lehman did not even guess!

The waltz came to an end. Evidently there was to be some kind of intermission, for waiters were busy filling glasses with champagne on a long side table. A sudden silence fell, and Jared, following the glances of others, saw that Frederick Lehman was about to speak. Probably it was the custom for a host to give formal welcome to his guests. Uncle Frederick, in his white vest and swelling a little, looked very important.

"Mesdames, messieurs," he began in his rotund voice—and with a gust of feeling, "*mes chers amis!* When one's heart is full of pride and happiness, it is hard to find words to express it. I am only a poor artist and not an orator. A few of you know, some of you suspect, but all of you will be delighted at the betrothal of my daughter, Clarice, with Captain Pierre Delart. I am unable . . ."

Frederick Lehman went on speaking for a time, but Jared did not hear him. He had gone sick at first, but gradually that passed. When his uncle had finished and healths were being drunk, he found a glass, raised it to his lips, even smiled. People were pressing about Clarice and Delart with congratulations; mechanically he joined them, as if he had become a puppet, moved by some external force. He did not really see her, as she stood flushed and radiant beside the young captain, though he spoke words which, for all he knew, were appropriate.

"There!" exclaimed Frederick Lehman, clapping Jared on the back. "You didn't expect this, did you, my dear boy— such an occasion? One of the best matches in Paris, I can tell you," he added confidentially. "How did you like my speech? It seemed to me that I said just about the right thing."

"Yes," agreed the other, "yes, indeed."

It was only when the dance had been resumed with increased zest, and as he stood against the wall, seeing nothing but a vague interplay of colored forms, that thought began again, fragmentary, but lucid.

He was struck by the cruelty of this thing. Why had the Lehmans not prepared him—when he had arrived that morning, earlier in the day at least? Why had they permitted him to be struck like this? But with a cold detachment, he understood and forgave them. How could they have known? They had intended only a pleasant surprise. He remembered that Clarice, with more insight, had been on the point of telling him that afternoon in the Bois, when they were interrupted. After all, what difference did it make? As compared with the devastation that numbed his mind, the manner of his awakening was merely trivial.

He could not face the ruined center of things, dared not. Not yet. Little by little, it would grow upon him. . . .

With an effort, he fixed his thought on his former plans. He would join Bert Gary in Italy, would telegraph tomorrow. But, oh, God, how desolate! . . .

"Aren't you going to dance with me, Jare? Do I have to run after you and beg for a dance myself?"

The voice was timid and faltering, but he did not realize it. He caught only the words and looked up a little vaguely.

"I'm so sorry . . ."

He intended no coolness. Like a bankrupt with only a few coins in his pocket, conventional phrases were all he had left. He did not even notice that he had hurt her.

Languidly, mechanically they danced. There was no longer the blending of colors, the sense of isolation apart from the others. Everything stood out clear and stark in the ballroom.

148

Around and around, as if in a circle of steel. The thought of the *Iles Fleuries* that afternoon. He thought of the first dance with her—breaths of cold from that center in his mind.

"What is it, Jare?" she exclaimed suddenly. "Why do you look like that? We'll have to talk this out. At least we've got to be honest with each other. We'll walk back afterwards alone."

She had stopped dancing, and drew away from him.

Startled, in spite of his numbness, he tried to make amends.

"I didn't mean to offend you, Clarice. I don't know what I've done. Please . . ."

But she had turned away. Someone else asked her to dance.

The interplay of colored shadows, the beat of the music went on, inexorably.

26

A sleepy *maître d'hôtel* bowed as the Lehmans went out, then closed the door and turned off the lights. The emptiness and silence of the park, the vague outlines of the building resembled an abandoned stage. It was still night, and the murmur of Paris had almost ceased, but the chill of the air showed that morning was not far off.

"Such a pity that Pierre couldn't have stayed to the end!" said Aunt Elizabeth, one foot on the step of her carriage. "He hated so to leave. The maneuvers start today. That's the penalty of marrying a soldier, Clarice. . . . So you're walking back with Jare, are you? I should think you would want to get to bed instead of tramping home."

"It's only ten minutes across the bridge, Mother. Just a breath of air. I have the key."

"Well, do as you please."

Mrs. Lehman climbed in, followed by her husband. The door of the carriage closed. They drove off.

"Now!" murmured Clarice, taking his arm.

Having drawn the hood of her opera cloak over her hair, she walked with Jared slowly through the park toward Cours la Reine. Their footsteps sounded distinct in the silence.

"Now we can talk," she began, but paused again; and they walked on without speaking down to the street, then crossed

149

it, and began following the embankment of the river under the arches of the trees.

He wondered that, in spite of everything, the old feeling toward her returned, the curious sense of oneness, as it had always been. He wondered that the touch of her shoulder against his should still quicken his pulses; that his now-hopeless love burned higher, more remorselessly. Would it always be so? He felt a sudden fear of the strange power that consumed him and equally a dread of losing it. The last was far worse. Better the ache of life than the chill of nothingness. And at least he had these moments with her now. Their footsteps numbered them as they walked on, each moment irrevocable.

Almost unconsciously, he drew her arm closer to his side. At last she turned her face towards him.

"Was it because you love me?"

For a moment, he could find no words. They had stopped, and were standing face to face. He could barely see her for the darkness of the trees.

"Yes," he said. "I have always loved you, Clarice, but I did not know what it meant until today."

She drew closer to him.

"I have always loved you too. I thought you had forgotten me. . . . Oh, Jare, why couldn't we have remembered!"

In passionate appeal, her hands rested on his shoulders. It was the cry of grief, of childhood, of the lost years.

"You, and then Pierre," she was saying. "You mustn't think that I don't love him. I was proud when he asked me to marry him. But if I had thought you loved me . . ."

It was as if she were pleading with herself rather than him.

"Now it can't be changed," she went on. "I have given my promise. I have no right to tear that in two and cast it back at Pierre because at last you and I have learned what might have been. . . . No right. Neither you nor I . . . We will never forget. I know how it will be. But we can't buy our happiness at the cost of someone else's."

He realized that for her this was true. No protest that his egotism could make would alter what had become finality for her. And yet in spite of the sense of doom, he felt a certain exaltation. In the confession of her love she had given him something imperishable.

"I thought you had forgotten," she repeated. "They wrote that you . . ." She stopped. "Am I to blame, Jared? How have you felt toward me?"

As in a ray of pitiless light, he saw his own past, its inconsistencies and shallowness, its lack of unity.

"No," he said, "God knows you are not to blame."

He could not say more than this, but he knew that he ought to say more—admit that the fault was his, confess the weakness that had led to this. And yet he could not.

"How have I felt toward you?" he answered. "I only know that when we meet, something deeper in me than anything else belongs to you. Today I learned for the first time what it meant. Tonight I know what it means to have made a mess of things. And I know that I love you and will always love you."

They stood face to face, wrapped in the darkness, conscious of their essential unity, of their frustration, prolonging this one moment of avowal which was also one of farewell.

Then slowly, close together, they followed the embankment to the Alexander Bridge. They paused in the center of it, gazing far off along the river at the outspread lights of the city. He covered her hand with his, as it lay outstretched on the stone balustrade.

"It's strange," he said, "how I feel myself already in the future, looking back to you and me standing here, trying to remember everything—all that over there, and just how you looked and the feel of your hand."

"Yes," she agreed, "I know that years from now I'll never cross this bridge at night without seeing the two of us here. . . ."

The shiver of mutability passed over them; the dread of change that they dared not confess, change in all things, in themselves, even perhaps in their love. For a moment, dimming the starlight, fell the shadow of that knowledge that nothing human endures, that no hour, even in memory, can be wholly recaptured.

"This summer," she went on, "must be filled for the future."

"No," he answered. "I'm leaving in a few days, Clarice."

With a low cry, she turned to him. "But you promised . . ."

"Don't you understand how it is?" he urged. "Do you think, after tonight, that I could be near you, see you with him, pretend, act as if I felt nothing? . . . I couldn't do that."

Her eyes fell.

"No," she murmured at last. "I understand. It was simply that I wanted you so much . . . so very much. It wouldn't be possible for us after tonight. Only . . . at my wedding . . . I would like to have you near me."

"Yes, I'll come back."

Hand in hand, they stood looking down at the stream.

"Promise you will write often when you are back in America, send me some little thing now and then, something you think I would like. I'll do the same from here. Will you?"

He found it hard to agree with a steady voice. He realized what it would mean in the hunger of Dunstable to be allowed to think that this or that might please her, and then count the days until he heard what she had thought of it.

The minutes passed. It was not the stream they saw reaching out into the city, but the still-dimmer intimations of the years to come, the mystery of time.

At length she drew back.

"This will be our good-by, then—the real one."

She lifted her face to his.

"Kiss me," she said.

He held her a moment close to him. "Good-by," he whispered, "good-by, Clarice."

Jared felt that what had been lost to him that night, what had been broken in him, would never be restored.

PART THREE

TOLBECKEN LEDGER

27

Though the interest and diversity of his career would have justified it, Rufus Tolbecken had never kept a diary. But from his twenty-first year he had kept something else which, if rightly interpreted, contained a record of his life. It was a double-columned ledger indicating on the credit side actual and gross income, and on the opposite, or debit, page actual expenses and gross ontlay. RUFUS TOLBECKEN, ESQ., *in account with the* FIRST NATIONAL BANK OF DUNSTABLE. It opened with an entry on July 12, 1852, when he had come of age, and it continued without break through four volumes down to April 1, 1912. According to custom, on this date he had set himself to balance his books for the preceding quarter.

The study lamp at Tolbecken shed a glow on the paper. His pencil crawled slowly up the columns of figures. After a while his hand began to tremble, and laying the pencil aside for a moment, he stretched out his fingers, regarding them absently. Then he resumed and finished his calculations, and he leaned back.

Actual income for the last three months: three thousand four hundred and some dollars—actual expenses: over five thousand. He turned back the pages of the grand totals of last year: there was an excess of expense over income of six thousand; the year before, about the same; the year before that . . . His hand fell away. The twelve preceding years showed a steadily increasing deficit. Then he took to comparing items: from his legal practice for the last quarter, about five hundred dollars; for the same period three years before, a thousand; fifteen years before, five thousand; but in '85, ten thousand; and for the whole year, thirty-eight thousand—it had been a great practice. On the debit pages of the last five years, two semiannual payments stood out among the lesser items—seven thousand dollars in local taxes on house and land . . . seven thousand dollars with an income of twelve.

Pushing his chair back from the desk, he sat with a hand on either arm of it, at bay. His lordly, generous years returned to haunt him. He had been worth half a million twenty-five years ago. He had earned much and spent freely. There had been gifts to charity, to the town, endorsements on the notes of friends, the education of his children, settlements on his daughters at their marriages, aid to his sons. But he had not been prodigal; he had understood the worth of money. In proportion he had spent no more than his father or grandfather; the Tolbeckens had always been freehanded. Between them and himself, however, there was this difference: that in each case an able son had lived to balance and more than balance their accounts, whereas of his own sons, the only one of ability had died. And there was this further difference: that the structure of American life had changed, was changing daily at an ever-increasing speed. Now men who had talked in thousands talked in millions; unheard-of luxuries had become necessities; taxes pyramided; competition, wrangling on every corner, demanded strength and youth.

He sat at bay, his great head bowed. "When thou wast young," he thought, "thou girdedst thyself and walkedst whither thou wouldest: but when thou shalt be old . . ."

The bitterness of his son Jared's death weighed upon him. Because of it he had, as it were, projected his life across the space of two lives, taxing himself to the utmost, bridging the gap, holding on by force of will, holding things together until young Jared's time. But the cost had been great; construed by the ledger, it had been in vain.

The cost of what? It seemed to Judge Tolbecken that he asked very little, nothing but to retain his home and the shreds of his practice, so that he might hand them over to the boy he loved, and for this he had spent his fortune and himself. He was no worshiper of money, but money, after all, denoted, in his case work, hard work, and former success. It scandalized him to watch this feeble bleeding away of his wealth. "We must retrench," he thought. "We must make a drastic cut somehow." The habits of a prosperous life were against it; the cherished purpose of his soul was against it;

the fatigue of age was against it. Reason told him it was necessary, but his will, tired out and clinging to possibilities, delayed. He would put on pressure at the office; young Jared, finishing law school, would take his bar examinations that summer. He refused to acknowledge that he no longer had strength for work, that his grandson's earning power would be negligible to start with. It sufficed that by next autumn the new firm name, Tolbecken *and* Tolbecken, would be stenciled on his office door. Now that the end was in sight and he could hand over the position held at such cost, he could not think of surrendering it. He preferred to go on faith, recalculate his assets, and give himself the advantage of every doubt. Future expenses were glossed over in the same way. The present deficit, like other deficits, led somehow to the assurance that next quarter, next year would be better. And so conjured, the dark hour passed, though it left an ache.

He returned to his ledger, absently turning the pages and letting thought drift back along the columns.

October 3, 1856. To James Hapgood . . . $62.00. That was for the Landsdowne poets on the shelf facing him, in their cloth and gilt bindings; it was for the set of Washington Irving in calf, the Waverley Novels, the blue buckram set of Byron, Young's *Night Thoughts*, and a few others. They had been stacked up on this same desk as a birthday present for his father. The old gentleman, in flowing side whiskers and a black stock, had picked them up one by one. "You positively overwhelm me, my dear boy. No gift on earth like books. . . ."

February 12, 1857. To Dr. Samuel Jones . . . $50.00. He could see the doctor's cutter now, racing up through the snow and stopping with a jangle of bells, while he himself, on the lookout, had thrown open the door. There was hush and excitement in the house, footsteps hurried back and forth overhead. And he paced up and down, up and down, below, looked out of the windows, listened in the hall, roved here and there in a sweat of nervousness. His mother appeared. "It's a boy, Rufus, it's a fine boy! You can come up." Except his wife and himself, they were dead now . . . all of them . . . dead long ago—his father, mother, the doctor, even the child. Long ago . . .

November 8, 1862. (This in his father's handwriting.) *To John Mally, for chestnut stallion, Ranger, remount for Capt. Rufus Tolbecken with the Army of the Potomac . . . $500.00.* A fine horse that, killed under him in the Battle of the Wilderness. He thought of his lusty, bearded companions,

155

with their gauntlets and high-crowned felt hats, the roar and youth of them. It seemed incredible that fifty years had passed since then.

May 9, 1870. To Joseph Kearns . . . $200.00. He smiled faintly, remembering his own dismay at such a bill for clothes. His diplomatic wardrobe.

Then followed a long number of entries representing drafts from Europe for two years. It had been a restless, homesick period. He was too thoroughly a man of action to savor the fussy, convention-bound life of foreign minister in a small European capital. He missed his house and neighbors, fretted about his practice, longed for his children, who had been left at Dunstable under the guardianship of their grandparents and Aunt Joan. He yearned for the stir and march of America. Even after forty years he could recall his delight and the peculiar tang of the air on entering New York harbor.

September 10, 1874. To the Pennsylvania Monument Company . . . $1500.00. It stood now thickly covered with ivy, the Tolbeckens' mausoleum, its bronze doors engraved with their names. "Soon," he thought, turning the page. He had no fear of death, but deeply rooted in life as he was, its mystery daunted him. There were times when he felt utterly naked and alone before its advancing darkness. As much as possible he closed his mind to it.

September 27, 1874. To the Treasurer of Princeton College . . . $150.00. And from then on that official appeared often in the ledger. It reflected the education of his children, the extravagances and scrapes he had paid for, the hopes he had entertained. To what end? In the light of retrospect, they seemed to him more faded than the yellowing ink that recorded them. And then the entries to milliners, tailors, caterers, jewelers, carpenters, gardeners, doctors, undertakers—the cryptic summary of joy, pride, and illusion. To what end?

The credit side of the ledger took up that challenge, the pages of fees or salary received for unstinted work, but more important the will to serve that underlay it. He must take the usefulness, the permanency of this on faith. If questionings arose, more passionate than doubt was confidence in the ultimate value of work. He scorned defeatists. The changing patterns of froth upon the surface did not reveal the essential current. And yet, there at the end was the deficit of human inadequacy, fading strength, outworn brain. His books would not balance after all; they must be balanced for him by a higher power.

He turned the pages. He was down to Jared's day now, and

156

he lingered over the entries, smiling and sometimes chuckling to himself.

1889—Rayberg and Co. Silver porringer, cup, and spoon . . . $25.00.

1896—Dr. J. M. Ellis. Services for little Jare . . . $100.00. Diphtheria. He shook his head and pursed his lips, remembering.

1897—D. L. Naylor. Pony saddle . . . $10.00. He chuckled over that. Then the first suit of long pants, the first dinner coat, bills from Lawrenceville, Princeton. His forefinger lovingly plodded on from item to item. *May 6, 1908—Tiffany. Pearl studs on Jared Tolbecken's twenty-first birthday . . . $250.00. June 22, 1909—First National Bank of Dunstable. Letter of Credit for Jared Tolbecken . . . $1000.00.* It had been his graduation present. He had spent all of it. Five hundred dollars on a pendant for Clarice Lehman. Five hundred dollars! The family had gasped; only his grandfather had stood up for him. "He did exactly right. No skinflints in our family. Spent his money like a gentleman." And now again the Judge felt a glow of pride.

Other items—monthly allowances, fees to the Pennsylvania Law School. *March 26, 1912—Rayberg and Co. Ebony cane to be presented to my grandson upon admission to the Bar . . . $50.00.* He had been unable to put off buying that cane any longer. He had thought about it ever since Jared entered law school, and at last stalked into the jewelry shop to ask for the best one in the store. It must take its place some day among the Tolbecken canes in the glass case in the hall— there was one for each generation. Now, its pommel carefully engraved, it was hidden in his study closet for him to look at and polish now and then.

Yes, Jared was almost ready. If, in spite of taxes, they could hang on to Tolbecken just a little longer, he would make the practice pay again, and the old house would stand for another century in defiance of change.

"My dear boy," the Judge thought, "my dear boy! Every dollar I've spent on him has yielded a hundredfold." He loved to think about the various aspects of Jared's character. "Afraid he'll never be a businessman, though. Too scrupulous. As he should be. Enough go-getters around—need some gentlemen. When it comes to brains, I'd pit him against any of 'em. Might be a little more regular at church. Ought to talk to him about that. Comes from this new skepticism at Princeton—Macklin and the rest. But he'll swing around. Can't blame him too much, with that fool Oliver in the pulpit.

157

"Wish he went out more; gets out of parties and dances. Too much alone. Not right at his age. Never the same since that visit to France."

He remembered his wife's and Joan Maylin's suspicions that Jared had fallen in love with Clarice. They kept harping on the weekly letters that he slipped into his pocket separate from the rest of the mail. Perhaps they were right, but Clarice had been married three years now—happily married, too, from all accounts—had her household and two babies to look after. The boy wouldn't be foolish enough to let an old fondness like that influence him too much. Of course not. But worried by the shadow of anything affecting his treasure, the Judge began to fidget, looked at his watch, closed his ledger, and grunted several times uneasily. It was all rubbish. Jare hadn't the time with his law-school work to go fiddling around in society. Good sense, too, nose to the grindstone. Besides, wasn't he out that very evening with a couple of friends at one of those newfangled cinemas? And he saw a little of the Oliver girl and others.

From the drawing room across the hall, came the voices of Rachel Tolbecken and her sister. He felt a sudden need to talk, and having locked his ledger in a side drawer, pulled himself up, leaned a moment on the desk to get his balance, and tottering a bit, walked out.

28

"What are you girls up to?" asked the Judge.

"Oh, nothing," said Grandmother at her needlework. "Joan's been reading the paper to me. Been balancing your books?"

He nodded. They had been reared in the tradition that it was almost indelicate for women to meddle with finances—a mere fiction, of course, for Mrs. Tolbecken and Aunt Joan guessed shrewdly enough how affairs stood, but they rather admired his reticence in such matters. It was a perquisite of the head of the house.

For once he conceded a little. "We ought to make a retrenchment of some sort; taxes have been excessive this year."

Joan Maylin cleared her throat. "There's no use talking about retrenchments. We've already retrenched in every possible way. We've given up the horses, all except Jare's riding horse. We've only Carrie now and myself for the cooking and housework. The garden hasn't been attended to properly for years; the house needs a great deal done to it. When I think of the way it used to be . . ."

"Well, do your best," interrupted the Judge, with an attempt at briskness. "There's no occasion for poor living. There's no reason why we shouldn't have an extra servant. I only meant . . ."

He encountered the gaze of his sister-in-law and looked away. She suspected more than he liked. There had been a defection on her part of late toward those of the family who counseled the sale of the property, and he feared that even his wife shared the same opinion. Women had often a colder, harder point of view than men. Was it a chimera he clung to, a false estimate of values? No, he would never admit that. As he looked about the room, every corner of it was filled with memories. The suggestion of life anywhere else seemed unthinkable; it hurt him that his own generation should weaken on this point of loyalty.

He changed the subject. "Jared not back?" he asked mechanically.

No, and it was time he was. The pictures must be over.

"Hope he hasn't been calling at the Olivers'," added Rachel Tolbecken.

"Why not?" said the Judge. "I don't see any harm in Frances. I've just been thinking that he didn't get out with young people half enough."

"Yes, I know, but we don't want him with her. She hasn't improved with age. What a bad little minx it is! There's no use your defending her, Rufus. You can't put her cigarette smoking and drinking and flirting down to youth any longer. She's twenty-three years old, and decent women don't do those things. Of course, she's a child of her parents, but that doesn't help matters. You'd have said three or four years ago that she could have married into any of the best families of Dunstable; she's getting a little shopworn now."

The Judge smiled. "How do you know, Rachel? You never see her."

"*I* see her," put in Aunt Joan. "I saw her the other night with that fast brother of hers, a cigarette in her mouth, coming back from the races in his automobile. And she was rouged to the eyes. Besides, we've both of us heard our fill about her."

"Gossip! You haven't spent all your life in small towns without knowing what gossip is, Joan."

159

"Yes, and not without knowing when there's something at the bottom of it."

"As to her smoking," continued the Judge, "don't you remember how pioneer women out West used to smoke their pipes?"

"Fiddlesticks!"

"Give a dog a bad name," he said.

"I've *never* approved of her," said Aunt Joan, after a pause. "I think she's hard and mercenary. But when she was in school and he in college, it didn't seem to be worth worrying about. Maybe it isn't now. Matter of fact, I don't think the boy's interested in her any more. But I know she's interested in him. She's forever gushing over me in the street and saying, '*Dear* Miss Joan, how is everybody at Tolbecken? I do hope Madam Tolbecken is well and the Judge. Tell Jare he's been neglecting us lately.' She gets a cold shoulder from me, I can tell you. But he does call at the Olivers' more than anywhere else—out of habit, I suppose—and when a girl like that sets her cap for a man . . ."

"Exactly," said Mrs. Tolbecken, "or a girl's mother. I think those two are absolutely unscrupulous. Their reputation is . . ."

"One moment," broke in the Judge, his eyes smoldering, "I will ask you to recall that you are discussing the wife and daughter of our pastor. I forbid that kind of talk in this house."

"Hoity-toity!" said Grandmother.

"I beg leave," he went on, "to request your attention. I am amazed at your attitude, madam." In his ire the vocabulary of the fifties crept back. "You make distasteful insinuations against the character of a young woman and impair your own dignity."

She looked up from her needlework and regarded him with a faint smile, her white lawn cap confronting his white beard. No one in his household bandied words with Rufus Tolbecken, but her smile was enough. He would come round.

"A mountain out of nothing," he continued. "You say yourselves that he's not interested in the girl. I wouldn't care if he were; I would have confidence in his choice. We have no right to interfere."

Mrs. Tolbecken went on with her needlework and Aunt Joan with her newspaper.

"We've no right to interfere," repeated the Judge on a note of decrescendo, "that is, even admitting there's something to interfere with." As a matter of fact, his conscience already troubled him. He fumbled with his watch chain a moment. "I didn't mean to be harsh, Rachel. Perhaps I lost my temper; but it did seem to me that you and Joan spoke a little indelicately."

"Yes," she admitted, "but it's simply because we love Jare so much. He's all we have. But it's on that account that we don't want to see him made a fool of. What earthly use are old people if it isn't for their experience? We haven't the right to interfere, but we have to advise; and I certainly intend to put Jared on his guard, if it ever seems to be necessary."

"Go easy then," said the Judge. "He has a mind of his own; we mustn't turn him against us."

A rapid footfall sounded on the driveway outside, mounted the front steps. "There he is now," said Aunt Joan. The front door opened and closed. A hat and coat were tossed on the hall settle.

"Hello, Grandfather and everybody! Still up?"

Jared took a seat and described the pictures, *Quo Vadis* by an Italian company. They had met Nan Oliver at the theater and dropped in at her house afterwards.

Mrs. Tolbecken and Joan Maylin exchanged glances.

"Who else was along?" asked Grandmother.

"Oh, Eaby Ellis, Josh Sedley, and Grace Armstrong. Josh and Grace are engaged, I think."

"He used to be fond of Nan, didn't he?"

"I suppose so—off and on."

Another exchange of glances.

"Do you see much of Nan these days, Jare?"

"Oh, not a great deal," he answered indifferently. "We're old friends."

"She's not as pretty as she used to be," observed Aunt Joan, with great artfulness.

"Perhaps not. I hadn't thought about it. . . . Well, I'd like to look over tomorrow's assignment on contracts before turning in. Good night, everybody."

He kissed them in turn, pressing his lips fondly against their wrinkled cheeks, and went out.

"I do believe there's nothing in it," rejoiced Grandmother.

"The dear Machiavellis," he thought, climbing the stairs, "still worrying about Nan!"

He turned on the lights in his room and walked over to the bookshelves. But before taking down the work on contracts, his hand wandered to another shelf of French bindings and pulled out a book, which he opened at random. It was a copy of Verlaine with passages marked here and there. But he felt tired and a little bleak. Mechanically he drew out a decanter of brandy from the lower part of his desk, filled and emptied a small glass. Then in the glow of it he read the marked passages, stopping at some marginal comment in Clarice's hand. He wandered on, and he found himself repeating some of the verses under his breath. It seemed to him that he could hear the tones of her voice. . . . It was odd how his vision blurred all at once. . . . Nan Oliver, indeed! He refilled his glass.

29

There was considerable basis for Judge Tolbecken's hopes for the law practice. Jared graduated with honor from the Pennsylvania Law School, and passed his bar examinations with distinction. It would be some years before his earning power could establish the fortunes of Tolbecken and Tolbecken, but he gave every promise of being a successful lawyer.

For a young man of even moderate ability launched in the town of Dunstable with the prestige of such a name and connections, it would have been comparatively easy to occupy an advantageous position at the start. And he had a good deal more than average ability. Other circumstances favored him. That, following his return from Europe, he had applied himself strictly to his law studies, had appeared seldom (though not too seldom) at the country club, had cultivated the society of older men, and had taken a small part (on the right side) in politics made a good impression in the best quarters. Dunstable was solidly Republican, and the name of Tolbecken had been identified with the party since its beginnings. He appeared in the Tolbecken pew of Dr. Oliver's church sufficiently often to retain orthodox esteem. He supported the cause of temperance if not of prohibition. Karl Kirschbaum, agitating for a new high school, which involved a real-estate deal in one of the poorer districts, featured him as a speaker on the education of youth at a couple of Businessmen's Club meetings, and was an enthusiastic sponsor.

In view of his young parishioner's budding prominence, Dr. Cary Oliver invited him to an occasional game of golf (an association that raised Jared's credit still further with the respectable element) and even suggested that he lead a youths' Bible class at the church.

"Now, wait," said Oliver, "I know what you are going to say. You don't subscribe to all the old-fashioned dogmas. Quite so. I have a great respect for honest doubt—even," he added hastily, "if I don't share it. To be broadminded is to be a Christian. But here's the idea. I want to attract boys to the Sunday School who would be repulsed by the pious sort of thing. You would be a drawing card. You were an athlete in college and belonged to a good club. I wouldn't expect you to teach the Bible at all—perhaps a verse or two for the sake of appearances—but talk about good sportsmanship, clean living, and so on, tell of your experiences in football or track. Keep their interest—that's the whole thing. They'll sop up Christianity without knowing it."

Jared shook his head. "I'll think it over, but I don't see myself in that picture."

"Remember," urged Oliver solemnly, "you would be fighting the good fight. Besides, you would have boys of only the better families, and that might lead to professional contacts."

For the mischief of it, Jared reported this conversation at Tolbecken and got the expected rise.

"Bible class and no Bible," snorted Aunt Joan, "preaching and no teaching, Christianity and no Christ—what's left!"

"Dr. Cary Oliver's left," said Grandmother.

The Judge groaned. "You wouldn't dream of abetting such a plan, Jared?"

"No, sir," returned the other, "don't worry. I wouldn't dream of it."

He wrote that evening to Clarice: *You don't know how much I'm coming to value a sense of humor. A nest of bumble-bees and myself as loud as any of them—that is Dunstable. Buzz, buzz.*

There was a good deal of indifference, an emptiness of heart, but no conscious insincerity in this development of a prominent citizen. Activities of one kind or another were more interesting than twiddling one's thumbs. Perhaps in the end the Tolbecken tradition would replace lost love. He might as well make a success of things while he was at it. And it pleased him mildly that he made a success. He might speak with more conviction than he really felt about the new high school. But who would blame him for that? It was a good cause. In the honest belief that temperance made for general well-being, and in deference to his family, he would

163

support the movement, without any qualms at all about his own drinking. He did not drink too much—at least not often. The church made for good citizenship, the Republican party for good business; he gave them more loyalty than most people. If, as a result of work and the right affiliations, Dunstable approved of him, called him steady, levelheaded, and a true Tolbecken, he could accept this praise with as much complacency as anyone. And if as time went on he compromised more and more with the old Adam on trifles of thought or conduct, he kept these slips to himself, like any other prudent man.

In the fall of 1912, America was convulsed by the periodical clash of parties; but this time, with more fervor than usual, Wilson had been nominated on the Democratic ticket. In politics as in education, his supreme faculty was to disentangle real from superficial issues, and to present principles rather than policies as the object of controversy. America responded with that earnestness which is never aroused except when ideals are at stake. Voicing the liberalism of the nineteenth century, Wilson was contending not for an economic revolution, but for a "new spirit, a new attitude" in human relations.

"It seems like the old days at college," said David Mansen, back from medical school for a week end. "He's carrying on the same fight nationally that he did there. I shouldn't wonder if he makes it a world issue before he's done. 'A new spirit, a new attitude.' Of course that's the one hope of the world, not the redistribution of wealth. But it would mean a revolution, all right—just about the biggest. I suppose," he added, "this is the first time a Tolbecken will ever have voted for a Democrat."

They were in Jared's room, Mansen's ungainly form outstretched in a chair on one side of the fire. His friend eyed him a little uneasily through the smoke of a cigarette. Jared inhaled again before answering.

"What makes you think that I'm going to vote for him?"

The other straightened up in surprise.

"I don't understand. You were a great supporter of his in college. Don't you believe in him—in his principles?"

Jared lit another cigarette.

"It's not a question of Wilson. I have no confidence in the Democratic party, that's all. I think America's safer under a Republican administration."

"Is that your honest opinion? I mean, is that your real reason for voting the Republican ticket?"

164

"Of course it is." And at the look in Mansen's face, "You don't seem to believe me."

The other stared into the fire. "I was wondering what effect your voting Democratic would have on your career in Dunstable, on your friends, family, and reputation. Don't get angry, Jare. It's pretty easy to rationalize. Because what you've just been saying makes no sense. It's just a catch phrase. Here you have a man far above the run of politicians, a man of proved ability whose ideals you share, and perhaps you have the one chance in your life of voting for a real issue. But you turn your back on all this, because you say the Republican party is safer. Safer for what? The vested interests. Isn't that it?"

No, it was not it. There were a thousand other things to be considered. Jared launched into a passionate harangue on the Republican party that would have delighted his grandfather. In the course of it, he poured himself a drink, two drinks. Mansen continued to stare into the fire.

After a while Mansen smiled. "I shall vote for Wilson myself, but if you are honestly convinced on the other side, I have no quarrel with you. You're trained to know about politics; I'm just a medical student, trained to know something about human beings. And I'm an old friend of yours. Do you realize that tobacco and alcohol, as you use them, tell tales out of school?"

"Tales of what?"

"Conflict and escape. And it seemed to me that your defense of the Republican party was rather a defense of yourself. A man shouldn't need to defend himself, Jare."

His words made Jared uncomfortable, but in the silence that followed, he felt no resentment.

"You know too much, Dave," he said at last hoarsely. "You ought to make a success in your profession. Conflict —yes. Ever since that time in Paris . . ."

David shook his head. "Don't romanticize yourself. Your conflict began long before then."

"I think I'd rather not discuss it," Jared said with some sharpness.

How could he ever tell anyone about that *via dolorosa* across the Alexander Bridge!

30

About this time, a protracted affair between Nan Oliver and Jared's classmate Bill Forgan of New York (the Forgan millions) came to an end. Forgan became engaged to someone else. It was an event that tried the patience of Mrs. Cary Oliver to the utmost. Men were as plentiful as green apples in Nan's life, but they could never be brought to ripen for her. They were generous with orchids and candy boxes, loved to take her motoring on warm nights, showed her a good time, and then faded out. In view of Nan's looks, charms, and wardrobe, it made no sense to Mrs. Oliver. Once, twice, or thrice, the man himself might be a cad and a bounder, but when it kept on happening, when someone like William Forgan dropped into the lap of another woman's daughter, Mrs. Oliver was bound to confess that there might be something wrong with Nan herself. Could it be that she did not take this marriage business seriously? Didn't she realize a marriageable daughter could not be kept groomed up to the proper pitch indefinitely? Nan could not be so stupid.

After an acid comment on the announcement in the newspaper of Mr. Forgan's engagement, Mrs. Oliver crumpled up the paper and asked Nan bluntly what the trouble was.

"I don't know," said Nan. "Perhaps he got sore that night when he found me sitting in the hammock with Lynn Welsh. He always was stodgy."

"Just so!" retorted her mother. "I might have expected it! I think William was justified, I really think so. When you knew how devoted he'd been, and how advantageous such a marriage would be, you insult him to his face. Really, I don't understand it. It's too much!"

"Don't cry about it," said Nan.

"I *will* cry about it! Here's your father and me been scraping for years—sent you to an expensive school, gave you a trip to Europe, pinched ourselves to keep good clothes on your back so that you could hold up your head with anybody—and what does it come to? You sit in the hammock with Lynn Welsh—and Lynn Welsh not worth a copper—and let William *Forgan* go! Well, I'm through; I'm sick of it! You can sit in the hammock with your Lynn Welshes till you're an old maid. That's what you can do."

"Mother, you're positively common."

"I don't care if I am," said Mrs. Oliver. "I'm tired."

She had done pretty well with herself since she married Cary Oliver in Xenia, Ohio, thirty years ago. Her voice and manner and friends had improved unbelievably, but at a moment of stress like this the native accent broke through. Nan was both shocked and impressed by her mother's spirit.

"I'm sorry," she admitted. "I didn't know Bill Forgan was coming that evening, and of course I don't care a snap for Lynn Welsh. But there's no use being tragic over it either. There're plenty of other eligible men in the world besides Forgan."

"Who?"

The savage directness of the question staggered Nan for a moment. She faltered and looked blank.

"Who?" repeated her mother.

"Well, I don't know—there's Jared Tolbecken, for one."

"Pshaw! You don't call him attentive, do you? You've seen precious little of him since graduation."

"Yes, but I think it's up to me if I want him. He proposed once."

"Proposed!" gasped Mrs. Oliver. "You mean he actually asked you to marry him?"

"Yes."

"Well, I never! *When* did he propose?"

"At his graduation."

"And what did you say, in Heaven's name?"

"Oh, I don't know what I said. I put him off."

Mrs. Oliver let her hands fall to her lap. "Now," she said, seething, "I'm beginning to understand. Now it's beginning to come out! And I've been wondering and thinking you were abused, and blaming nice young men . . . and you've been putting 'em off! Oh, really, it's too hard . . ."

"Stop it," said Nan. "I'm getting tired myself. He couldn't have married me then, could he? You wouldn't have wanted me to hang around for years till he was through law school. Lovely time I'd have had! Matter of fact, I'd just met Bill Forgan that very evening. But now . . ."

She fell to musing, her deep eyes intent on vacancy, and Mrs. Oliver meditated too. When she spoke again, her tone was different.

"Of course, darling, that's right; I understand perfectly.

167

You've always been very fond of Jared, I know. I believe you've really been waiting for him all these years. That's it, isn't it? No, don't interrupt, I know how it is. Down deep in your heart you were caring for him. Well, I can't blame you. He's a charming boy—not as desirable in some ways perhaps as William Forgan, but an attractive young man, good family, and so on. You could accept him without the slightest hesitation. Judge Tolbecken can't live much longer, and I understand that dear Jared is the principal heir. It would be quite suitable, dear, if you wish it."

Nan's look of bewilderment turned slowly to admiration. That phrase about waiting for him all these years! In some ways her mother was a genius.

"But the question is, does he wish it?"

Mrs. Oliver raised her eyebrows. "That remains to be seen. As you say, it depends a little on us—I mean, on you. Naturally he can't know that you care for him unless you show it. Not too obviously, of course. You'd be the last person in the world to throw yourself at anyone. When you refused him that time, you weren't sharp or final, were you?"

"Oh, no, I simply put him off. I even—kissed him."

"Precious lambs!" exclaimed Mrs. Oliver in high approval. "Mother'll have to help a little. Don't worry, I'm sure it'll all come right in the end."

Nan shot her a suspicious look. "What do you mean by 'helping'? For the love of goodness, don't you go and mix in. I can take care of myself."

"Don't worry," repeated Mrs. Oliver airily.

Her mental comment was that Nan, having made a botch of things so far, inspired no confidence. She required a mother's technique and experience.

"Will you let me give you a piece of advice?" she went on. "If you're really fond of Jared, you'll be willing to sacrifice little things for him—not make up quite as much, leave off cigarettes and slang, and talk about serious things. You know, he's as old-fashioned as his family."

"Piffle!" said Nan. "I refuse to look like a frump. Jare's not so much of a fish as all that—don't you believe it!"

Mrs. Oliver squared her jaw. "When it comes to getting married, men are queer. I can't see that all your primping has helped you much with any of 'em. When you're married you can do as you please. And another thing! You'd better be awfully nice to his family."

"Dear Judge, *dear* Miss Joan," mimicked Nan.

Her mother's eyes blazed. "Now, I want you to get this

straight, Frances: your papa and I aren't going to stand for any more fooling."

It began to be noticed after that that Nan had changed. She gave up rouging, at least noticeably. She no longer smoked, or at least no one saw her smoke. She said *Dear* Miss Joan" when they met on the street, and she made a point of talking to Judge Tolbecken after church. The old gentlemen, secretly charmed, beamed at her through his spectacles, and could not for the life of him see what people had against her. Even Jared noticed vaguely that she seemed different, and made conversation about it once at a chance meeting.

"You ought to know the reason," she said cryptically, then added that she supposed it was age, and that she felt "kind of deserted" sometimes. Why didn't he call more often?

When he did call, there was great to-do and a warm welcome, pleasant enough on lonely evenings. It flattered Jared to feel that the Olivers liked to have him; he and Nan gossiped about mutual friends and joked each other a bit. It amounted to nothing but that, even when once as a joke Nan laid her head on his shoulder and Mrs. Oliver, who happened to come in at that moment, said jovially, "Bless you, my children," smiled, and walked out.

But it amounted to a great deal more than that when one evening Mrs. Oliver entertained him alone in the sitting room before Nan came down. In spite of her affectations, which seemed to him a little pathetic, he rather liked Mrs. Oliver; she was so sprightly and hospitable. But tonight she looked depressed.

"Jared," she began, "I don't want to be intrusive—Nan would never forgive me—but I'm really worried about her. She's very unhappy."

He asked why.

"Promise that you'll never breathe a word of this to Nan?"

"Of course, Mrs. Oliver."

"Well, then, to be frank, it's on your account. She can't understand and, as a matter of fact, neither can her father nor I understand why, now that you've finished law school, you never make any reference at all to your engagement."

"What engagement?"

"Why, your engagement to Nan, of course. She's beginning to wonder if you've stopped caring for her, and the thought of that almost breaks her heart."

"But we're not engaged!"

The temperature of the room dropped to zero; Mrs. Oliver stared at him in blank amazement.

"Would you mind saying that again, Jared? I'm not sure I heard clearly."

"Why, I said that Nan and I are not engaged."

She stiffened slowly; her look became ice. "Oh?" she said. And after a pause, "I'm to understand then that you did not mean it when you asked her to marry you!"

"But that was four years ago, Mrs. Oliver. She refused me. I didn't dream . . ."

"One moment, if you please. I know all about that from Nan herself. You're technically right—being a lawyer I suppose that may be enough for you, but it is not enough to save my daughter from inexpressible grief. If you'll pardon me, she did not refuse you; she left you free, and that is a very different matter. Nan is like that—utterly unselfish. She thought only of you; she did not wish to bind you at a time when you could not marry her. Far from refusing, do you remember what she did? She gave you her lips. When a girl like Frances kisses a man in answer to his proposal of marriage, it means that she gives herself to him heart and soul forever. I will ask you to think a little about that."

Jared realized that in this pitiless view he stood guilty of an unpardonable offense, a mean attempt to sneak out of a serious commitment. His cheeks burned; his ears rang.

"She left you absolutely free," repeated Mrs. Oliver. "She would never dream of pursuing you—I should think not! But when you continued to call—even though it hurt her that you called so seldom—and when you did not seem attentive to any other girl, it's hardly to be wondered at that she believed you still cared for her. And then the other evening when I found you both, with her head on your shoulder, I can't tell you how happy I felt."

"But, please," interrupted Jared, "won't you let me explain . . . ?"

"She left you free," intoned Mrs. Oliver, "but she considered herself bound. As I said, she had given you her silent promise. It has always been you since that moment. Other men, a great many other men, as you know, have wanted to marry her. There was Sedley, Kay Grafton, James Dennis, William Forgan, men of great fortunes. But she would not even consider them. It was always you, only you. And now you tell me *that you are not engaged*. Well! What am I to think?"

The Reverend Cary Oliver himself could not have made a more skillful speech, on the whole, or one to which a reply was less possible. Mrs. Oliver had brought herself to the point where she actually believed three quarters of what she said; a woman might be permitted a fourth quarter of hyperbole. The manse, too, was a good setting for truth, and the pastor's wife a convincing witness. Jared knew of the men who had paid attentions to Nan, and that nothing had come of them. He remembered her answer in the street: "*You* ought to know the reason."

But for all that, he was struck by the absurdity of this charge, and felt nettled. The fact remained that Nan had not engaged herself to him four years ago, and that she had given small evidence of devotion since. The sensitiveness of boyhood that would once have responded to Mrs. Oliver's maneuvers was not all lost, but it had become alloyed with a strong measure of common sense. Right or wrong, he did not intend to be dragooned into marrying Nan Oliver because of an ancient proposal that had been declined and that he had had no reason to believe had ever been taken seriously. As for love, he would not have stained its memory by thinking of it in this connection. Mrs. Oliver had just a little overplayed her part. There had been undertones of vulgarity and coarseness which jarred with the Tolbecken sense of propriety. She waited, dabbing her nose, proud of her efforts. The quarry's confusion passed, and he stood up.

"In that case, I shall discontinue my calls."

But as Mrs. Oliver, frozen by her defeat and at a loss for words, stared at him, Nan entered the room in her newest chiffon dress. The light glimmered on the ripples of her blond hair, caressed the smooth roundness of her arms and neck. She seemed all buoyancy and innocence, but she contrived to look daggers at her mother before greeting Jared.

"*So* sorry to keep you waiting. But the country-club dances never do start on time, anyway. Been having a chat with Mummie? . . . Why, what's the matter? You both look so queer. Has Mummie been crying?"

"The matter is," said Jared coolly, "that Mrs. Oliver has given me to understand that you have considered yourself engaged to me during the last four years . . ."

"The idea!" exclaimed Nan. "Mother, how *could* you!"

"You promised," quavered Mrs. Oliver, "you promised you wouldn't tell her. . . . Oh, you're dreadful. . . ."

And she dabbed her nose again.

"Well, I forgot," admitted Jared. "But at any rate this thing must be cleared up." And to Nan, "When I proposed to you at graduation, did we become engaged or not?"

"No, Jare."

171

She looked at him tenderly, and her eyes fell.

"But you kissed him," protested Mrs. Oliver.

"It was only a kiss," said Nan bravely.

"Have you imagined that we were engaged?"

"No, Jare."

Wistful fortitude sounded in her voice. Jared felt an unreasonable twinge of conscience.

"I don't want to come here under false pretenses," he went on. "I think I'd better not come again."

Nan caught both his hands, swinging them gently in the frankest, gayest fashion. "Why, you old silly, what *are* you talking about! *I* know we're only good friends. Everybody knows that. Of course, if you don't want to be . . ."

"You know I want to be."

"All right, then. . . . Let's go to the club."

But she contrived to have a moment alone with her mother before setting out.

"Now that you've made a hash of things," she raged, "will you please keep out of my business? Of all the dumb, left-footed ways of tackling him, that was the limit. As if Jared Tolbecken could be roped in like that!"

"Frances, you're forgetting that I'm your mother."

"You're too darn much my mother, if you ask me. You might have been a little delicate about it. I can handle him, but not with you butting in."

"Very well," croaked Mrs. Oliver, "*very* well, we'll see."

"Yes, we will see," retorted her daughter, and hearing a movement on the front porch, "Right along, Jare. I'm just kissing Mummie good night."

Light-footed, airy, and radiant, she rejoined her escort outside.

"Such a pother," she confided. "Mother's awfully queer sometimes. You simply have got to make allowances." She slipped her arm beneath his with a little squeeze. "We're friends, aren't we?"

31

That night she danced no more often with Jared than with others of the young set who crowded around her. But there are different ways of dancing. Little by little, she set him at

172

his ease, lulled whatever suspicions might have arisen from her mother's bungling, was perfectly gay, sensible, and confiding. They talked about mutual acquaintances, laughed over old times.

"Whatever happened to Angus Grey?" she asked.

"I don't know. The last time I heard of him he was in the Mexican oil fields."

"Bill Forgan told me about the fight you two had. I don't blame you at all. He was a pretty bad egg underneath. And to think I used to be *impressed* by men like that. Seems so long ago." She looked away, adding casually, "I've learned better since."

But she let something else glint through, not enough to disturb, but to be remembered—an accidental pressure of her body against his that a flush or a smile apologized for, a look that changed in mid-career from one of tender adoration to one of good-fellowship. They drank some glasses of punch together. There was a good deal of stick in it, and he suddenly found himself delighted with her, awfully glad they had come—he was having a good time.

"You're losing your clothes again, Nan."

"That darned old shoulder strap," she laughed. "Do you mind fixing it for me, Jare? I think I can find a pin. . . . Not here, silly—out on the veranda where no one will see."

He followed her across the floor. . . . What a body the girl had! In a shadowy corner, she turned her back to him with an embarrassed laugh.

"You see what I mean . . . shorten it a little behind and then pin it just under the edge of the dress. Do you think you can?"

He felt the smoothness of her skin, and recalled a night in June some years ago when they had been alone in her garden. . . . She felt his hand tremble.

"Hurry, Jare . . . please," she said in a faltering whisper.

Then she was once more a good pal, smiling, just a little embarrassed. Later, at her door, he seemed to want to linger, but she did not ask him to stay.

"I've had such fun. Do call in again when you have time. I'm being very domestic these days—hardly ever out. . . . Such fun," she repeated, withdrawing her hand quickly, but almost with a quick caress, from his. And with a little wave she was gone.

He walked back to Tolbecken with fever in his veins. Imagination prolonged it, heightened it, as the days passed. He called the same week and frequently thereafter. But she remained the good, sprightly friend, an ideal companion for the country club or an occasional drive, always beautifully dressed, physically attractive, but making no advances. It touched him that, now and then, when a warmer tone crept into her voice, when her shoulder pressed a little too long against his, she covered it up quickly and with a certain confusion. He could see that Mrs. Oliver had been right, that Nan had taken his proposal more to heart that he had thought, but she was perfectly sensible about it, and did not wish him to know how she felt or attempt to inveigle him. Her behavior showed, instead, a reserve and delicacy which he found admirable. She had changed a great deal during the last four years, he thought.

He was himself to blame, certainly not she, that her shape and movements, certain postures, an accidental carelessness of dress at times exerted an almost hypnotic effect. He condemned himself for this, set his will against it. He had no intention of marrying; he would not call again, must not call when his thoughts degraded her like that. Nonetheless, he continued to dangle; and his fever grew because of her very reticence and natural allure.

"Well," remarked Mrs. Oliver bitterly one day, "I can't see that you're getting anywhere, Frances. Just a lot of icing and no cake. You'll never get married this way."

Since her defeat of a month before, she had remained critically in the background, much given to pursings of the lips, ominous sighs, and head shakings.

"What way?" said Nan.

She was seated at her toilet table, polishing her nails, and now held them up for inspection.

"Why," exclaimed Mrs. Oliver, "I never heard of such a thing! The other evening on the porch, when he crossed over to sit next to you, you stuck in your corner like a *fool*, never gave him an opening, kept talking about the Armstrongs and the Sedleys . . ."

"Listening, were you?"

"I happened to be in the drawing room," said Mrs. Oliver with dignity. "I was shocked. I thought you had some sense about men. But you're either a simp, or you just want to go on hanging around being bridesmaid to all your friends. Don't you know how old you are?"

Nan examined her nails, was satisfied, and gave a pat to her hair.

"Nan, don't you see . . . ?"

"Yes, I *see*. For Pete's sake, Mamma, cut it out. You're a perfect headache. I don't want to talk about it any more, thank you." The sapphire eyes looked steely as Nan swiveled around on her chair.

"You ought to be spanked," blazed Mrs. Oliver.

"Oh, hurry up," Nan directed, "and take a stitch in the waist of my white dress, will you? He'll be here in a few minutes."

"I have already done so, and ironed it," replied her mother. "Where'd you be, if I wasn't forever darning and patching and picking up your things for you?"

She went dutifully to the closet, however, and brought back the dress in question, which Nan proceeded to slip on.

Mrs. Oliver gasped. "But Nan . . ."

"What's the matter now?"

"You've forgotten your corset."

"Don't be so old-fashioned."

She was adjusting her dress in front of the cheval glass.

"You mean to say you're going to a *dance* at the *country* club like *that*? I won't hear of it."

"Don't be a dodo. The smartest girls are doing it everywhere. Dunstable needs to ʷake up."

"What will people think?" protested Mrs. Oliver. "Your papa's position . . . Frances, you must not. I won't have it."

"Piffle! I'd like to see you stop me. You know it looks well."

"I could understand it," continued Mrs. Oliver, weakening a little, "if a girl had a *boyish* figure, but you—and in a dress as snug as that one . . ."

Nan turned from the glass, radiant in the white shimmer of the dress, her hair a pale gold coronal, her eyes vivid jewels, and in the sheer exuberance of self-approval, gave her mother a kiss.

"You do look stunning tonight," glowed Mrs. Oliver completely melted. "But when you're dancing with a man like that . . ."

Her voice died away on a tone not of protest, but of regret—regret of liberties that her own youth had missed. As she admiringly watched Nan moving here and there, collecting her vanity case, her scarf, comprehension began to dawn in Mrs. Oliver's mind. There was no use expressing this even to herself—she remained officially correct—but she felt a vicarious excitement.

"Mind you, I don't *approve*," she went on, "I think it's very *extreme*. But then I suppose you've got to follow the fashions. And I admit it's becoming."

"You're a good sport," declared Nan. "There goes the front doorbell now. So long, Mummie."

They were once more at one by virtue of an intuitive understanding. From above, Mrs. Oliver watched Nan descend the stairs—a descent that grew more deliberate as the front hall came into view—heard the fluted gaiety of her greeting.

Frances Oliver's costume that evening was more than a personal experiment; it denoted symbolically the beginning of a new era. But the Dunstable Country Club did not think in terms of symbols. The young lady made a deep and favorable, though unarticulated, impression on the masculine element, and roused corresponding censure among the ladies. Looks were exchanged and eyebrows raised by matrons whose own daughters would be as corsetless as Nan within a few months.

But to this, Frances herself seemed to be indifferent. She used the confidential style with Jared more innocently than ever, and, of course, could not be expected to read behind his pale dark face and ballroom correctness. She talked among other things about her brother, Jim Oliver, a handsome, blond-haired youth, at that moment leading his partner with the brilliancy of a professional.

"I wish you could do something for him, Jare. He's such a problem. Didn't get through college, you know. And between you and me, he doesn't seem to have any principles." They had stopped for a glass of punch, and stood watching the other dancers. With her shapely hands she smoothed down her dress along the sides. To Jared there was something peculiarly disturbing about those hands, the outstretched fingers.

"What do you think I could do?" he asked.

"See something of him. Your example would help a lot. You've got such a splendid reputation in Dunstable, and he looks up to you. . . . Golly, I've a thirst tonight. Ladle me another glass, won't you, *please?*"

She gave a curious turn to the "please," one of those forgetful notes of tenderness, which she corrected with a smile.

They drank to each other, her eyes on his. And without warning he saw a flicker of invitation in them that tightened the pulses of his forehead.

"God, you're lovely tonight!" he exclaimed.

Once more the outstretched fingers smoothed the sheath of her dress. He refilled their glasses.

"Here's looking at *you.*"

"And you, Jare."

It seemed to him that a cord was being twisted around his head. He went on in a constrained, casual voice.

"It's terribly hot in here, don't you think? How would you like to go outside for a moment?"

"*Love* to, later." There was no question of the casualness in *her* voice. "I've got this next dance with Eaby Ellis. Hello, Tom. Hello, Bill. . . . No, I can't. I promised Eaby. Honest I did. . . ."

Jared walked away. He found himself with Grace Armstrong and mechanically invited her to dance. After Nan, it was like holding some rigid dressmaker's dummy. They were old friends, and she pumped him a little about the masculine reaction to Nan's attire.

"She's awfully popular tonight."

"Always has been, hasn't she?"

Actually he was wondering whether they would stroll together outside, and if so, what then? His pulses went on throbbing. Nan swept past, vivid, lithe, intoxicating.

"Yes, but especially tonight," urged Grace. "I suppose you men find her especially attractive tonight."

"What do you mean?"

"Oh, well, if you haven't noticed anything . . ."

"I don't understand."

Grace knew he was lying, but did not particularly care. She had been answered, anyway, by the mothlike gyrations of the men around Nan. She felt deeply shocked, as she kept telling herself, that the daughter of a minister should dress like that, and was all the more shocked upon reflecting that her own plumpness made it inexpedient to follow Nan's example. It was as if the latter had taken a mean advantage, had broken a time-honored treaty that gave all girls equal chances up to a point. Perhaps, thought Grace, if she dieted, it might be possible. She resolved to try. But meanwhile it wasn't very nice or respectable.

To Jared, the dance seemed endless. Why did the orchestra have to keep it up forever? But when it was over, he did not seek out Nan or wait for her. One of those languid moods, when a man, tired of a dilemma, leaves the decision to the toss of a coin, had stolen over him. He walked out on the half-deserted veranda, lit a cigarette, and stood gazing off at the Delaware, which bordered that side of the golf course. Under a full moon, its expanse shaded from vivid silver to misty grey, a pavement of light untroubled by the warm south wind breathing from the sea. If Nan did not come out, well and good. At least, he would not pursue her. That was one face of the penny. If she joined him, it was the other face. But instinctively he knew what would happen. Something deep in his consciousness kept pounding, slow and heavy like the beat of an advancing drum. He could not think at all for the quiver of it, could only feel its approach.

"What a heavenly evening, Jare!"

"Isn't it! Shall we walk down to the river?"

"Yes, let's," she answered. "I'm tired of dancing."

It seemed to him that they were reciting words learned by heart, composed by someone else, as if they were figures in a play already written and remaining only to be acted. It belonged equally to the stage directions that they should turn right from the club and follow a path through the pines leading to the river. It belonged to the same directions that they should meet several couples, exchange greetings, and stroll on. Then they were alone, and the beat of the drum was closer. They came to a preordained path, a smaller one, branching further to the right.

"There's a little sand beach down yonder," he said. "Have you ever been there? It's quite shut in by the pines."

"No. What fun! Do show me."

A hundred yards brought them to a steep bank above the sand of the cove.

"I can't," she objected. "I'm in dancing slippers and I'm wearing my best dress. It would be ruined."

"I'll carry you," he answered, though he could hardly hear his own voice above the thunder of the drum. "Will you let me?"

"Of course, Jare."

When he had brought her to the beach, she stood a moment, smoothing down her dress and smiling up at him. Then he took her once more in his arms.

*   *   *

It was late when they drove back. "We ought to be married soon, Jare—" her head pressed against his shoulder—"not later than the early fall. What do you think?"

"You know it's for you to decide," he answered.

Thus reassured, Nan went on. "I'd like to announce our engagement at once. I'm so proud of it, I can't wait to tell. Do you mind?"

"Of course not. I'll let my family know tomorrow."

He would not have drawn back now, even if it had been

178

honorably possible. Desire is not the same thing as love, but at times it is hard to distinguish between them.

"Darling!" she said proudly.

As luck would have it, the Olivers were still up when they reached the house. There were lights in the study. The reverend doctor, of whom it could not be said that indolence was one of his defects, sat working over next Sunday's sermon. His wife, with the intention of waylaying Nan when she got back, dozed on the sofa; but at the sound of footsteps on the porch she was wideawake. Then her heart beat a little faster. Instead of whispering good nights outside, they had entered the hall, were approaching the study door. With the quickness of intuition common to mothers, she guessed that it could mean only one thing, and answered the knock with her sweetest tone of voice.

"Come in, dear."

A glance at Nan told her what had happened, though she would not have permitted herself to guess beyond a certain point.

"I hope you'll forgive my intruding like this," Jared was saying, "but the fact is . . . in short, Nan has consented to marry me, and we both wanted you to know at once."

"My dear fellow!" exclaimed Cary Oliver, glowing like a harvest moon. "My dear fellow!" He was in his shirt sleeves, but to honor the occasion, slipped on his coat. "I'm de-lighted, delighted!"

Mrs. Oliver folded Jared and then Nan to her bosom. The glance of mother to daughter expressed with the quickness of light a number of things—pride, praise, comprehension, the deference due to talent, and hallelujah.

"This is a very beautiful, a very sacred moment for me," she said. "I feel, as Shakespeare says, that God's in his heaven and everything's all right. It's a very sweet sentiment, isn't it?"

"Browning," said Dr. Oliver, "and misquoted, but I agree. In honor of these dear young people, I shall introduce those verses into my next sermon." And more jocularly, "Now that you're in the family, Jared, I'm afraid you'll have to lead that Bible class. . . ."

It was only when he was back at last in his room at Tolbecken, and even the echoes of the drum had died away, that Jared could look at himself in the mirror which his restored sense of reality held up. He was not so much of a hypocrite that he could go on indefinitely confusing love and lust. There was no use dishing up for himself way-of-the-

179

world arguments spiced with biology. As he looked around the familiar room, he would not admit, but still realized that he had sold incalculable values, and had mortgaged others, for a mess of pottage. He and the Tolbecken tradition had failed each other at every point except one: at least he would not attempt to go back on the bargain.

Pausing in front of his desk, he took up a letter which he had begun that afternoon to Clarice, and reread it—it presented a flattering portrait of himself, as he wished her to think of him, as an intellectual, something of an idealist, above all as a gentleman. With a grimace of disgust, he tore the paper into shreds and tossed it into the wastebasket.

32

The news fell upon the ladies at Tolbecken like a thunderbolt, leaving desolation behind it, and a sense of doom. Mrs. Tolbecken and Joan Maylin suspected that he had been victimized by an arrant piece of matchmaking; they saw through Mrs. Oliver and Nan with perfect ease; but in their veteran wisdom they perceived equally that nothing could now be gained and much could be lost by hard words. Above everything else—disappointment, disapproval, apprehension—the family must hold together.

Of course, if the match had been disgraceful, they would have opposed it valiantly for Jared's sake; but they had nothing tangible to urge. Nan Oliver had been fashionably educated, she was the daughter of a leading clergyman in the state, and a noted beauty. They were perfectly aware that no one in town would criticize such a marriage. What they feared were precisely those essential, personal factors which in the circumstances could no longer be discussed.

Judge Tolbecken, however, actively approved. He got up from his chair, and putting his arm around Jared's shoulders, gave him a hug.

"I'm delighted, sir," he exclaimed heartily. "Frances Oliver is the handsomest young woman in Dunstable. A most engaging young woman! I declare that I'm half in love with her myself. It gives me the greatest satisfaction, Jared. I shall make a point of calling on her and Mrs. Oliver at once."

And to the ladies in conclave afterward, "I never knew a

girl yet that the women of her future husband's family didn't pick to pieces. You women violate the first principle of law by considering a girl guilty until she is proved innocent. As for me, I think she's an uncommon fine young woman."

"I hope you're right," observed Mrs. Tolbecken, intent on her crochet, "but right or wrong, we'll have to make the best of it."

Aunt Joan did not listen to the Judge's defense of his favorite. As he talked, her square face took on a squarer cast. She was becoming convinced that she had one last duty to perform at this point, an unpleasant duty; but she was not one to dodge an issue. In the end, she got up and walked out of the room as if on some household errand, for she did not wish to make a point to the others of the talk she planned with Jared. He had given them the news in the late afternoon, and had then withdrawn to get ready for supper. Knocking brusquely at his door, she entered to find him seated in a chair next the window. One glance at her face warned him that he had not altogether escaped the ordeal he had feared.

She came to the point with customary bluntness, after seating herself opposite him. He thought not irrelevantly of Gibraltar.

"I hope you realize by this time," she said, "that I love you."

"I'd be pretty dumb if I didn't, Aunt Joan."

"Well, then, you ought to know that the questions I'm going to ask you are for your own good and the family's—but principally your good. Do you love Miss Oliver?"

"I wouldn't have asked her to marry me if I didn't, would I?" he evaded.

"That's not answering my question."

"All right. Of course I do." He felt small and unreal before the keen old eyes and stern lips that concealed so much tenderness. "Why do you ask?" he added to cover his confusion.

"Because men very often ask girls whom they don't love to marry them. As an example, you don't have to look any farther than your own parents. Your father *thought* he loved your mother. The fact is she set her cap for him and flattered him. I've never talked to you like this before, and I wouldn't now, if I didn't think it was necessary. But there's no use being sentimental even about the dead. He married her—and you know what came of it."

His position was too weak for an answer to this. It seemed to him that he did not have even the usual choice between truth and pretense. To tell Joan Maylin that he had seduced

Nan and must now make it good by marriage, that in spite of his rationalizing he knew perfectly well that he did not love her in the sense that his aunt used the word was unthinkable. He dared not expose his weakness, defeat, and bewilderment to the people who idolized him. On Nan's account as well as his own, pretense was the only wise, the only possible thing.

"And who suffered?" she went on. "They did, of course; but I wonder if we didn't suffer more—especially your grandfather. That's the trouble with a sham, even if it's unconscious. It festers, spreads, works itself out in suffering somewhere—usually for a lot of people. That's one of the facts of life that we always try to get away from and never do. If you and Nan really love each other, if you're sure of it, I'd be the last person on earth to interfere. But if you're not sure, if there's any other reason"—Aunt Joan looked at him steadily—"it'll be a bad match, Jared. And don't think for a moment that you and she will be the only ones to pay. The rest of us who care for you will have to do a great deal of the paying."

He stared at her, daunted. "Come," she seemed to be saying to him, "show yourself as you actually are, not as we believed you to be, our paragon and pride. Show yourself beneath the level even of the ordinary young fellows we used to contrast you with. Oh, you orator on the education of youth, you distinguished young man! Here lies your only way of escape—by the Valley of Humiliation." What she actually said, having laid one of her gnarled old hands on his knee, was: "You'll forgive me, won't you, Jare?"

Then he made his decision, out of respect for everyone but himself and his own pride. He had no right to destroy their opinion of him. He had no right to let a breath of suspicion fall on Nan. There was no use making a tragedy out of it; few marriages were perfect anyhow. And if a mistake had been made, it was exclusively his and Nan's affair. He did not choose to believe in vicarious atonement.

"I really don't know what the fuss is about," he answered, working up a little anger. "I know you and the family don't like Nan . . ."

"That has nothing to do with it," put in his aunt sharply. "The point is whether you love her."

"I've told you I do," said Jared, "and I repeat it."

Aunt Joan got up, her face somber.

"That's all I wanted to know," she answered, shaking her head, "and that's all I wanted you to know. To tell you the truth, I don't believe you. But I've said my say. From now on, I'll not mention it to you or anyone else again."

He began to protest, but she would not listen. "I've told you what I thought," she repeated. "You must do what you think best." And added, "Now, hurry up; don't be late for supper."

Then she marched sturdily to the door and went out.

So on the whole his engagement passed muster with the family more easily than he had expected. Where it fared worse was with himself—the necessity of explaining it over and over to his own mind, the shadow of derogation that clung to him, the tendency to drug his thought with desire and call it love.

But the real test came when he set himself to write about it to Clarice. Suddenly it seemed to him ghastly in its commonplaceness. Thought drifted away to haunt the one memorable episode of his life. Yes, he had had his glimpse of Arcadia before the gates were closed. Until recently he had had the right to dream of it. Now, the sooner he forgot, the better. It startled him when the pen he held snapped between his hands. Finally, he wrote a constrained statement, praised Nan briefly, and let it go at that. He could not help adding: *You won't stop writing, Clarice? Your letters will mean as much to me now as ever—perhaps more.*

He could not know how much she would be able to read between the words.

33

"We're in luck," confided Nan several weeks later. "We can take our time about the wedding, darling—not that I want to. But it's nice not to be hurried." She smiled her demure smile, looked beguilingly embarrassed and fitted herself into the curve of his arm.

"Mummie believes that it ought to be in October," she went on. "That'll give me just time enough for the invitations and trousseau."

Indeed, Mrs. Oliver, mindful of the adage about the cup and the lip, resolved to take no chances. Autumn, she insisted, was the best season in the year for weddings.

"There's splendid weather at first," she declared, "and after that it's so cozy in one's own little nest."

183

When she talked about little nests, she used an ecstatic soft note that made Jared wince.

"Don't you think so, Jare?"

"Yes, very pleasant."

"Then *that's* settled," beamed Mrs. Oliver.

But one or two things hung fire. Nan pouted a little to her family at the idea of living at Tolbecken, which she described as antediluvian, but she was secretly flattered by the prospect of ruling—for she intended to rule—that historic mansion. When she called on Grandmother and Aunt Joan, her eyes roved a bit, and once she asked Jared to show her over the house, and spent an absorbed half-hour dreaming of removing partitions, replumbing, redecorating, cashiering old furniture, and generally renovating, at an approximate cost of at least twenty-five thousand dollars.

"Spying out the land," smiled Aunt Joan, listening to the footsteps overhead.

"Yes," said Grandmother, "but she has a surprise coming."

For that evening Rachel Tolbecken absolutely refused to consider living under the same roof with her.

"I'm an old woman," she remarked, "and I don't intend to be disturbed in my habits. Neither does Joan. Jared and Frances must have a separate establishment."

"But Rachel . . ." protested the Judge.

"No," maintained Grandmother, "I mean it. Young people have to solve their own problems, and on the other hand, I won't have them interfering with mine. I'd do anything in the world for Jare's real benefit, but there's nothing sillier than weak self-sacrifice. There's no use talking about it, Rufus, I'm going to have my say in this."

Naturally the Manse felt hurt and in its own privacy talked with indignation about spoiled old women with one foot in the grave; but Nan consoled herself easily enough by making plans for a fine house on the Ridge. There were several furnished houses to be rented at about three hundred dollars a month, until they could have Tolbecken, and one—the one Nan pined to have—at four. The real-estate agents treated her like a queen.

"Before you get in too deep," said Dr. Oliver, "you'd better find out what Jared can afford."

"He's so vague about money," complained Nan. "He said he thought perhaps the four-hundred-dollar one would be all right, but he would have to ask Grandfather. Papa darling, don't you think you could talk to him about it?"

Dr. Oliver agreed. He thought it was high time they knew

something definite about his future son-in-law's prospects, and he did not feel quite as sanguine as Nan about the four-hundred-dollar house. He broached the matter over a cigar in his study, when Jared dined with them a day or so later.

"By the way," he asked jovially, "where are you going to live next winter? Nan has set her heart on the Cummings house."

"Rather high rental," murmured Jared.

"Exactly. I say so too. But it all depends on your income." The query in Oliver's tone could not be evaded.

"At present," said Jared, "I'm on a salary basis." He did not think it necessary to add that this was two hundred dollars a month, and that for the first year out of law school, it represented a good deal more than he actually earned. "But," he went on, "in view of my marriage, Grandfather has promised to take me into partnership with him this autumn on a basis of fifty per cent."

"Very generous," approved Oliver, "very generous indeed! You ought to have at least two thousand dollars a month to afford the Cummings house. I assume that your share in the practice will easily exceed that figure."

"I haven't the faintest idea," said Jared.

"What! Do you mean that you don't know what your income will be?"

"No, I don't. Grandfather never told me, and I haven't liked to ask him."

"I see."

Dr. Oliver began to think about unhatched chickens and birds in the bush. He liked to deal in certainties. "Well," he observed, "don't you believe, in view of your marriage, that you'd better discuss finances with the Judge? I don't want to seem intrusive—far from it!—but you and Nan won't be able to live on love."

But when Jared, having nerved himself to the point of approaching his grandfather on the subject, put in a question or two, he was met with a vague "We'll see" and "Plenty of time to think about that," which left him more at a loss than ever. Although he was aware of a decline in their way of living, he had only a nebulous idea of the family resources and even about the earnings of the firm. There was less business than he had expected, but there still seemed to be a good deal. He did not know how unremunerative most of that was. Partly from pride, partly from an inherent reluctance to discuss his personal finances, Rufus Tolbecken had put off the evil day of admitting his weakness. As they had never talked about money before, Jared had no precedents to go on. He had always been generously supplied with whatever sums he needed. The condition of being well off seemed to belong to the Tolbecken status, and not even the Olivers had taken it more for granted than did he. But on one point the Judge was definite enough.

"Four hundred dollars a month for rent!" he exclaimed with a flash of anger. "Absolute nonsense! You must tell Frances to get that out of her head at once. Even if you could afford it—which you certainly cannot—no young couple should start life on a scale like that. It's pretentious and unseemly. A hundred dollars a month will be your outside limit, and I'm not sure . . . well, we'll see. We'll have to go slow. There's no hurry."

"A hundred dollars a month!" exclaimed Nan later with equal vehemence. "I never heard of such a thing! What *do* you mean—that we should live in some horrid little unfashionable shack? Jare, dearest, you wouldn't ask me to do that?"

He argued that there were a number of perfectly adequate houses at that price even on the Ridge itself, and that if they could afford nothing better, they would have to put up with it. She looked and felt on the point of tears. The galleon she had brought to port was beginning to turn out a dud.

Like many another prominent family, the Tolbeckens were supposed locally to possess at least ten times as much wealth as they actually had. It was this reputation that had whetted Mrs. Oliver's eagerness when the pursuit of Jared had first been launched, and her triumph when it was brought to a successful conclusion. To be dashed suddenly from such heights seemed intolerable.

"I won't believe it!" she exclaimed. "It's just plain, ordinary closeness."

"I'm not so sure," demurred Cary Oliver. "You can see that Tolbecken itself is in need of repairs. Perhaps I ought to have looked into this before . . ."

"You certainly ought to have," cut in his wife, glad of a scapegoat.

Cold silence fell in the drawing room, while Mrs. Oliver, her husband, and daughter stared into space. With the singular unity that characterized them, they were all thinking along the same line, though convention forbade expressing it. On their side as well, the marriage was beginning to look like a mess of pottage, and they weighed the expediency of escape.

"Perhaps," said Mrs. Oliver at length, with strained casualness, "the wedding might be put off awhile—until later in the winter, that is, or even next spring. You were invited to the Kirklands' at Tuxedo in November, before this came up. Do you think Jared would mind waiting?"

But Nan had a profound sense of reality.

"I don't believe it would work," she replied. "That is, if we really expect to get married."

As if it had been put into so many words, her mother understood the gist of Nan's remark perfectly. Jared would not mind waiting—not in the least. That was the trouble. She heaved a sigh.

At times like these the family looked to Cary Oliver to express the common conviction.

"What's your idea, Papa?" Mrs. Oliver asked.

Dr. Oliver put on his pulpit expression. "I was just about to give my opinion. It seems to me that in Nan's perhaps legitimate disappointment we have been forgetting other factors than mere wealth—far higher factors. Haven't we been forgetting romance, the love of these two young people for each other?"

"That's true," nodded Mrs. Oliver piously.

Nan lit a cigarette, and stared at the ceiling.

"Haven't we been forgetting," continued Dr. Oliver, "that love often means sacrifice nobly, gladly endured? That's true romance, *Christian* romance."

"Yes, Papa," agreed his helpmate, "I guess you're right. But I hope Jared has the sense to realize what Nan is doing for him. I think you ought to make him understand that, Nan."

The latter, exhaling gently, smiled.

It was unfortunate that Jared could not have overheard this conversation. But echoes of it, at least, filtered through. From that time on he was not worshiped quite as much at the manse. He began to hear a great deal about the Forgan millions. Subtly and to various tunes, it was borne in on him that he ought to be humbly appreciative of Nan's sacrifice to love in a cottage, when she might have had a mansion. Mrs. Oliver no longer wore her best dresses when he came to dinner. But a certain masterful and incalculable quality in him restrained this process a little; unconsciously they stood in awe of him.

"What was the name of William's yacht?" reflected Mrs. Oliver on one unpleasant occasion. "The *Daphne* or *Diana* or something? Must be a floating palace. He wanted to rechristen it the *Frances*."

187

She had discussed the Forgan house on Fifth Avenue, the Forgan shooting estate in Florida, the Forgan villa at Newport. Jared looked up.

"He calls her the *Patricia* now."

Mrs. Oliver sagged a bit. "Yes, poor William! He married a Patricia Gale. But how did you know about the name of the yacht?"

"We were rather chummy in college," Jared explained. "We happened to meet the other day in Philadelphia, and talked about various things."

He did not add that Forgan had taken too much to drink and talked very freely indeed.

But to Nan, when they were alone, he said, "I think I'll ask you to drop the subject of Bill Forgan."

"Why?"

"Because forever talking about what a man owns seems to me rather ill bred."

"Jealous, darling?" she flushed.

"No," he returned in an odd voice, "not jealous."

A girl less adroit than Nan would have blundered at this point. Instead she began to wonder about that conversation in Philadelphia, and guessed that she could not afford to make a scene.

"Bill always was something of a rotter," she remarked.

"Yes, I think he is."

"Well, then, let's forget him."

Snuggling close, she appealed to him with her lips and eyes. The crisis passed, but after an anxious tête-à-tête with her mother, the Forgan millions were withdrawn from conversation.

34

Meanwhile, the Olivers, Jared, and everyone else concerned in the forthcoming marriage speculated on Judge Tolbecken's curious silence. It was unlike him to be enigmatical and reserved in his own family. He had taken to spending longer hours in his office or behind the doors of his study; or he rambled alone through the garden. He seemed to be avoiding Jared, and when they were together, sat lost in thought. An unwonted impatience would break out if anyone questioned him, and Grandmother, terrified, reported that at night when he thought she was asleep, he would get up and sit looking out of the window. "What on earth is the trouble?" she demanded. But he put her off. Actually he was engaged in the supreme struggle of his life.

During these days he thought more than once of his letter to Jared urging the profession of law as a career. "I talked him into it," he muttered, "on the pretext of making a living. What kind of a living! A young man has the right to think that he'll be able to support a wife. I asked him to give up what he wanted to do, and now I'm to tell him that he can't get married! That's not fair. I won't stand in his light. I won't have him waiting for me to die."

Or he consulted his ledger. "Fifty per cent of the practice!" he thought. "What's that figure down to? Fifteen hundred—two thousand a year, perhaps. The boy can't live on that."

Or at the bank he counted over the depleted securities in his safe-deposit box. "If I died tomorrow, he wouldn't have enough to support a wife and keep the property, not to speak of providing for Rachel and Joan. He'd have to go on using the capital or sell the place."

Everything led back to that; turn as he might, the sale of Tolbecken seemed to present the only solution. Daily, hourly, whether he closed his eyes to it or not, he confronted the possibility which seemed to have become a necessity. It stalked at his side as he walked, through the clamor of the crowded streets, about the sagging fence of his domain. It peered over his shoulder at the pages of the ledger. It grinned at him in his clientless office. It mocked him on his turns through the garden. And opposed to it stood love—love of every inch, of every stone, shrub, tree, blemish or beauty of his home. Wealth, pride, consequence in the world were slipping away from him, slipping through his fingers. And in the background stood death.

If Jared waited—well, perhaps by some miracle of success at law the place might be saved, but probably at the cost of everything—his youth, his marriage. No! The Judge would not accept that. Sometimes he thought weakly that if he could only be allowed to die where he had lived, that would be enough. But he would have no premium set on his death. The sale of Tolbecken, and that only, would solve everything. It would provide for Jared's marriage. It would compensate for the nakedness of the practice that pride had so far led him to conceal. It was the only just, the only wise thing to do. But he still shrank from the knife at his heart. He could not

189

discuss it with his family. He wanted no suggestions, no sympathy, no babying. His struggle went too deep for that. Above all he would ask no favors or advice. He had always managed his own affairs and he would manage them to the end. Days came and went; he knew that escape was impossible; but still he lingered on, struggling, brooding.

There was one palliation on the other side. Having reached the point of admitting that the place would eventually have to be sold, he warmed himself with the thought of Jared's happiness, grew a bit sentimental over Nan, and cherished the idea that he might live to see their children. He believed in young marriages and in young love. The thought of giving Jared such a boon softened his sense of the sacrifice. In the end it was this that turned the scales. The simplicity of old age blinded him to much that might not have escaped him thirty years earlier.

He realized that if Jared suspected such a motive for the sale of Tolbecken, he would oppose it; in any case he would feel to blame. He must not know, therefore, however much he might guess at it later on, when the poverty of the practice could no longer be kept from him. It would be too late for objections then; he would be married and happy. Rufus Tolbecken disliked the idea of any fanfare of martyrdom. He would announce the sale to the family as a *fait accompli* to which he had been forced for strictly business reasons. The idea of his having to reconcile Jared to the loss of the property afforded him a certain bitter amusement.

No one saw him that morning when he gave a final nod at the empty desk in his office, reached for his hat and cane, and stumped down the stairs, a beaten man. But in the struggle with time he was not altogether beaten. He retained something that not even time could destroy.

Karl Kirschbaum did not haggle at the Judge's terms of three hundred thousand dollars. No doubt he saw the uselessness of haggling, but beyond that, there was a solemnity about the supreme deal of his life that he did not care to cheapen.

"I can regard the matter as closed then?" asked the Judge.

"You can, sir. I consider the property worth your figure."

"The fellow's almost a gentleman," thought Rufus Tolbecken. He sat a moment looking across the room. Then he held out his hand. "You've won, Mr. Kirschbaum. Let me tell you that I never thought you would."

"And let me tell you, Judge, that in a way I'm right sorry."

But when his caller had left, it may be forgiven the real-estate man that his gaze sought the pink map opposite with its green, stubborn eye. On an impulse, he tipped up his red-ink bottle, extracted the cork, and shambling over to the wall, smeared out the green circle of Tolbecken. The new Dunstable was complete.

"Did my marriage have anything to do with this?" asked Jared that evening, when the first excitement of the news had passed.

"It did not," returned the Judge, in one of the few deliberate equivocations of his life. "Whether you married or not, it would have been the same. It was time that made it necessary to sell Tolbecken—time alone."

35

To Jared, the sale of the property meant a revolution so complete that he could not grasp it all at once. The bitterness of it kept filtering through his consciousness for the rest of the summer. He felt that he ought to have been consulted, or at least warned, and even his grandfather's assurances, coupled with those of Aunt Joan, that it was the only sensible course to have taken left him unconvinced. The sale of the place had been mooted from time to time ever since he could remember, but only as an unlikely possibility, and he felt, not without reason, that if affairs had reached the pass where a sale became necessary, he should not have been allowed to live in a fool's paradise.

Hitherto, he had belonged not to Dunstable but to Tolbecken. From the humdrum routine of law school or office, he had been able to return to an aristocratic world of his own; now the entire background of his life, which had seemed so permanent, was splintering down like old hoarding. Hereafter he would belong only to Dunstable.

Drop by drop, the significance of the change filtered through. Local newspapers featured the news of the sale on their front pages. Reviews appeared of the history of Tolbecken and of the visits there of famous men; it was lyrically compared with Mount Vernon, Monticello, and the White House. The whole town sighed over its passing with windy sentimentality. Then, too, there were exaggerated reports of its price—from eight hundred thousand up to a million and a half. For if Tolbecken had to go, it would be creditable to everybody to have it go for a great sum. The Judge, already rich in the popular imagination, became a magnate. For several weeks, Jared could not open a newspaper without the extent or the irony of his loss being thrown in his face.

Or he would come back from his office through the streets —smell of coal smoke, factory chimneys, motors, trucks, and tram cars, advertisements on billboards and posters—to his room at the house with its old mahogany four-poster bed, its pictures and bookshelves, the soft light distilled through the elm leaves at its windows. And he would reflect that very soon this refuge would cease to exist for him, that he would never enter these doors again—indeed that the doors themselves, the stately house and garden would be blotted from the faces of the earth, would be as insubstantial as memory, as a dream.

He felt the beginning of disintegration in the family as well. When the Reigers or the Vincent Tolbeckens called, their attitude toward the old people was not quite as deferential as it had formerly been. The estate had represented a fortune; sold and divided, it no longer inspired the reverence due to possessions. It was one thing to be Rufus Tolbecken of Tolbecken, and quite another to be Rufus Tolbecken who might be living anywhere. He was still beloved, but no longer essential; in fact, if not in sentiment, he had become negligible.

Of the proceeds of the sale, one hundred and fifty thousand had been settled on Jared, so that he came in also for a certain amount of envy. It had long since been understood that he would inherit the homestead, and each of the Judge's children had already been provided for; moreover, at the Judge's death they would share in his remaining assets; but it chafed them that one grandchild only should profit at this time by a transaction which implied a loss for them all. For, as long-accepted things are taken for granted and their value minimized until they are gone, so Tolbecken, which, in family criticism of the Judge, had been called a white elephant, began to grow in importance. They remembered the entertainments and receptions that had been held there. The rooms became more spacious as they thought of them. They discovered that the house was a manor, "a regular château," which had practically been given away for three hundred thousand dollars. None of them felt quite the same assurance as before. Mary wife of plebeian Albert; Vincent, drudging in his cage at the bank, had each enjoyed the consolation of a private hauteur at the thought of Tolbecken, the palpable evidence of their gentility. Now they were down on a level with everybody else. And in exchange for this no one but Jared was to receive anything. By degrees, the remembrance of the taxes, the up-keep, the Judge's failing income, even their own persuasions to sell faded out and were eclipsed by the conviction of Jared's selfishness. They did not openly reproach him—they even forgave him—but he was to blame nevertheless. He had shown himself just a bit disloyal.

"You're a very lucky boy," said Aunt Mary. "Your marriage ought to be a success, when a place like ours had to go into the making of it."

"But Grandfather assures me that my marriage has nothing to do with the sale."

"I hope you don't believe that, Jare."

So that in addition to everything else, he had the misery of learning that his affair with Nan had been sealed at this cost to the family as well as himself; while on the other side, Nan pouted at the slender income they would have, scoffed at the poor little hundred-dollar-a-month house they rented, and felt herself generally ill used.

The work of moving and the decisions to be made now fell, of course, to Joan Maylin's share. Rooted in her philosophy of seeing things as they were, she showed a hard front to the plaintive Mrs. Vincent and Mrs. Albert, scolded them when they shook their heads about Jared, talked of spilled milk when they gloomed over Tolbecken, and utterly routed any attempt of theirs to dictate to her. But at dead of night, she kept vigil with her own thoughts. She had reached the age of little sleep, and would sit for hours looking out the window into the darkness, or, huddled in her wrapper beneath the lamp, would turn the pages of her heavy old Bible. As she had bade farewell to so much and so many that she had loved, she now bade farewell to the house she had tended for forty years. Wiser than the others, she realized it had to be, for life had taught her the necessity of renunciation, and that all things are given only on loan.

The colors of thought subdued by age may be more ex-quisite than those of the hopes of youth. Direct and dauntless spirit that she was, she sighed a bit over her vanished world —she had been proud of Tolbecken—but unafraid she awaited the future, and faced the situation realistically.

It was she who decided where the Judge and her sister should move in the autumn. There was a new apartment building on Elm Street with an elevator, hot-water heating,

193

good janitor service, and a southern exposure. It had baths communicating with the bedrooms, cement and hard-wood floors, garbage chutes, and up-to-date kitchenettes. Her practical soul reveled in these details. She chose an apartment with four bedrooms (one as a den for the Judge), a parlor, a dining and a servant's room. Outside and inside the building looked modern, impersonal, and efficient.

"There's no use taking a house," she argued in private conference with Rachel Tolbecken. "It couldn't replace this one, anyway, and would be a lot more trouble and expense. In a flat there're no stairs to go up and down, no furnaces to tend, and there's hot water handy in case of sickness. Besides," she added with characteristic Maylin frankness, "it can't be for very long, and a flat's as good to die in as a house, and more convenient."

To this her sister agreed, and they began sounding the Judge.

"A flat on Elm Street?" he mused.

"Yes, in that new building, you know—the one Mr. Kirschbaum put up."

"Oh, yes, that one."

"Though of course," continued Aunt Joan, "there's the house on North Street I told you about. It's a block nearer your office and the rent's not much more."

"That's true," said the Judge.

"But *I* advise the flat. No repairs and more comfortable all round."

"That's true," said the Judge.

"When would you like to look it over? We shouldn't put it off. . . . I said, when would you like to go there with me?"

"Where?"

"Why, the flat. Rufus, you haven't been listening to a word I've said. Aren't you interested in where you're going to live?"

The old man roused himself. "Pardon me, Joan. I was a little preoccupied. No, I'm not interested really. You and Rachel decide. Any place will do. But if you want, I'll go around with you this afternoon."

And later he followed the agent and his sister-in-law through the apartment, was shown bathrooms and kitchenette, inspected the naked bedroom destined as his study, agreed that the view southward was pretty fine. "No, Judge, I don't mean from here," said the agent, steering him from a contemplation of distant warehouses. "If you'll just stand to the side and crane your neck a little, you'll be able to see the trees along the river. There you are, sir."

194

"I don't believe," said Aunt Joan to her sister afterwards, "that he paid the slightest attention to anything."

He spent a great deal of time in the garden that summer, drifting here and there, and to the outrage of the thrifty, especially Dr. Oliver, he made a considerable outlay on the upkeep of lawns and hedges. "He's diddering," said Oliver. Aunt Joan herself ventured a timid objection, but a look silenced her. He liked directing the men he employed at their cutting, trimming, and weeding. Not in years had the grounds of Tolbecken looked so green, cool, and pleasant as they did just then.

But he was whimsical in his gardening. Once Jared, to please him, did some work around the roses that had languished recently and stood in need of tending.

"I'd rather you didn't," said the Judge, coming up. "They'll die this winter. I've a fancy they'd rather die here and not be pulled up by the roots."

It was a restless summer for everyone. By the terms of the sale, the house was to be handed over on September 15. Meanwhile, room by room and in the attic, Joan Maylin sifted the accumulated possessions. Indifferently the Judge left it to her and Jared. Old bundles of correspondence came to light, autograph albums, keepsakes, cotillion programs, broken toys, photographs and daguerreotypes of dimly remembered persons in once-elegant costumes, silken ball slippers, broken fans, canceled checks. Back of the stable a fire smoldered all day long. Aunt Joan, making short work of sentiment, called it the funeral pyre; but she sighed often enough before tossing this or that into the condemned hamper.

And gradually the house took on a gaunt and alien aspect. Rugs stood corded in bundles, bookshelves gaped empty, boxes cluttered the floors, patches on the walls replaced the well-known pictures, the furniture was allocated to various members of the family. The apartment on Elm Street would hold only a fraction of the family chattels. Everyone was considerate, of course; but such a division invariably hurts somebody's feelings. Mrs. Albert wanted the highboy in the northeast bedroom and had to put up with the dresser; Mrs. Vincent felt that she might have been given the colonial cupboard and sofa. Nan Oliver hoped that Jared would insist on his rights, especially to the Chippendale set she coveted. "You're too modest, darling," she complained. There were strains and stresses here and there. Altogether, it was an uneasy, feverish summer.

At last the moving began.

"Why don't you go away, Rufus?" begged Aunt Joan, alive to what this would mean to him. "You haven't had any vacation at all this year and now's the time to take it. You'll only be in the way hanging around. There's Senator Brooks, who has invited you to visit him in West Virginia goodness knows how often. We'll pack your bag for you, and you go and get a good change for two weeks. We'll be settled by then. You can come straight back to the flat. Perhaps you could take Jared along with you," she added as an inducement.

The Judge hesitated a moment, his gaze on the naked walls of the drawing room. Huddled in forlorn groups, chairs and tables seemed to have resigned their functions; they suggested nothing familiar or livable.

"Do as I tell you," coaxed Aunt Joan.

"No," he said, "I think I'll stand by."

She protested for form's sake; but she understood and secretly approved. It would not do for Rufus Tolbecken not to be present at the surrender of his house or to evade the final gesture.

So he stood by while vans backed up to the steps and sweaty movers scuffled and grunted through the halls, hustling the forlorn furniture out. It looked unexpectedly shabby and decrepit, stacked in the vans in broad daylight. He saw the bed his mother had used, where in far-off days he had cuddled to sleep in her arms, tossed up piecemeal. He saw the table, around which so many joyous gatherings had been held in the long dining room, hauled out to the tune of jokes and grunts. He saw the velvet armchair from the drawing room, the tall clock from the landing, which had ticked out the annals of a century, carried down the steps and away. Each article had its history, its inexpressible memories. He saw his life bundled out and stood impassive, or with a stern "Be careful of that" supplemented Aunt Joan's entreaties.

Finally, the house being gutted, he walked with her and Jared through the naked rooms to see that all had been taken. None of them spoke. Their footsteps rang vacantly along the floors. At last, on the outer threshold, he stood for a minute looking back, then closed the front door, locked it, and supporting himself on his cane, descended the steps.

He handed the key to an agent from the real-estate office who had been waiting.

"Everything's in order, I think. My compliments to Mr. Kirschbaum."

The four of them moved slowly down the driveway between new-cut lawns, crossed by the afternoon shadows of

196

the elms. A stillness had fallen on the place, that strange stillness of abandonment.

"It's a fine property, Judge," piped the agent. But Rufus Tolbecken merely nodded and walked on.

His wife, already installed in her chair at the apartment, greeted him briefly.

"Well, then," she said, "it's over?"

"Yes," he answered, "it's over."

36

The wedding of Frances Oliver and Jared Tolbecken took place at the North Street Church on October 5. The bride's father performed the ceremony, her brother gave her away, and all the notables of Dunstable, with a sprinkling from other cities, looked on. Afterwards there was a mammoth reception at the manse, with salad, ices, wedding cake, and punch.

Even Nan agreed that she had done fairly well in the matter of wedding gifts. Of a thousand invitations, approximately two hundred had yielded something. In private the tribute, as it came in, had been shrewdly appraised and its adequacy passed on; but no one could accuse her of being unappreciative in public.

As for the bride herself, all that art and nature could supply had been delivered. Her beauty, vivid and emphatic, overshadowed the bridesmaids'. The *point de Venise* of her gown had cost Dr. Oliver his next year's increase of salary. Her complexion still had the glow of eighteen; her full lips were still delicate. Her triumph was unquestioned.

The bridegroom, in his role of impresario to the prima donna, looked well too—a regular Tolbecken, people observed, with his wide forehead, dark eyes, and somewhat stern, angular face. He stood half a head taller than Nan, herself well grown; they made a distinguished couple.

Thus everything proper to a wedding was fully in evidence.

Toward the latter part of November, Jared and his friend Ellis, meeting at the Dunstable University Club, went in to lunch together.

"Where have *you* been?" asked Eaby, as they sat down. "I

haven't seen you for a coon's age. You weren't at the Duncans' or the Talbots' or the Sedleys' or the Armstrongs'. Nan was there, of course, looking like a million."

"Yes," said Jared, "I daresay she was."

"You weren't even at home," continued Ellis, "when the crowd dropped in on you last Thursday evening. We had a hell of a good time—you certainly missed it—hope we didn't break anything. But everyone's been wondering what's happened to you. How about it? My wife shoots me an earful about the duties of a husband if I take an evening off once a month. Is anything wrong?"

"No. I've been busy, that's all. There are new cases. Nan and I were at the Bowmans' when you and Beatrice didn't show up. The 'crowd' wondered about that, too. But if you really want to know—I've declared my independence."

"What from?"

"The 'crowd.' "

He had declared it secretly a month ago after putting up with the Dunstable young-married set during the three weeks following the Virginia honeymoon. As individuals, he had known its members all his life, but as a pack running together, he'd had, because of college, law school, and the seclusion of Tolbecken, no protracted experience of it until then. It was the typical hydra-headed smart young crowd of a second-class business town with some fashionable pretensions, frequently swelled by visitors from Philadelphia or New York. It flitted from house to house and country club to country club. It was composed of young women and their lackey husbands with or without a business, and was adorned by a few unmarried hangers-on. It was forever phoning its members or dropping in on them for poker or bridge or phonograph dances. It rolled back rugs, spilled whiskey and soda around, left half-burned cigarettes sticking to tables or mantelpieces, and consumed everything in the icebox. It used its own pet phrases, chattered endlessly about itself, frequented the same places summer or winter, and shared the same ideas and outlook. It made privacy in home life impossible.

"Plain living and high thinking for you, eh?" joshed the other. "What's Nan have to say about that, Jare?" Ellis asked more seriously. "Beatrice wouldn't stand that kind of thing from me for a minute. Do you think Nan will in the long run?"

Jared shrugged. "She'll get used to it," he answered. "I'm not a fanatic on the subject; I'll show up now and then; but

198

I don't intend to make these social goings-on my only form of amusement."

"What else is there to do?" returned Eaby.

"Well, there're books, conversation, music, the theater. You know," Jared went on, "I used to have some such idea as this: you come back at night to a pleasant house, bathe, get into your dinner things, have a well-served meal, and then sit with your wife in front of the fire and read together or talk." He broke off with a laugh. "You know—that sort of thing."

He recalled his homecoming the night before. Nan was out; the servant had forgotten to turn on the lights in the hall. It was a wet day, and stains not yet wiped up encroached over the sill upon the rug. An empty bandbox stood open on one side. Upstairs he had picked his way through a disorderly bedroom where Nan's shoes, stockings, and underclothes trailed about. The servant had come up with the report that Madam was out motoring with Mrs. Sedley and that dinner would be late. . . .

"I get you," said Ellis sympathetically. "I used to imagine the same thing—a real little love nest."

"Don't use that word," snapped Jared. "It's vulgar."

"The trouble with you," retorted the other, "is that you always were and always will be a highbrow. But we won't scrap over words. I know what you mean—I wish myself that there wasn't so much all-fired rushing around."

He sighed impatiently. He was a good-natured, thick-skinned man, born to be a drudge for his wife, who in return for his servitude made him blissful by an occasional pat on the head. He could never get over wondering and being grateful that such a superior woman as Beatrice had married him. He slaved all day to keep her in funds and acted as her handyman in the evening; but no matter how much he did or gave, he always remained in her debt. It never occurred to him to ask why; she kept him too much alive to her superiority for that. Without thinking much about it, he assumed that it was the lot of all good husbands to give everything and be thankful for crumbs.

"Well," he concluded, "marriage is a great game."

"Yes," said Jared, "I learned that from the 'crowd.'"

There was that first quarrel with Nan about her habit of spending most of the morning in bed while the household drifted as it would, and he had his cheerless breakfasts alone in a room stale from the party of the previous night. He had carried his point there, but he put up with a good deal to avoid the sordidness of vulgar little squabbles. It had startled Nan to have duties to perform, not occasionally, as a gesture, but every day, as a matter of course. She had not supposed that married and single life would be different, except that, as a married woman, she would have wider scope for self-indulgence. What else was a husband's income and a house of her own for?

The struggle between them was still latent, a friction between two different principles of living. Nan wanted to enjoy; she used continually to repeat, "Why don't you let yourself go, take things easy, have a good time?" Jared, more and more since the sale of Tolbecken, wanted to succeed. He would atone by success for his initial blunder, and if he could not restore the homestead, he would at least uphold its traditions. "Don't you see," he would reply, "that taking things easy isn't a career?" But as yet Nan's physical attractions and vitality relieved most of the strain. In her other relations with him she sought and gave pleasure with the same abandon with which she motored or danced. They were still intoxicated with each other as lovers; Jared refused to admit the essential, widening, cleavage between them. Only sometimes, on a dreary day like this . . .

"We're speaking in general terms," he added hastily. "I don't want you to imagine . . ."

"Oh, no . . . of course," said Ellis, piously. "But don't you think you're tackling a pretty big thing—American Womanhood, you know, and all that?"

"I'm not tackling anything," retorted Jared. "I simply believe in give and take on both sides."

Ellis felt worried. He was fond of Jared, but he admired him even more. He always felt flattered and distinguished by being in Jared's company. In the company of others, he let fall more often than was strictly necessary the fact that he had had lunch with Jared, or had visited him, or simply been talking with him, but he did not like the twisted line of Jared's mouth today; his old friend had changed in the last two months. Besides, Beatrice considered him a martinet whom she herself wouldn't tolerate for a moment.

"Women won't stand for much these days," he hinted. "We have to go slow and baby them a little."

But as Jared answered nothing to this credo, but went on with his dessert, the subject lapsed.

"By the way," said Ellis, "I ran out to the hospital the

200

other day on that lighting deal and happened to bump into David Mansen. I didn't know he was an intern out there—and, say, what a reputation he's got!"

Tolbecken nodded. "Yes, I know. He graduated at the top of his medical-school class just as he did at Princeton. He's so taken up, though, that I've hardly seen him this fall."

He didn't feel it necessary to explain that he had made no particular effort to see David, and that he felt uncomfortable with him; unconsciously he avoided considering why he did. He still thought of him as his best friend, but their paths lay increasingly apart.

"What a reputation!" repeated Ellis, reverential of success. "Just my knowing him gave me a boost with the superintendent! He told me that he's ace high with all the doctors there. They think he's going to make a national name for himself."

"I have no doubt," agreed Jared a little coldly.

Why was a man who cared as little for recognition as Dave Mansen forever outdistancing a person like himself who cared so much?

"He's queer, though," continued Eaby. "He's worked out some kind of a newfangled religion or psychology or something that he uses with his patients. A sort of reintegration process, as the superintendent explained it. Sounded phony to me."

"No," said the other, rallying against any criticism of his friend, "I know all about it. It's only Christianity. But that's newfangled enough if you start practicing it."

Ellis stifled a yawn. "Say, that's a fact, isn't it! But I'll have to admit, though, it hasn't cramped his style much. When I think of what a little rabbit he used to be when we were kids and what he is now, it's a regular miracle. Remember the time I caught him outside your back fence and how you and the French girl . . . What's ever happened to her, Jare?"

"Oh, she got married. She has two children, and lives at Versailles."

"Kind of a cousin of yours, wasn't she? Remember how you used to be sweet on her?"

"Yes."

The air had somehow grown cold. Eaby, reflecting that a recent bridegroom might be touchy about ancient loves, added with what he thought to be great tact, "It's certainly queer how things work out for the best. Gives me a chill to think of some I might have married before Beatrice turned

201

up. Guess it's the same with you, isn't it? Nan makes the rest of the field look pale."

Calling a waiter rather abruptly, Jared signed the check. "No, it's on me this time," he said, at Ellis's gesture.

"But, look here," protested Ellis. "What's the trouble? You're not peeved about anything, are you?"

"God, no! Why should I be peeved?" He stood up, and leaning over, patted Ellis on the shoulder. "Good old Eaby! See you later." Then he turned on his heel and walked out, leaving Ellis alone, to puff on his cigar and speculate on his friend's oddity.

37

It was a gray afternoon outside with a raw wind whipping the papers and rubbish in the streets. Jared turned up his coat collar, and threaded his way mechanically through the after-lunch crowd on the sidewalk. There was no reason, he told himself, why he should have seen red at Ellis's mention of Clarice in the same cigar puff with Nan and Beatrice. As a matter of fact, he felt not so much angry as stifled. It was all of a piece with the daily vulgarizing of life, the endlessly drab prospect before him, whether he made a success of things or not. Up and down the streets of Dunstable, helloing to people, hanging about the courthouse, proving titles, thumbing law books at the office, looking up deeds, briefing a more or less routine case; then back in the evening to his impersonal little house on the Ridge, a dose of the "crowd" or, to escape from that, a call at his grandfather's apartment on Elm Street (haunted always by the contrast between his present way of life and the dignity of life at Tolbecken), and, at last, bed fellowship with Nan, gossip or caresses, and sleeping to forget. It was humiliating that he should even cling to standards or memories; it would show more strength to chuck them and join up heartily with the backslapping, boosting, clamorous present. But for all his personal ambitions, he was not trained for such a gesture; its insincerity would still have betrayed him as unregenerate.

Today, for the first time, he sympathized intensely with his father, who had solved the problem by running away from it.

But for such an escape he needed Maylin's naïve ruthlessness; for Jared it was unthinkable. He climbed the musty stairs to his office, with its new, brave lettering on the glazed door—*Tolbecken and Tolbecken*. There was no running away from that.

When he entered, the stenographer lowered her magazine, and announced that the Judge had phoned that he would not come back that afternoon—he had some engagement or other.

"Anybody call?" he asked.

"No," she yawned. "Only thing that happened, a man came up to have his signature notarized."

Having closed the door of his room, he sat for a moment drumming the desk with his fingers. There was no longer any secret, of course, about the practice; his grandfather's pathetic subterfuge had been uncovered in all its bearing on the sale of Tolbecken. "I didn't want to tell you before, Jared," he had explained humbly. "No use troubling your happiness. But I'm an old man and haven't been able to keep up. . . . I feel worn out these days. You mustn't judge me too harshly. The best I could do was to hang on and keep the firm name for you. But now you're here," he added, rubbing his hands, "things will pick up, I'm absolutely confident." He had mailed announcements of his grandson's partnership to all his friends and former clients; and as a matter of fact there had been an increase in business—the Kirschbaum realty company, for example. "You wait," the Judge would say. "It takes time. In a few years you'll be surprised."

Years!

To occupy himself, Jared began tinkering with the brief of a case which was due to come up for trial next month. It was an affair of disputed boundary lines between two farms to the north of Dunstable. He had gone over his argument till he knew it backwards, but once again he checked up references and precedents.

"The legion," he thought suddenly, recalling for no apparent reason his talk with Professor Macklin at college, "keeping step with the legion." Well, he was doing it in spite of the professor's forebodings. He would continue to do it. But to what goal did the march lead? That was the miasma which had begun to creep across his mind. What incentive was there for all the effort, sound, and fury in the streets outside that rattled the windows of his office?

The incentives of the older Tolbeckens had been clear—development of a virgin country to meet human needs; the development of certain principles of justice; the confidence in unlimited progress, physical and spiritual, that dominated the nineteenth century; the expectation of some divine event toward which creation moved. Progress was still advertised on every corner, but the meaning of the term had subtly shifted to the material side of the human front. What progress had come, actually, to mean for the majority was unlimited increase in the physical appliances of life, expressed in sensuous terms of size, convenience, and uniformity. The legion tramped on toward this more-of-everything, and earth trembled with the thunder of their progress. Thicker newspapers, bigger schools, quicker transit, huger markets, more machine-made products. But was that the point of living? Would that satisfy him when he came to die? Perhaps it was the coal smoke sifting through the windows, perhaps it was something else that stuck in his throat.

No, to give zest to "progress," the belief in the divine event had to be retained. Otherwise humanity would choke to death. In President Wilson's national program there was still a vision and a pilot star. There, at least, was an idealism that made sense, Jared thought.

In this connection, the thought of David Mansen troubled him. He grudgingly admitted this supremacy, envied the peace, power, and effectiveness of his friend's life. But how had Mansen achieved it? By the elimination of self? By a kind of suicide? His formula of utter consecration to the will of God seemed mystical, unnecessarily demanding, whereas Wilson's ideals struck him as being practical and at the same time inspiring. They dealt with liberty, social justice, a new spirit among men, national reform—all of which Jared could support; it came within the normal frame of experience. Was it not only a pettifogging business to be concerned, as Mansen was, not with the mass, but with the individual, the reform of oneself? It seemed a trivial enough preoccupation.

No, he would fight this growing sense of futility that numbed him by an earnest devotion to the President's political and social projects. Jared glowed a little with the spirit of the new resolution.

There were several callers that afternoon, among them no less a person than Karl Kirschbaum himself, on a routine matter of mortgage foreclosures.

"The Judge isn't in, I take it?" asked the real-estate man casually.

"No."

"Well, I'm glad he isn't, Jared. He's so tenderhearted that the idea of foreclosing a mortgage makes him sick. I'll bet he's lost thousands of dollars by simply not taking what he ought to have taken. And that's not business. Here's the list."

Jared looked over the names of the condemned. He knew a couple of them—forlorn elderly people who had hung on for years and were now destitute.

"I suppose," he ventured, "that in the case of Mrs. Peters it wouldn't be possible to give a little more time?"

"No, sir," replied Kirschbaum bluntly, "it wouldn't."

Leaning forward, he tapped Jared on the knee with a long forefinger.

"Now, I know what you're thinking," he went on, "and it's to your credit, but softness in business won't do—ever. Life all along is a proposition of paying up. You foreclose the mortgages."

"I'll attend to it," sighed Jared.

A new spirit among men indeed!

But Kirschbaum seemed to be haunted by the Judge's vacant office.

"How old is your grandfather, Jared?"

"Eighty-two."

"What a wonderful man!" pronounced the other. "There's no one on earth I respect more. But I've never understood him, you know—I've never known what's kept him going. He doesn't do anything the way other people do. Isn't it queer?"

At half past four, Jared closed the office and turned home. Passing along the front of Tolbecken, he noticed that the work of demolition had begun. One of the elms was down and several others with ropes attached showed the bite of the saw. A huge placard on the lawn announced that the L. T. Morelli Company, Wreckers, were in charge of operations. The house no longer looked merely abandoned but dilapidated, a derelict awaiting execution. It would be a relief, he thought, to have it down and the place built over. In the meantime, he resolved to walk some other way. But now, on an impulse to see the last of it, he turned through the gate, followed the cart-rutted drive, and then by habit the path between the hedges leading to the rear garden.

Desolation hung over everything, a desolation more oppressive in the autumn twilight. Matted leaves, drifted into heaps, cumbered the path; branches blown from the trees and newspapers left by workmen were strewn about. The dead eyes of the house stared down on all.

205

The dreariness of this place evoked its ghosts for him in a confusion of recollections, the spindrift of the past. He walked for the last time through his forfeited birthright, mocked by the sense of loss, sick with a yearning for what could not be restored.

Here he and Clarice had nailed steps for climbing to the lower branches of an oak. Even now fragments of the rotten boards still clung to the trunk. Here and here he had first read such and such books. Here were the initials he had cut —his own, Clarice's, and David's—long ago. An unevenness on the ground beneath marked a pet's grave. He stopped by a cluttered heap of stalks and leaves where the roses had stood.

Then, looking up, he suddenly realized that he was not alone in the garden. Someone was standing on the oval of lawn behind the house, but in the half-light he could not tell who it was. He was startled, and felt almost an uncanny dread of the long-coated figure, leaning slightly forward. But when it straightened up and moved slowly away from him toward the circle of trees beyond, he recognized his grandfather.

Stopping now and then to look up at the house or at the burnished crowns of the elms, the old man crossed the lawn and continued falteringly along the farther path leading to the rear gate. A tree had been freshly nicked by the ax to mark it as next for destruction, and Jared saw him pause, running his hand over the place. Finally at the path's end, he turned and with bowed head, his hands joined on the knob of his stick, he stood lost in thought. Silence, dusk, autumn, the downward fluttering of leaves, the deserted house—they created a vision of such loneliness that Jared felt the cold of it close around his heart.

He drew back into the shadow of the hedge, retracing his steps, his breast constricted by an almost physical pain. For the sake of his marriage, he thought. His marriage!

He clenched his fingers until the nails bit into the palms.

He found Nan, contrary to her habit, seated pensively before the drawing-room fire. Unexpectedly too, she wore the same dress as in the morning. She looked curiously white and forlorn.

"How was the Bowman reception?" he asked, warming himself. "Everybody was there, I suppose?"

"Probably. I didn't go. I didn't feel like it."

"What's wrong?"

"Oh, nothing."

He was unprepared for the outburst that followed after a brief silence. The whiteness of lassitude became all at once a whiteness of anger. She grasped the two arms of her chair.

"Everything's wrong," she cried. "Everything! I can't stand it. I won't stand it. The plans I'd made . . . all the good times I'd looked forward to! It isn't fair! I'd like to kill myself!"

She seemed on the point of hysterics, her mouth drawn, her body shaken with sobs.

"But, Nan, what on earth's the matter?"

"You might as well know. I wouldn't believe it at first. I'd tried so hard to be careful. I'd kept hoping. But Dr. Guerney told me today."

"What?"

"Can't you understand? Why are you so stupid? I'm going to have a baby."

"But that's splendid—it's wonderful!"

At a stroke the gloom and misgivings of the past hour vanished. After all, of course, *this* was the solution, the ever-repeated miracle uniting a man and a woman in something entirely their own, a living bond.

Stooping down, he raised her from the chair and held her close.

"Oh, Nan, I'm so glad," he said tenderly.

She stared at him, bewildered for a moment, and then thrust him back. "Don't touch me—glad!" she repeated. "You can afford to be glad. You don't have to give up anything. You can sit back and let me suffer. You don't have to drag about for months looking like a fright. You won't have a nasty little kid on your hands, spoiling every bit of fun you care about. What about our trip next summer, and all the clothes I've made for this winter!"

She burst into tears and flung herself on the sofa.

"Don't," he begged, following her. "Anything I can do . . . I'll help you, Nan. Don't feel this way. You should be happy about it."

A ray of comfort crossed her mind; it was an aspect of the affair that had not yet occurred to her.

She looked up with a wan, patient smile, accepting his caress.

"You'll be very kind to me, won't you, Jare? You've got to be!"

38

Baby became an irresistible master word from then on. There was, of course, no longer any question of Nan's getting up in the morning if she chose to lie in bed; irksome household duties ceased entirely; in view of her coming ordeal, no one but a brute would have denied her any reasonable, or even unreasonable, pleasure.

For a young husband already aware but constantly being reminded of his obligations, nine months in these circumstances is a long time. Cheerless breakfasts and pick-up meals, constant errands, unlooked-for expenses, and unremitting attentions were the order of the day for Jared during this interval. His declaration of independence from the crowd had to be recanted, or at least postponed—for who would be so heartless as to neglect a wife at such a critical period? Nan intended to enjoy her last fling, as she called it, to the utmost. She brought an elegant gown, a new runabout. She absolutely forbade that any but the immediate relatives be informed of her condition, and she managed so well that up to the last three months none of her friends suspected anything. Now and then Jared's devotion cracked a little under the strain.

"You must humor her, Mr. Tolbecken," said the Philadelphia specialist, who had been appointed field marshal of the campaign. The first child, you know—it's a very critical period in a woman's life."

"But I wonder, Doctor," ventured Jared, "if so much dancing and so many late nights can be very good for her."

"Dancing is an excellent exercise," said the specialist, "and if she sleeps late the next day, there's no harm done by staying up. I wouldn't be surprised," he added shrewdly, "if it did you more harm than it did her, but that's one of the penalties of being a husband, isn't it?"

"You must humor her, my dear boy," said Judge Tolbecken, when Jared in a fit of discouragement reviewed his mounting expenses. "Any sacrifice you can make for a woman at such a time is nothing in comparison . . ."

"Pooh!" interrupted Grandmother. "That's just nonsense.

208

Birth is the most natural thing in the world. What's all this fuss about it?"

"I agree with you," put in Aunt Joan. "The idea of that doctor talking about *dancing* as exercise! What Frances ought to be doing is housework."

Rufus Tolbecken, catching Jared's eye, shook his head slightly. It indicated that allowances must be made for Spartans like his wife and sister-in-law.

"You'll have to manage somehow," he declared. "Of course, I'll advance any sum necessary."

"You'll do nothing of the kind," retorted Jared. Privately, however, he resolved, rather than sell another bond, to get rid of his mare, Astarte. At ten years, she would still fetch six hundred dollars.

"But humor her," insisted the Judge. "It's a special occasion in both your lives."

"You should be very sweet to Nan," prompted Mrs. Oliver in her turn. "Of course no *man* could possibly realize what such a visitation means to a woman—all she has to give up, the tremendous unselfishness, the terrible suffering she has to go through. And for the sake of what? Just love. . . ."

Jared murmured his sensibility.

"Nan has so set her heart on that little wrist watch at Rayberg's," Mrs. Oliver continued. "She was saying to me only yesterday—and you can't imagine how faint and tired she looked—'Do you think Jare will give it to me, Mummie? Every day when he comes home from the office, I sort of hope he'll surprise me with it,' she says."

"But that watch," protested Jared, "costs three hundred dollars."

"I believe he's perfectly callous," she told her husband later.

Of course in the end Jared bought the watch, and sold another bond together with his horse.

"So you're an active member again?" gloated Eaby Ellis at an assembly of the crowd. "That for you, Mr. Independent! What was I telling you about American Womanhood! You're doing the lock step now, all right, along with the rest of us. She's brought you to heel, boy, in good shape."

It was hard, when the time came, to give up Astarte. Since the sale of Tolbecken, Jared had kept the mare at a livery stable not far from his house; he rode her late afternoons or early mornings along the few remaining country roads. The upkeep and care of horses had become increasingly expensive;

he reflected that she would have had to go soon in any case. But when, after clinching the sale, he walked around for a last look at her, the farewell cost him more than he anticipated.

As usual, at the sound of his step, she neighed and lifted an eager head over the back of her box stall. He opened it, presenting his tribute of sugar and an apple. She nosed for more, plucking with her lips at his pockets, then lifted her head, stamping a little, her eyes alert. It was her invitation to the ride.

"Not today, girl," he said, working at a tangle in her mane.

The breath of the mare on his cheek, the warm odor of her were like an emanation from his youth. Suddenly it came over him that this was the last of it, not only in a personal sense, but of the world to which his youth belonged—the simpler, unmechanized, horse-drawn world. He would never see it again. The smell brought back Gregory, the harness room with its leather and steel, the phaeton and the surrey with its fringed top; it brought back the sweet, smokeless air of the past. He thought of his rides with Clarice. They had bought Astarte in his sophomore year, the year before she had come back on that visit. How tall and gallant she had looked in the old-fashioned habit!

"You were young, too, then, weren't you?" he said aloud.

It was dark in the stall. He laid his cheek against the mare's neck.

Coming back from his office on an afternoon in March, he stopped to admire a sparkling, low, high-powered Hispano-Suiza roadster drawn up in front of his house, parked behind Nan's runabout like a falcon behind a wren. No doubt it belonged to some caller in the apartment building next door. It was painted a battleship gray and had gray leather upholstery. A car like that, Jared thought, with its special body and all the rest, could have cost no less than fifteen thousand dollars. With its swank, dash, and power, it had a personality of its own that reminded him vaguely of someone. Yes, of Angus Grey—it was the Angus Grey of cars. He smiled at the notion, imagining the former paragon with his reckless face, joyous grin, and the cold devil in his eyes seated here behind the wheel. *There* was a man who never faltered, doubted himself, or turned aside—in that respect he was curiously like David Mansen, his opposite in every other way. Jared wondered where he was now. The *Alumni Weekly* had reported that from Mexico he had gone to the Orient in connection with some oil concessions. "Set him somewhere east of Suez where the best is like the worst," the class secretary had quoted aptly. Yes, wherever he was, Angus Grey would be riding the crest of the wave unconcerned by any of the Ten Commandments.

With a final glance at the car, Jared entered his house.

There was to be a dance at the Reigers' that night, he suddenly remembered, a grand assembly of the crowd. He could picture Nan at that moment grappling with the problem of the evening's dress amid a landslide of frocks and lingerie. He would have to bathe and get ready himself. . . . Well, five more months. But as he entered the hall, Nan's laughter, rippling from the drawing room, stopped him.

"That's the best ever," she exclaimed to someone. "You're a perfect case!" And, hearing the click of the front door, "Come in here, Jare. We've got a caller."

As he crossed the threshold, a once-familiar voice startled him.

"Well, well, well," it said, "old Befo'-de-war, his very self!"

A figure, seated beyond the hearth and visible only in the subdued light of a table lamp, rose, swinging across the room to meet him. Struck by the oddness of the coincidence, he exclaimed:

"Angus Grey! By Jove, I was just thinking of you!"

"Speak of the devil, eh? But let me look at you, Befo'-de-war. Nan, couldn't we have a little light, please?"

"It *is* dark," she answered in the curious social voice she used for special occasions.

As she turned the switch, it seemed to Jared that Grey stood out of the twilight with a sudden hard vividness. But the very abruptness of his appearing scored the change that five years had made in him. The essential, remembered traits were there, more clearly defined. He had grown a little massive. His handsome nose, the strong curve of his lips, the challenge of his eyes were more forceful, more prominent. His native assurance of manner had been polished by experience into the ease of a man of the world. Tanned dark by the tropics, perfectly dressed as ever, his physical fitness combined, Jared felt, to put his own office pallor and dinginess into sharp contrast.

"Well, well," repeated the visitor, "there you are. We both look older, don't we? But not venerable yet . . . same old Jared. By the way, congratulations." His smile included Nan. "Didn't know a thing about it till I picked up some mail in

211

Canton, and found out that one more prize had gone to the wrong fellow. That's a fact, Nan. You know I was terribly smitten in the old days, still am, but grieve in silence. . . ."

"Oh, really," she drawled, coloring a little.

They sat down once more beside the fireplace.

Angus leaned back, exhaling cigarette smoke.

"Well, give me the news. Nan was saying that your place here had been sold. I drove into Dunstable and asked for Tolbecken. 'Tolbecken Square?' says the man. 'I guess that's right,' I told him. Then he directed me to drive through Tolbecken Place, along Tolbecken Avenue, to Tolbecken Square. And I said to him, 'You people around here don't seem to have much imagination in names.' But when I got to the square, Tolbecken itself was gone, like the center of an onion —nothing but grading and construction work. Don't wonder, because of the site . . . but it must have been an interesting old place."

Jared could feel his guest's eyes sweep the narrow limits of the commonplace room, all the smaller because of the old-fashioned furniture in it. But there was nothing patronizing in the glance; there was only cool appraisal. He explained about Tolbecken, and told Angus about his law work.

The story of Angus's fortunes was much more diverting, the story of a successful man. He had traveled in Texas, Mexico, then China, Indochina, Persia, Africa in the incessant pursuit of new oil fields, new prospects. The acrid spice of the East, a hint of the changing panorama of his life clung to his somewhat bald narrative. Grey had never much enjoyed talking about himself; he could impress without that. His vanities were subtler, stronger. . . . Yes, he admitted, with grace, he had risen in the company; he had done fairly well.

"Still unmarried?" put in Nan. "Weren't you engaged to Betty Andrews of New York?"

"Oh, that," smiled Angus. "It seems a long time ago. She deserted me like all the rest of you girls. No, 'He travels the fastest who travels alone,' and I've had to travel fast. Not," he added with a wink to Nan, "that I haven't sometimes rested. But now seeing you and Jare so domestic in such a pleasant house, I really have twinges of envy. Besides, it looks as if I'd be settling down for a while."

"Where?" asked Jared.

The other beamed. "That's just the point. Here in Dunstable."

"Here?" repeated Nan, a more intent look in her eyes.

"Yes. I've been appointed general manager for this section beginning next fall. This is by way of a scouting trip—I've a few people to see, some contacts to make. I thought you might help me, Jare. I wanted to ask your advice about a firm of lawyers. We want to retain someone who will handle the corporation's legal business in this state."

"Jare!" exclaimed Nan breathlessly.

"I'll give you what advice I can," said Jared. "Kent and Hume are probably the most active firm in town. I could suggest them without hesitation. Then there's Kennedy, Vail, and Robson, who are about equally important. I don't think you'd make a mistake with either firm, but on the whole Kent and Hume are perhaps better known. . . ."

Nan flounced on the sofa. "Lord!" she muttered.

"Yes," nodded Angus, "typical, isn't it? Befo'-de-war, you certainly run true to form. But I don't see how you're going to build up a practice that way. How about Tolbecken and Tolbecken?"

"You asked my advice," returned Jared. "Our firm used to be the most prominent in the state; but Grandfather is almost finished, and I'm just starting. I take it that your company wants the most experienced man they can get, and I'm not that man."

"Of all the fools I ever heard of," burst out Nan, "I think you're the limit—just a perfect duffer!"

"Wait a moment," soothed Angus, his shrewd glance wandering from Nan to Jared and back again. "Suppose the company wanted your firm, suppose the name meant something to them—on my recommendation—what then? The retaining fee would be considerable."

There was something in Angus Grey that had always reminded Jared of a poised rapier, despite, or perhaps because of, his always winning smile. What answer could there be to this proposal except assent? The Mutual Oil business would mean everything to him and to his grandfather. It would be a great step up the ladder to success. Why should he go on suspecting Grey, why keep up the rancor of that silly quarrel at Princeton? Angus seemed to have forgotten it, in that respect was behaving better than he himself. After all, they had been friends once.

"It's very tempting," he answered. "You know what the facts are. If in view of the circumstances your company selects our firm, of course . . ."

"I can answer for the company," put in Angus.

"Well, then, thanks a great deal."

"Bravo!" said Grey, leaning forward to shake hands. "We'll consider it settled."

"Great! . . . Great!" Nan exploded. "You're a peach, Angus. It's certainly wonderful of you. We'll have to have a drink on that." She sprang up, excited, and gave Angus's shoulder a squeeze. "Jare, mix us up one. Let's have an Old Fashioned. I'll ring for ice . . ."

The Mutual Oil business! Jared could see his grandfather's satisfaction when he heard the news. The tide had turned.

They clicked glasses.

"Here's to happy days," said Angus.

"Here's to *you!*" fluted Nan, her eyes like blue stars.

"Thanks again," said Jared. And when they had refilled the glasses, "By the way, where are you stopping?"

"Nowhere as yet."

"Well, then of course you'll stay with us."

"You don't mind? It'll only be for a couple of nights."

"Mind!" exclaimed Nan. "But I hope you won't object to a dance tonight. You'll meet everybody who counts for anything in Dunstable."

"Not in the least," smiled Grey, "provided you dance with me, hostess."

"And won't I just!"

They went out to the car for Angus's bags, while Nan in her best society drawl apologized for not having a butler. Secretly she resolved that on the strength of the Mutual Oil business they would have one from then on.

Upon re-entering the house, Grey opened a brief case. "I'd almost forgotten," he said fumbling. "I brought you a wedding present, Nan, something I picked up for you at Colombo—ah, here it is—"

With flushed cheeks, she tore open the little package he presented.

"Lordy!" she whispered in an awed voice. "Lordy! . . . Jare, look . . . *look!* It's *too* magnificent! . . . No, let me have it. I want to put it on."

It was an enormous star-sapphire ring with a tiny knot of brilliants on either side that covered her third finger from knuckle to knuckle. She stood with her arm stretched out beneath the lamp staring at it. Then, turning, she flung her arms around Angus's neck and kissed him.

"You are a darling," she cried, "a perfect darling!"

"Just a token of admiration," he said, bowing.

Jared protested. "But you shouldn't have done that. It's a great deal too much. I don't think we ought to accept that."

"We?" returned the other. "I wasn't aware that I gave it to you. It belongs to Nan—it's a trifle, anyway. Of course, if she doesn't want it . . ."

"Not want it!" she echoed. "I'd like to see anyone get it away from me. I *am* so appreciative—though of course, as Jare says, it was much too generous of you."

And she returned to the lamp, once more stretching out her arm.

"I bought a good many jewels in Ceylon," continued Grey. "The shops there are fascinating, Nan. When I move here in the fall, you must let me show you my collection."

Jared felt helpless, as if an invisible net were being spun around him. He saw his independence being forfeited to these repeated favors, in spite of himself, and in so insidiously natural a way as to make defense impossible. He could hardly reward kindness with suspicion.

Already feeling somewhat like a pensioner, he accompanied Grey to the guest room.

"It's awfully good of you," said Angus casually, as if aware of the embarrassment he had caused and intent on putting him at his ease, "to take me in like this."

"It seems to me that the goodness is all on your side," returned Jared, a little formally.

"Oh, no." Angus leaned against the mantelpiece. "But you're sure it's convenient? You're sure you want me?"

"Of course."

The other gave one of his gay laughs. "Well, remember the devil never comes unless he's welcome. By the way, whatever became of Mansen?"

"He's an intern right here at the hospital. He had a splendid record at medical school."

"So he's here, is he?" Angus's face had grown rigid. "The damn saint!" he burst out suddenly, but checked himself. "I'm sorry; I remember he's your friend."

It was strange that a man apparently so well controlled should give way to such childish anger. A grimace twisted his mouth. He brought his fist down twice on the mantel. Then the fit passed, and he smiled.

"Curious, how some people stick in my throat. Well, I don't want to see him, that's all. He won't be there tonight, will he?"

"No, I think not."

But to Jared, the strangest part of the occurrence had been his awareness of a note of fear in the other's voice.

Angus Grey made a deep impression on Dunstable society that night. A new star had risen upon the town that dazzled young and old, men and women alike. The Reiger ballroom, which formed a wing of their Gothic mansion, had never seen a more brilliant affair.

Jared had a reflected part in all this glory. As Nan confidently informed one friend after another of the new windfall, his importance among the crowd rose point by point. The Tolbecken arms were being regilded. Jared could taste the heady liquor of success, of personal recognition, as he never had before. Eaby Ellis, more deferential than ever, whispered congratulations. "My word, some people have luck!"

They stood watching Nan pirouetting in the arms of Angus. She wore the sapphire ring, and Jared noticed how good a pal she seemed to be with him. Nan was as good as her word and danced a great deal with her guest that evening.

She sang his praises to Jared that night after they had gone to bed.

"I thought you once told me that you were through being impressed by men like Angus Grey," Jared said.

"Did I ever say that?"

"You certainly did."

She was silent a moment. "Well, I'm not an idiot, if that's what you mean. I know his sort all right, and I'm not impressed the way I used to be—the way that fool, Mary Reiger, is, for instance. Did you see how she tumbled for him! Fat little prune! I have to laugh. . . . No, I'm not impressed that way any more. He's a pretty carnivorous animal—but you can't deny he has a powerful personality."

She fell silent again, and turned over, snuggling into the pillows. Jared, unable to sleep, stared up into the darkness of the room, in a confusion of thoughts reflecting the events of the day. Outside, the old clock from Tolbecken wound itself up to strike the half-hour. He was startled when Nan spoke suddenly.

"At any rate, I'm glad he's leaving day after tomorrow, and won't be back until October!"

"Why? What difference does it make?"

"Oh, nothing. You don't believe people notice anything yet—about Baby, I mean?"

"Not a thing. You looked splendid this evening."

She sighed. "Well, good night. You are a dear sometimes."

39

The June heat clamped down on Dunstable with its usual mugginess. Shirts stuck to backs; street odors thickened; the very air felt greasy on the face. But hot weather had its advantages. Toward the end of the month, Nan departed with the Olivers for an obscure mountain resort far from the public eye, taking her martyrdom with her. The weeks preceding her departure had been cloistered and hectic. An unwilling mother, Nan found some satisfaction in involving her husband and relatives in her travail. When he had seen his wife off, Jared remained in town with a sense of holiday.

Returning from the station to supper at the club, he joined a group dangling their evening papers in the reading room.

"Any news?" he asked casually.

"Some archduke or other assassinated in Servia. Headlines about that." Jared picked up a paper in his turn and read about the murder of the Archduke Ferdinand. It seemed terribly remote—just another mess in the Balkans. Where was Sarajevo, anyway, and how was it pronounced? Then he had a cocktail, and went in to supper with a crowd who discussed Travers and golf, Fritzi Scheff, and Wilson's Mexican policy. Afterwards they had a sound evening of auction undisturbed by conjugal bickerings.

Years later he would look back to that summer with astonishment. On the public stage, Huerta and Carranza, a murder at Freeport, Long Island, the Irish-English row, the trial of Madame Caillaux furnished the papers with copy. The shooting of Mrs. Bailey occupied a great deal more space than that of the Austrian prince, which dropped out of sight within a week. He would recall an eventless month of office work in the mornings, followed by golf or tennis and relaxed evenings. There were a couple of letters from Clarice, mentioning vague rumors. "The same old saber-rattling," he thought, much more interested in the Delarts' removal to the garrison at Grenoble and in Clarice's description of the Grande Chartreuse. Imperceptibly, the hour of universal dissolution crept up on self-absorbed humanity and cast no shadow. Drowsy with summer, in a world grown old, civilization drifted toward the precipice.

217

Even when the roaring from the abyss began, few recognized it. July 24: AUSTRIA READY TO INVADE SERVIA, SENDS ULTIMATUM (one front-page column in the *New York Times*). It was the old story. July 25: EUROPEAN WAR IN THE BALANCE (another column). Well, it had been in the balance a long time. July 26: AUSTRIA BREAKS WITH SERVIA (four columns by now), STOCKS FALL. That was bad. But July 27: LONDON STILL HOPES FOR PEACE. Of course. It was the usual false alarm on a big scale. July 29: AUSTRIA FORMALLY DECLARES WAR ON SERVIA; RUSSIA THREATENS, ALREADY MOVING TROOPS; PEACE OF EUROPE NOW IN KAISER'S HANDS. Still, the editorial was full of hopefulness. Then July 30, 31, and thenceforward, rising to a flood, the tide swept over the whole front page. RUSSIA EXPECTS WAR, MOBILIZES 1,200,000 MEN; KAISER CALLS ON RUSSIA TO HALT WITHIN 24 HOURS; ENGLAND AND FRANCE READY, BUT HOPE FOR PEACE. (Why, the thing was incredible. What was it all about, anyway?) STOCK EXCHANGE CLOSED; GERMANY DECLARES WAR. (Headlines by now, streaming across the page. Type at its blackest as the world tumbled down the first cataract.) ENGLAND AND GERMANY CLINCH; GREATEST OF WARS BEGINS; EIGHT NATIONS, FOUR NAVIES AND 17,000,000 MEN ENGAGED; KAISER ATTACKS BELGIUM; FRENCH SHIPS DEFEAT GERMAN; GREAT ENGLISH AND GERMAN NAVIES ABOUT TO GRAPPLE; RIVAL WARSHIPS OFF THIS PORT AS LUSITANIA SAILS.

Well, it was over there, three thousand miles away. Thank God, over there, and that we had nothing to do with it! A damnable, cruel, king-made absurdity, from which we had been saved by the foresight of our ancestors in emigrating to an enlightened country. Everyone gloried in this heaven-sent isolation, and bought the amazing extras, which made such intensely interesting reading. The outrage could not last long in any case—six months at most; Lord Kitchener was crazy with his talk of two or three years. The banking kings of Dunstable together with greater kings elsewhere could demonstrate on paper the impossible expense of it.

Meanwhile a spindrift of passion drifted across the Atlantic. That sympathy with the underdog which lies deep in the American consciousness began fermenting, and the Belgium of 1914 replaced the Cuba of the nineties. The kinship with England in language, institutions, and point of view, the common attitude toward sport, the common law, the King James Bible became operative. The funeral pyre of Louvain could be seen around the world. And stories of brutalities and executions, equally effective whether true or false, began circulating. Frightfulness raised its head with a clamor of phrases calculated to impress, but serving only to enrage. Scraps of paper fluttered about in the public mind along with statements from the German Embassy.

"Read this, will you!" exclaimed Joe Sedley over a newspaper at the club. "Bernstorff got this out in Washington: 'Civilians of the Belgian town of Louvain made a perfidious attack on German troops while fighting. Louvain was punished by the destruction of the city. . . .' Damned if I get it. An army marches into Dunstable, and you and I take pot shots at it. All right, that's our funeral—let 'em shoot us. But why burn the public library, churches, and Y.M.C.A.? Can anybody show me the sense of that?"

"I can," replied Karl Leittner of German parentage and hitherto a popular young businessman. "Germany's fighting for her life. She had to make an example, strike terror . . ."

"Well, do you know how that strikes me?" interrupted Joe. "It makes me want to go to Canada and enlist."

"But, see here, Germany's got to live, hasn't she?"

"If what we read is true," retorted the other, "I don't see the necessity."

There were cold looks and level eyes focused on Leittner around the table; when he began a somewhat ponderous defense of his father's native country, Joe Sedley got up and walked away; the others buried themselves in their newspapers. From that month on, the Fritzes, Heinies, and Karls, who had once been hail fellows, felt an increasing chill. Rudyard Kipling's war poem which ended, "Who lives if England fall, who dies if England live?" kindled the blood.

Of course, it was passion, therefore irrational; far deeper, and more dynamic, than reason. If the German apologists had reasoned like seraphs, their arguments would have availed nothing against the flames of Louvain and the human heart. In the splendid isolation of America, the germs of war were multiplying, multiplying . . .

Clarice wrote of her husband's departure for the front with his regiment, described the station platform crowded with women and children, the last embraces, the strange emptiness after the train had gone. There could be no question of Jared's partisanship. He bought a map, exulted over the first reports of Allied victories, and then with a sinking heart followed day by day the wavering lines of Belgians, English, and French as they moved back. Already many of

219

Pierre Delart's regiment were dead; he himself was wounded. The rivulet of red in France was fast becoming a river. The woes of a continent could be heard across the ocean.

Nan wrote from her mountain resort: *I tell you this thing of having a baby is just one big nightmare. But never again! I can promise you that! You ask me what I think about the war. I don't think about it. It's enough to worry about myself, thank you, as long as nobody else cares for me.*

Rufus Tolbecken, who, with Grandmother and Aunt Joan, was spending July and August at the shore, wrote sadly: *We are distressed beyond measure by the war. It weighs on us day and night, though we don't like to talk about it. You know what I think of war—I was with Sherman on the March to the Sea. Poor, sinful, pitiable humankind! The President's attitude and appeal for neutrality commands my heartiest approval. . . .*

Jared set this down to old age. It was not his view of the struggle. War might be terrible, but it was also heroic; it purified a nation. Now that the dust of the onset had cleared away, the issues became evident—barbarism and tyranny on one side, enlightened freedom on the other. Who could remain neutral in such a conflict?

One afternoon, reflecting that he had not seen David Mansen for some time and eager to hear his opinion of affairs, he drove out to the hospital.

"What do I think of the war?" David rumpled his hair back in a way he had. "Well, I think that pretty nearly everybody past or present has been to blame."

"What do you mean?"

"Only that nations are made up of individuals. The destructive forces in you and me, when multiplied, are the cause of war. It's just the suppuration of the world abscess."

"Are you serious?" retorted Jared. "You mean to say that you can't see the magnificence of a thing like this—that it's a struggle between right and wrong, civilization and barbarism?"

"I'm afraid I can't."

"And I suppose you think," Jared continued, "that the people over there aren't dying for their ideals?"

"I think they are false ideals."

"Well, then," said Jared stiffly, "I believe we'd better not discuss the matter."

But David went on. "Don't misunderstand me. To my mind the terrible thing about it is that so much courage

220

and self-sacrifice is being devoted to a miserable sham. The men who *honestly* believe in a humbug and die for it are blameless, but that does not keep them from dying in vain. Can't you see that any principle which requires the lies, brutalities, and hatreds of war must be false?"

"No," burst out Jared. "I believe in patriotism. I believe in the defense of one's country."

Mansen shook his head. "I do not believe in anything which entails cultivating the brute in man."

"But war cultivates the better qualities too. You spoke of courage and self-sacrifice. There's discipline, comradeship, physical hardness. All these things are good."

"And yet ultimately," said David, "they are put to the service of hate. I don't believe you would maintain that the morale of this country was improved by the Civil War."

Jared had no answer to this. He could only retort that a civil war was different from others. "But at any rate," he continued stubbornly, "all I know is that I wish this country could take its stand beside England and France. There's where we belong. It's the great adventure of our times, and I'd like to have a part in it."

Mansen leaned back in his chair, his gaunt, homely face rather stern, his eyes abstracted.

"I just wonder if it isn't just that—the adventure—as much as the so-called principles, that appeals to a lot of people. War's a good excuse for getting away from routine things."

It was this thought that remained with Jared after he had driven home. He believed in the Allied cause, was thrilled by the challenge of the issue. But at cooler moments, faced by the humdrum of his life, he half admitted that a personal interest colored his passion for freedom and civilization. Right or wrong, the war still retained a lure of romance; it presented an avenue of heroic escape.

40

A battery of doctors and nurses, the best room at a maternity hospital in Philadelphia (the resources of Dunstable being considered inadequate to such an event) gave all that modern science and comfort could give to render Nan's supreme sacrifice as endurable as possible. A false alarm brought her down from the mountain resort to the hospital ten days in advance—days of intense emotional expenditure on her relatives' part. Everybody (always excepting Grandmother and Aunt Joan) pitied her, were expected, and indeed compelled, to pity her; but her own self-pity, keeping the lead, could never be quite overtaken or satisfied. She continued to absorb pity and roses, chocolates, novels, and gifts of every kind, but she continued also to suffer in a callous world that failed really to understand the extent of her sacrifice.

"Everybody is so darned cheerful," she protested, "as if it weren't anything at all! I'd like to see *them* in this dreary hole day after day; they wouldn't be so chipper and sunny then."

"But, Nan," he argued, "there's no reason why you shouldn't be at home if you'd rather. I'm sure we could get over here in time . . ."

"That's an example of what I mean," she burst out. "You don't care whether I take chances or not; you're not taking them. You don't have to face any danger. What you're really thinking about is the expense, and I know it."

Jared flushed. He could not help thinking about the expense somewhat. It was mounting at the rate of a hundred dollars a week. How did women get along who could not afford such an outlay?

Nan flushed in her turn. "I'll remember that," she said icily. "Counting the pennies as usual!"

Her voice and lips trembled, and she stared out of the window.

"You know I don't grudge you anything," he groaned, but was aware that no protests would help in the least. It was one of her pet charges against him. "Only," he added, "you were complaining of the hospital a moment ago."

"And haven't I the right to complain?" she retorted. "Look at me—at what a sight I've become!"

"Of course, Nan, I realize how uncomfortable you must feel. There are billions of people in the world, though; and they have all been born. Surely it can't be as dreadful as all that . . ."

"There you are!" she raged. "That's consolation for you! Why don't you go on and tell me about the millions of women who have died, who have become invalids for life, who have lost their looks!"

He would keep silent, telling himself that in her condition she was not quite responsible, but his silence was equally provoking. If he brought her gifts, she was too languid to enjoy them. When he called, she considered his visit perfunctory; if he stayed away, she accused him of neglect. And she poured out her wrongs into her mother's or Dr. Emerson's sympathetic ears. Jared would return home through the August heat to Dunstable with the sense of having been crushed in a mortar, and could look forward only to a renewal of the ordeal the next day.

On one occasion, Joan Maylin made the pilgrimage to Philadelphia, taking with her some delicacies of her own baking.

"So good of you, Aunt Joan," murmured Nan, having glanced into the basket. "I'm sure the cakes are delicious, but I have very little appetite these days. Of course, the nurses will love them. Here you are, Miss Clayton—will you please take this away? I'm rather sensitive to odors just now." And leaning back in her chair with closed eyes, "How is Madame Tolbecken? Well, I hope."

"Very," returned the other. "And I'm glad to see you looking so well too. A good color, and you've put on weight as a girl should in your condition."

Nan opened her eyes, and looked coldly at the visitor. "Not having had a child of your own, I suppose you don't understand how ill . . ."

"Nonsense!" laughed Joan Maylin, winking at the nurse. "I've been helping babies into the world for the last fifty years, and I've seen women a good deal frailer than you have a raft of them. You're a strong, healthy girl. You may have a hard time because it's your first, but you won't think of it afterwards."

"My first?" exclaimed Nan. "Do you suppose I would ever dream of having another?"

"Now, now," Aunt Joan said soothingly, "we won't talk about it."

Nan burst into tears. Here was another Job's comforter arrived to torment her with a pat on the head. Tears were, as a rule, an unfailing means of rallying whatever decent feeling human heartlessness was capable of. But this time the charm failed. Aunt Joan's square face showed no sympathy; she settled back in her chair, and waited for Nan to stop crying. What a ninny the girl was! Poor Jared!

"Cheer up," she said, "this nonsense isn't good for the baby."

"What do I care!" cried Nan, her voice choked with frustration and rage.

"The trouble with you," continued Aunt Joan, "is that you've been on a diet of sugarplums all your life. You never developed teeth for biting into anything real, like bearing a child."

Nan could hardly believe her ears; to her, Joan's words seemed incredibly brutal. She stopped crying and stared at the other for a minute. Then the real hardness that lay beneath her self-indulgence came to the surface.

"What makes you think," she flamed, "you know what I can or can't do? I can take care of myself without advice. You're rather tiresome, really. If you've come here to lecture me, just save yourself the trouble, because I won't stand for it."

Her eyes, now tearless, shot fire, but it struck vainly against the granite of Joan Maylin's stare.

"I can make some allowances," Aunt Joan answered, "for your condition. I know that women at such times aren't altogether accountable, and as a matter of fact I'd rather have you saucing me than sniveling like a child. What you think of me makes no difference. A girl like you needs truth rather than soothing syrup, even though she mayn't like it."

"Will you please go!" Nan cried angrily.

Aunt Joan shook her head. "Not until I'm ready. And all the tantrums in the world won't trouble me in the least. You're sick from selfishness, my girl. That isn't the proper frame of mind for bringing a baby into the world. It'll make it harder for you and it won't help the child. Hate me all you like, but try to remember that you're about to be a mother. A childless woman has missed a good deal in life. Nothing ever quite makes up for it. Try to deserve what's being given to you."

Whereupon she stood up, and with great deliberation drove home the two hatpins that held her bonnet.

Nan stared at her. She had never in her memory been so talked to, and curiously enough the experience had a bracing effect. She felt better, lighter somehow, and surprised herself by murmuring, although in a pinched way, "Well, perhaps you're right."

Joan Maylin nodded emphatically. "Of course I'm right. You've got spunk if you had a mind to use it."

As she turned to the door Nan called to her:

"Aunt Joan."

"Well?"

"Would you mind being here . . . when the time comes? I . . . I'd like to have you near me."

It was the instinctive acknowledgment of strength: her weakness clung to it in spite of her hurt vanity. Some people, like Joan Maylin, are born to serve as the bulwarks against the fears of others. She had done so all her life, and was used to such an appeal. Her face softened as she walked back to Nan's chair.

"Of course I will. Don't you worry at all. Aunt Joan'll see you through."

Nan looked up at the rugged features with a strange respect.

"It's good of you," she said.

Gently, Joan stroked the other's hair an instant, then drew away.

"Well, good-by. I'll be back when you need me."

And with that she tramped out.

For a while Nan felt a curious glow. Of course her self-pity returned with the nurse, the doctor, and Mrs. Oliver—it was easier to breathe on that level than on the upland of Aunt Joan's courage—but she kept a special place for the latter in her mind, and astonished Jared by announcing that she considered his aunt a peach.

Nan's pains began suddenly at night on the first of September. Roused at one o'clock by the telephone, Jared collected his mother-in-law and Joan Maylin, and drove the thirty-odd miles to Philadelphia.

There was considerable coolness on the part of Mrs. Oliver in the back seat.

"I'm sure it's very nice of you, Miss Maylin, but it really isn't necessary."

"Maybe not," said Aunt Joan, "but I promised Nan to be there."

"It's curious she should want anybody except her own mother, Miss Maylin. . . ."

Jared's heart was in his mouth. The doctor's words over the telephone had sounded ominous.

"I'm afraid the labor is going to be harder than I had expected. Her nervous condition isn't all it should be. However, don't be alarmed, my dear fellow."

Jared had communicated this to Aunt Joan before driving to the Olivers'.

"The man's a fool," she remarked. "He may be a great specialist, but he hasn't any common sense. All those dances, late nights, and everything else he permitted! In my time, an old-fashioned country doctor would have been shocked. Besides, he's babied and petted her into being afraid. But don't tell her mother, Jared. The woman's as soft as putty."

At the hospital, they were informed that Nan had been taken to the delivery room. Jared had a glimpse of her there —her moist, chalk-white face, and eyes that barely recognized him for the fear in them. She lay between the white-clad attendants surrounded by all the efficient instruments of science. She seemed already unfamiliar, translated out of their common world into a region of terribly bright light and polished steel, shut in by impersonal things—a vulnerable living being waiting for its dread and pain to be dealt with expertly.

Catching sight of Joan Maylin, she reached out a hand toward her.

"I want you to stay with me. I don't want anyone else."

"But, darling!" urged her mother.

"No, I want Aunt Joan."

Her voice grew shrill. A nurse escorted Jared and Mrs. Oliver to the door.

"I can't understand," the latter whimpered, wringing her hands.

"She isn't herself, madam," said the nurse. "Just a notion she has about Miss Maylin. She mustn't be excited. I'll let you know when she wants to see you."

Vivid against the glare of a lamp, Jared could see the resolute face and broad shoulders of Aunt Joan bent over Nan's bed.

"That's right. You hold my hand hard—harder. That's right. Good girl. Aunt Joan'll help you."

Mrs. Oliver, weeping, betook herself to the sitting room at one end of the hall. Jared walked up and down the corridor. By the strange alchemy which occurs at such times, the remembrance of past coldness, friction, and estrangement was blotted out. He thought only of Nan's beauty, the pleasure they had had, their tender hours together. Now especially he felt at one with her, suffered with her, yearned over her. In the pain of this night, he felt that their lives were being forged together. If there had been mistakes, wrongs, grossness, and selfishness in the past, that was being sublimated, burned away tonight. The future would be different.

Now and then a cry reached him in spite of the muffling walls. And once when the door half opened, he could hear Aunt Joan's voice, comforting and yet masterful. Why was it, he wondered, that everyone still turned to her—after seventy-three years? Why did Nan in her day of need cling to her, a person she had always been inclined to make fun of and dislike? Why did Nan not depend on him, or her mother? After all, he knew the answer to these questions. "You can't bluff about value," he thought. "It's there or it isn't. But what makes value? All sorts of hidden things in one's self that no one sees, but that everyone feels. Integrity —it comes back to that." And the test of such integrity was that people did turn to you, did depend on you.

Well, the past was past; the future would be different. The window at the far end began to show pale. How much longer could it last? He thought back over the preceding months—overshadowed by the expectation of tonight, as if it were a perilous gorge in the mountains through which he and Nan must pass to another landscape. All women who bore children must travel this way, some in courage, some in fear. What of those millions whom medical science did not shield as it shielded Nan and her child, assuring them of the maximum ease and safety? Even so the ordeal was terrible enough. But what of the countless others? Life kept perpetuating itself across the continents, whether science lent its aid or not. Mysterious, unknown life!

Now and then he stopped to exchange a few words with Mrs. Oliver in the waiting room. The distracted, helpless woman fidgeted about, apparently more oppressed by Nan's choice of Joan Maylin than by anything else. At intervals she would haunt the door of the operating room, open it and croon baby talk at Nan through the aperture, only to be once more excluded, and return whimpering to the waiting room, a picture of futile devotion.

Once Aunt Joan came out for a few minutes. She looked tired and grave.

"They're giving her a breath of chloroform," she said, "this

227

twilight-sleep business. Perhaps they're right—I don't know. You see, it's a question of the will. Frances has never been used to making an effort, and now when she has to, she can't. Poor girl! I've never seen a harder time."

"But you don't think, Aunt Joan . . . I mean, there's nothing serious, is there? What does the doctor say?"

She lowered her voice. "Of course he doesn't say anything. Acts as if he knew it all. But I don't think he's too happy. He's not the Lord of Life. After all, we can only do our best and pray. But don't worry." She put her hands on his shoulders. "You look faint. Go out and get a breath of air."

"You look done up yourself," he muttered. "I wish I could do something. Can't you rest a moment?"

"Oh, no," she smiled, "I'm used to it." A faint cry sounded. "Well, I must be getting back."

He heard her voice from within, cheerful and brusque as ever. "That's the girl. That's fine. No nonsense, now . . ." And a shrill answer, "Oh, Aunt Joan . . . I can't. . . . Oh, Aunt Joan . . ."

He shrunk back along the corridor. Not the Lord of Life —but Dr. Emerson was a noted obstetrician. He had assured him that everything would go well, and he had at his command every known improvement and convenience.

With a thumping heart, Jared followed his aunt's advice and went outdoors for a few minutes. The September dawn, a little chill and foggy, sifted through the trees along the sidewalk. Presently a car drove up and Dr. Cary Oliver emerged. He was smoking his morning cigar and looked pink and new-shaven.

"Well, well, well," he hailed, "am I to congratulate a proud father?"

Jared told him how matters stood.

"So much the better," beamed Oliver. "We'll greet the happy event together. I was afraid I might be late. There was no use in both my wife and myself staying up, and I need my sleep. You look worried, my dear boy, but you should really imitate me. This is the time for Christian faith." He gave a victorious puff on his cigar and rounded his chest. "We should all feel very grateful. I'm especially conscious at this time of the divine love. I don't feel like a grandfather, though," he added humorously. "I did the course yesterday in eighty-six."

They went inside. Aunt Joan had come out of the room and was walking toward them along the corridor. Something in her face made Jared go cold.

"Nan?" he breathed.

"I believe she'll live. But, Jare—the baby was born dead."

Stricken, he leaned back against the wall. Not grief, at first, but a sense of irony, cosmic and mirthless, drab as this gray corridor, overwhelmed him. He stared at Joan Maylin, echoing stupidly, "Dead?"

Cary Oliver, his pink face drawn now with concern, looked deflated and bewildered. His wife, who had joined them, burst into tears.

"Darling," said Aunt Joan in a broken voice, looking up at Jared. Her face in the half-light looked like a lined mask.

"Can I see Nan?" he asked.

"Not yet."

The minister straightened up.

"We must thank God for what He has preserved to us," he began in his rich voice.

A flame of rage shot through Jared. "Don't babble," he shot at him, and walking to the end of the hall, stood gazing out of the window.

He did not hear the heavy tread which paused a moment in the corridor as Aunt Joan whispered the news, and then came on. It was only at the sound of his name that he turned to face Judge Tolbecken. The old man's head was up, but he leaned a little on his cane.

"My poor boy!" he said. "My dear, dear boy!" And moving closer, he drew his arm around him.

The embrace conveyed to Jared the realization of something deeper than human sympathy.

A month later Dr. Emerson's bill gave an official ending to this episode. "To Jared Tolbecken," it read, "for professional services rendered—$1000." Science as well as death had claimed its own.

41

For his residence in Dunstable, Angus Grey selected a house in the best location on the Ridge. It was an example of the newer modern architecture, and perfectly appointed. One large reception room and the dining room covered almost the whole of the first floor. Grey's years in the Orient had yielded a rich loot—the silks, lacquers, rugs, and ornaments he had

229

brought back gave a distinct character to the house; it was in no sense a museum, but it had about it an aura cool, sensuous, and slightly exotic.

Grey's servants confirmed the impression. A Chinese majordomo, silken as a cat, who had been his head boy in Shanghai, ruled and recruited the rest of the Oriental household, concerning which Dunstable never learned much, however earnestly it gossiped.

Wealth, charm, and good looks are always enhanced by a breath of mystery; men who paid lip service to moral taboos elsewhere felt at ease and relaxed in Angus's tolerant drawing room. Women, married or not, were thrilled to be escorted by him or invited to his small parties. At once, without dispute, in Dunstable as in Princeton, he became the paragon and magnifico. In the course of the winter, he gave a series of dinner dances, which for cuisine and music, innovation and dash enraptured the younger set. His stag dinner party in the autumn, to which only a select number of the leading citizens of Dunstable were invited, established him with the magnates. He made only one error on this occasion: he invited Judge Rufus Tolbecken.

It was true that he could not without offense have excluded him from such a gathering, for the Judge, though shorn of his manor house, retained an almost legendary name in Dunstable and was, in addition, officially the legal adviser to Grey's company. Jared, knowing both Angus and his grandfather, was to blame for the mistake; but he assumed that the Judge, who no longer went out of an evening, would decline as usual. To his surprise, he accepted, with a certain relish, and no hints of the probable wetness of the party availed in the least.

The old gentleman had been delighted at the accession of the Mutual Oil business, which confirmed his prophecies about the future of the firm under Jared's leadership. He had been equally pleased by an interview with Angus Grey, who was too much a man of the world not to adapt himself to the Judge's age and attitude.

"An attractive young fellow," pronounced the latter. "You know, Jare, he reminds me of some Virginians I used to know in the fifties when I went South to visit my classmate, Jack Powell. Same ease and good manners. Not our type, perhaps—too much bourbon and cards—but fine men."

If Jared felt a certain patronage in Angus and something of the employer's manner, a familiarity with Nan when he

230

called that grated a little, he kept it to himself, excusing it on the ground of his own sensitiveness. Judge Tolbecken saw nothing of this; on the autumn night in question, he looked a very stately figure in his high silk hat, a foreign ribbon in his lapel.

Jared, escorting him with considerable apprehension, drew up before Angus's lighted windows. His concern was not lessened by the roar of voices from the drawing room. From the very outset, the evening promised strains and stresses. A hush fell as Rufus Tolbecken entered, the hush both of respect and constraint. Mr. Dunning of the distilleries made a wry face over the edge of his tumbler at Mr. Belknap of the press. Albert Reiger, who had been chuckling at a ripe story by Karl Kirschbaum, snapped his face back into its accustomed grooves of propriety. The Judge bowed to the twenty-four or -five other guests, most of whom he knew; he was the only one of his generation present, a lonely and somewhat incongruous figure among the businessmen.

Angus Grey hurried forward with his best manner.

"Delighted to see you, Judge. I understand you're making a great exception in my favor tonight, and I'm truly flattered. Chang, a cocktail for Judge Tolbecken."

The other, smiling cordially, raised his hand. "No, thank you, I seldom . . ."

"Now, Judge, for once and to please me. . . . I'd like your opinion. It's a new brew I'm launching in Dunstable. Very harmless . . ."

"Well, sir, if you insist. But I'm afraid my opinion . . . To your good health, Mr. Grey, and your success here!"

He raised the palish liquid to his lips and tasted it.

"Very pleasant. Absinthe, I see—and lime juice. But not exactly harmless."

The mischief in Angus's eyes dimmed. It would have been a lark to get the old fellow lit before he knew it.

"You're a connoisseur, Judge."

"Oh, no, but I've lived in France in my young days. What do you call this particular mixture?"

"A Dr. Funk," said Angus. "Picked it up when I was in Tahiti."

"My compliments to the doctor," bowed Tolbecken. But when his host had moved on, he set down the still-full glass on a table.

For launching his party with a bang, Angus could not have chosen better. The innocent, mild fluid that slipped down so

231

pleasantly and had been served in tumblers blossomed into a sudden glory of high spirits. Even the prudent were tricked in spite of themselves into heavenly exhilaration. Brakes were off. Voices rose. Laughter exploded. Acquaintances took to one another like old cronies. The company floated into the dining room on a rosy cloud.

Champagne started with the terrapin soup—limitless champagne that projected Dr. Funk on a gay crescendo to the tune of a Hawaiian orchestra screened in one corner. "Aloha. . . . Aloha. . . ." Kelly Rogers tossed a rowdy joke across the table. Roars applauded it. "I gotta better one than that," called Belknap.

Judge Tolbecken had the place of honor at Angus's right, but to Jared's concern, Dunning sat next his grandfather on the other side, and Dunning was three quarters drunk. As for Angus, the familiar red band had crept out around his forehead.

"Happy days, Judge!" he said a little carelessly, lifting his champagne.

"Your health, sir," replied the other, with a sip. "I've never tasted a better Pol Roger than this. I recall that my friend, Mr. Livingston of New York—it was in 'seventy-three—used to serve a champagne . . ."

But Angus, turning away, beckoned a waiter. "You tell those Kanakas to put some ginger in it. We're having too much of the dreamy stuff. Let 'em give us a hula."

Judge Tolbecken waited a moment, and then leaned back with a smile. Angus, forgetting him, had addressed Mr. Giddings, a railroad superintendent, on his left. "Speaking of hulas," he said . . .

Paul Dunning, sagging in his chair, confined himself to his right-hand neighbor so that the Judge ate for some minutes in silence.

"You're not drinking," said Angus when he had finished with the railroad superintendent.

The old man's sobriety irked him—all the more since he found the entire crowd suffocating. "Provincial bores!" he thought gazing down the table. He recalled other dinners, his freebooting companions of Malaysia. And here he was in Dunstable seated between a businessman and a church deacon. God!

"No," said the Judge, "at my age I find one glass sufficient."

The muscles on Angus's jaws stood out in spite of his smile. "Must be rather dull?"

Tolbecken overlooked the irony in his host's tone. "No, I find life interesting—too interesting these days in view of the war—a little lonelier perhaps, as one gets along."

"How old are you?" asked Grey, stifling a little yawn. He had reached the stage of drink where he did not choose to exert himself in politeness. What was Judge Tolbecken anyway but a name that had been bought and paid for to the profit of Mutual Oil? It was pleasant also to get Jared where he wanted him after that Princeton affair—take him down a little. He had not finished with him yet.

"It's a question of higher mathematics," smiled the Judge. "I was born in 1831. That makes it eighty-three years."

Angus whistled. "Good Lord! Well, life doesn't owe you anything. I suppose you've seen a good many changes."

"Yes, a good many."

Strange, thought Tolbecken, that young Grey should be using this tone with him. It hardly mattered, except that he had considered him better bred, and felt annoyed at his mistake. There was no resemblance after all to the cavaliers of Warrenton. If Angus recalled other dinners, so equally did the Judge, and with a still more passionate regret. But however his host might behave, that did not absolve him from his duties as a guest. He made another effort.

"Almost too many changes, Mr. Grey. Sometimes they rather bewilder me." And searching for an example that might be supposed to interest the younger man, he launched out on a review of the differences in dress from decade to decade of his life. He exerted himself to be amusing.

Angus sipped his champagne with wandering eyes, and overhearing a talk on his left about the German atrocities, burst out, "That's nothing. Speaking of rape, I'll give you an example of what goes on in China."

The Judge stared at him in amazement. "I beg pardon?" Then as Angus launched into his anecdote, he murmured, "I see," and once more leaned back.

He felt increasingly annoyed. It was a comfort, looking down the table, to see Jared, and to know that there was at least one person present who understood him. Jared had been right; he ought not to have come. The scant respect to himself he could overlook as beneath his notice, but the whole affair insulted his fastidiousness. The memory of his dining room at Tolbecken, and of the men and women who had gathered there, made his heart ache.

If the evening had ended at this point, it would have had

233

no further consequences as far as Rufus Tolbecken himself was concerned. But his lips tightened when, after coffee and brandy had been served, a couple of Hawaiian dancers began entertaining the company. It was merely one of those novelties upon which Angus prided himself, and which he managed in spite of Dunstable limitations. He explained that they were native dances, much more modest than the ones usually seen by tourists. And they were indeed that. The young women wore the colorful *pareu* of the southern islands which clothed them from knee to shoulder. They danced quietly, gracefully. But even so, Polynesian dances of that kind have a single theme, perhaps emphasized all the more by art and reticence. Under drooping eyelids, Rufus Tolbecken observed them, and then watched the faces of his fellow guests in their various expressions of intentness. At length, he leaned back serenely, absorbed to all appearance by his cigar.

There was not much dancing. After twenty minutes, tables were brought out for poker and bridge. The *pareu*-clad girls vanished. They had served merely as a liqueur.

But the Judge still reclined in his chair, watching the smoke eddy in front of him. Jared could not understand why he deferred the signal to leave.

"Would you like me to drive you home now, Grandfather?"

"No, thanks, I'll finish this, while you play a rubber."

Actually he was observing Angus Grey, who sat at a nearby table; and he evidently admired the other's cool fashion of play, his assurance in betting and handling the chips, for he nodded slightly once or twice. In the end, he got up and sauntered about the room, examining now a print, now a shelf of handsomely bound books. One of these he pulled out, glanced at the illustrations, then clapped it to, after which, noticing that Jared had finished his rubber, he beckoned that he was ready.

"Aren't you saying good night to Angus?" inquired his grandson, as the Judge walked out.

"No, I'll not disturb him. You may, if you like."

He drove back with Jared in silence, except that to the question as to how he had liked the party he answered, "We'll discuss that tomorrow."

The blow fell next morning at the office.

"Will you come in here, Jared, and close the door?"

The Judge leaned back in his revolving chair, the tips of his well-shaped fingers together.

"I have always allowed myself one professional luxury,"

234

he began, "and at this late date I do not propose to forego it. I have steadily refused any permanent connection with a client whom I distrusted and of whom I thoroughly disapproved. Not to do so would be unfair both to the client and to myself. It is clear to me that Mr. Grey is a blackguard, and I intend to sever connections with him at once."

A warm current of pride swept through Jared, but he felt almost equally a countercurrent of prudence.

"Don't you think 'blackguard' is a pretty strong term?"

"Perhaps it is. I'll withdraw it if you like. Let me say that I have absolutely no confidence in him."

"May I ask why not, Grandfather? If you are going to reject every client, these days, whose personal habits you dislike, I'm afraid we'd better close the office."

The Judge shook his head. "I'm not unreasonable. Except for Dunning or Belknap, there was no one there last night whom I would not take as a client. They were ordinary men having a night off in a foolish fashion, but that's not my affair. I draw the line at a man who identifies himself with evil and promotes it. My estimate of Grey is cumulative, and it's final as far as I'm concerned. God knows, I can forgive a weakling. The point is that Grey has a strong mind and will. I could overlook one thing or another—his trick of the absinthe, his attitude toward me, his talk at table, his women dancers, his professionalism at poker, his rotten books. But putting all this together, he makes a distasteful impression. I think you wondered that I stayed on last night. It was to see more of him, and I've seen enough. Our firm's connection with him ends today."

"And with it twenty thousand dollars a year," put in Jared. "I suppose, sir, you remember that—as well as other business that the connection would have attracted?"

The Judge raised his eyebrows. "My dear boy, the client's yours; you brought him in. I'm past retiring age; and if you want him, I'll be glad to step out. But while my name's on the door there, I hope you won't talk to me about the size of a retaining fee in an issue of this kind."

It seemed long to Jared since he had heard just that tone; it brought with it the half-forgotten idealism of youth. For an instant, he caught within himself a glimpse of the ruined fortress.

"You're dead right," he returned. "As for your retirement, you must have a poor opinion of me even to mention it on such a point as this. But what excuse can you give him?"

"Excuse?" echoed the other. "I'm not in the habit of giving excuses. I shall tell him that I do not wish to continue the connection. If he asks for reasons, I shall tell him exactly what I have told you."

Needless to say, Jared dreaded the coming interview with Angus; but when it occurred that afternoon, there was none of the acrimony he had expected. Never did Grey's adroitness and self-control show to better advantage. He met the Judge's bald announcement with a cordial smile.

"I was expecting this," he observed.

"Oh, indeed?"

"Yes, Judge Tolbecken, I had heard of your scrupulous sense of honor (which, believe me, I value a great deal) and I had feared that you would realize the inadequacy of your firm to handle my company's business. My friendship for Jared made me eager to stretch a point or two—perhaps not altogether in justice to Mutual Oil. Your stand is a relief to me, Judge, and does you credit."

Jared was boiling with anger, but to his surprise, his grandfather relaxed into a smile and then burst out laughing. His amusement made him look ten years younger. He removed his glasses, still chuckling as he polished them.

"God bless me!" he said, using his strongest oath. "You're an amazing fellow, Grey. Thanks for your testimony to my character. However, as you know perfectly well, my reasons for severing our connections weren't quite that."

"No?" returned Angus. "Well, whatever they are is a matter of indifference to me. I will ask you, Jare to turn over our files to Kent and Hume."

Not a shadow appeared in his good humor, as he rose and paused to light a cigarette. It was only when Jared happened to encounter his eyes a moment that he was startled to see the passion in them.

"See you soon," he added. "Good day, Judge, I'm grateful for this brief association with you. I shall not forget it."

When he had gone out, Rufus Tolbecken shook his head. "He's a remarkable devil. Look out for him, Jare."

After Jared had personally conveyed the Mutual Oil files to the offices of Kent and Hume, he went home to face Nan's fury.

42

Since the stillbirth of her child in September, a change had taken place in Nan Tolbecken. Physically, it could be described as transition from the soft glow of youth to a harder, more brilliant glitter. Restored by several weeks at the sea, she returned to Dunstable with her beauty undiminished, except that there was a hint of strain about it. It demanded a longer time at the mirror; it required more vivid colors and a more extreme fashion. In spite of artfully used cosmetics, the rich curves of her mouth had lost some of their delicacy.

To Angus Grey she seemed more charming than ever. He showered her with attentions—consulted her about his house, showed her his collections, called incessantly, and made himself at home as an old friend. The two were naturally congenial. On her side, he fascinated her; but strangely enough, as time passed, she talked of him less often.

Of course gossip began at once, the usual whispering and hints, hearsay and prophecies, of which, as might have been expected, Jared heard nothing. He knew of Angus's calls at the house, and occasionally disliked his manner, but there had been nothing to make an issue of, even if he had greatly cared. The death of the child had left behind it an apathy too deep for trifles, and he had reached the point of considering most things trivial.

On the afternoon of Judge Tolbecken's break with Grey, he went home chiefly concerned by the thought of the inevitable quarrel. They were frequent nowadays; they added to the general chill and tedium of life.

"Do you mean to tell me," Nan burst out now, "that you are going to give up most of your income because a childish old man gets peeved at a dinner party?"

"I'll ask you to speak of Grandfather with respect," he retorted.

"I'll speak of him as I please. And I suppose you expect me to give up our extra servant, and skimp along as we did last winter?"

He nodded. "Certainly we'll have to economize. There's no other way."

"Oh, isn't there? No other way except for us to be the laughing stock of everybody in town? Here you were with your broken-down firm, hardly able to make ends meet, when Angus gives you a start in the world. Whereupon *Grandfather* turns up his nose and we go back to scraping and saving. No, thank you! I'm through that."

"What are you going to do about it?" he asked coolly.

The question stopped her a moment. She sat trembling with anger, and white except for the drawn line of her mouth. On the point of defiance, she choked it back, but at last went on in an almost toneless voice.

"I guess you'll be telling me next that we have to break off with Angus ourselves—the one interesting man in town—the only one who knows how to live, who can put tang in things. I'm so tired of the whole business . . ."

Jared shrugged. "*I* certainly am. As for Angus, he had the gall to pretend that we were severing relations because we didn't feel ourselves up to handling his work. If he spreads that line around town, there'll be war. If he doesn't, I have no quarrel with him. That's Grandfather's affair. But I have no particular love for him either, and I'm glad to be off the payroll of his company."

She remained silent a long while—so long that Jared had turned to go out when she addressed him in the same thin voice.

"Just a moment. There's something I want you to understand too. You may fool Dunstable with your honorable, pure, high-minded Tolbecken bluff, but you don't fool me. We know each other too well for that, don't we? Whatever Angus Grey is, he isn't a hypocrite. You are."

The shaft struck home, upsetting his poise, which thus far he had been able to keep. Truth, more than injustice, rouses anger. Jared was no more of a hypocrite than most people. But, like most people, he was aware of private compromises which, if known, would invalidate the esteem in which he was generally held.

Jared boiled inwardly, but could think of no defense except a countercharge. He bridled his answer not so much in self-control as in distaste for mud slinging.

He merely said, "Before passing judgment on me, you might examine yourself."

She gave a short laugh. "I'm a good deal more sincere than you are. I know what I am and what I want. However I may act with other people, I don't pretend to myself—like you."

After his heat had cooled, he acknowledged the truth of her claim. She had the integrity of a selfishness without regrets, just as Angus had. He could not say as much for himself.

Angus Grey called that evening, the very incarnation of good humor. To Jared's relief he admitted guessing Judge Tolbecken's reasons for the break.

"I saw him looking at my edition of Aretino. The illustrations are pretty warm, I confess. I'll show them to you sometime. Your grandfather isn't hard to read. When he barged off with never a good night, I knew what he thought of me. But put yourself in my place. If he had called me hard names, I'd have had to protest as a matter of form—not" (he added with a glint of steel behind the smile) "that it would trouble me personally. Then, from one thing to another, we might have had more and worse, because I'm not too humble. As to my flank attack, I couldn't resist it."

"That's all right," said Jared. "I've seldom seen Grandfather more amused. But it would be unfortunate if others in town got the wrong impression."

Angus nodded. "They'll get no impression at all from me, except that Judge Tolbecken and I differed. Of course, I can't be responsible for rumors. I'm not to blame if your grandfather puts himself in a false position."

It was true enough. Anyone who heard of the shift to Kent and Hume would interpret it only to the prejudice of Tolbecken and Tolbecken. The Mutual Oil Company was not the sort of client that any law firm would willingly surrender.

"But what interests me," Angus went on, "is your attitude. I take it *you* don't share the Judge's outrage at the flesh and the devil?"

Nan, entering at the moment, heard the question and smiled. Under the circumstances it was a hard one to answer in terms of yea or nay. Jared would have liked to range himself flatly on Rufus Tolbecken's side; but he had star witnesses here as well as his conscience to refute him. It was the usual dilemma of the two masters.

"No," he admitted. "But I think he's right from his standpoint."

Angus shrugged. "We're not discussing his standpoint. Are you and I going to stay friends?"

Short of absurdity, there was no reason for answering no to this. And who dares to be absurd?

239

"As far as I'm concerned," Jared replied coolly.

He did not catch the wink that Grey directed at Nan or the dry tone of his voice.

"Well, that's delightful. By God, I've never seen you look better than tonight, Frances. Rose is your color, my dear. How about a drink?"

As the winter passed, Jared's forebodings about the effect on his practice of the loss of Mutual Oil were progressively realized. Just as one rich client brings the next, so the loss of one is apt to detach another. Obscurely (he could never tell how nor through whom) the impression spread that Angus Grey, in justice to his company, had been forced to engage the services of a more experienced and aggressive firm. Business, instead of growing, began to ebb; the prestige of six months ago faded out.

Late in February, Jared, having cleared his desk of the morning's docket, sat in thought about this problem. If the present decline continued, the office would not be worth maintaining in a couple of years. Except for the sake of his grandfather, who might not live so long, the prospect, curiously enough, exhilarated him. Definite failure here would give an excuse for starting somewhere else, doing something else. Or perhaps by that time America would be forced into the war.

Yes, that would be good-by to the known, the tedious, and the small. How much nobler, how much easier to fight for a great cause in France than to drudge in Dunstable! Over there, the fetters of the past were struck off; one could begin again.

It was a wet-weather day. A drizzle of melting snow turned the sidewalks to slush and smeared the windowpanes. He got up, looking down at the vague scuffle in the streets, listening to the endless torrent of wheels and footsteps. What was the use of it? he thought, with a sudden pang of disgust. He fell into the mood of retrospection. After all, he pondered, the fading of his practice agreed with the whole pattern of his life. He thought of the distinction of Tolbecken, the standards it implied: they had been cheapened to correspond with the invading vulgarity of the times. He recalled his intellectual interests at college: one by one they had atrophied in the interest of professional expertness, leaving a narrower, barer outlook. In still more vital directions it had been the same—the blunder of his marriage, the sale of Tolbecken, the present emptiness of domestic life. Symbolizing everything else, the stillborn child haunted him; it had been stillborn, like every other hope, at the point of its fruition, as if he were bound

240

by some relentless enchantment. He looked down on the swarming street, conscious of a refrain in its tramp and rumble more eloquent than any form of words, the surge of humanity, restless and forever seeking an outlet from the blind alley of its limitations.

The summons of the telephone recalled him to his desk. "Yes," he replied woodenly, "Jared Tolbecken speaking." "Can't you guess who it is?" returned the voice.

An odd delusion possessed him, one that made no sense.

He faltered half to himself, "No, I'm afraid not."

A laugh strangely familiar replied, "I don't blame you. I can't realize it myself!"

"Clarice!" he exclaimed.

A sense of dream, of unreality, closed around him.

"But how . . ." he stammered. "I can't believe it. . . . Where are you?"

"At the station. I telephoned to your house. . . . Will you come over for me?"

"I can't believe it," he repeated. "*You* here? Here? Just a moment, I'll . . ."

He hung up the receiver and was struggling into his coat as he crossed the outer office. "What'll I say . . ." began the stenographer, but his footsteps were already on the stairs. . . . And just as a dream has no transition, he found himself in the waiting room, his gaze circling the white patches of faces, until suddenly it stopped at the far end, and he swung across toward the figure standing at the door there.

It might have been Paris again—the kisses on either cheek, the dark flash of her eyes almost on a level with his, the modulations of her voice.

She was explaining about Pierre, their eyes eager upon each other. Wounded at the Marne, he had been temporarily assigned to the Service of Supplies. He was in America for the purchase of munitions, was at that moment in Philadelphia, but would spend the night at Dunstable. It was only a brief visit. . . . She had begged so hard to come, all the more as he was still far from well. . . .

She had grown taller, Jared thought, but that was an illusion, caused, as he soon discovered, by a subtle change in her features and bearing. A soldierly quality, the sense of hardness and training which was spiritual rather than physical, impressed him. As they crossed the station, he noticed how people glanced back at her, despite her plain dress.

They used the ordinary phrases that cover emotion.

241

"Not just a night," he was protesting. "Now that you are actually here—though I still don't believe it—you'll surely give me—I mean us—more than that."

She shook her head, smiling, and answered something about the urgency of Pierre's mission—that she had to be with him. But her thought was on Jared. She noticed with a pang that his shoulders drooped a little and that the corners of his mouth were drawn down. There was already a touch of gray at his temples. With a sudden warmth, she thrust her arm beneath his and drew close. It was a simple act, but one that startled him by making him realize how unused he had become to warmth.

"Of course you'll be staying with us," he insisted. "Everybody will claim you, but mine's the first claim."

"Of course it is," she agreed, aware of the hunger in his face. "But Frances . . ."

"Nan will be delighted," he put in conventionally.

Even now that they were in the car together, the dream impression continued. It could not be real that on this dismal winter's day he had with him, threading the streets of Dunstable, her for the sight of whom he had yearned five long years. He could not bring it clearly into the focus of his mind.

She gave a sudden exclamation. "No! It's not possible. Wasn't this the place . . . I mean, wasn't Tolbecken here?" She pointed to a façade that included the new Wellington Hotel and the Acme Trust Company.

"Yes." He nodded without looking.

They drove on silently toward the Ridge through a tangle of trucks and cars. Business gave way to residences, new and opulent, with only here and there a brick relic of the past lingering on.

"It's incredible," she mused after a time. "Everything is changed—everything!"

As they approached his house, reality began to impose itself. He reflected that it was perhaps unwise to take Clarice here rather than to Aunt Mary Reiger's or to the Tolbecken apartment. It had been an instinctive impulse on his side in order to keep her as much to himself as possible. But what, after all, would be Nan's reaction to the Delarts? Clarice's arrival, successful surprise as it was, had the disadvantage that it had given no time for maneuvers and preparations. Also, he winced at the notion that she should learn too much about his relations with Nan. In the end one thought determined him. He recalled that Nan had mentioned lunching out with one of her friends. This meant that before the round of family welcome began, there were perhaps two hours in which he and Clarice could be alone—the only probable time during her stay. And these two hours were worth all the rest.

"Here we are," he said drawing up before the small front next to the flat building; more than ever he was aware of its contrast to Tolbecken. He felt that she too was aware of it as they walked to the door. Seen through the drizzle of snow, the place looked smaller and more forlorn than usual.

The house had an unlived-in impression in spite of the good furniture, which Jared saw Clarice felt. A giant clock, too high for the ceiling, stood in the hall ticking vacantly.

"Wasn't that on the landing in Tolbecken?" she asked. "Do you remember how it sounded at night, Jare, when we were small?"

She did not add that it looked like an exile.

Yes, Madam was out, reported the girl who answered Jared's ring. The servant hadn't expected company for lunch and wished she had known about it, but would do her best.

Alone in the guest room, Clarice strove with the weight at her heart. So this was where he lived? Her woman's eyes saw more than even Jared feared—the lack of warmth and care in this house—the absence of signs of love, imagination, interest.

Alone before the fire in the drawing room, they each felt the impossibility of bridging five years in their two hours. But there was more than time between them. He read in her eyes a search for someone else, bewilderment at not finding him, and then a flash of joy at recognizing him here or there. That was the trouble: she had not altered save in the progressive, the splendid sense. He had dwindled from what he had once been. The gradual realization of this on his part, if not on hers, widened the chasm. It brought no lessening of the adoration he felt for her; but it brought also the sense, as never before, of self-erected, invincible barriers. He realized suddenly that whereas she talked with the old-time frankness about herself, he, on the other hand, felt somewhat on the defensive, tried to keep up appearances.

"I've done fairly well at the law," he said. "It's a long road, of course, has its ups and downs, but the practice is growing."

He could not bear having her regard him as a failure simply because of the Mutual Oil fiasco. The statement was not altogether false, nor was it entirely true. But he intended it to leave a better impression than the facts warranted.

"I'm so glad," she rejoiced. "But I knew you would succeed in anything you did. I only hope you haven't so many clients

243

that you can't accept another—the French Government, for example. Pierre desires some firm to manage his contracts for him when he leaves. I proposed you."

"Great!" he returned. Something of the professional manner helped him to conceal how much this windfall meant. "Did you ever know of any firm who had too many clients? Besides, I'd consider it a service to the cause."

He grew eloquent about liberty and civilization, condemning the President for his neutral policy.

She shrugged. "The *Boches* are also talking about liberty and civilization. I've seen too much war. Your President looks far beyond it. You do more for the world here behind your desk than behind a cannon."

But when he contested this with a certain parade of ideals, she remained silent, then changed the subject. She was eager to see Da-vid, and plied him with questions about him, most of which he could not answer.

"Aren't you friends any longer?"

"Oh, yes, but we're both so busy."

"Too busy for friendship?"

She leaned toward him. "Are you happy, Jare? I know that no one is altogether happy, but I have the fear that you . . ."

"Happy?" he repeated. "Oh, quite. Naturally, the trouble this autumn about the child . . ." His voice fell away.

She nodded. "Yes, but there will be other children to take its place."

Across his mind, like a dim vapor, drifted the thought of Nan's resolution and of his compliance with it, of their relationship, degrading, sterile.

"I hope so," he answered.

So the time passed. They were interrupted by Nan returning from her lunch. She stared at the tall figure that rose as she entered, noting the chic of the stranger's hat and dress. But the name startled her.

"This is Clarice Delart," explained Jared. "She and Captain Delart will be our guests tonight."

"Well!" said Nan. "I don't need to say that I've heard a lot about you. Isn't this a charming surprise! I can't tell you how much we've enjoyed your sweet wedding gift." She had dropped at once into her "society" accent. "*So* nice you're going to stay with us, Madame Delart. Such a treat for Jare!"

"Do call me Clarice."

"Oh, may I? Thank you *so* much."

They were a study in physical and spiritual contrasts as

244

they stood there; Nan's beauty, direct and flaming, and Clarice's restrained elegance and poise were at opposite poles. His wife's affability did not deceive Jared; he knew the ice beneath it.

"Please sit down," continued Nan. "Won't you have a cigarette? No? Well, I will if you don't mind. Bad habit, I suppose." Cold-eyed, she studied her guest through the smoke, exhaling as she talked. "Jared doesn't approve. Good old Jare! By the way, I'm simply *mad* about your hat."

It turned out that Nan knew a great deal more of the fashions than Clarice. The topic dwindled, was replaced by an exchange of polite queries.

"I'm afraid," said Clarice, "that I'm taking too much of your time, Jare—I mean, on a busy afternoon away from the office!"

Nan made a slight grimace. "You needn't be concerned about that," she laughed. "Busy afternoons in his office are pretty rare, aren't they, Jared?"

He got up from his chair in some confusion.

"I think it's about time we were calling on the family, Clarice," he said.

43

As much entertainment as possible took place during the next twenty-four hours. Aunt Mary Reiger led off with a family dinner that evening, followed by an impromptu reception for such friends as were available, to meet Captain and Madame Delart. Aunt Joan, mindful of her reputation, spent the following morning hot-faced in the kitchen, producing with the help of old Carrie a lunch abundant in popovers and feather-weight rolls, scalloped oysters and mince pie. Aunt Sophia and Uncle Vincent, who were denied any other opportunity, offered breakfast, with a battery of grapefruit, Maryland sausages, codfish balls, fried potatoes, and waffles—an array that astonished and somewhat daunted Pierre Delart.

More than on Clarice, it was on him, thus far unknown to the family, that attention was centered. In his tight-fitting, double-breasted serge suit and long, square-toed shoes, no one could mistake him for anything else than a French officer *en civil*. He showed the effects of the war only by a certain fatigue about the eyes; otherwise, in his straightforward, quiet manner, which remained unruffled amid the babble of a foreign tongue which he had learned to speak only haltingly, he made the same impression on Jared of virile gentleness that he had in Paris.

He represented the blending of the Catholic and military traditions. At five o'clock next morning (it happened to be Sunday) Jared, after too brief a night, was roused by footsteps in the hall and down the stairs. Going to the window, he saw Pierre and Clarice moving off through the gray light in the direction of church, several blocks distant.

"What is it?" muttered Nan sleepily.

"Nothing. They're going to Mass."

"Good Lord!" she exclaimed, turning over.

But when he had gone back to bed, he could not sleep. The incident revealed so much—the secret value behind his guests' distinction, the quality of their life which so contrasted with his own. They were victorious, not defeated. But their victory had not been granted them on easy terms. Taking a long view of it, he reflected, life showed an eerie sense of justice.

The Tolbeckens, particularly those of the older generation, thoroughly approved of Captain Delart. Grandmother praised his manners, Aunt Joan his modesty, the Judge conferred on him the highest title he could think of: "A gentleman, Clarice." And raising his glass to Pierre at dinner, "I drink to France, sir, who is so happily represented by you." He and Delart were as much together as time allowed. In conference with Jared, they discussed the munitions contract, though it was only with reluctance that the Judge would hear of a fee in that connection.

The younger Tolbeckens were disappointed that Pierre talked so little about his war experiences. They could not draw from him any battle descriptions or exciting stories. Once he spoke wistfully of his expected return to his squadron, which had been delayed by the slow healing of his wound.

"I suppose," said Uncle Vincent with a show of spirit, "that you are keen for action, Captain, want to tackle the Germans again, eh?"

"No," answered Pierre flatly. "I want my friends and my horse."

"Doesn't sound like much of a hero to me," Vincent later declared to Aunt Sophia.

From Jared's standpoint, the Delarts' visit, engrossed as it was by the family, was tantalizing enough. Minutes, hours

246

passing; the pittance of Clarice's stay dwindling to an end—and no further chance came to be alone with her. He consoled himself with the thought that yesterday he would have considered the prospect merely of seeing and hearing her a miracle. After all, what would they say if they were alone? But having had something, he wanted more. It was not a question of speech, but the sense of intimacy that the presence of the others excluded. Now and then, as his compensation, he caught a spark of that when their eyes met.

There were other grains of comfort spread here and there. He exulted in her superiority to members of the "crowd" at the Reigers'. Dressed in a black evening gown, her hair worn low, and with no ornaments except a rope of pearls, she stood at one side, inevitably apart.

"What an interesting time you must be having in France," said Mrs. Ellis. "Real excitement! Nothing ever happens around here. I wish Captain Delart was wearing his uniform. I was just telling Eaby last night how becoming a uniform would be to him, and that he ought to get into the militia. Guess I'm a born militarist. Do tell me about the war."

But when Clarice made an effort to describe the whirlwind in a few words, Mrs. Ellis's gaze wandered toward a group of her friends who had lowered their voices about something. She wondered what it was.

"Madame Delart, don't you think we ought to be in it?" demanded Grace Armstrong. "I declare I'm ashamed of America. That's because we've got a college professor for President who would rather hear himself talk than fight. It's all such a tragedy, I can't think of anything else. By the way," she said, turning to the elder Reiger girl, "who do you think I saw last week in Philly? George Butts. And he said to remember him to you. . . . No, I don't think he's going to be at the Parkers'. He doesn't care for Susan. . . ." And the tide of local gossip marooned Clarice, until a newcomer had to be introduced. But now and then she exchanged a smile with Jared.

For him the brightest event of the evening centered about Angus Grey. When Angus, arriving with the air of a man who expects nothing, caught sight of Clarice, his bored look changed to interest, then to astonishment; he repaired his charm and made haste to come forward.

"We are old acquaintances, Madame Delart."

Puzzled for a moment, she shook hands, hesitating. "I'm not quite sure . . ." Then coldly, "Oh, of course. Princeton. Mr. Grey."

"That's it," he beamed. And conveying a compliment in a glance, "We have both changed since then."

His assurance missed the dryness of her answer.

"I hope so. Pierre—Mr. Grey; my husband, Captain Delart."

But Angus was not to be put off. Having exchanged bows and a word or two with Pierre, he returned to the charge with all the resources of his ease, good humor, and address. Few could resist him when he chose to be agreeable. Perhaps there was a shade of malice and the thought of outshining Jared, who stood silent nearby, but as an expert in women, he admired her elegance, and he resolved to monopolize her. He hung on with sprightly chat, undiscouraged by half smiles and vague nods, rather stimulated by her coolness, which he thought would be fun to melt. People came up and retired, but Angus lingered. Noticing his infatuation, Nan Tolbecken's eyes hardened.

Clarice listened absently, looked over his shoulder, and fingered her pearls. But he thought he was making progress. Moving conversationally from one thing to another, he had launched into an anecdote of Indochina, and told it so well that even she had begun to pay attention, when, without warning, she interrupted him with a brief "Pardon" and walked off toward the door. At a loss, Angus stared after her. Then his face flushed. An ungainly, tall figure in an ill-fitting dinner coat was coming across the room toward Clarice, hands outstretched.

"Da-vid!" she was exclaiming. "I wondered if you were never coming. . . ."

Angus, turning away, caught Jared's smile. From then on, Clarice, in talk with Mansen, forgot him.

Late next morning during a lull of hospitality, when the Judge, after church, for once broke the Sabbath to confer with Pierre and Jared at the office, and Aunt Joan was devising lunch, Grandmother and Clarice sat alone in the drawing room of the Tolbecken apartment. Clarice sat on a low stool beside Madame Tolbecken. Their heads were on a level, the snow of Grandmother's cap contrasting with the black gloss of the young woman's hair. More than proximity lessened the half century dividing them. They thought curiously alike about most things and were devoted to each other. For Rachel Tolbecken, this hour of chat alone with one whom she habitually called her favorite girl was an inexpressible reprieve from the tranquil loneliness of her books and embroidery. Her round little face glowed with contentment; her old eyes, their blue turned to gray, rested on the other in affectionate approval.

They had discussed the Delart children—little Pierre's sturdiness and little Marie's naughtiness, which Clarice regarded more sternly than Mrs. Tolbecken.

"She's such a trial, Grandmother—a perfect little tomboy."

"So were you, my dear."

"Not like Marie, I hope. She has a really bad temper. I can't keep her in clothes—she ruins them so fast."

"So did you, Clarice."

"Sometimes," smiled the other, "I'm at my wits' end. Punishment doesn't seem to help."

"Don't be too strict," counseled Mrs. Tolbecken earnestly. "Of course, I don't approve of these wishy-washy modern ways with children, but the ways of my time were much too hard. Love and common sense is the only plan."

They discussed, with a great deal of head shaking by Grandmother, Frederick Lehman's illness, that kept him and Elizabeth on the Riviera. Mrs. Tolbecken took a darker view of it than Clarice.

"Do you know of your mother's plans, if anything should happen?"

"I think she would come home. She hasn't been happy in France. But I hope you don't believe that Father will . . ."

"No, no," Mrs. Tolbecken reassured her. "I simply meant *in case*. One of the truest proverbs ever made was about crossing bridges."

She took Clarice's hand, shapely and dark against the faded ivory of her own frail ones, stroking it gently, conscious of its warmth.

Clarice, bending over, pressed her lips to the other's withered fingers. Then after a pause, "Do you remember how you used to read to Jare and me when we were children, Grandmother—*Ivanhoe, The Talisman?*"

"Of course I do. I can see you just as plain as day—you and he on that sofa yonder, only it was at Tolbecken. You, with your scratched legs and black bang, sitting close to him. You were both dears."

Still fondling the smooth hand, the old lady sank into thought, her eyes brooding. When she spoke again, it was in a different tone.

"Clarice, I want to ask you something."

"Yes, Grandmother?"

249

"You used to care for Jared once. Maybe it was even more than that?"

"Yes"—the other's glance faltered—"it was more than that."

Mrs. Tolbecken cleared her voice. "At one time I hoped that you and he would marry. It would have been . . . Well, we won't discuss that. You chose wisely. But I was thinking of him as a boy—what he might have become. . . . I wanted to ask your opinion, dear, because you care for him and have good judgment. Do you find him changed?"

Her lips trembling a little, Clarice nodded.

"Lost is the word," Mrs. Tolbecken went on bitterly. "He thinks we don't see it when he's here of an evening, and sits there looking at the fire. We try not to let on. But sometimes I can't sleep afterwards. Lost, commonplace, like so many of the others here, when once he had such promise . . ."

"Don't!" exclaimed Clarice. "Please don't! He's not that—not that to us who know him. But he has changed—faded . . ."

"Very well," said Grandmother, "I want to know what we can do. You have clear eyes. He's still young." But when Clarice remained silent, she added, "You can speak frankly with me. No one will know."

There was a long pause.

"It's not that, Grandmother; but there are certain things that I—especially I—oughtn't to say. And perhaps, after all, they aren't necessary to say."

Mrs. Tolbecken pondered.

"Yes, you're right. It isn't necessary. We all know—at least, Joan and I do—but we're afraid to admit it even to ourselves. He must separate from Frances, divorce or not. Think of me suggesting a thing like that after the stand we took with Bella! But there you are." And Grandmother, appalled at this admission, flushed. "You know, Clarice, now that I'm old, I think I see things more clearly, at least more unselfishly. Perhaps not, perhaps it's just weakness. But when the time comes, I'll not oppose him as I did Bella and Maylin. There was a good deal we used to call principle once that was only pride." She broke off. "But that's not all. I've never understood *why* he married Frances. Is it only his marriage that's wrong? I'm afraid not. I'm afraid it's something else, something deeper . . ."

Her voice dwindled off. Clarice answered the appeal in her eyes.

"We mustn't be afraid, Grandmother. That won't help."

Aunt Joan entered.

"What are you two talking about?"

"Oh—this and that," said Grandmother evasively.

A few days later, Jared saw Pierre and Clarice off in New York. Before the midnight sailing, they had dinner together at a small French hotel. Pierre was in high spirits at the prospect of home. He believed that he would shortly be re-assigned to his regiment, and kept wondering how it had gone with various old friends in the past month. He brought up one name after another, smiling fondly over the peculiarities of one or the other. Jared, in his civilian isolation, envied him the comradeship of the army.

"Do you think it will be a long war?" he asked.

"Yes, it is war to the death, and Germany is a strong nation. . . . By the way, this is excellent Burgundy. Do you remember, Clarice, how Henri Lambert liked Chambertin? He had a keen taste in wine. *Pauvre vieux*. . . . Even he would have enjoyed this."

It seemed to Jared that Clarice, submissive though she might be, felt her own exclusion from this band of friends. After all, it had preceded her in Pierre's life and unconsciously absorbed him now. Sometimes, as he talked of the regiment, a certain loneliness showed in her eyes. But because of their common exclusion, Jared felt nearer to her. If Pierre had his world of the messroom and garrison, they had shared one of their own that was closed to him. Not that Jared had any illusions. He knew that Clarice's loyalty to her husband took precedence of anything else in her life. But something of her, however small, belonged to him and to none other.

They dined leisurely, and minimized the element of fare-well.

It was late when Pierre, having consulted his watch, threw a questioning glance at his wife.

"Yes," she nodded. "But you mustn't forget my gift to Jare. Or rather it's a gift from Father and me. Pierre has one like it; I wanted you to have this one."

"*Parbleu*, yes," said Captain Delart, feeling in his pocket and bringing out a small, flat package. "*Mon cousin*, let me add my part to the gift. My wife has told me of her affection for you. I want you to accept mine."

But when Jared was on the point of opening the package, Clarice laid her hand on his.

"Not now. Not till I'm gone."

251

There was a moment of farewell at the steamer.

"You don't realize," he told her, "what seeing you has meant to me."

"It's been the same with me," she answered. "It's been worth all the miles and days just to see you again. After the war," she kept saying, "it'll be your turn to visit us in France."

Et sans faute! added Pierre heartily.

"Of course," he agreed. "Some day . . . if I ever can."

Out of the darkness of the wharf, he could see her figure at the rail grow dim and at last vanish as the steamer backed out. Once again it was carrying her away from him into the years.

With a leaden heart, he returned to his hotel, oppressed by the thought of the next day in Dunstable and of the days beyond that. The moment of rebellion had not arrived, but he felt its approach. There would come the time when he would refuse to go on along the parching, endless road. But not yet. He did not care enough about anything even to rebel. It was easier to put up with tomorrow.

Then he remembered Clarice's gift, and eagerly drew the little package from his pocket. It was like her to realize how forlorn he would feel that night. The wrapping contained a leather case and a written card. *Au revoir again! And that something of me may be with you always.*

Opening the clasp, he found a miniature, a frame of blue and ivory out of which shone the vividness of her face.

44

That same evening, Nan Tolbecken excused herself from a dinner at the Sedleys' on the plea of a bad headache, on which account, as she told her hostess, she considered it more prudent to stay at home. With unusual thoughtfulness she gave her servant an extra night out, and paid the girl's way to the cinema. She then changed to a luxurious dressing gown of wine-colored velvet, carefully drew the curtains of the living-room windows, set out a decanter and a siphon, lit a cigarette, and proceeded to enjoy ill health in front of the fire.

She thought in terms of the great world—a mistlike drifting of pleasant things and places: the terrace of a villa at

Palm Beach; the grand stairway of the Opéra in Paris; New York shop fronts; the deck of a yacht thronged with fashionable guests; a long, magnificent dining room; exotic, far-off cities. And everywhere herself, on terrace or stairway or yacht, in dining room or bazaar, a capricious queen with the world at her feet.

One element, however, distinguished these pictures from earlier dreams of a like sort: that she shared them in fancy with another whose presence added an unusual glow. This spelled danger; for selfishness, like any other principle, should avoid compromises. Watered by love, it is apt to lose its cutting edge.

She had never felt just this way before, and it disturbed her a little. It was as if a person, splashing in warm shallows, relaxing in the caress of the water, were suddenly to be caught in the grip of a swift current flowing toward unknown depths. Something not altogether of her own will, not altogether egoistical, imposed itself on her vision—something that brought her a novel sensation of abandon. She told herself that she must keep her head; this was the time for strategy, not idle dreaming.

And yet, cheek in palm before the fire, she let her eyes soften, looked again and again at the minute hand of the clock that crept too slowly around the dial, and more than once caught herself in a sigh. Nan was suffering something more serious than a headache; for the first time in her career, she felt an ache at her heart.

Attentive as she was to every sound on the street, she heard a light step before it reached the door, and hastened to open it.

"A wet night," said Angus slipping off his raincoat, "wet and cold, which makes you seem all the more like a flame. I've been pining for this."

With a gallantry she loved, as something new and foreign, he raised her hand to his lips.

"Tonight you are not charming, my charmer—only gorgeous, enchanting, marvelous!"

She fixed drinks, and as they stood silent for a moment before the fire, glasses in hand, their eyes met, and held.

"To the future, Nan!"

"To the future!" she answered.

He slipped his arm about her shoulders as they sat together gazing into the fire; but when he tried to draw her to him, she held back slightly.

He leaned back, studying the flames. Then he said, "We

253

understand each other, Nan. By the Lord, I sometimes think that's better than love. We were made for each other. You don't expect me to go on philandering, do you? I want you. Do you want me?"

She turned suddenly to face him.

"Yes."

"Well, then?"

"If you understood me so well," she returned, "you could realize that it isn't as simple as all that." She laid her hand on his knee. "I'm not content to play hide-and-seek like this. I hope you're not."

"No, of course not," he murmured.

In point of fact, the same dilemma that troubled Nan confronted him also to a less degree. Among the women he had known, she was more congenial than any—congenial to something other than whim or desire. He thought of her at times almost as a mate rather than as a potential mistress. But his common sense recognized the folly of such extravagance. Here she was, hinting again at marriage following a divorce. What did she on her side have to offer except good looks and congeniality? Nothing. Grey's ambition and strong will reserved marriage as a trump for the queen of diamonds. He was not the man to waste it on a low card of hearts. Women as playthings or even companions could be had at a cheaper price. But Nan, he confessed admiringly, was no fool; she presented a fine problem in tactics.

"I must get a divorce," she went on. "But that's not too easy. You know the Tolbeckens. Still, there's always Reno."

He nodded, his thought, like a chess player's, on the move ahead.

"Which takes money," she added.

Angus shrugged. "You needn't be concerned about that." This time she let him draw her closer.

"But after I am divorced, what then? I'd have to be sure . . . What I mean," she concluded, "is that I don't care to be left in the ditch."

"You're priceless," he smiled. "You know I love you, I want you. Don't you trust me? I'm afraid no written contract we could draw up now would be legally valid afterwards —you might consult Jared on the point."

"Don't joke," she returned passionately. "But you're always vague. You've never told me in so many words that you would marry me. If you love me, can't you be definite?"

"No," he answered, resolving on a bold stroke. "Of course,

holding you like this, intoxicated with you, hungry for you, I'll tell you anything you like. But I'd rather be frank. Why do you women always bother about marriage? What has love to do with it? Not a thing in the world. When you boil it down, what it amounts to is security. I'll provide for your security—but I don't intend to put on handcuffs—and that's flat. You may not think it, but I'm paying you a compliment, Nan. I usually lie to women."

"Thank you so much!" she drawled, getting up from the divan. "But you've made a mistake not to lie to me."

"No, I haven't," he smiled. "I think you're a realist."

She faced him, blazing, conscious of a world that had suddenly grown small and poor.

"Perhaps I misunderstood you. You weren't suggesting that after my divorce I should trail around as your woman, were you?"

He sighed, shook his head, and opened his cigarette case.

"What an idea! How could you imagine such a thing! When I'm madly in love with you! That rather hurts me. Let's talk about the wedding. Church? Or at home?"

"At least," she raged, "you might care enough not to sneer."

Once more he shook his head.

"There you are—if I lie, you suspect me; if I'm frank, I insult you. What can I do?" Then with a sudden ardor, "Divorce or not—it makes no difference to me. Tonight or tomorrow or when you're through with the courts, I want you. While I'm talking of life and love, you stickle about marriage. I won't promise you that, but I'll promise you more —travel, glamour, passion—the whole world, Nan!"

Despite his real glow, he studied her, and saw that her lips had parted.

"By the way," he went on, "I meant to tell you—I'm leaving in a few weeks. Even *you* can't redeem this place. I've applied for the foreign field and got what I wanted—the East again. Are you going to stay behind in Dunstable?"

"Leaving?" she repeated. She felt numb and stricken. Her anger drained away. "But I thought . . ."

"I know, but it isn't good enough. No promotion in the company would pay me to live here. I own shares enough to do as I like. The fellow who took my place doesn't thrive in the Orient. I do, and I'm going back. How about it? I want you with me."

She stood pallid, gazing into the future without him—the

255

future that had grown stuffy and paltry because of the dreams he had kindled in her; she thought of the round of stale parties with the stale people she had always known. . . .

"Listen," he continued, pressing his advantage, and drawing her down once more beside him, "listen, Nan. I'm playing fair with you. As I said before, we understand each other. You know that I've loved a good many women, and I know that you've played with a good many men. But I love you more than the others, just as I think you're more beautiful than any of them. Don't let's be silly and stick at words. We can give each other pleasure for a long while. And that's what counts. You'll have everything you want, and I'll have you. Think! We two out there! *Living* every moment—in the world or alone, on the sea, or in cities. But *living*—squeezing the juice out of things, keen for the next deal of the cards, the next sailing. By God, you're lovely, Nan! I want to see you in the East. That's the background for you. You can forget this half life here! Are you coming with me?"

She sat leaning against him in the full grip of the current. It was carrying her away from the shallows, into the depths. More than ever, the hearth, like a magic window, yielded vision upon vision.

"But afterward?" she murmured. "Afterward—when the fun's over?" The cold half of her mind presented a different picture. She straightened a little. "What would be the last sailing?"

"I'm no prophet," he answered. "You know as much as I do. You might bury me or I you. We might drift apart. We might even decide to marry. What interests me is the fun we can have beforehand." And taking her suddenly in his arms, "What about tonight?"

Dread swept over her, dread of his masterfulness, dread that for once the game was out of her hands, dread also of herself that she loved him the more for mastering her.

"No!" she cried. "Angus! Not tonight! Please . . . please not tonight. . . ."

It was amazing, as he thought of it later, that he had yielded—it was unlike him. But a sudden odd whim had possessed him, a queer tenderness of a kind he had never experienced. For once he did not savor the fear and the submission, preferred the quarry still unwon, enjoyed the flavor of postponement. Having achieved the victory, he conceded her the battle. Unconsciously he was wiser in this than he supposed.

256

"Of course," he said, releasing her. "I'm sorry—it's just that I love you. By Jove," he added dryly, "I didn't know that I loved you so much. How about some music? I think it would be better."

As he played and sang in his clear, rich voice, she stood looking at him, aglow and with a softer light in her eyes than had ever shone there.

"I can't lose him," she thought. "Whatever happens, I can't do without him."

When they parted at last, she gave him her lips willingly.

"Think it over, Nan," he said. "I must have you with me in the East. You must go with me."

"I'll think it over," she answered. And when he was gone, she stood for a while motionless, staring at the closed door.

To the Dunstable prophets a separation between Jared and Nan Tolbecken had seemed probable for some time. Gossip had started not long after the marriage, had gained headway at the stillbirth of the child, had become strident after the arrival of Angus Grey. It invaded the Tolbecken family circle as well as Cary Oliver's study at the manse, creating a destructive atmosphere which would have stifled a more promising union than this one. Singularly enough the notion had occurred last of all, perhaps, to Nan and Jared themselves. In her case, the attentions of Angus Grey had precipitated it; with Jared it had been Clarice's visit. Discontent with what was took flame from the re-evoked memory of what might have been.

But for several weeks the moment of revolt he had foreseen that night in New York gave no sign of arriving. Nan, for one thing, was gentler and more conciliatory than she had ever been with him. He was unaware that she was wavering between prudence and adventure, and while coquetting with ideas of the latter, was making sure of her anchorage in case she decided to play safe. Indeed, once after a wrangle with Grey she resolved in a passion to give him up, and expressed her delight to Jared at the prospect of his leaving.

"His self-importance!" she scoffed. "His airs of owning everything and everybody! I'm glad he's going—I'm tired of him."

Half unconsciously, the thought of Angus's departure relieved tension and revived a faint prospect for the future. It seemed easier to Jared, after all, to run in the old groove than to wrench free of it. What would be gained by separating from Nan provided they could live tolerably together? Nothing but tedious scandal, nothing but an independence he did not know what to do with. If they could keep up appearances between them, it would be less trouble than anything else.

But the explosion came suddenly and was set off unspectacularly. It had been a black day at the office. The blight of the last few months had reappeared in a new form. The French military attaché in Washington, Pierre Delart's superior, had regretted to inform Messrs. Tolbecken and Tolbecken that his office believed the interests of his government would be better served by a firm in Philadelphia with which the office had had previous dealings. He felt certain that Captain Delart had acted in ignorance of this fact, and while eager to make any adjustment of fees which might seem equitable, he expected that Tolbecken and Tolbecken would submit such data as they possessed to the Philadelphia firm, and begged to remain faithfully theirs.

It was a disingenuous letter, because Pierre had discussed the choice of the Dunstable firm with Washington by telephone. Between the lines of it showed clear as day that the attaché's office, checking up on the legal reputation of the Tolbeckens, had heard the same disparaging reports which had damaged their practice that winter. Or perhaps someone in town had volunteered information. If so, it was easy to guess, though it would be difficult to prove, who that might be.

In a dark mood, Jared drove home for lunch, and found some unexpected bills of Nan's awaiting him. As a rule, he would have taken this philosophically, but today he ventured a mild protest which called forth a tirade which in turn led to a full-blown quarrel.

And suddenly, as he looked at her face, turned hard and vixenish, he realized that he was through. They were both to blame in this instance, they were both being petty, and about a nonessential thing, but as a last drop overflows the cup, their altercation brought home to him the unbearable sordidness of their life together, the emptiness of his home, the sterility of his marriage, the blankness of the future. And he came at once to a final decision.

He bit off a sentence in the middle, strove with himself, managed to keep silent. Nan too had become silent, and when he rose to leave the room, her eyes did not follow him.

He would postpone the final talk with her until they had both cooled, he thought. As he went out, he stated merely that he would dine with his family that evening. She answered with a cool nod, and went by him and up the stairs. He spent the rest of the afternoon at his desk, preparing himself to break the news to his grandparents and Aunt Joan. In view of the sacrifices they had made for his marriage, that would be the hardest part of the ordeal.

It was not until after dinner, when the little circle had gathered in front of the fire—the Judge with his newspaper, Grandmother with her fancywork, and Aunt Joan chatting of the day's events—that he finally blurted out, "I've something important to talk over with you," and then balked at the last leap.

"Eh?" said the Judge, looking up sidewise from his paper.

The two women, warned by Jared's voice, sat in a mute apprehension.

"I've decided to separate from Nan," he went on with an effort. "Probably it will mean a divorce. . . . I wanted you to know," he concluded lamely.

In the silence, he could hear the loud ticking of the clock on the mantel. The Judge lowered his newspaper. Grandmother's glance, meeting her sister's, expressed a grim sense of fulfillment.

Rufus Tolbecken cleared his throat. "Please be a little more explicit."

"Very well," returned Jared. "It's simply that I've reached the limit. My home's a farce and always has been—no love, no children, no expectation of either—just a rotten pretense that I can't keep up any longer. I'd rather die than put up with more of it. Nan . . ."

"Jared!" interrupted the Judge. "You've got to learn to put up with things. That's what life is. Nan, indeed! What about you? Look for the beam in your own eye."

"Of course you don't understand, or rather you won't understand—I expected that. But whether she's to blame or not, our marriage is over. I'm sick of the treadmill, and I'm through with it."

For the first time in his life, he was aware of a chasm opening up between him and his grandfather, a chasm deepening, widening. The sensation daunted him.

"In that case," said Rufus Tolbecken, "there's nothing further to discuss. I'll add this, however. You say I don't understand. Believe me, I understand selfishness when I see it. I understand self-pity and self-indulgence . . ."

"Rufus—" put in Grandmother.

"One moment, if you please," insisted the Judge. "I am fundamentally opposed to divorce, and you know it, Jared.

But to talk of it after a year and a half of marriage seems to me not only odious, but puerile—the chatter of spoiled children. Whatever your grievances, you could be expected to remember your vows to this woman. Because you can't be patient, can't attempt to win and guide your wife, you are prepared to drag our name through the scandal of a divorce."

The Judge's voice reverberated in the room, his head was raised in the old leonine fashion, but Jared noticed what he had never seen before, that his grandfather's hands trembled with a sudden palsy. To his surprise and Rufus Tolbecken's, an unexpected champion took up the defense.

"Mr. Tolbecken," said Grandmother in her most stately manner, "I do not share your opinion, and I believe Joan agrees with me. You talk about beams, but do not apply Scripture to yourself. You uncovered your own weakness when you spoke of our name and the scandal of a divorce. What is that but pride, Mr. Tolbecken, and what is pride but selfishness?"

"Rachel!" gasped the Judge. "I'm amazed at *you* . . ."

"Yes," continued Grandmother, "I know, it's very inconsistent. But I can't help thinking of Maylin and Bella—it's strange how I keep thinking of them these days. They wanted a divorce. But, no—you and Joan and I and all the rest of us wouldn't allow it. Their lives were wasted on account of our name and the fear of scandal—please don't interrupt me. That's the essence of it, though we gave it the fine name of religion. You and I are close to the end, Rufus. You know I don't approve of unnecessary divorces. But I won't have other lives on my conscience because of a formula, however respectable it may have seemed."

". . . amazed," repeated the Judge, in an altered voice. "Joan, I can't believe that you . . ."

"Yes," said Aunt Joan in her blunt manner, "I do agree with Rachel. If a mistake has been made, it's got to be dealt with. Bad as it is, there's no use making a worse tragedy of it. Frances Oliver was a mistake from the beginning. I warned you at the start that you wouldn't be the only sufferer, Jared, and now we'll have to face the music with you. But *why* did you marry her?"

Why had he married her, indeed! Was he to dig up from the past his old lust? Show them the fraud he had been forced to practice? Admit that he, craving a divorce now, had been no better than she? It was all too sordid to admit, and would do no good, but the thought left him defenseless. He did not answer Joan Maylin's question.

260

Rufus Tolbecken got up, and with a hand gripping the mantel, stood looking down at the fire. At last he said:

"I must beg your pardon, Jared. Your grandmother is right. While I was accusing you of selfishness I was thinking along old lines—family honor, family reputation. I keep forgetting, keep holding on to things that are already gone. I wonder if there is anything more to go. Yes—my faith in you. I don't want that to be taken. But my life is nearly over. Yours is your own affair. Come here, my boy."

With an affection that cut his grandson to the heart, he laid his hand on Jared's shoulder, his deep-set eyes searching him.

"Do as you must," he said. "I'll stand behind you."

"No," returned Jared abruptly, "I'll try to go on . . . as long as possible . . . as long as I can. . . ."

"Do as you wish," repeated the Judge. "I mean it. I don't *want* you to think of me." And returning to his chair, he attempted a wan smile. "How about reading a little to me from that new life of Disraeli? It's queer how blurry my eyes are nowadays. Did I ever tell you I once met Disraeli? Yes—back in the seventies. An odd-looking old fellow, Lord Beaconsfield . . ."

Jared drove back home undecided. Perhaps, after all, something could be saved. Perhaps the wretched misunderstanding could be patched up. He would have a talk with Nan. As never before, he was struck, when he came in, by the feeling of silence and emptiness in the house.

"Nan," he called.

There was no answer. Even the servant had gone. Climbing the stairs, he found the bedroom in disorder, empty drawers half open, the closet stripped of Nan's dresses and shoes, some express labels scattered on the floor. Bewildered, he stood looking about him; then a letter, displayed on the dressing table, caught his eye. Though it was addressed to him, the writing was not Nan's. Tearing it open, he read:

My dear old Befo'-de-war,
Though I'm a little drunk, I wanted to write just a line of farewell, as we're not likely to meet again. I am taking your wife with me as the only souvenir of Dunstable I want. Nan and I will talk of you now and then with proper respect. For legal details, apply to Kent and Hume. I can think of nothing else but to wish you good-by without au revoir, from your indebted friend.

Through the bold scrawl of the signature, Angus's face grinned up at him. But another sheet detached itself; it contained a few words in Nan's writing. The note ended: *I got tired of pretending and have decided to live.*

At the moment, he grew aware of the sound of the telephone, and mechanically answered it.

"Well?"

"This is David Mansen, Jare. I'm calling from the hospital. I'm sorry to tell you that there's been an accident. Nan seems to have been in a car with Angus Grey . . . they were brought here. . . . Nan . . . is dead."

45

"Not yet," said Mansen to Jared at the door. "You shouldn't see her now. They'll have finished in a little while. I called up the Olivers, but they're out of town for the night. If you'd like to see Angus, he's down there."

David pointed to a gray panel, numbered 14, along the corridor.

A sudden hot surge broke over Jared's numbness. He found it hard to speak.

"Yes, I'd like to see him."

Mansen gripped his arm.

"Not in that mood, Jare; I thought you understood. The man's dying."

Jared swung around. "What!"

"His back was broken in the collision. He won't live the night out. I'm keeping him under morphine, but he's still conscious."

Somehow, the thought of Angus Grey coupled with death seemed grotesque, preposterous. It gave an added unreality to the dim corridor.

"There's no use my seeing him," Jared muttered.

"He asked for you," said Mansen. "You may regret it if you don't."

"Very well."

But it was hard to enter the slate-colored door with its black number.

A shaded lamp gave light enough for him to make out the dim figure on the bed whose labored breathing sounded across the room.

"Are you awake?" asked Mansen in a low voice.

"Yes. Who is that with you?"

"Jared."

"Ah. Turn on the lights, Professor. It's dark as a grave here. That's it."

Angus's face appeared out of the dusk. It was marble white, but more handsome than Jared had ever seen it. The mangled and broken body was covered; the head and shoulders, half raised on pillows, seemed untouched.

"Well, Befo'-de-war," he brought out haltingly, "we meet again after all. It's right funny. You and the Professor and me! I never expected that. Nan . . . how is she? Tell me!"

So he didn't know. Jared's hands closed on the footrail of the bed. He looked a question at Mansen, who nodded.

"She was killed," he answered.

Grey closed his eyes.

"Yes, I expected it. . . . God, what a crash! Must have been doing seventy when I hit whatever it was. Not altogether my fault, but I suppose I'd had a glass too many. . . . How's Nan? . . . Oh, I remember. . . ."

He lay silent a moment. Then he said:

"Professor, give me another jab, will you? It's beginning to hurt like hell." And while Mansen filled the hypodermic Angus stared at him, as if he were incredulous of the pain.

After the needle had had its effect, he said:

"You're a queer bird, Professor. In your place, I'd have rather enjoyed seeing me squirm. Lord, how I've hated you, fellow! You were the only one who ever licked me. I could settle things with Jared here, but not with you. Nothing to take hold of. And now, of all the men on earth, to have you tinkering with me! Heaping coals, eh? What a damn fool world!"

He lay mumbling a moment. Then he added:

"But I respect a man who is one thing or another—the whole way, no fuzzy edges. You were one thing, I was the other. But neither of us tried to straddle. What do you say?"

Sitting down by the bed, David took the other's pulse.

"I'll admit you nailed your colors to the mast," he answered. "I admire that part of it, as long as you wouldn't hoist mine."

"Hell!" grunted Angus. "Yours? No, thank you. And I haven't any regrets. Get that, Professor. Except . . ."

He fell silent.

"Except what?"

Angus grinned. "Except that I lost my grip on the steering wheel." And as Mansen removed his hand, "Have I got a chance?"

"No."

Something flickered in the other's eyes.

"It's just as well. I'll grant you this, Professor. A man like me oughtn't to get old. It spoils the game. Besides, I'd have missed Nan . . . she was a beautiful woman."

He started plucking at the sheet restlessly, his gaze on the ceiling. Then rallying, he looked at Jared.

"Oh, yes—I wanted to tell you something—I really cared for Nan, you know. We might even have got married. It's a mistake to fall in love. Spoiled my luck and hers. . . . I have no apologies to make. I'd do it over again. But I thought I'd give you the satisfaction of standing there and looking at me. Seemed the sporting thing after what I'd done. So, go on and look."

He tried to smile, failed, let his head sink back. In his twisted fashion, he had made amends. Apologies meant nothing. In Jared's place, it was the pleasure of looking at a broken enemy that he would most have valued. Suddenly Jared felt a grudging admiration for Angus; the metal of him gave the same tone to the end.

"What a pity!" Angus exclaimed all at once, in a voice that showed delirium. "*Commedia finita est.* That's all the Latin I know. It's enough."

He was back in college. Familiar names of classmates and friends crept out from the drift of his thought. Jared was surprised that his own name appeared so often. He had not believed that he occupied much of a place in Angus's thoughts. Once he was evidently singing, but the words came out in a confused whisper, of which Jared caught only a phrase or two. Then the scene shifted to the Orient—apparently he imagined himself there with Nan. "Look," he told her, "how fast the sun sets. It gets dark before you know it. But behind us, Nan—you see?—the moon is already there."

As he showed pain, David Mansen prepared another hypodermic, but he was given no time to use it. Suddenly the delirium passed.

"David!" cried Angus—he had never called him that before—"David! Hold me, will you? That's it . . . hold me. . . ."

264

There was a rasping sound that Jared had never heard. The hands clinging to Mansen's arms relaxed.

"That's all," said David after a moment. "How strange that it should have been me."

In Room Number 18, Nan Tolbecken lay, as beautiful as she had been in life. Her hair, concealing the wound, was spread about her on the pillow, like fine-spun gold. She was beyond love or hate, thought Jared, beyond even the bitterness of memory; she had crossed the threshold.

PART FOUR

BEYOND THESE VOICES

46

During the years 1915 to 1917, screaming headlines became the normal speaking voice of the press. As the conflict abroad shot its sparks nearer, the cry rose shriller, became more incessant. Battle on sea and land, atrocity, devastation, and massacre, new weapons that revealed the ingeniousness and depravity of man, new methods of warfare reaching far beyond the battlefront, shafts aimed no less at the mind than at the body, perversions of justice, of reason, of truth— all were screamed across the blackening pages. The confusion of the Somme, the long agony of Verdun shrilled through the East, crossed the plains, overswept the Rockies. The heat of world passion, more inflaming than the blast of any furnace, grew steadily hotter. The policy of no entanglements wore thin, became at last an ostrich slogan mocked by reality. The sparks fell thicker, struck home at last, stinging, infuriating.

Lusitania and *Sussex* and *Arabic*. How the names reverberated! Have done with polite notes of regret! Have done with patience! Have done with the vision of mediation that still haunts the statesman in the White House! Day and night, drums beat in the minds of thousands—drums of fury—drums of adventure, of indignation, of crusade. Day and night, month by month, the volume of them swelling.

UNRESTRICTED SUBMARINE WARFARE. More blood of ours!

And the drums beat louder. WILSON GOES TO CONGRESS.

The world listens. The hour has struck. And the headlines, filling their lungs for the climax, announce:

WAR.

Its flame, so long baffled, leaps the Atlantic, completes the circle, and girdles the earth.

Up, Manhood, for the great cause! Liberty summons. Freedom lies in jeopardy. Democracy faints. America draws her sword for an ideal. The rights of man, O Lafayette, O Washington! She wages a war that shall end all wars.

"Our God is marching on."

At Camp Mead several buck privates of K Company, Nth Infantry, National Army, sang a sort of battle hymn:

> "Mad'moiselle of Armentières, parlez-vous,
> Mad'moiselle of Armentières, parlez-vous—
> We won't get pinched if we're not too tight,
> We'll come for supper and stay all night.
> Hinky dinky, parlez-vous."

Then they sang:

> "Pack up your troubles in your old kit bag,
> And smile, smile, smile. . . ."

They felt that they had a particular right to these songs, as they were due for embarkation that week. They were proud of themselves and their outfit. They held the best company record on the rifle range. And their captain, J. L. Drackenford, old top sergeant in the regular army, had been overheard on a hike remarking to First Lieutenant Jared Tolbecken that he was damned if all things considered, he didn't think the damn rookies would shape up nicely. They swaggered a little as they walked down the company street past their officers' shack.

Hearing them, Jared Tolbecken, who was enjoying comparative Sunday leisure stretched out on his cot, grinned over at Second Lieutenant Eaby Ellis engrossed in an old letter from his wife. By a peculiar stroke of luck they had both been assigned to the same outfit after training camp at Fort Meyer, and would probably see a part of the war together.

"Listen to this, Jared," said Ellis. "Beatrice had that snapshot I sent her enlarged. She says, 'I've fallen in love with you all over again, now that you're in uniform. I wouldn't have you any place else but the army these days, though I don't

268

know what I'd do if anything happened.' Gee, she's a sweet kid. If it hadn't been for her, I don't know that I'd have joined up—business going so well, and the children just getting interesting. I'd have had deferred classification in the draft. But she was dead right. I wouldn't miss this show for anything. Would you? Makes life seem bigger somehow. Gives it a purpose, doesn't it?"

Jared nodded. He would have found it difficult to express all that the army had meant to him. The Dunstable dreariness seemed years instead of months away. He felt young again, for one thing, and physically fit. The temptation to escape boredom in drink had passed. He enjoyed the comradeship of the men. But these were but the effects of a much greater benefit. For the first time since college, he could give himself enthusiastically to a cause he believed in, one that unified him—he had an ideal. What could be more inspiring than to spend his life for a better world, a world in which the autocracies that had caused the horrors of this war would be impossible, a world made safe for the works of peace? He agreed with every particle of Wilson's vision, and could not understand his grandfather's and David Mansen's skepticism. What if men did die, was it not worthwhile in order to build the Golden Age? Moreover, saving honorable wounds and death, the army did not demand a great deal. There had to be discipline, of course, but men were thereby relieved of much personal responsibility. He considered it wonderful that this multitude of people, many no better than himself and many worse, a mass of human weakness and passion, could be welded by discipline into a force for ideal purposes. Though he was unable to solve his own personal problems, he would happily give his life to solve the problems of the world. And it seemed to him that the army of men like him, secure in the guidance of its leaders, was dedicated to the same issue.

"Yes," he agreed, "it does give life a purpose. And besides that, it's interesting. I'm glad we're sailing!"

Ellis filled his pipe. "I'd be a little happier about it, if it wasn't for Beatrice and the kids. I'll sure be missing 'em. . . . By the way, where do we pick up our extra lieutenant —Calkus, Balkans, whatever he is? Drackenford told me that someone like that had been assigned."

"Theodore Balkus," said Jared. "We may pick him up in New York."

Eaby chuckled. "Old J. L. had a good laugh over the chap's papers. Harvard . . . a literature major. What a crew!"

He broke off at the entrance of a mail orderly, who clicked heels and saluted.

"Telegram for Lieutenant Tolbecken."

Somewhat nervously, Jared tore open the yellow envelope. With people as old as his grandparents, one never knew. . . . It was a day letter from Dunstable. He stood staring at the typewritten lines.

"Anything wrong?" asked Ellis after a pause, and when there was no answer, "Bad news?"

"Terrible," muttered Jared. "You remember Captain Delart?"

"The one we met at the Reigers'? Yes."

"He's been killed in action. . . . Pierre, killed! God, how awful."

The knightly figure of Delart, steel-tempered, rose before him—he felt the pity of his irreparable loss. One more sacrifice for the future world. He had never been reduced to the meanness of envy toward Pierre. He suddenly realized, in this concrete and personalized instant, the terrible cost of war.

"Clarice is coming to America with the children," he went on, "so as to be with Aunt Elizabeth. She sails on the *Rochambeau* on October fifth, just after we leave. I'll have to cable her."

Mechanically buttoning his tunic and taking up his cap, he walked out, still a little dazed. Beyond the shock of Pierre's death, he felt a more immediate disappointment. He had looked forward to meeting Clarice in France. Perhaps it would be years now until he saw her again, or perhaps . . . For the first time the chill of his prospect sobered him. He had not realized how much Clarice had had to do with his eagerness for embarkation. And yet—even as he banished the notion as unworthy, he could not avoid the lilt of a future hope. Who could tell—when the war was over and its goal had been achieved, when present sorrow had lost its vividness, when he returned with his duty accomplished—who could tell but that then . . . ? No, it was despicable to think of that now. In another sense he dared not think of it. Meanwhile, by the death of Pierre Delart, he had acquired one more incentive, a personal one this time, to serve the ideal represented by the war.

Before embarkation, he and Ellis had a night's leave in Dunstable; they were the heroes of the moment. Beatrice Ellis had arranged a dinner at the country club in her husband's honor, and showed herself to be a good sport and a patriot. She was, in fact, proud rather than grieved. Her electrical-supplies salesman had suddenly become a romantic figure to her, but privately she wept a little before seeing him off next day. Eaby was deeply moved; he treasured those tears in secret, and was to take comfort from them many a time.

Jared made calls of farewell, and spent the night at his grandparents' apartment. It was an occasion for all the favorite dishes, a last heaping of his plate. The ache of love that was present there could not be expressed except indirectly by look or tone of voice.

"Have a little more of the chicken, Jare. Carrie fried it that way just for you. And one more piece of the Sally Lunn. Of course you can."

Now and then he would glance up to find Aunt Joan or Grandmother or the Judge looking at him, neglectful of their own dinner; flustered at discovery, they would try to disguise their feelings. Once, Aunt Elizabeth, who sat next to him, squeezed his hand under the table and smiled at him through sudden tears. Somehow, in spite of his own convictions, it was a relief that they made no pretense of being completely cheerful.

The death of Pierre lay heavy upon them. Clarice had wished to remove her children from the atmosphere of war for a while. Whether or not she would remain permanently in America had not yet been determined.

The only invited guest was David Mansen, clad in carelessly fitted medical officer's tunic. He was at present assigned to a military hospital in Philadelphia.

"So you've been converted, you old pacifist?" said Jared when he greeted him.

"If I know what you mean," answered the other, "I have not. I'm less converted than ever. But the world's at war. My profession will be used to build up rather than tear down."

"And send people back to the front," countered Jared.

Mansen nodded dryly. "Sometimes. At least give them a breathing space. But I'm to be on the psychotherapy end. The people I work with aren't likely to go back. For the last year, I've been reading up on war neuroses. It isn't pleasant reading. That's a side of the mess that most people don't hear about."

Then, noting the pain in the face of Judge Tolbecken, who stood near, he broke off.

"Well," remarked the Judge with an effort at cheerfulness, "I have my war work cut out for me—which is to keep the office open for you. I thought I had about finished with that; but when one Tolbecken goes, the other at least has to attend to the mail."

Jared was on the point of urging that there would not be much mail to attend to, and that the firm ought definitely to be dissolved, but he stopped himself. The office represented to Rufus Tolbecken his last illusion. His worn face looked momentarily proud at the thought of being of service. Jared could only thank him with a warning against too much work.

"Pshaw!" exclaimed the Judge. "Work never hurt a man. I could still lick you and Dave put together, in spite of your uniforms."

But when dinner was announced, he walked unsteadily into the dining room, and asked Jared to do the carving.

"The Tolbeckens always have taken part in things," said Aunt Joan. "But don't get into battle if you can help it. All the patriotism on earth won't make up for a wooden leg."

"You wouldn't want me to be a slacker, Aunt Joan?"

"No, but I'd rather have you alive than dead. I hope it'll be over by the time you get there."

"I hope not!"

"Pass Jared the preserves," interrupted Grandmother, changing the subject.

Afterwards, in the living room, they talked about old days at Tolbecken, laughing again over time-worn little anecdotes until the Judge took down his battered copy of Bryant's *Poetry and Song* and read aloud some of his favorites. Unintentionally the evening became a kind of memorial, even to the point of Aunt Joan's falling asleep during the reading of Gray's *Elegy*. Later, she came into Jared's room when he was in bed, as she used to do, added another cover, and stooped over and kissed him.

Yes, it had been an evening he would long remember—a memorial to steadfastness greater than the courage of battle, to a love and tenderness that would sustain him always.

47

They were in luck. Of the American millions, they belonged
to the first few hundreds who entered Paris. Lafayette, we
are here! This was the poetry of war, the grand gesture and
the dress parade. The men were in the pink of condition,
bronzed and lean from their training camps; their uniforms
were spick and span. In the eyes of the French, America
had never sent ambassadors comparable with them. They
were hailed as deliverers, they were acclaimed in the streets
as heroes. For most of them, it was the whole of their ration
of glory, had they but known it, and they used it up in one
day.

Compared with the luminosity of Paris as Jared remembered it, the city, darkened against air raids, looked dismal
that night. Having freed himself from the others, he followed the Seine up to the Tuileries; he crossed over into
the vague space of the Concorde. Then he found himself under
the trees of Cours la Reine. He had set no goal for the walk,
but something other than his conscious self guided him. As
phantoms may be supposed to haunt places where once they
lived the most intensely, so, lost in memory, he followed the
pavement wet with fallen leaves toward the Alexander Bridge.
There to the right, felt rather than seen, was Le Doyen's,
silent now and desolate. Nearby was the spot where he and
Clarice had faced each other that night with the confession of
their love and the knowledge of its necessary frustration. He
could still hear the tapping of her heels as they walked, and
grew faint again with the old longing.

Yes, the pilgrimage had been inevitable, he realized. Back
of consciousness, his younger self long since exiled still lived
and had claimed this hour. "Oh, God!" he thought, suddenly
weary of the years since then, the days and the ways and the
bitterness of them.

Then with the same feeling of compulsion on him, as if it
had been in a dream, he turned left upon the bridge, and
crossing to the middle of it, stood looking eastward upon the
blackness of the city. How jeweled it had looked then under
the stars! Now mass upon mass of shadow, it rose funereally

toward the low-hanging clouds. He sensed rather than saw the river before him. The world of his youth had ended here. How prophetic his vision had been then of what must be his life without Clarice! His hand clenched passionately above the stone coping. But however defeated, even disloyal, he had kept something that had not changed, something that could not change. It might yield no fruit, it might remain sterile, but the beauty of it would not vanish. It was to this tenacity that he made his orisons, there in the darkness.

It was not surprising that fatigue, mud, rain, horror, lice, rats, and high explosives should obscure once confidently held ideals; it was amazing rather that in spite of them men could sometimes rise above the animal level. Concepts of romance, adventure, nobility soon faded. Tedium, cynicism, aching nerves, and apathy settled down, thicker than the winter mist. But a residuum of better times remained in the belief of most of the men that they were fighting for something—not victory merely, but peace; not peace merely, but the annihilation of war. In proportion as suffering increased, the conviction grew that all this hardship must have a purpose, that the thought of its having none would be more intolerable than the war itself. That purpose could be only a world forever free of such catastrophes. More even than discipline, more than hatred for the enemy, it was this faith, often inarticulate, that sustained men through their infinite agonies.

From the parapet of an observation post in February, Jared stared out into the frozen blankness of the night. It was a cold that rasped the throat, the cold of a graveyard. He had the impression of peering out of his grave to make sure that the other cadavers were remaining in theirs. A flare from behind to the right suddenly opened a chalky, spectral pool in the darkness, showing the distortions of wire and gaping earth like a jumble of tombs unsealed at Judgment Day. Even when it had died down, the picture remained for a moment on the retina.

He lowered himself to the duckboard. "I don't see anything. We were wondering about that racket over there."

"Guy must have lost his nerve," said the sentry, "must have took to hearing things. It's kind o' lonesome up here. All I've heard is nothing."

He replaced Jared on the step-up. Several bulky forms a shade blacker than the night indicated the rest of the post.

"Say, Lootenant," muttered one of them, "I wish you'd tell me something."

"What is it?"

"Well, it's this: how've they stood it? I don't mean us—we've only been muckin' around for two or three months. I mean them—them foreigners. How've they stood it—for years?"

"You know as much about it as I do, Crane. I suppose they've stood it because they had to."

They were all shivering beneath their layers of wool. The breath of the earth soaked them to the skin. They were lumps of cold, vermin-infested flesh, drooping with sleep, but held upright puppetwise on the string of discipline.

"For years," repeated Crane wonderingly. "I don't see how they've done it. I'll tell you what, Lootenant, I've figured out that human beings are the toughest nuts on earth."

It occurred to Jared that the poet Henley, who had thanked indefinite gods for his unconquerable soul, had come to the same conclusion.

"That's true, I guess," he answered. And he sloshed back along the communication trench to the main line.

Here, at regular intervals, the half-numbed members of his watch stamped and shuffled through the hours. He inspected a second observation post and returned. That done, there was nothing else to do but wait, spacing off the time with cigarettes, one every five minutes.

Now and then an electric torch flashed between the mud walls, or a match lit up some face. Now and then a flare threw a leprous light on them before it vanished. The scuttling of a rat sounded occasionally. The trench was infested with them, white fellows, large as kittens. In the dugouts he had been unable to overcome his dread of their quick, thudding movements around his bunk.

He tried to think consecutively, but felt too cold for that. To his right a steady dribbling of earth down from the wall into a puddle reminded him of young Peterson's death there two days before. An enemy whiz-bang had torn out that section of the trench, which had not yet settled after the repairs. Peterson had been disemboweled by a fragment. None of them had ever seen a man bleed like that. The earth kept on splashing down.

Before daybreak far off to the north a rumbling began. It was too far distant to catch the riveting of smaller guns—only a remote thunder, as of giant rollers, reached them. A raid or a strafe somewhere on a big scale. The sound reminded him of scene shifters one used to hear at work behind

275

the curtains of theaters. And somehow the comparison stuck and developed in his mind. Titanic scene shifters in the night, resetting a stage—not merely the stage of war. Years of such rolling, myriads of lives, tons of gold, to prepare for a new act, new actors, different properties. Well, they were fighting for just that—another world; whether they lived to see it or not, whether or not they would feel at home there, the lives of all of them were dedicated to that hope. And unless so dedicated they were of all men the most miserable.

Slowly the rumbling ceased and he began to be aware of light, of the profile of the parapet, of outlines of figures propped like his own against the wall.

Something screamed through the air a hundred yards to the left. "Watch yourselves!" he yelled, throwing himself down. It was a "quiet sector" at present, basking in mutual forbearance, but the artillery on both sides exchanged a few shots now and then to keep their hands in. A shell whizzed overhead and burst behind, shaking the trench. Explosions sounded down the line and from the rear, where French and American batteries opened up. Then the demonstration languished.

"Everything all right?"

"All right, Lootenant."

They scrambled up, cursing apathetically, and wiped their hands.

"Chow's ready, sir," reported the mess sergeant.

It was the official notice that one more night had passed.

The German offensive, the counteroffensive, in the spring and early summer of 1918, swept its steel sleet over K Company, as over other units of the A.E.F., and buried a third of it. A third more were in hospital. Sixty-four derelicts answered the roll call in their rest camp. Of the officers, Drackenford had dysentery and Ellis an infected leg wound. Balkus had transferred to the staff long ago. Jared, assisted by two temporary officers, remained in charge for the time being.

The derelicts were now veterans. They had seen more war than had some of the French or English, and they were not particularly elated. Fatigue in battle reaches the point where it leaves indifference. They retained only their habit of humor, cracking jokes to convince themselves that they were still alive. Hollow-cheeked, grinning skeletons, in baggy, strangely clean uniforms, they loafed about their billets until food and rest should fatten them up. Before them extended bleaker than ever the vista of the war.

They were no prophets; they could not know that this last offensive marked the limit of the German reach. Still efficient, the field-gray legions hammered front to front. America with her millions was on the way; replacements filled up the company. They let the new men talk. In ancient days, a year ago, they too had looked forward to meeting the Heinies and counting them out. Since then they had breathed their gas, been scorched by their *Flammenwerfer*, endured their barrage, encountered their charge. They were unacclaimed heroes to the newcomers, but were not puffed up about it. Secretly they pitied them and, being full of ineffable memories, they talked little of what they had seen or done. When they were out of the trenches, they spent most of their pay on brandy and *vin rouge* at the village *estaminet*. "It probably wasn't so bad after all," the rookies thought.

Meanwhile, billeted with the local pharmacist, Jared communed with the phantoms projected by his raw nerves. Terrors of all sorts assailed him, to be held at bay only by the sheer force of the will. He feared to remember, he feared to look ahead. There were times when he bitterly envied those of the company who had been done out and were thus discharged from further apprehension. For them there need be no more the conflict of shrinking flesh and exhausted spirit, no more the makeshifts of clinging to life, the involuntary grovelings and abasement. He had come through without a scratch so far, but he was stricken invisibly. It was the future more than anything else that appalled him. How with his present knowledge of what it meant, with his cringing nerves and weakened body, could he face another ordeal like the ravines and wheat fields of Soissons?

At company inspection, outwardly cool, lean, weather-hardened, and with the ease of long custom, he walked down the lines an object of admiration. The company plumed themselves on him, bragged about him in the regiment. They did not know that he flinched like a girl at any sudden noise. At night when the will relaxed, specters of sleep or of half consciousness rose. At times with the sense of pushing back some palpable, strangling web, he would get up, drink a tumbler of cognac, and pace back and forth. He recalled his activities in the preparedness campaign at home, the slogans and high spirits and zest. War had turned out so much bigger, so much worse, different, than he had dreamed.

He was due for leave but could not take it until Drackenford's or Ellis's return. He craved relief as he had never thought it possible to crave anything. To get away from the men, from rifles, ammunition, supplies, and the everlasting discipline—to get away from the smell of the army! To return, if only for a week, to Paris and to rest!

But a month passed. The company moved on to a training camp at Vaucouleurs. Foch's counteroffensive seemed to be getting up steam. Neither Drackenford nor Ellis returned. Jared hung on, more stale with every day's passing. Bayonet drill, bomb throwing, rifle practice, more rifle practice. Up and down the lines with comment, praise, reproof. "Squeeze that trigger—don't pull. Squeeze when the sight nicks the bull's-eye. What the hell do you think you're doing, jerking like that!" Up and down, day by day, keeping his temper, forcing himself to relax, forcing himself to smile. The men, vaguely sensing his condition, wondered at him. He wondered a little at himself and how long he would last.

He could hardly keep his voice steady when in the end he announced to the company, "You men will be glad to know that Captain Drackenford is due back tomorrow."

That evening he packed up and also put in his request for leave.

Jared lay awake that night for once with pleasure. It would be good, too, to catch a glimpse of Drackenford before leaving. Dear old J. L.! They had only the war in common and yet he loved him more than any man on earth. There had grown up an intensity of affection between them such as a lifetime of peace would never have produced.

It was not until late the following morning that in a last conference with the top sergeant Jared saw the latter snap suddenly into a grinning salute and at the same time received a shattering clap on the back.

"For Pete's sake!" roared the familiar voice of the captain.

They stood a moment muttering before their hands shot out, and there were white stripes across their fingers when they let go.

"Well," said Drackenford. "I'm sure glad to see you. Damn me if it don't put hair on my chest to have a look at you. Howdy, Sergeant! Shake! How's the boys?"

K Company began drifting up, old ones to the fore, new ones hanging back. There was a round of salutes, handshaking, and delighted faces. Drackenford passed from one to the other. Then, turning back to Jared, he said, "Come on. Where's your shack? I want to get the news." But when they were out of earshot he laid his arm on the other's shoulder.

278

"I can't tell you what I feel," he said, "about your playing the game like you've done—sticking with the outfit, I mean. It's been a rough deal on you, but it's meant a lot to me having someone to hear from. Understand? I'm never going to forget it."

"That's all right, J. L." At a stroke the past months faded out. "I was glad to stick around."

Drackenford gave him a squeeze before straightening up. "And now," he said, "I want you to go off and have one hell of a good time. Give the dames in Paris a whirl for me."

At mess Jared's leave formed the chief topic. They pictured him in the theaters and rubbed their hands over the thought of the restaurants he would visit. The captain went in person to get the leave papers.

"Have to see the adjutant, anyhow," he said, "and maybe I can jog him up some. If you start early you might reach Paris tonight."

But an hour passed, then two hours, and he did not return. With his kit roll buckled and ready, Jared fidgeted, walked up and down, and watched for him. At last he determined to go over himself. It was too late now to make Paris, but if they thought they could keep him here for another night they were mistaken. It was unlike Drackenford to let a man down like that.

At the turn of the road, however, he met the captain walking slowly, his eyes on the ground.

"Well," Jared said, fuming, "you've taken your own time about it! I didn't think you'd treat me that way, J. L."

Drackenford shook his head. "Don't blame me. Couldn't help it."

"Well, where are the papers?" And as the captain moved on without answering, "Didn't you bring the papers?"

"There's been some delay," faltered Drackenford.

"Delay! I'll see whether there's going to be delay. I've delayed here in the regiment while every officer has had leave. I'll go to headquarters if necessary. I'd have thought you might have done that for me."

"I did," muttered the other. They had reached the door of Jared's shack. "Come in here," said Drackenford. "I want to tell you something." He thrust his hands in his pockets and drew them out, he hooked them on his belt and let them drop.

"Well," said Jared, "what is it?"

"I'd rather take ten lickings," Drackenford burst out. "I

279

never felt so rotten about anything before. But the fact is, all leaves have been canceled. Everybody's to report back. The big push is on."

Jared stalked over to the table with its files of company papers and sat down. Outside in the summer light, khaki figures passed back and forth, but he saw nothing. He had only the sense of being caught in a gigantic trap. There was to be no leave for him. In a haze of fatigue he must plod on toward an effort that men at their best could hardly face. He could see himself unpacking his kit. There would be no evenings in Paris, none of the gay, careless activities he had so often anticipated.

A spasm shook him. He buried his face in his outstretched arms.

Drackenford stood over him. "Don't take it like that. Just another heave—you and me together—and the job's done. Don't give up now on the home stretch. You've got to make the grade."

"I've lost my nerve," muttered the other. "I'll go out there and be shot for a coward."

The door opened. Drackenford flung round. "What do you want?" he roared.

"I'm sorry," came a voice.

"Take yourself out!" The door snapped shut. "Now look here," went on the captain turning back, "a man's always got one last kick left. You're going to go through with this. And you're going to go through it with bells on. We'll be together nip and tuck." He thrust out his hand. "Shake!"

Jared got up. A spark leaped through him from the clasp of that square hand.

"You and me," said the captain, "don't count for much in this man's army. But I reckon we count for something to each other."

It was pleasant and new at least to take the field again a part of an American army. The days of brigading with the French were past; the A.E.F. had to stand on its own feet now. It was pleasant and new also to feel the heat of enthusiasm in these new divisions. Four years ago, the French and English had gone in with like spirit. Now they were experts at the job and were tired. But it was especially pleasant and new to be the assailant and not the assailed, to know that the Germans in their turn were staggering back. "It'll soon be over over there," they hummed. Peace, the better world, mankind forever free from the plague of war by the sacrifice of its millions who had endured this one.

On such a novel and invigorating stream Company K drifted from the short, fierce victory of St. Mihiel toward the Argonne. Once more the gaping ranks had been patched together by fresh replacements; once more the survivors, incredulous of their endurance and their luck, turned exhausted toward the next venture. They were driven by camion a part of the way and then hiked. Apparently most of the world, a slow-moving, mud-colored tide, rolled in the same direction. Flatcars, trucks, artillery, ambulances, field kitchens, staff automobiles, field batteries, ammunition wagons, interwoven with the endless queue of the infantry stretching beyond both horizons, crept forward incessantly, thundering to the east. It was scene shifting on a grand scale. As an exhibition of the complexity of modern warfare, they had never seen the like.

Then, heard even above the rumble of transport, rose clearer and nearer the roar of the guns. Planes, like a gathering of eagles, thickened overhead. At night the dancing fringe of flares grew brighter. It was the old, familiar front, the coast of war. But instead of the plains, here was a country rolling upward, ravines and tablelands. Instead of open fields, a darkening of splintered woods. An eerie country into which the mud-colored stream flowed and disappeared.

As they drew closer, the vibrancy and tension of nerve began, the suppressed excitement, as if invisible fingers were screwing them up to the right pitch. Ambulances began to dribble back with their loads. Beyond shellfire for the last time, they camped in a ruined village.

"Better get a barrelful of sleep," said Drackenford. "There won't be much of it handy where we're going tomorrow."

"Or maybe too much," Eaby grinned to Jared when the company fell out. He had joined up again after St. Mihiel. It had been good to see the familiar, broad, bulldog look of him.

They spread their blankets in a barn that still retained part of its roof. A cold, late-summer rain dripped outside and filtered through upon the rotting boards where they lay. The place crawled with the lice of unnumbered transients who had occupied it.

" 'Night, all," said the captain. "We're pushing on at three in the morning." A moment later his snoring announced that cold, rain, fatigue, and vermin had no further power over him.

Jared envied him that. He envied him in most things. He seemed the proper man for war or peace; of practical wisdom he had more than all the books ever printed could teach.

281

He had balance and stamina; too many like him had been destroyed during the last four years.

Eaby Ellis chatted for a few minutes. He had recently had a letter from Beatrice full of Dunstable happenings. "Can't you just see that fairway up to the fourth hole?" he said. "Green and soft, with the Delaware back of it! Won't it seem strange to remember this sometime? I used to think that I loved Beatrice and the kids—I didn't know what loving them really meant."

At last he slept.

One would think that after such a day's hike anyone could sleep. But Jared was too exhausted to relax. Would he be able just once more to go through with it? He rolled from one stiff side to the other, wrapped in a shirt of crawling, stinging insects. He was tired, tired! His mind reeled at the thought of tomorrow, but outside the guns thundered like a refrain. He turned over on his back and lay staring into the darkness.

As he lay there, it suddenly seemed to him that a hand was laid gently on his forehead. It did not startle him; instead, it brought a feeling of release, of peace. He realized that he had been ill and was lying on the sofa at Tolbecken. A summer storm rumbled far off. Aunt Joan bent down over him; her face was as he remembered it from years ago. Her eyes smiled. No, he was looking out into the darkness. She had gone. But there seemed to him nothing strange in this. A feeling of ease passed over him and at last he fell asleep.

An hour's stumbling over what once had been and still was used as a road brought the battalion to the near side of the low ridge they were planning to take over. There, scattered about in foxholes, they waited. Drackenford crawled from one to the other with a word for everybody, and took stock.

The battalion commander appeared, similarly crawling, and lay for a moment head to head with him. "Major Henderson's been hit," he roared in his ear. "You'll take over on the right, J. L."

He drew a tattered map from his pocket and switched on an electric torch. "Give that another look and don't get tangled up. This sector of woods to the right across the valley—take it and hold it. You'll have to bomb out the machine-gun nests. We're going to lay a barrage along the whole stretch, but it won't knock all of 'em out. Don't worry about what anyone else is doing. You grab that hundred-yard line and hold it until ordered to advance." He shifted the light to his watch dial. "Set yours by mine. Let her rip at five-thirty-five sharp. Good luck."

He crawled off turtle-fashion along the line, while his orderlies checked up and passed the word to every outfit. A telephone squad from the covering batteries reported to Drackenford and ensconced themselves in a shell hole.

Darkness had now faded to a pale gray. Peering from the rim of the crest, the men could make out the blur of the opposite woods, an undulating line on the further side of a shallow valley. At its extreme tip to the left lay a different sort of blur which was probably a village. At its right in a long sweep forming a bay, it rejoined a sector held by the French.

Suddenly the artillery fire from behind tripled in volume, and shifting its range from the enemy gun positions, laid a barrage along the fringe of woods. A torrent of steel screamed over the crest, while driblets of it, falling short, burst in the valley.

"Fix bayonets!"

In his shell hole, Jared noted the haggard faces from which at the moment every aspect but strain had disappeared.

Five-thirty. Five-thirty-one, thirty-two, thirty-three. Five-thirty-four. They stood up, quivering like sprinters on the line, their mouths working or drawn taut.

Five-thirty-five.

"Let's go!"

Then consciousness split up into sensation—of sliding and plunging down the slope, concussions, panting outstretched on the earth, the cracking of whiplashes next to the ear, glimpses of men spinning topwise and pitching forward. Jared saw a figure stumbling toward him.

"Where do you think you're going?"

"I don't know," quavered a faint voice.

"Well, this is the way."

He whirled the man around, shoving him forward.

They were across the valley now, entangled in fallen trees, splinters, and brushwood. Steadily ahead of them somewhere crashed the barrage.

Drackenford appeared suddenly.

"Keep going!" he yelled. "Keep going, and for God's sake scatter out!"

Here and there figures stalked between the bare tree trunks. A clump of gray-blue was stuck aloft in a tuft of leaves. At the crack of a rifle a man on Jared's right pitched forward. The gray clump detached itself, thudded down, was caught on a branch and doubled across it.

Even more ominous was the riveting of machine guns opening up in front, to the left, and even from the rear. Wounded and sound alike flattened themselves. As he lay prone, Jared's pack jerked with the impact of bullets. One from the machine gun behind glanced off his helmet. Helpless and cut off, the doomed gun squad hung on.

Worming himself around, Jared waited for a lull in the firing and then leaped several paces behind a bank. Bullets immediately spattered the earth down on him, but he worked his way forward, crouched again, then leaped again for cover. His heart pounded, he drew his breath in gasps, but he crept nearer. It was beyond, from what seemed to be a pile of fallen timber, that the stinging bursts were coming. He could see the emplacement now, but he must circle behind. At this point the underbrush grew thicker; he thought he had lost his objective, when near at hand someone laughed and spoke German words.

Parting the branches of a thicket, he saw the camouflaged entry of the dugout, crept closer, drew a grenade from his belt, hurled it, and fell flat as the heap of timber heaved itself, burst open, and then sank in.

Elsewhere in the blind wood similar encounters went on. As Jared regained his company, he could take note for the first time of what had happened—on all sides were strewn drab-colored figures, pressing face down into the earth. Others, the wounded, turned their heads from side to side, or lay with jerking hands and legs. Drackenford, with a torn shirt and bandaged arm, estimated that half of the two companies had gone down.

"You've been hit, J. L.?"

"Aaagh," growled the captain, and finished detailing the stretcher-bearers. "Well?" he asked an artillery sergeant of the telephone squad.

"It's no good, sir. Wire's been cut. It'll take time to repair it."

"Very well; you, Richards, and you, Piltz, beat it back. Get in touch with Major Guthrie or someone. Hah, here we are!" A runner appeared, saluted, and handed over a field message. "Orders to join up with outfits on our left," said Drackenford. "They've swung round and are tackling the village. We're to leave this point and get into contact.

"Ellis, round up officers and men and communicate orders. Tell 'em to keep in touch with me as a center. I'll blow my whistle in ten minutes. Tolbecken, get the stretcher-bearers started. We won't have one full company left."

Comparative silence had fallen after the barrage, so that individual sounds could be made out—faint cries among the trees, a distant rumble of firing, the drone of planes. With silence came reaction; the weight of reality following excitement. Stretcher-bearers and wounded were lucky to be getting out of it. The others watched almost with envy as they stumbled off.

A whistle sounded and once more the scattered line filtered to the left through the woods.

Except for a possible gun nest that had been overlooked, there was nothing to be apprehended in the present advance. The dead of the neighboring companies pointed to a similar struggle and success. At any moment they would undoubtedly come into touch with the rear of the units which had swung to the left, and of which some, to judge from the firing, were at present already engaged around the village. But after a space there were no more dead and Drackenford whistled for a halt.

"Queer business," he pondered, and walking down the line, consulted with Captain Bell of H Company. "How's it strike you? Doesn't seem to have been a scrap around here at all."

"Probably wasn't defended," said the other. "Heinies beat it."

"Yes, or maybe our crowd swung in toward the village and gave this a miss. At any rate, I'm going to throw out skirmishers in front. These woods are too thick to please me."

"Won't do any harm," said Bell. "But don't you think if there were Germans around, we'd be apt to hear from 'em?"

At that moment they heard.

It was a concentrated, deadly fire that mowed down a third of the line without warning. Rifles and machine guns mingled in one long-drawn rattle. Then more scatteredly, on the right flank and to the rear, came further shots. It was impossible to see ahead because of the brushwood, but looking behind, Drackenford caught a glimpse of gray uniforms between the trees.

"Push ahead!" he yelled. "We'll try to cut through!"

His whistle shrilled in the lull of the firing.

Beyond the screen of bushes, they found themselves facing a knoll from the hollow top of which came the main blast.

They made it somehow. Some, that is, made it, throwing grenades over as they charged. With those inside they formed a trampling, stabbing, smashing crowd. Automatics, fists, bayonets and rifle butts went to work at the same time. In the end, they cleaned the place of any living creatures but themselves, and lay gasping among the wounded and dead.

Drackenford peered over the lip of the knoll. "Game's about up," he panted. "We're pretty well cut off. Now we've got 'em coming in force. Looks as if our attack was messed up. Why in hell didn't we make sure of the woods before bothering about that damn village!"

He backed away. "Get busy," he shouted. "We've got four German machine guns here—any of you men know how to work 'em?" Several who had had machine-gun training pushed forward. "Set 'em up at intervals to cover us all round. And the rest of you grab every rifle and bomb you see and keep 'em handy. I'm going to fight it out," he told Jared. "Whether we get off or not, it will give our crowd over there notice of something happening. Otherwise they'll have these ginks on their rear."

It was amazing how quickly he organized the defense, charging the others with his own energy.

The German counter attack was advancing cautiously. The fracas of firing around the knoll might have meant success for the defenders or not. They were closing in and as yet had drawn no fire, which was encouraging, but they paused to throw out skirmishers and to send snipers aloft for a clearer view. The snipers' bullets began cracking.

American marksmen answered with good effect, but it was impossible to keep the branches clear. Eaby Ellis went down, shot through the head, and lay on his face. He was dead before Jared could reach him.

Drackenford aimed high and fired at a clump of leaves from which a body plunged forward. He nestled his rifle again in the way he had, as if it were a violin, and fired again. "He was a good fellow," he said. "This hellish business!"

If the Germans had had time they would have wiped out the defense at long range, or perhaps would have broken its morale, for nothing is worse than to lie inactive under fire. But they were in a hurry and charged the knoll in force. Machine guns and rifles smashed their first charge, and a second. A third wave reached the parapet before it was driven back.

"We ought to be hearing from home," gasped Drackenford to Jared, "if we're ever going to hear."

The attackers had dragged up a trench mortar from somewhere, but the first two shells were duds. A third, which wasn't, knocked out eight men. A fourth fell short.

"Here they come!" yelled a rifleman.

286

At the same moment another shell thudded and burst.

"Hold 'em!" came a voice through the smoke. "Hang on!" Drackenford was down, blood trickling from his mouth. "We put up some scrap. Don't bother about me, Jared. Soak 'em again! I'm . . . all . . . right. . . ."

Something snapped in Jared's mind. He saw Drackenford's eyes suddenly open wide and stay fixed. He saw Ellis's outstretched form. He saw the heaped-up bodies. But he did not care. A red flame crossed his eyes. He did not know that he shouted, laughed, yelled at the men in his turn to hold on, and took his place at the last machine gun against the upswelling flood of the German rush.

The world split in two, became an infinite glare. Then a wave of blackness pounded down. Then, nothingness.

* * *

Through the drawing-room windows of the little house in Dunstable, the drab autumn light rested on the figure of Clarice Delart, her face buried in her arms outstretched on the table. One hand still held the yellow sheet of paper marked PARIS and signed DAVID MANSEN: JARED SEVERELY WOUNDED. LITTLE HOPE. WILL KEEP YOU INFORMED.

Her fingers closed upon the yellow paper; the cold light shone down.

48

Out of the depths where Jared Tolbecken lay, he could not call. Not will or desire, but powers deeper than consciousness must decide the issue for him—inherited vigor, on one hand, wounds and exhaustion, on the other. The chart above his bed registered the trembling of the scales. For no apparent reason, life or at least a shadow of life, continued day after day. "This can't go on," said the doctor. "He's been unconscious since they picked him up two weeks ago. It's a miracle he's held out till now. I'd give anything to save him, if only for Dave Mansen's sake, but it doesn't seem possible."

"Was that Dr. Mansen who came over from Paris?" asked the nurse.

"Yes, he's a great chap—I knew him in Philadelphia. This patient is his best friend. Well, let me know if there's any change."

"Very well, Doctor."

The nurse stifled a sigh. In her experience in that ward—an officers' ward for serious casualties—there was not much chance. The cots emptied, filled, emptied, but they were emptied as a rule because the men in them died. She saw them die, or saw them carried out to the operating rooms, but not to return. She nursed them, wrote letters for a few, saw them carried out, and felt the black tide rising higher.

The lines on the charts above the beds wavered up and down. Often when she closed her eyes, she could see them like incandescent threads burning in her mind. They represented the days and nights, the fear, hope, and pain. In this case, they had managed to spin themselves on uncertainly, but at any moment they might stop.

The crisis came one night.

Another hypodermic. What was the use, she thought, of flogging the tired heart on for a few more beats.

"That will be the last," said the doctor. "I'll leave him with you."

The struggle went on. After a while the breathing grew fainter, stopped. She drew herself up and waited. Then another breath came, and another; the breathing suddenly had a different quality.

At dawn he opened his eyes.

Of course, life still hung in the balance. After the depths followed purgatory—a series of muscle-knitting and bone-patching operations, which took the rest of the winter. They were painful and discouraging, but in the end successful enough. He would never again be able to raise his left arm above his shoulder, and would always walk with a limp; otherwise, when shock, exhaustion, and stiffness had been surmounted, he would recover, the experts said—in time.

But these were not the memorable things. The probes, stitches, and bandages, the smell of anesthetic and antiseptic, the various surgeons, the routine of convalescence, all were eclipsed by one fact—the consciousness of peace. More even than the first cablegrams and letters, the paean of joy, relief, and thanksgiving from home, the thought of his welcome there, or, rather, with all this as a part of the greater happiness, remained the triumph of peace.

He could never forget that moment in November when even the quiet village where they were was shaken by a roar, the blowing of horns, ringing of bells, shouts, and the sound of people running.

"I'll go and see what it is," said the nurse. She came back in a moment paler than usual and stood leaning against the foot of his bed. "The war . . ." she began breathlessly, "the war's over. They've signed an armistice."

"Over!" he repeated.

It had come at last, the dawn of a new age, the future of peace and good will. Before him rose the faces of dead men who had made this possible. Their blood had purchased it, lives beyond reckoning, tears beyond measure; ruin and heartbreak and desolation had sealed this covenant.

The horns sounded, the bells clanged, the cheering grew.

He thought of Drackenford, Ellis, and the others in the Argonne wood. . . .

Again, there were the accounts of Wilson's arrival in Paris, his visits to England and Italy, the acclamations and hero worship of an exhausted world. Had any human being ever occupied such a pinnacle? Had America ever dreamed of such pre-eminence among nations as now under his leadership? The masses of humanity looked to him, beyond their war lords and politicians, to keep faith. The oppressed and hope-less peoples sent him their delegations, used his name as a watchword. Even the enemy, desperate, crushed, and blood-sick, began to dream of a liberalism inspired by him, pinned their hopes to him as their only possible savior. Had he not declared that "there shall be no annexations, no contribu-tions, no punitive damages"? Had he not announced "impar-tial justice"? Was not an era of friendly cooperation among free peoples to replace old enmities and connivances?

Jared read these descriptions over and over with the glow of one who had contributed his full share, however modest, to make the glory possible. The futility of his life had been retrieved by it. It was *his* peace, and the letters he dictated to home reflected this elation.

Nothing—no illness of body or defeat or bafflement—had been able to divert the forward drive of Wilson's spirit. The rejection at Princeton had merely given him wider opportu-nity; the scope of the college had been exchanged for the scope of the nation and that in turn for his present unparal-leled primacy in the world. But his ideals throughout had been the same; his appeal to human aspiration the same. In each case he had brought the institution or state he served to an equal eminence with himself. Princeton had been raised to a position of leadership she had not had the vision to hold; now it was America, guided by him, who stood supreme among the nations, who was to be sponsor and dispenser of the new order: America would not fail to wear the crown.

In Wilson, thought Jared, the political idealism of the nineteenth century had found its last and mightiest prophet. The divine event toward which creation moved was at hand. The righteousness of democracy had been established. The spiritual forces of charity and justice had been proved superior to the weight of selfish nationalism.

How this serenity faded, he would never know definitely. It was a change of light that began after the opening of the Peace Conference, so that gradually the sky became less blue, and at last, though with patches of azure, a cold gray.

Perhaps his conversations with David Mansen, who at times ran over from Paris, gave the first pause of doubt to his assurance. David, realizing what the peace meant to his friend, was not callous enough to discourage him, but he did not join heartily enough in his enthusiasm.

"The real trouble with you," said Jared, chafing, "is that you don't want to admit you were wrong. You pacifists hated the war. Not that I blame you for that, but the war was necessary—you can only suppress force with force. Now that the air has cleared, and the war made a whole new order of things possible, you like to pick flaws and hang on to your theories. Why don't you have more faith in Wilson's vision? You used to preach to me about it."

But when David remained silent, Jared insisted.

"Don't treat me like a sick child. Why won't you ever discuss anything that matters? I'm well enough for an argument."

"But I don't want to argue, Jare. As you say, perhaps the war was necessary in the same sense that disease is necessary. As to Wilson's vision, I agree with it in part. But this talk of a new order to be brought about by international agreements, when human nature is just the same as it always has been, doesn't fill me with confidence. The President makes a splendid appeal to human idealism; but that kind of mass idealism doesn't change the human heart. Really, it's often only sentimental. Look at Princeton. It was all right until it came up against pride and money, until the cost of it began to hurt. Wilson's whole edifice is built up on individual men and women. If they are sound, it will stand, if not, it will fall. Besides one can't help hearing things in Paris. They say he's beginning to compromise on the Fourteen Points in order to get French and English support for his League idea. But is that honest from the standpoint of Germany?"

"You and I seem to have shifted sides," said Jared. "Personally I believe in Wilson."

"And so do I," agreed David. "He's the greatest man of our generation. But I had a glimpse of him recently—he's become very much older. He shows the strain—he looks positively ill. Men wear out, Jared, and sometimes the brain betrays the heart. However, I'm probably wrong even to be afraid. I hope I'm wrong."

Then, in support of Mansen's doubts, began to accumulate newspaper rumors from America, rumors of revolt in the Senate and public disillusionment—a growing clamor to have done with the world mess, get the boys home, and let Europe stew in its own juice. The No Entanglements policy burst from its tomb as glib as ever. Provincial watchwords of "common sense" and "the main chance" replaced slogans like "war to end wars." The fashion of generosity was passing like other fashions, and the jag of idealism, like other jags, had been found to leave a headache. Spring had not yet covered the graves of the A.E.F. with green when the war seemed already far off and its emotions silly.

Then too, when Jared could once more get about in a wheel chair and mix with others, there was the hospital gossip, the clear expressions of the conflicting attitudes.

"By God," said one patient, "when I think of these damn Frogs, I sometimes wonder if we weren't on the wrong side. Now they even want us to pay for the trenches! Tom Nelson writes me from Coblenz that he's met a lot of Germans, and that he feels at home with 'em—they're honest and friendly, he says."

"He can have 'em!" interrupted another. "Do you figure I've forgotten everything in six months? The damn, murdering devils! I hope they skin the last nickel from them in the peace treaty. And I hope they hang the Kaiser. You've got the French all wrong. I was billeted with some people at Gondrecourt . . ."

"Oh, cheese it," broke in a third. "Don't tell us about that woman again. I say to hell with 'em all. Just give me home—little old America. This ought to be a good lesson to us not to mix into rows or anything else over here. League of Nations! League for getting next to Uncle Sam's bank account—that's what it looks like."

"Look here," said Jared, "don't you remember what brought America into the war—what we were talking about just six months ago? It wasn't simply to beat the Huns. It was for something bigger than that."

"That was big enough," remarked another. "But I know what you mean, Tolbecken, and I hope to God they fix it so that there won't be any more wars. But the fact is we were screwed up to talk and believe a lot of guff—just guff. Most of us are too tired to think, anyway. What we want is rest and fun—oceans of it. I intend to get mine. There won't be any more wars for me, anyhow. I'll let other people do the worrying. . . ."

Fun, oceans of it. Transferring to a small convalescents' hospital at Fontainebleau, Jared began to have his first glimpses of Paris. The city had lost its radiance of years ago; now it had a hard glare. The chestnut trees along the Champs Elysées looked as if they were dying; hotels or shops had replaced the former mansions. Cafés swarmed. Montmartre had begun its gilded decade. The music halls competed in nakedness. Prostitution abounded. Champagne flowed.

Oceans of fun. The whole world danced. Fat and lean, youth, middle age, and decrepitude fox-trotted together, as if in a chase to get away from memory. A remark of old Clemenceau's went the rounds, that in all his life he had never seen rumps so happy and faces so sad.

Decency, like the slogans of the war years, had been debunked. Sex was now the master word—sex consciousness, sex fulfillment, sex in behavior, art, and clothes; there was a constant patter about sex between the sexes.

"What did I tell you?" said Teddy Balkus, whom Jared encountered one afternoon at the Café de la Paix. "Remember when I told you that Freud was the apostle of modern times, and you laughed at me? Well, he certainly has carried his point. We're through with repressions now."

Balkus had prospered greatly by his transfer to the staff. He was now a lieutenant colonel and aide to one of the American statesmen at the Peace Conference. His breast was gay with French, English, Belgian, and Italian decorations. He had as many service stripes as Jared, and his silver oak leaf eclipsed the humble captain's bars on the other's shoulders. The only way in which Jared had outstripped Balkus was in the acquisition of a crutch and a wound stripe. And Drackenford and Ellis had outstripped him, thought Tolbecken, in death. The waiter, who had ignored Jared in the crowd, danced reverently to the snap of Balkus's fingers.

"Yes, no more repressions," continued Balkus, sipping his *apéritif*. "Wait till you see my new book, *Tolerance House*. There's realism for you! Covers just three hours in the mind

292

of an American soldier in a bathouse. I bet you it will set the pace when it comes out."

"You mean to tell me," exclaimed Jared, "you've had time to write a book?"

"Yes, while you people were scrambling around in the mud, I've been in a position to study life. It takes brains to get the most out of living, Tolbecken; it doesn't take any to get shot."

"No," murmured the other, thinking of Drackenford, "it only takes guts."

But Balkus was only amused at this sally. He patronized Jared, invited him to dinner, and introduced him to several Peace Conference delegates. It was from these that the atmosphere enveloping the deliberations became vividly apparent.

Jared talked with an American who raged about the iniquities of the French, English, and Italians, the squabble for mandates, indemnities, and annexations. He talked with a Russian who gritted his teeth at Bolshevism, a Communist who railed at the bourgeoisie. He talked with a German whose veins stood out on his forehead at a mention of the rumored conditions.

"Do you think we'll put up with a Polish Corridor?" he exclaimed. "The loss of our colonies? With being the milch cow of Europe, wage slaves for generations? We, a people of seventy millions?"

All this, Jared told himself, was only the hum of war excitement that had not yet died down, but at all events it held no promise of that end of war to which men at the front a year ago had looked forward as a consummation. At great cost the scenes had indeed been shifted and the stage was new—new and strange—but it was hard to see how the world had profited.

Feeling very venturesome, he sought an audience with the President, and to his surprise obtained a few minutes at the house on the Place des Etats-Unis. Like Mansen, he was struck by Wilson's appearance of age and frailty. There was the same keen eye and resolute face that he remembered, but it was an old man who greeted him and, as it seemed to him, a man at bay.

The President asked about his wounds, shook his head over Jared's brief account of them, inquired for his grandfather.

"He has a great character, a *staunch* character. That is what we need nowadays, Jared—principles, and staunchness in support of them."

The other summoned courage to answer, "It was your principles, Mr. President, that made the war endurable for most of us. The hope that they would prevail kept us going. If anything were to happen, if it turned out that they didn't prevail, it would have been better for us not to come through. We wouldn't have much left. I felt that I owed it to some—some friends of mine who were killed—to say this, Mr. President."

He was unprepared for the sudden emotion which showed in Wilson's face.

"I know. There's nothing I feel more deeply than that. I shan't break faith with them. Whatever happens, you may depend upon it." He paused a moment, then added, "This will be the greatest triumph or the supremest tragedy in history, Jared. Mankind is at the crossroads and will have to choose. But I believe in a Divine Providence. The direction of the affairs of this disordered world does not depend on our finite intelligence, but on divine mercy and good will."

He rose, ending the interview, but as Jared struggled a little with his crutch, he said, "Let me help you," and lent a streadying arm as the other got up. "Remember me to Rufus Tolbecken."

Strangely enough, for the first time his grandfather's remark about Wilson, made long ago, recurred to Jared: the sort of man who at last would go on alone. It was this impression of an infinite loneliness that he took with him out into the garish streets of the city—Wilson was an old, resolute, lonely man, keeping faith with the dead in a world eager to forget them, defending ideals that had become a joke, proposing a covenant of peace that no one wanted. The first scene of the new world play had a flavor both of Don Quixote and of Calvary.

"Done at Versailles, in a single copy which will remain deposited in the archives of the French Republic, and of which authenticated copies will be transmitted to each of the Signatory Powers."

As Jared read the summaries of the treaty contained in the papers, he had the sense of a world-wide spiritual collapse that involved him personally. Was it to produce this that millions had died? Was this the bitter end of heroism—this Magna Carta of hate and avarice? He read it incredulously, clause after clause dictated by the lust for vengeance and for gain; clause after clause a seed of future war ripe to bursting. After years of moralizing, fine sentiments on liberty and fair

294

play, hymns to justice and groans at German duplicity, could the Associated Powers draw up a document that gave the lie to every article of their avowed creed? What of the Fourteen Points? What of "no annexations, no contributions, no punitive damages"? What of anything that had been regarded as a promise by the enemy at the time of the armistice? Sold out and forgotten. Done at Versailles.

Not only Germany had been sold there, but the conscience of mankind, the whole principle of truth, the future of the world.

And what of Wilson? What of the man who had been acclaimed six months before as savior and dictator? Expediencies and compromises on every page of the treaty discredited him. The plea that it was the best peace which could be had under the circumstances rang hollow and feeble. He of all men ought not to have compromised. That had been the tragedy.

"No," said David Mansen, concerned at his friend's disillusionment, "he compromised, of course, but he's not a traitor. Don't you believe that for a moment. He did wrong for the sake of right—it was a slip not of the heart, but of the mind. Remember what he has saved after all, at the cost of everything else—the League of Nations. And by saving that, he believes that the wrongs can be retrieved, will be set right. Not a traitor, Jared, or a hypocrite, but a man who has set everything upon a single hope."

Yes, after the vortex of the war, after the mockery of the peace, one dream of a better world remained.

49

"Do you remember when the old seventy-first got back in 'sixty-five?" Joan Maylin asked her sister one evening. "I mean, what was left of 'em. No, you wouldn't remember, either, because you weren't in Thebes. I was struck then by the way they acted. Boys I'd known full of life four years before. Now they just lounged around on the porches along Main Street and chewed tobacco. Even when they worked, they seemed to have no pith in 'em. And yet there wasn't anything wrong physically with most of 'em. What ailed 'em was that they felt sold out. Some of 'em got over it, and some didn't."

"Yes, I remember," said Judge Tolbecken, rousing himself unexpectedly. "It was the same here in Dunstable with the Hundred-tenth. Same with me, for that matter. I used to wonder if the darkies had been worth it, and if Thad Stevens and the gang in Congress deserved dying for."

During the last year, he had fallen into the habit of long, empty silences before the hearth of an evening, silences which actually represented vacancies of mind over which Joan Maylin sorrowed. His present interruption had almost startled her.

"Well," she added, "that's the trouble with Jare right now."

The old man straightened up.

"I'll have to speak to him about it. Remind me, Joan. I told him once that the worst part of war was the peace, but he wouldn't believe me."

"He's taken that defeat of the League of Nations to heart," put in Grandmother. "You'd think he had as much interest in it as the President."

"The truth is," said Aunt Joan grimly, "it was about all he had left to be proud of. At least, I gather that's the way he feels. You were in a better position after the Civil War, Rufus. You had a wife and children, a career, and a big, growing practice in your father's office. I don't believe Jared's doing anything to speak of in the law these days. . . ."

"Business will pick up," declared the Judge mechanically. "Now that he's back, I'm confident of it."

"If only Clarice and he . . ." began Rachel Tolbecken, but stopped.

"Yes," sighed Aunt Joan, "do you remember how she looked forward to his arrival and how happy she was? Now that seems to be all over. I don't understand it. When I try pumping him, he shuts up. Lizzie tells me that he calls sometimes. But he wouldn't live with them at his own house, or here with us. I don't approve of a man's living at a club. And there's another thing I've noticed: he hasn't been to church once since he got back—not once—and that's nearly a year ago. You ought to speak to him about that too, Rufus."

So they worried about their one treasure, half understanding, half bewildered. After all, their world was the past. No ghosts could be more alien than they to this strange, busy, cynical America of 1920.

Jared had no intention of stewing to no purpose about a

career simply because it was proper for a man to stew. He would hold on until his grandfather's death to avoid disappointing him, and he then would drift. He would have money enough if he lived carefully—at least enough to buy drinks with. An army friend of his had gone to the South Seas and wrote invitingly. That or somewhere else might be amusing.

Religion for him? He was too indifferent even to argue the point. What was the use discussing it, anyhow? He had had his fill of the Divine Providence, and let others fool themselves if they pleased. In a world of hoaxes, the divine hoax seemed to him especially pathetic.

And Clarice? Oh, brightest of the lost dreams! But love is not enough if one has nothing else—no belief, no faith, no purpose. Love must have the thought of giving, not merely of receiving. If it is really love, it will not crawl lazarlike to the door of the beloved, pleading entrance for the sake of nursing and consolation. It must come a suppliant, indeed, but bearing gifts, at least, of hope and courage. With his patched-up body, shaken nerves, and spiritual bankruptcy, he would be an outrage to play on her compassion, all the more so as for that very reason she would find it harder to refuse. His own weakness had that much pride that it did not choose to cling to her for strength.

As a result, he raised a barrier between them that she did not understand. To be honest would have been to beg. He could only pretend indifference and let the concealed fire burn. Gradually it had become harder for them to talk together, his constraint imposing a like constraint on her, until their whole relationship was affected by it, a kind of bleak enchantment which he did not know how to throw off.

Daily at his office or at the club, in his room at night, the thought haunted him of how different it would have been if he could have returned home with the assurance that the war had not been fought in vain, that his own effort and sacrifice had contributed to something else than the next harvest of dragon's teeth. He could then have faced the world proudly and confidently. As it was, the war had produced only a worse chaos in which the bloodstained objectives he had worshiped had proved a sham.

One evening in the late winter, he called at his former house on the Ridge, now occupied by his aunt and Clarice, and was struck as usual by its transformation. What in his time had been a conventional, unlived-in place had become strangely vitalized. The same furniture had acquired a personality which it had never had in the past, the same once rejecting rooms now made him welcome. Especially tonight as he entered, he felt the warmth and cheer of it as compared to the outer cold.

Mariette, Clarice's French maid, greeted him in the manner reserved for the family. Madame Lehman was out. She would inform Madame Delart. Would Monsieur take place by the fire *en attendant*?

He stood with his back to the flames, glad of the heat on his leg, which still ached in such weather, and let his eye wander about the room. No doubt the exquisite fabrics explained much of the difference, but not all. A faint breath of that Paris he remembered years ago clung to the place.

"Makes me feel old," he thought. "And yet it's only eleven years. Can't be! Yes, that's all—only eleven damned centuries."

Then his heart stirred at the sound of Clarice's footstep on the stairs.

She looked tired tonight, and explained that she had been putting the children to bed, and that they were a handful sometimes.

"I'm sorry they're in bed," he complained. "I don't see them half enough." And drawing a couple of small packages from his pocket, he handed them to her. "Put these beside their beds when you go up. It'll be a surprise for them in the morning. And remember, next Saturday they're coming to the movies with me."

She flushed a little with pleasure.

"Uncle Jared's the grand event of their week, you know. They chatter about you all the time."

"Honestly," he answered, "they're the event of my week too—I can't tell you how much so. It shows a fellow's getting on, when he begins to care for small children."

She changed the subject suddenly. "Is your leg hurting tonight, Jare?"

"Yes, a little. How did you know?"

"I simply felt that it was. Let me arrange the pillows. Sit down now."

"That's good," he sighed, "but you mustn't spoil me."

He read pity in her look, too much pity, he thought, and his pride rebelled. Sensitive to his own great need, he interpreted every glance or phrase of hers as a reflection on it. Already he felt the now-familiar absurd constraint drifting between them.

"What news?" she asked, when they were installed in front of the fire. "I hope some big case has turned up since you were here last."

Was that another hint of pity—this time at the destitution of his practice?

He shook his head. "No, I have just enough business to remind me now and then that I'm a lawyer. But don't let's talk shop. I had a letter today from Kit Curtis, a fellow who was with me at the base hospital—an artist. He's in Morea now, an island beyond Tahiti. He's married one of the native girls and expects to remain there. He wants me to join him."

Something in his tone disturbed her. She glanced at him, startled.

"I'm tempted," he added. But at the question in her face, "Oh, not just now, of course. Sometime. Later. I shan't go on with the law indefinitely."

"You mean just a visit, don't you?"

"Well . . . a long visit. Perhaps . . . who knows? . . ."

"But, Jared, you couldn't do that?"

"Why not? Eventually there'll be nothing to keep me here." Again he misread the pain in her face.

"Perhaps not. But even so, don't you think it would be running away? Isn't that true of your friend Curtis? Would you care for life in terms of escape?"

"Escape from what?"

"Your race, your traditions."

So she regarded him as a quitter, did she? Well, he admitted it. He was beaten. He saw no virtue in the philosophy of carry-on. Carry what on? Where to? Why? In the general débacle of all ideals, *sauve qui peut* had become the only sensible watchword.

"Our race!" he exclaimed. "Why shouldn't I want to escape from it? What on earth has our race to say for itself? Fifteen million dead, four years of destruction, every oath broken and every possible crime committed. Good Lord, the less we talk about our race the better! And my traditions? I haven't any. They're gone. There aren't any left to live by. I don't mind escaping from a grave."

She remained silent, without courage for argument. He was right in thinking that she pitied him; but her pity had no tincture of self-righteousness; it was far more grief.

"Your friends," she ventured at last, "the people who love you—don't they mean anything, Jare?"

"You and David," he answered, "of course. But who else when the family are gone? Classmates, people at the club,

299

around town—I'm afraid they don't mean very much. An
you have your children, and David has his profession . . .

In her bewilderment she found nothing to say. On his side
fearful of exposing himself, he veered off, pride, misname
reserve, playing as usual its divisive role.

"But there's nothing immediate about it," he added, "jus
a notion. I'll probably hobble along the streets of Dunstabl
a long while yet. Speaking of Dave, have you seen his nev
office?"

She nodded absently, her eyes on the fire.

"And what a practice he has!" Jared went on. "Not tha
the money end means anything to him—I doubt if he ever
collects his bills—but it shows what people think of him. Al
that Dave needs now is a wife and family." He smiled at th
idea. "Do you think he'll ever get married?"

She hesitated a moment. "I don't know. He asked me t
marry him today."

It took more courage than Jared knew he possessed t
answer casually, "So?" It showed him what, in spite of every
thing, his own subconscious hope had been. It was like writ
ing *Finis* at the end of his life. And yet how inevitable i
seemed! As in the case of Pierre Delart years ago, the bette
man, the victorious man, deserved the reward of victory. Wa
he to protest against it or to stand in their way?

"Yes," she continued, "but I told him no, that I did not lov
him in that fashion . . . that he would always remain m
dearest friend . . . that the memory of Pierre . . ."

Her voice broke off. But her answer, though a reprieve
had brought little comfort. Her "dearest friend . . . th
memory of Pierre." What place, then, did she reserve fo
him? As if their source was frozen, he brought out his word
stiffly.

"Of course. But you may change your mind. If any ma
on earth is worthy of you, it's David. He's a great man, an
he'll have a great career. You think alike. . . ."

He did not know that his coldness cut her to the quick
that for once her understanding of him was at fault, that sh
set down to indifference what was merely the faltering o
despair. And in her turn she drew back. For some strang
reason the old relationship between them had ceased. Sh
would not demean it by clinging to him.

"Yes," she agreed, "David is the finest man I have eve
known." And then she turned conventionally to somethin
else.

They had suddenly become almost strangers to each othe

300

As if on a formal call, he lingered out the proper time, while they talked on indifferent topics, each conscious of pretense. Then at last he struggled up, found his cane, made a joke about it, and limped to the hall. With smiles and aching hearts, they bade each other good night. The door clicked. She heard the starting of his motor. Driven by a sudden impulse, she opened the door again, ran out on the steps, and called, "Jare—wait a moment, Jare." But he had not heard her. His car faded in the darkness. She stood looking after it, baffled and miserable.

"Yes," he thought, when he had turned on the light in his room at the club, "escape. Why not?"

It was a sort of reflex thought expressing nothing but a kind of numbness. Mechanically also he poured himself a drink, emptied it, refilled the glass, and drank again. Alcohol, as a rule, gave him some respite from the sense of chill that haunted him these days. But tonight, though he emptied glass after glass, it produced the opposite effect. As he sat vacantly by the table, he became conscious of a growing, indefinable horror. To combat it, he got up and brought Clarice's miniature to the light, and sat pondering it. But this too failed of its magic. Its beauty mocked him. Like everything else, it too belonged now to the past, to the whole order of what might have been that had eluded him. The fire and courage of her face had nothing in common with his own surrender. Justly she had passed him by.

Well, then, escape. What right had she to question the only course remaining to him? Escape from this new, ugly, vulgar, scrambling world, bent only on forgetting. Somewhere there was sunlight and color, leisure and rest. The five senses were still his to use, and distant places there were below the horizon where they could still be used without shame. He tried to conjure up diverting pictures of distant coasts, but the blue and ivory of the miniature broke through and dispelled them. They remained tawdry and unreal, essentially uninviting. They offered him escape, indeed, just as his liquor did, down at the animal level; but that was all. It was not good enough.

The horror grew. He realized that no island, no savage continent lay far off enough to give him refuge from his own shadow. To escape from that he must escape from life, and for that no travel was necessary. He had not coquetted with the thought of suicide, but recently he had become more and more aware of the automatic which he kept in the drawer of the table. From the fringe of his mind the consciousness of it had

301

gradually worked toward the center. Now, as if under som
hypnotic influence, he pulled out the drawer and began ab
sently fingering the weapon, slid out the clip, shot it home
toyed with the safety catch. Then he put the thing down, stil
looking at it, filled and emptied his glass.

And suddenly, as such moments come, the disgust of lif
took him by the throat. Yes, of course, irrevocable defea
dishonor, cowardice . . . the mess to be cleaned up . .
fear of the blinding crash in his brain . . . the cruelty t
those who loved him. But he had had enough. He could no
stand it—not any more of it. Madness? Yes, put it down t
that.

His hand closed on the butt of the automatic; he pulle
himself closer to the table, raised the barrel . . .

Someone knocked at the door. Instinctively, he clappe
the weapon back into its place. His heart racked him with it
wild pounding; the room wheeled.

Again the knock was repeated.

A voice curiously detached from himself answered, and h
looked up to see David Mansen on the threshold.

50

"Come in," Jared said dully, and as the wheeling of hi
mind steadied, he got up, though he still gripped the edg
of the table. "It's good to see you. I was getting lonely. To
damned lonely, in fact. Have a drink." The neck of the bo
tle rattled against the glass. "No? Well, if you don't min
. . ." He drank the brandy himself as if it had been wate
"Ah, that's better. Pull up a chair. . . . I'm *very* glad to se
you, but what brings you here at this time of night?"

"I had a late call," answered David. "On the way back,
saw the light in your window, and I thought I'd drop in."

He seated himself unconcernedly, but Jared knew that th
trained eyes of his visitor missed nothing—not a twitch o
his fingers as he lighted a cigarette, not a line of his palli
face.

"And a good thing too, I should say," Mansen added.

"Why do you think so?"

"Because you look as if you had been entertaining a ghos
—in other words, you look a wreck."

"I'm all right. A little blue maybe." And conceding a bit for the sake of appearances, "My nerves have been pretty well shot since France. Maybe you could help me."

"Maybe."

"I've been meaning to look you up professionally," Jared went on, feeling that he was covering his tracks. "I suppose you'd advise me to give up liquor, wouldn't you? Maybe even tobacco?"

To his surprise, Mansen laughed.

"I don't think that would help. In the first place, you couldn't do it; and in the second, if you could, you wouldn't need to."

"I don't understand."

Clasping one knee, Mansen leaned back in his chair, but his keen gaze was on his friend's face.

"Did I ever tell you about the time I was on the point of committing suicide?"

He noted the sudden flicker in Jared's eyes, the involuntary tightening of the lips, and judged that the probe had struck home.

"You!" exclaimed Jared. "No . . . I can't believe it."

Mansen nodded. "Yes. It was in medical school. I was working at terrific pressure, and began using cocaine to pep me up. I was set on leading the class, and, believe me, there was *some* competition."

But, Dave, you and drugs! It doesn't make any sense. It's incredible."

"You see," laughed the other again, "I've had a pretty good camouflage too. But there you are. I was taking a shot now and then to keep up. One habit led to another. I was losing my grip. Molehills became mountains. Pretty soon I felt I was a failure and knew I was a hyprocrite. I was pretending to be a good sort of man and was actually a mess. All the ground I had gained in college was lost. What I had believed in began to seem unreal. And at last one night it came to me suddenly that I couldn't stand it . . ."

"Suddenly?" Jared repeated. All at once he blurted out what he had been at pains to conceal a few minutes earlier. "God, I'm glad you came tonight. You know I was on the very point . . . I had the gun in my hand when you knocked."

"Yes," agreed David without apparent surprise. "That's the way it's likely to come—suddenly."

"But what happened in your case?" asked the other.

"Well, I had decided for opium as my out. What stopped

me was remembering something I had heard a long time ago. I hadn't thought of it for years, and then, just at that particular moment, there it was. Somebody once told me that if ever faith seems unreal, it is because a man is unwilling to pay the price. That started me thinking."

"The price?" said Jared.

"Yes. You know what I believe in—a great personal, creative current that fills a man and works through him, provided there's nothing in the way of it. I had let my contact points get foul. I had become ambitious for myself—I wanted to be thought well of—I wanted to lead. It wasn't the creative force of the current that mattered any more; it was me—my ego, my ambition. That led to strain; that led to drugs; the whole thing led to hypocrisy. And there I sat with a glass of water in one hand and the opium pills in the other. But the core of the whole trouble was dishonesty—being one thing and appearing to be something else."

"Well," asked Jared intently, "what did you do?"

"I decided to give my belief one more chance. Of course, the first thing to do was to get rid of the dishonesty. That meant owning up to a couple of people who believed in me and thought I was a model young man."

"What do you mean—owning up?"

"Letting them know me as I knew myself. It wasn't easy."

"Who were they?"

"One was my chief rival in the class; the other was a professor who had done a good deal to help me along. And mind you, I had a lot more to tell them about than just the cocaine. I tried to squirm out of it one way or another, but I saw that I couldn't. That's how the price presented itself to me."

"And what happened?"

"Why, instead of being a model young man, I became a close friend to both of them. That's the way it usually works, though not always. I had to take the chance."

"Was that necessary?" argued Jared. "Wasn't it enough to turn over a new leaf without exposing yourself?"

"Not as long as there were two people I felt distinctly uncomfortable with because I had fooled them."

"It sounds morbid and introspective to me," objected Tolbecken.

David smiled. "Call it what you like. I called it that and a lot of other names while I was trying to wriggle out of it. On the other hand, you *might* call it ordinary frankness. At any rate, it wasn't quite as morbid as the opium pills."

"Did it work?" asked the other.

"It worked fine. Sacrificing pride to honesty did the trick. My contacts were clear again, and I was working with the current instead of by myself. Of course I had to use my will, but that came easier. The long and short of it was that I felt unified and free."

"And since then?"

"Oh, I've got a long way to go yet, Jare. I keep picking up dirt of one kind or another, and it's got to be cleared out. But the chief thing is that I'm free from the biggest danger of all, which is doubt. I know that God is, and I know a little of what He is, and I know that if I choose to do His will and keep paying the price, He will show me enough of it to steer by. And that's all the light I need."

Jared brought his fist down on the table.

"I'm tired of this God stuff, Dave. I admit I'm sunk. I'm like a lot of beads when the string's broken—just rattling around. I realize now that it used to be the old-fashioned American attitude I was threaded onto. Well, that faded out. Then it was Wilson's vision, the whole war idealism, that seemed to give life a purpose. You know what happened to that. And each of these principles included God. He played the leading role in both. But what did He do for either of them, after all those lives were sacrificed, all those people were left stranded? Not one thing."

"So you're a victim of circumstances—is that it, Jare?"

"Call it that if you like. People of our generation were born either too late or too soon—a kind of threshold generation. Intellectually we belong to the past. We have no place in the world as it is. We can't adjust ourselves to it. We're just survivals who are permitted to live on sufferance."

David consulted his watch. "There are a good many people who feel that way nowadays," he agreed. "You have plenty of company. Well, I've got to be going."

Jared stared at him. "In other words, you're not enough interested in me to want to talk. I need help, Dave. I'm at the end of my rope. You don't seem to realize it."

"Oh, yes, I do," David said, "but there's no use wasting time. If it would help you any for me to hold your hand, I would sit here all night."

"I'm not asking you to hold my hand."

"Yes, you are, as long as you consider yourself the victim of circumstances. Of course, it's a lot more poetic to saddle your failures on the age and to pose as an exile of the old regime. But fundamentally that's just moonshine. When a man

305

reaches the point of saying, 'I'm to blame; I'm responsible; I made the mess I'm in and I can't get out,' there's something to take hold of. As for the God stuff, as you call it, it isn't God's fault if His name is hauled in to give respectability to human enterprises. The greatest mistakes in history have been made by those who thought they knew what God's purposes were for other people, for masses of men, for the world. The individual is forgotten in the crowd. But it's only the individual that counts, the individual that God works through. Don't hitch Him up to American tradition or to the League of Nations or to any human system. Hitch yourself to Him and see what happens."

"All of which means what?"

"Something very simple: honestly try to clean up your own dirt—the things you know are wrong in you—and ask His help."

"That's pretty naïve, isn't it, Dave?"

Mansen got up. "Yes, it's pretty naïve. Wallow around in sophistication if you want to."

He stood smiling, relaxed, and at ease, confronting the other's baffled defeat. As never before, Jared felt his vitality and power. In contrast with it, he felt too, as never before, his own feebleness. Far more than anything Mansen had said, it was *himself*, the overtones of his personality, that carried conviction.

"Lord," Jared exclaimed suddenly, "I'd give anything to be you for just five minutes!"

"Nonsense!" returned David. "Be yourself. What would you give for that?"

"What shall I give? What *can* I give?"

And at the note of entreaty in his voice, Mansen's face grew very gentle. Rounding the table, he laid a hand on his shoulder.

"Everything, Jare. In the long run, everything. But to begin with, you have to give your pride."

"How? In what way?"

"Is there anyone between whom and yourself you feel that your pride is a barrier, to whom on account of pride you would not turn for charity, to whom on account of pride you would not show your weakness and your failures? Of course there are a number, but I mean one above all others whose good opinion you value?"

Jared nodded slowly. "Yes. And of course you know who it is."

306

Mansen picked up Clarice's miniature from the table, and looked at it thoughtfully. Then he laid it down.

"Well, you must go to her. Whatever in your life has come between you, the things you have never dared to tell her, the things you are ashamed of, the compromises, as far as you know them—tell her all of that. Will you do that?"

Jared grew rigid.

"No . . . I couldn't. It wouldn't be right. I mean it would hurt her. I mean . . ."

"You mean it would hurt you. I know. It will hurt a great deal. But if you're in earnest, it's the only way."

"To what?"

"To life."

"No," Jared repeated. "Anyone but her. I know I've been dishonest, self-indulgent, a compromiser, full of self-pity. I know that I've been a vague idealist who never faced himself. Isn't it enough to realize it?"

"No," said David, "it's not enough. What does it cost you to realize that? It's your pride we're talking about. It's honesty between you and the one to whom it most matters. It's the first step in the new process."

"But I haven't your faith."

"You'll never find it, Jare, unless you are willing to make a venture in the dark. And that venture means sacrifice."

For a long while, Jared remained silent. Then the bitterness of his need rose up within him like a cry.

"Very well," he said at last, "I will. And I'll pray to something I hardly believe in for help to do it."

"When?" asked David relentlessly.

Jared looked at the clock.

"Tonight. I wouldn't have the nerve tomorrow. It's only half past ten. I'll call her now."

"Good," said Mansen. "My car's outside. I'll drive you over."

Jared got up and walked over to the telephone, then paused, irresolute. David's eyes narrowed. The hands clasped behind his back tightened. Then he breathed again. Jared had taken off the receiver.

"Clarice? . . . Yes . . . I want to speak to you tonight. . . I'll be right over."

"Now," said David, when he had hung up, "I can tell you something that may make it harder—or easier. I have always loved her, as you know. Today I asked her to marry me."

"Yes," replied the other absently, "she told me about it."

"Did she tell you why she refused me?"

"Yes, on account of Pierre."

"Not altogether. She said it was you she had loved all her life. That's what I came here to tell you this evening. You weren't fit to hear it until now."

Jared nodded. "Harder or easier? Perhaps both. I don't know. At any rate, it doesn't matter, because this means the end."

"That's the chance you have to take," said David.

51

Jared stood facing Clarice in the little drawing room. The logs on the hearth had crumbled into embers. Pale with concern for him, she had pushed forward the armchair he had used earlier in the evening.

"What is it, Jare?" she said. "You look so strange and ill."

Now that the moment had come, the ordeal seemed harder than he had expected. Now that he knew of her love, he must deface her belief in him, make clear to her that what she loved was a creation of her own fancy and of his pretense. But one thing helped him: that he had reached the point of admitting the necessity of it, that what he now did was literally a choice between life and death. And something else helped him, a faint glow different from anything he had yet felt and that he could not account for.

"I had to speak to you tonight," he said, gaining the chair. "I hope you'll forgive my keeping you up. . . ."

The words stuck in his throat. She seated herself on the divan close to him, and leaned forward with anxious eyes, noting that he gripped the chair arms to keep his hands from shaking.

"You ought to have rest," she urged. "You started in much too soon after your illness. You ought to have let us take care of you."

He shook his head. "It isn't that, Clarice. I wish it were . . ." Then, after a pause. "Do you remember the time you and Aunt Elizabeth visited Princeton?"

"Of course."

"Do you remember that when we came back that evening

o the inn you said there was something in me you didn't understand any longer, that we didn't know each other as we used to, and you asked me what it was, and begged me to be honest? Remember?"

"Yes." She nodded.

"Looking back," he went on, "it seems to me that that was the turning point of my life. I had the feeling then of a part of my mind that was locked up and cut off from the rest of it, full of things that I didn't want anyone to know about—least of all you. If I had only dared throw the door open, everything would have been different—my whole life. We wouldn't have drifted apart, for one thing. . . . As I see it now, it didn't amount to much—only a boy's foolishness or grossness of one kind or another. But I didn't dare. . . ."

She laid her hand on his.

"Then later in Paris," he continued, "even that night after the dance, I wasn't honest with you. I didn't dare tell you why I hadn't written. I made all sorts of excuses to myself. It was prettier to think that we were just unlucky. But that wasn't true. I was entirely to blame. . . . The locked-up part of my mind kept on growing. After a while it came to seem natural. I wasn't even aware of it any longer. Then suddenly I realized tonight that all of me was locked in, and it seemed that there wasn't any way to get out but one. . . ."

He made a gesture with his hand. Her face had gone white.

"That's why I'm here. But don't think I'd have had character enough to come by myself. It was David. He made me see that I had one chance, that there was one thing left to try to believe in . . . that's why I'm here. Because it hurts more with you than anyone else. Because maybe God, if there is a God, would . . ."

He broke off, tried to smile.

"I have to talk openly with you—if you'll let me."

He felt her hand tremble.

"It isn't necessary, Jared. Whatever you have thought or done makes no difference as far as I . . . You understand what I mean."

"I know you think so," he answered. "But that doesn't let me off. I haven't any great crimes to tell you about. I wish I had. They would show a certain amount of courage, and at least be interesting. It's just an average life, full of all sorts of little, mean, cheap, hidden things."

So, faltering and with dry lips, he showed her his life in concrete terms, the things it most hurt him to talk about. He felt

309

a constant temptation to varnish and soften, but he fough against it. Snobbishness, hypocrisy, cowardice, disloyalty had their various examples; dissipation and the front he had set up to hide it, the whole truth about his marriage and his relations with Nan, the concealment of that truth from his family other concealments were set forth one by one.

"There I was, posing as a gentleman," he exclaimed, "and so regarded in the town—Jared Tolbecken, representing everything my family had stood for. But all the time Nan knew what a bluff it was. You can hardly blame her for being cynical."

Or again:

"Fighting for a better world! Believing in the millennium I remember a German at Soissons who threw down his rifle and begged for mercy. I shot him down. . . . I remember once in a shell hole a wounded chap asked for water. I figured out that I wouldn't have enough for myself if I gave him any So I slunk off. I'll never forget the look in his eyes. But that very day I got the *Croix de guerre*. . . . A fine candidate for the better world! Drinking myself stupid to keep my nerve up. Drunk and fooling around with a woman outside the rest camp. Then writing home to you and the family in the role of a fine young officer. Dave Mansen was right. A house is no stronger than the bricks it's built with. I was one of the rotten bricks in the better world."

When he had finished, there was little left of the Tolbecken façade. He felt curiously humbled and small without it, did not wonder that she had drawn her hand away.

"That's all I can think of," he said at last, "except that the poor idealist, having been cheated by his hopes, has become a good deal of a sot recently—in private, of course—and was on the point of shooting himself tonight as a final treachery to the few people who still care for him."

He had not dared look at her for some time, and sat now with his eyes still on the last embers of the hearth. As what he had said unwound itself across his mind again in a vivid scroll, his heart turned to water. She would never want to see him after this. All he had left to do now was to slink away

And yet strangely enough he did not feel like slinking. He became suddenly aware of a measureless relief, a curious sense of freedom. He felt too a new energy vibrating through him—something so new and tonic that it hardly seemed part of himself. Almost in fear, he recalled Mansen's talk about the current. Shame there was, of course, for the past realization of how he must appear to Clarice; but that could not be helped. He had a sense of the past crumbling off, dropping astern.

A sound startled him, and he looked up at last to see that there were tears on her cheeks.

"I know," he said, struggling to his feet. "I'll be going now."

"What do you mean!"

"I know what you must think of me. You were good to listen. . . . I'm sorry to have caused you pain. I'll remember your—our . . ."

"Pain?" she burst out. "Do you think I'm crying because . . Why, Jared, don't you see that it's pride?"

"Pride?" he repeated.

"What else could it be? While you were telling me all those things, do you know what the echo was in my mind? I can't describe it, but it was like a far-off trumpet sound. It was courage, victory—every splendid thing. It was like our childhood come back again—only so much more. . . ."

He stared at her incredulously.

"Do you mean," he faltered, "that you . . . that in spite of everything you still . . ."

She drew close to him. "I can't forgive you for doubting me, for believing one moment I was such a plaster saint that I wouldn't understand. I'll tell you about myself, Jare, some day, and then it will be your turn. But after all you weren't altogether honest."

"Not honest?"

"At least I hope not. All that time, I waited for you to tell me the only thing that mattered and will ever matter to me. But you didn't."

Their eyes met. The light in hers answered him.

"That I love you?" he said. "That I love you!"

She was in his arms. Around them, above them, it seemed to him, leaped the flame of a new life.

52

The next day, Mrs. Rufus Tolbecken and Miss Joan Maylin, with the shrewdness of their age and sex, had occasion to suspect something. Why had Jared called up from the office and proposed a family party that evening, including Elizabeth Lehman, Clarice, and David Mansen? Why had he blandished Aunt Joan about her scalloped oysters, and given her a rigmarole about how pleasant it would be if they could all spend the evening together? They were delighted, of course, but it was so different from his recent unconcern about the family or anything else that the novelty of it startled them.

"And then his voice," marveled Aunt Joan. "I actually didn't recognize it at first. It had such a ring, he sounded so gay . . ."

"Joan!" exclaimed Grandmother. "Do you think . . ."

"I don't know," mused the other. "I don't want to let myself get worked up. It would be too wonderful."

But that evening Madame Tolbecken dressed for dinner as if it had been Sunday. She put on her newest and starchiest lawn cap and her satin dress with the black beads.

"You know," she counseled, "I believe I'd serve a little sherry tonight, just in case. . . . I mean, just for a treat."

In her suspense, she forgot the evening paper, and sat round-eyed and solemn awaiting the guests' arrival.

"What's it all about?" queried the Judge, who felt something unusual in the air, and had found his ceremonial broadcloth coat laid out for him.

"Oh, nothing," answered his wife evasively, "we just felt like having a real party."

The excitement of the old ladies quickened at Jared's appearance, and this in spite of the fact that, for the sake of the surprise he intended, he was doing his best to copy yesterday's manner. He tried to look indifferent when Clarice arrived and to press back the signs of happiness that kept breaking through. But the disguise failed. He was confronted by two master detectives who were not easy to put off.

"Did you notice his eyes?" murmured Grandmother in a whisper to Aunt Joan, while he was talking to the others across the room.

"Yes—like they used to look when he was a boy. He's entirely different. I can hardly wait . . ."

"Sssh, we mustn't let on."

Their nervousness increased during dinner. Grandmother said afterwards that she could hardly stand it. It was like sitting on pins and needles. But Jared made no move. He did not talk to Clarice more than usual. He kept drawing David Mansen out about his practice, or encouraging the Judge in his favorite anecdotes. It was only when dessert had been served that he took advantage of a momentary silence.

"I have something to say that I know you will be glad to ear."

At last!

Grandmother's face actually turned pink. She exchanged an xcited glance with her sister.

"I want to tell you that Clarice and I are going to be mar-ed day after tomorrow."

The announcement lost none of its effect because of the dies' anticipation. Grandmother drew a long breath and aned back. Aunt Joan's eyes grew suddenly moist. The idge stared at his grandson, bewildered, through his spec-cles. It was he who first broke the silence in a somewhat certain voice.

"Jared, as you know, I don't hear quite as well as I did. o you mind repeating what you said?"

"I said Clarice and I are going to be married."

The old man leaned forward.

"I . . . Well, sir. . . . Well, sir!" And half to himself, never expected God to be so good to me."

Then the gates of joy burst open. Everybody was up. Clar-e's cheeks were rosy before they were through with her! ven old Carrie, who had been listening in the pantry, claimed r share. How the room vibrated and sparkled with what uld not be expressed!

It was on the full tide of this happiness a month later that rs. Rachel Tolbecken fell asleep one night and never awak-ed. At the moment of death, perhaps some pleasant dream ad crossed her mind, for she still smiled. Her folded hands the day of burial looked as dainty as the linen of her cap. er face had lost some of its lines and seemed younger.

"Thank God for His infinite loving-kindness!" said Aunt an, looking down at her.

"Amen!" said the Judge from his chair close by. He sat in in hand, his eyes brooding. He had spent hours in the rkened room, silent, wrapped in his own thought; but he owed little grief. Indeed, it was his children and grand-ildren who sorrowed more than he and Joan Maylin. For ief is a tribute to the future; those who with good courage me to the end have left tears behind them. To such a man, e death of his wife meant everything and also nothing. She ad shared his bed for sixty years; they had grown to be one fe; her death foreshadowed his own. It meant all of that; it eant only that.

Doubtless, as he sat communing with her, studying her ce, the stretch of time seemed short. The girl of sixty years

313

ago and the woman of eighty were one to him. The changin
scenes of his life, the interests and cares were unified by he
There would be only one more scene for him to play alon

During the months of that spring, he appeared more reg
larly at his office than had been his custom of late. He lik
to sit in the familiar room, turning over papers that Jare
made a point of putting before him, discussing an occasion
problem of law, and dozing a good deal. A few old frien
climbed the stairs to chat with him.

"Hope you're not busy, Judge."

"I'm never too busy to see you, sir. Matter of fact, I b
lieve I had closed my eyes for a moment just before yo
came in. Privilege of old age. I can recommend these cigars

And on the way out, they would whisper to Jared, "Stro
as ever, your grandfather is—he'll live to be a hundred."

But to those who knew him best, there were significa
changes. Politics had always been a consuming interest wi
him; but now that the papers were full of the oncomin
campaign, he never read them.

"Thorns under a pot," he said once. "Tiresome! Wh
does it matter?"

For the first time since the Civil War, April 1 went by wi
his ledger unbalanced. He took it down, to be sure, and i
scribed the month, then looked back over the last quarter.

"Here, Jare"—he laid the pen down—"total up these figur
if you want to. I won't bother." And when Jared had finishe
he told him to put the ledger back in its place. "You'd bett
carry on from this point. It may interest you to look ov
now and then."

Stranger still, he gave Jared the key to his safe-depos
box at the bank with a careless "You tend to those things

What he craved most was the companionship of his gran
son, who managed to spend a part of every evening wi
him, often reading aloud from such favorites as Gray, Gol
smith, and Irving; but sometimes the Judge preferred to ta

Once Jared mentioned the age of the Tolbecken law offi
in Dunstable, hoping to draw his grandfather out on a congeni
topic, but was amazed when he answered, "Oh, yes, old nar
in Dunstable, if that means anything. What's Dunstable!
the way, Dick Kent dropped in the other day when you we
out. He said he was moving his firm to Washington to jo
up with Judge Hale. Going to call it Kent and Hale. Has
much income-tax and interstate-commerce business there, an
way, that he thinks he'd better be on the spot. Said you cou

314

have a partnership if you wanted it. Better think that over when I'm gone."

"But, Grandfather, do you mean to say that the firm name here means nothing to you? You've made great sacrifices for it. I thought you desired especially that I should carry it on."

"I made sacrifices," returned the other slowly. "I did desire, as you say. I was brought up in the belief that old names and old houses like ours lasted, that they were useful to America. But America doesn't want old things; she wants new ones and newer ones. Vain sacrifices!" he added after a moment. "Childish desires!"

"You mean that those things had no purpose?" Jared asked.

"I mean nothing of the kind. I mean that externals wear out in the end—as they should."

It was in ways like this that he showed the effect of his wife's death. Fiber by fiber, the roots snapped, the great old tree leaned toward the earth. In May, clouds began to cross his mind, which had hitherto remained clear. He startled Jared one morning by starting to discuss a case of which the latter had never heard, but caught himself up with the remark, "No, I remember, that was years ago." More painful still were references now and then to his wife as if she were still living, followed by the silence of recollection.

In his office one day at the beginning of June, he lost consciousness, and wakened with a startled "What's the matter? What are you here for, Dr. Guerney? Can't a man take a nap without having you show up? Jared's getting as nervous about me as an old hen."

"It's nothing much," soothed the doctor. "Your heart's a little weak. You'd better not come down to the office for a few days, and you'll have to give up those very good cigars of yours. But it's not serious—a fainting spell might happen to anybody."

"Fainted, did I?" grunted the Judge. He gave his hand to Jared and pulled himself up, swaying a little. "Guess you're right about the office, Guerney. Can't have me fainting around here, giving trouble. But when it comes to the cigars, I defy you, sir. I won't have the faculty of Physicians and Surgeons cudgeling their brains how to keep my heart twitching a little longer. None of your tricks when the time comes, remember! No oxygen or hypodermics! No need to be cruel to an old man. Let him off easy on the score of eighty-nine years."

He leaned on Jared's arm, and looked around the office—the books, at Daniel Webster above the mantel, at his desk.

315

"Eighty-nine years," he repeated. "Well, let's go." He paused as usual in the outer office to say, "Good evening, Miss Walton," before putting on his hat.

By evening, he had brightened remarkably, and sat as usual in his armchair. It was a gusty night of rain outside.

"Here's a letter," he said, "that came today from my old friend Donald Craig. Remember him, Jare?"

"But, Father," put in Elizabeth Lehman, "is he still alive?"

"Yes, just as much alive as I am or just as little. He's living with a nephew in Michigan." He tapped the letter with one finger. "Full of Works, Faith, Justification, Sanctification Staunch as Tolbecken Oak was. I envy him. I've been a backslider myself, an unprofitable servant."

After a while, he went on. "Those words don't mean much to you, but to me they bring back the past. They stood for something that changes but goes on. My chief happiness nowadays isn't only your marriage, Jare. It's the thought that you are lined up with that. . . . You know, thinking of Donald reminds me of an incident I haven't recalled for years It was at Manassas in 'sixty-two—or was it in the Wilderness in 'sixty-four? Queer, I can't think which it was. The Zouaves were going in. See 'em now. They'd been cut up badly, flags in ribbons, companies no more than a handful—not a battalion of 'em left. But going in. They hadn't a chance. Counterattack across clear ground against the Rebel guns. Gallant I can tell you, my boy. We cheered 'em. They knew they were a forlorn hope, and that they would never come back from the charge. Well, Donald Craig and others like him have been like that in another way—pretty much of a forlorn hope committed to a magnificent cause—magnificent!"

He drew a long breath, his hands tightening on the arms of his chair.

"Only a few," he added. "It's always been only a few Jared—against the world. But all the truly distinguished men I've known belonged to that company. Creeds? I don't know . . . Backsliding, I guess. . . . But I've kept the faith. You keep it. There isn't any other. . . ."

He sat with bowed head, staring across the room

"Well, read me something. Seems to me we started *The Alhambra*. It's on the table."

A half-hour later, Aunt Joan whispered, "Wait a moment he's breathing strangely."

They listened to the hurried, heavy intake of breath. Jare and Mrs. Lehman half rose. But the Judge opened his eye

"Getting bedtime," he said in a remote voice. "Rachel will scolding me for sitting up. That you, Jare?"

"Why of course, Grandfather."

"Listen to the elms outside. Regular high wind. Makes me seem good."

He leaned forward, breathing fast.

"Rufus!" cried Aunt Joan.

"Yes," he answered, as if to a call, "in a moment."

Clarice bent down. "Do you need help, Grandfather?"

"Help? Why? Listen to that storm. But Tolbecken has seen any of 'em. They knew how to build in those days . . . 'ong walls, oak beams, beautiful rooms. . . ." He looked oudly about the narrow apartment. "This drawing room . Stately, sir, our house."

He tried to rise, but sank back. "I'm feeling strange . . . ak!"

His hands slipped from the arms of his chair.

Late that night, just before dawn, he died. In the bleak ht of the new day there was this at least of comfort to ose around him: that death, more merciful than life in its usions, had restored what was lost, that after all he died at olbecken.

So, for the last time, his name stood conspicuously on the ont pages of newspapers. His achievements were rehearsed d his dignities recorded. Even the national press remem- red him. Telegrams poured in from younger contempo- ries, themselves old men, or from the sons of contempo- ries. The Grand Army, the bar associations of Philadelphia, ashington, and Dunstable passed resolutions of respect and gret. He was eulogized from the local pulpits.

This spontaneous veneration, the well-nigh public funeral th its impressive ceremonies revived for Jared the signifi- nce of Rufus Tolbecken's life. It was glorious, he reflected, have earned such a tribute of respect; his grandfather uld not be forgotten.

A month later he visited the grave with Aunt Joan and arice. A damp wind drifted the city smoke over the ceme- y. They made their way along sodden paths through the yrinth of monuments to the Tolbecken mausoleum. Even new lettering looked already old. He read: RUFUS TOL- CKEN, BORN JULY 29, 1831, DIED JUNE 16, 1920. There re no people, no wreaths, no speeches. All that had very ditably been tendered and was now done with. The three them stood mute in the desolate, vast place. The grave

317

seemed to have dwindled and grown small. A factory sir
hooted in the distance.

But before turning back, Aunt Joan pointed to a young tr
that grew close to the monument, its branches vigorous,
new leaves full and strong.

"Do you know what that comes from?" she said. "I trar
planted it in 'ninety-eight. It's from Tolbecken Oak."

4 Thrilling Bestsellers by Thomas B. Costain... Packed with Love and Intrigue, Passion and Power

CONQUERING FAMILY
Unforgettable drama of a powerful family who sought to sweep the whole world before them. 352 pgs. "Fascinating," N.Y. Times.

MAGNIFICENT CENTURY
Costain vividly recreates the turbulent and passionate era of Henry III. 383 pgs. "Magnificent," N.Y. Herald Tribune.

CONQUERING FAMILY

"Costain has brought all the skill of a prime storyteller. He riots amid the actual happenings in perhaps the most richly dramatic and romantic country we know...A thrilling narrative."—Salt Lake City Tribune.

THREE EDWARDS

"So colorful and gusty is his style, so filled with phrases that grip and hold, no fiction he ever wrote holds the breathless interest of the reader more tightly."— Miami Herald.

MAGNIFICENT CENTURY

"Fascinating...thoroughly enjoyable...history at its best... written by a man who combines a love of his subject matter with an understanding of the all-too-often overlooked fact that history—accurate, factual history—is the most fascinating tale of all."—San Francisco Chronicle

MAIL ATTACHED COUPON NOW →

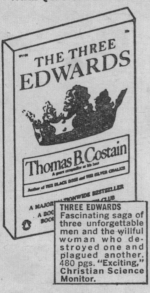